THE ONE SAFE PLACE

By Ramsey Campbell from Tom Doherty Associates, Inc.

Ancient Images
Cold Print
The Count of Eleven
Dark Companions
The Doll Who Ate His Mother
The Face That Must Die
Fine Frights (editor)
The Hungry Moon
Incarnate
The Influence
The Long Lost
Midnight Sun
The Nameless
Obsession
The One Safe Place
The Parasite
Waking Nightmares

THE ONE SAFE PLACE

RAMSEY CAMPBELL

A TOM DOHERTY ASSOCIATES BOOK/NEW YORK

For Peter Lavery,
in celebration of such lunches

THE ONE SAFE PLACE

This book is printed on acid-free paper.

A Forge Book
Published by Tom Doherty Associates, Inc.
175 Fifth Avenue
New York, NY 10010

Forge® is a registered trademark of Tom Doherty Associates, Inc.

Library of Congress Cataloging-in-Publication Data

Campbell, Ramsey, date
The one safe place / Ramsey Campbell. —1st ed.
p. cm.
"A Tom Doherty Associates book."
ISBN 0-312-86035-8 (alk. paper)
1. Criminals—Fiction. 2. Violence—Fiction. 3. Family—Fiction.
I. Title.
PR6053.A4855054 1996
823'.914—dc20 96-2635

First U.S. edition: August 1996

Originally published in Great Britain by Headline Book Publishing

Printed in the United States of America

0 9 8 7 6 5 4 3 2 1

CONTENTS

	Acknowledgments	7
	Boys	9
1	Violence	30
2	Meaning Business	37
3	Pictures	49
4	A Scream	63
5	Customers	72
6	A Trial	80
7	A Verdict	96
8	Nasties	108
9	Family	119
10	Characters	130
11	Voices	139
12	From the Past	146
13	Messages	156
14	Self-Help	164
15	Living	173
16	Law	181
17	Fame	189
18	Not There	199
19	In Broad Daylight	207
20	Unknowing	221
21	Ma and Da	234
22	Inquiries	249
23	Night	257
24	The Message	269
25	Game	277
26	The Call	289
27	Already, However	301
28	Having Seen	313
29	Getting Rid	321
30	Made in America	331
31	Last Chance	345
32	The Look	355
33	The Killer	364
	A Man	377

ACKNOWLEDGMENTS

My wife, Jenny, had even more to do with the book than usual. Once it was done, the excellent Lorraine Beare—alas, now gone to Norwich—saw it through many stages, and it was also given an improving read by Nancy Webber, the kind of copy editor I imagine every writer dreams of. Nor have I forgotten Peter Lavery, as the dedication shows.

I must thank the Adair family for the Florida episode: Gerry for inviting me there in January 1993, Marion for her great hospitality, Jason for lending me his room, and Michael for making sure I was okay.

Ina Shorrock and the, sadly, late Bob Shaw were the weapons advisers.

Eight months after writing chapter one, I was invited onto an edition of *Granada Upfront,* an audience participation show, to discuss video censorship. The resemblance is obviously coincidental. Susanne's teaching in this book owes something to Martin Barker's study *Video Nasties,* an essential book, which might usefully be read in conjunction with John Martin's *Seduction of the Gullible.*

B O Y S

It would be his last walk. A few hundred yards from the house, alongside the chain-link fence which separated the grass of the backyards from the ankle-length grass that bordered the lake, Marshall Travis became aware of holding everything still. An egret lowered its long beak and longer neck imperceptibly to prey among the reeds a quarter of a mile across the bowl of sky that was the lake. A pair of hawks hovered above the forest of palm trees and Norfolk pine between the suburb and the Interstate. Five lizards were frozen where they clung at intervals along the fence, the nearest so close that he could see its left front claw raised an inch, the digits curled like the tips of a fern, and the tiny gray-green bellows of its sides heaving in and out. Then an airliner rose majestically from West Palm Beach, drawing thunder in its wake, a sound which felt as warm and lingering as the touch of the January air. One hawk fell out of the sky, the other swooped after it, and as Marshall took a step toward the forest the lizards were lost in the grass, with only a jingle of the chain-links to show where they had been. He picked his way through the grass, faltering twice as breezes which might have been snakes made it writhe, and climbed the bank which separated the lake from the shallow canal at the edge of the trees.

Workmen had destroyed the bridge he and his friends had built, but now someone had wedged a log across the water that was just too wide for jumping. As Marshall slithered down the cracked earth bank, a frog plopped into the canal. Twigs and Coca-Cola cans bumped the drenched log as Marshall edged across, holding out his hands on either side of him as though feeling for the ropes of a bridge over a ravine, a fancy which reminded him that he would be much higher above the ocean before the sun went down. At once the bark of the log felt loose and slippery, and his need to grab a handhold was robbing him of balance. He had to close his eyes so as to dash to the far end of the log, where fallen branches tore at his legs through his jeans as he sprawled into a giant claw of tree-roots exposed by the bank.

His eyes stung, and a salt taste began to trickle into his throat. "Knock it off, you wimp," he said through his teeth, having sucked in his breath so hard it felt like a dentist's hooks between them, and scrambled up the bank without letting himself rub the ache out of his shins. From the top he could hear the suburb: a car traveling so slowly he guessed that a turtle was crossing the road in front of it, a rotary mower buzzing like a fly close enough to swat, the repeated clop of a jumping skateboard, the old lady who lived down the block from the Travises summoning her cat Bess, the hollow snarl of a motorcycle being tuned in a garage. The car stopped, and Marshall waited until he heard it move away at speed, the driver having carried the turtle to the sidewalk; then he slithered down the far side of the bank toward the first of the ponds which seeped up out of the marsh underlying the forest and the suburb, and made his way along a white sand trail.

The forest touched his bare arms with spider-threads which glinted as they drifted through the air. Bark rattled as lizards fled up trees. Butterflies displayed themselves alongside the path and then fluttered out of reach as though the vegetation was expelling blossoms. Ten minutes' walk brought him to the power lines that stalked through the forest, cables transformed into an abacus by balls of moss. Ahead a dirt road led to the Interstate, which was paralleled by a canal whose banks were studded with shells that would one day be sand. He liked to sit dangling his legs over the bank and watching the denizens of the water, and the notion of saying goodbye to his favorite place seemed to be gathering into an emotion keener and perhaps more lasting than grief.

When the sky began to grumble he hesitated, wondering if this was the approach of one of the T-Storms the weather report on News Channel 5 had announced were Possible. It was a plane, so large or so low that he expected to see the cables vibrate, dislodging the moss. The sound expanded, overwhelming his senses until he thought he could hear other sounds in it. Just as he raised his hands to cover his itching ears the gigantic roar began to shrink, and the illusion of muttering voices dwindled in proportion. The scents of flowers and pine and green water were able to reach him again, and he'd taken a stride toward the power lines when he heard a smothered laugh behind him, and an opened beer can hissed like a snake.

He didn't have to turn. Although the air seemed to have solidified as its humidity joined with his own sudden sweat, he could keep walking. The one thing he absolutely mustn't do was run. He slid one sandal forward, sand grating under his toenails and between his toes. He heard the snap of a branch, and the voice he was dreading to hear said loudly, "Who's that waving his ass at us?"

"Wants us to think he don't know we're here."

"Maybe he's too busy reading a book," a third voice brayed.

Marshall felt small as a lizard, paralyzed with one foot raised as he tried to judge how and when to move. "That right, Marsh?" the first voice called. "Been stealing books from daddums' shop?"

"That's not my name," Marshall said, and forced himself to be audible. "I don't steal."

"He don't steeyill," the second speaker wailed. "What don't he steeyill?"

Marshall was still facing forward, struggling not to turn. "And I don't talk like that," he blurted.

There was a splintering thud as someone dropped from his perch to the ground, and another. "I'll tell you what he stole," the first voice said.

"You tell it like it is, George S."

"His name, ain't that right, Max? Marshall's a name you only give someone when you know they're going to grow up to be a soldier like my daddy."

"He never stole your dad's name."

"You better believe it, Vic. Or his folks stole it for him. Maybe his momma because her and her kind think the army shouldn't have a say in things no more. Should just do what campus bitches like her say and the world'd be a peaceful place."

"Yeah, full of wimps like Marsh."

"Say, I thought a marsh was something you pissed in."

"Watch, he's going to make us chase his ass."

"Or he's going to stand there 'cos he's too dumb to know George S. is just behind him."

George S. hadn't sounded so close when he'd last spoken, but suppose he'd crept nearer? All Marshall could hear now was his own blood. He mustn't let himself flinch from the impression that a hand was poised to seize the back of his neck. If he could just move slowly enough that they wouldn't notice—He inched his left foot along the path and felt his weight shift forward. Then something sharp thudded into the ground behind him, spraying his legs with sand, and he spun round, his ankles scraping together.

George S. and his cronies were at least fifty feet away, leaning against three pines at the edge of the clump of trees and bushes from which they had watched Marshall pass. George S. was popping his inappropriately soft brown eyes at the beer can he'd just thrown and poking his cleft chin forward and grunting out laughs without moving his face, Max was slapping his thighs stuffed into Bermuda shorts and shaking his belly and breasts and chins, Vic was forcing bursts of air so hard between his pursed lips that Marshall wouldn't have been surprised to see Vic's permanent sunburn flake away around the mouth. The sight of them filled him with a mixture of hatred and contempt and panic, and he didn't know which emotion might get the better of him.

Max patted his stomach as if he'd just finished a meal and was ready for the next one. "Some dance, Marsh. Show us that again."

"And smile when you do it," said Vic in a voice almost as raw as his face.

"We don't want to see no tears in them big baby eyes," George S. said, scraping the heel of his boot down the trunk he was leaning against and tearing off chunks of bark. "You better start learning to jump when you're told, boy. Get in training for going to school with us."

Marshall tried to imagine that the bark was Vic's skin peeling off his face, but it didn't work. He felt as though George S. had injected tears behind his eyes, and if he tried to smile to hold in the tears he would be obeying Vic, but if he didn't move he would feel that his tormentors had taken control of him in yet another way. He heard his mother telling him that his body was nobody's property but his and that he must never let anyone do anything with it he didn't want them to do, but they already were—they were making his eyes and the scratches on his legs sting with sweat, and a nerve turn his left cheek spastic. Max emitted groans of mock sympathy as Marshall rubbed his eyes, and the nerve dragged at the corner of his mouth. Even his expression was no longer his to choose, and his helplessness made him clench his fists and speak. "No."

A wind breathed through the topmost branches and tried to strum the power lines, and he heard a man calling "Shemp" in the far distance, and the creak of relief the tree gave as George S. pushed himself away from it. "What did he just say?"

"He said a little baby word," Vic assured him.

"Sounded more like we made him fart to me," Max said, and began to shake open-mouthed and stare at his companions to encourage them to laugh aloud before he did.

"That's to look forward to." Though George S. was visibly disappointed with his cronies, that only added to the dislike he was focusing on Marshall. "What did you say, Marsh? You want to sound like a soldier, speak up like one."

Marshall didn't know if he was obeying or refusing, but his face wouldn't stay still. "No," he mouthed.

"He said it again, George S."

"Thinks we're so stupid we can't see."

"Nobody says that to me except my daddy." George S. drained another can and crushed it in his fist to aim at Marshall. "Know what pain is, boy? Know what hell is?"

Max and Vic were poised like hounds waiting for their master to give them the word. Vic's face was mottled even redder, and Max was actually panting. Marshall was afraid he might burst into hysterical laughter at the sight of them, but restraining himself wouldn't help: they had already decided his fate. He felt his mouth say "No" and heard Max squeal with mirth. "Maybe that's the only word his momma taught him," Vic crowed.

"He'd better learn not to say it to us," George S. said. "Pain and hell are what you're looking at, boy, and that's what we'll be all the time you're at our school if you don't do what any of us say."

"Let me give him a taste," Max said.

Vic rubbed a hand over the lower half of his face, and Marshall was sure he saw skin float into the air. "Tell what you're going to do, Max."

"Gonna sit on his face and give him a blast of my personal home-made perfume."

"If you're lucky that's all he'll give you. And when he's through, seeing as how your name's Marsh, I'm going to—"

"You're disgusting," Marshall cried to shut Vic up. He saw Max take that personally, shoving his chin forward in a furious imitation of George S.'s favorite stance, though the jowls of which a good deal of his face was composed made him rather resemble a lantern-jawed fish attempting to catch a fly. George S.'s hand rose snake-like and cocked back, aiming the can at Marshall's head, and Marshall knew the talk was over. He twisted around and threw himself toward the only other path which looked as though it might lead home.

"He's ours," George S. shouted, ending with a grunt as he flung the can. The whole of Marshall's back felt like an exposed nerve as he skidded along the sandy path. He jerked his hands up to protect his head and neck, too late. The can cut into him just below his shoulders, and he thought it had cracked one of the discs of his spine. The pain almost blinded him, but he had to keep running before any of his tormentors could retrieve the missile. Then a black dog bounded out of the trees to his left and raced straight at him, and his shins collided with its torso, which was solid as a fallen tree. He went sprawling, and the path dealt his forehead a gritty thump.

As he raised his aching head the dog came for him. Its large broad sawed-off face met his, and it opened a mouth that looked and smelled full of blood. He heard its owner calling "Shemp" again, much closer than the trees had made him sound before. As it set about licking his forehead clean, he wrapped his arms around the barrel of a torso and muttered, "Sic them, Shemp. Enemies. Kill."

His bare arms began to tingle with the dog's low growling. Otherwise the animal stayed still, having closed its jaws and peeled its snail-colored gums back from its stained teeth, and Marshall had time to wonder if, since it had never seen him before, it might turn on him. At least the three had halted some yards away, and he hugged the dog tighter, lending more of an edge to its growl. When it tried to pull away he held on. His arms had started to shake when a man dressed only in sandals and shorts jogged into sight on the path beyond the dog, and stopped at once. "Whatever you're trying to do, son, don't," he called, barely audibly. "Let go of him slowly and then stay absolutely still."

It wasn't just the thought of being robbed of protection that made Marshall hang on, it was the unfairness of his being suspected of maltreating the dog. "I was trying to save him," he protested, losing the struggle to keep his voice even. "They were throwing cans at him, look."

"That's not the case, sir," George S. said. "If you want to know—"

"We were only having a bit of fun," Max interrupted.

"With his little brother," Vic added.

"Just so you leave my dog out of it. Now, son, I told you once—"

"They're lying," Marshall cried so shrilly he could barely stand hearing himself. "They would have hurt Shemp."

At the sound of its name the dog swung its head toward him and opened its mouth. Lunging at him, it knocked him onto his back and planted its front paws on his chest before panting hotly in his face as a preamble to licking his chin. "He knows who his friends are," the man said. "I'd advise you three to be making tracks before he decides he's in a hunting mood."

"Sir, I give you my word—"

"Can't use it. All I need is not to see you three around here again, ever."

"Come on," George S. ordered after a pause. "It isn't over."

That might have been intended for Marshall or for the dog's owner, who held up one hand in a gesture that made Shemp tense and the three retreat hurriedly as Marshall let go, stretching out his arms on the hot sand. When the sounds of branches being snapped were lost among the trees the man paced forward and stood looking down at him. Marshall saw the weave of the black hairs on his legs and torso, and the bulge of his denim crotch. The dog had lifted its head to its master, its tongue lolling, its paws still pinning Marshall down. "If you know my dog I should know you," the man said. "Whereabouts do you live?"

"Along from the 7-Eleven," Marshall said as loudly as the dog's weight would allow.

"Shemp." The man patted himself between his legs. "I should run home if I were you, son, before your friends come back to use you for whatever they were going to use you for. Me and the beast, we'll be behind you."

He had to pat himself again before the dog responded by floundering off Marshall, who sat up gingerly, rubbing his spine where the can had struck it. "Did he bruise you? Let's take a look," the man said. "It's just that we like to play rough."

Marshall shoved himself onto his knees. The exertion and his sudden closeness to Shemp's owner filled his nose with the oily scent of the man's suntan lotion. "I'm okay. I have to run now," he said, springing to his feet despite a surge of dizziness.

"Illegal in Britain, you know."

When Marshall glanced at him the man pointed at the dog. "Keep us in mind if you want a romp."

He'd meant the breed was illegal, Marshall decided. "Thanks," he called over his shoulder.

He was settling into a rapid stride homeward when the dog crashed after him through the undergrowth. It seemed content to keep bounding across his path and back to its master, until a shout of "Shemp," more distant than Marshall would have expected, took it away for good. By now Marshall was almost home. He rounded the last pond and clambered up the bank which separated it from the canal by the lake. Someone had removed the log which bridged the canal.

It didn't matter, he could jump. He'd told himself he would one day, and this was it. He wavered at the top of the nine-foot slope, telling himself he mustn't close his eyes, just count to three, no, ten. His foot slipped, and he was slithering toward the canal, and a heavy branch flew past him and smashed into the opposite bank. "Should've been his head," Max said. "Your throw, Vic."

They and George S. had sneaked out of the trees above the pond and were standing at the top of the slope. Marshall's left foot plunged into the canal. The sun pierced his eyes, turning Vic into a silhouette which swung at him an arm several times the length it ought to be. He staggered aside barely in time for the thick branch to miss his scalp and scythe past his ear with a low whoop. Then Vic lost his grip on the weapon, which thumped down the slope and stood on end before falling across the water. The current pivoted its far end toward Marshall, who sloshed into the canal and trod on the branch as it reached him and sprang onto the opposite bank. His fingertips scrabbled at the hard earth as he began to slide downward, scraping his knees, and George S. said,"Time to stop playing. This is a gun, Marsh. Get your ass over here."

Marshall had often heard shots fired in the woods, and once he'd found bullet cases beside a path. He knew that George S.'s father had taught him how to use a gun, but would he let the boy take one out with him? Maybe he didn't know George S. had. Marshall peered over his shoulder, pain jabbing his neck, and saw a dark gun-shaped object glinting in George S.'s hand.

Even if it was a gun he wouldn't dare shoot it at him, Marshall tried to think. They wanted to prevent him from reaching the safe ground in sight of the houses, and if he let them head him off . . . The prospect sent him scrambling up the bank.

Sunlight fastened on his back. Earth dug under his fingernails and stung the quick. The strap of one sandal slid down over his heel, and he thought he'd lost the sandal. He flung up his hands as if he was surrendering, though only to seize the ridge, and missed, and skidded down the bank. "I warned you," George S. called. "You take one more step . . ."

Marshall pressed the raw palms of his hands against the earth and hitched himself upward, and straightened his legs as the toes of his sandals dug into footholds so shallow he was afraid to look down, and then his head was above the ridge, in sight of the lake and the rear of his house at the far end of it. He rammed his chin into the stubbly earth, and heaved himself up until his forearms were over the ridge. He levered himself onto his knees and rolled down the far side of the bank.

He was lurching to his feet when he heard two thuds behind him, followed by a splash and a curse as Max failed to achieve the leap. Marshall only had to run, because he was within a hundred yards of the nearest house. Although there was nobody to be seen, he only had to shout for help if he needed to, assuming that the roar which the latest plane was draping over the suburb didn't blot out his voice. He sprinted through the thick grass toward the end of the fences, on the lakeward side of which someone had abandoned a length of hosepipe whose random curves gleamed black. He heard his pursuers thudding up the bank, and glanced painfully back to see George S. storm into view, brandishing the piece of wood which no longer even looked the color of a gun. Marshall put on speed, hunching his shoulders up and ducking his head to present less of a target. Then the hosepipe lifted its head and extended its forked tongue and came writhing fast at him.

His ankles bruised each other as he stumbled backward. He heard Vic arrive at the top of the bank with a snarl of triumph and Max labor after him, cursing with every breath. He couldn't let them drag him back. He launched himself at the three-foot snake, and in the moment of jumping he saw it was farther away than the canal was wide. He felt himself falter in mid-air, legs waving frantically. Then his feet snapped grass several inches beyond the snake, and kept running, but only until George S. shouted, "Run while you can, Marsh. You won't be able to run away from us much longer."

Marshall swung around and held onto the picket fence while he filled his sandpapered lungs with air. The snake was less than a foot away from him, and stretched across the margin of the lake almost as straight as a line he might have drawn with his heel. "Yes I will," he said, and raised his voice. "We're going away today and never coming back."

George S.'s chin wagged from side to side with frustrated rage, and Marshall burst out laughing. He didn't move when his enemy slid down the bank, spraying the grass at the bottom with dust. If George S. wanted to come for him now, let him come and take whatever consequences he stirred up. But Vic yelled, "Watch out, snake."

George S. saw it, and skated to a halt on the grass. He brandished the piece of wood as though it was a wand whose use hadn't been fully explained to him, then pointed it at Marshall like the gun he'd wanted it to be. "Pray to die if you're lying, Marsh. And if you're not, I'll pray that worse than us is waiting for you where you're going."

Marshall turned and walked away, refusing to be panicked into running. He didn't look back until his lungs had ceased to ache. George S. was watching from beyond the boundary of the snake while his cronies lurked behind him. "So long, Georgette," Marshall said. "Mumble away, Maximum. Hasta la vista, Victim." By now he was facing away from them and waving to his mother, who had come to their fence. The sight of George S.'s face, moving its chin like a goat chewing on frustration, had convinced him that leaving was the right choice—made it seem like the start of an adventure he couldn't begin to imagine.

Darren Fancy was cycling through traffic on one of the roads into the center of Manchester when he forgot where he was and where he was going. A gush of sunlight through the low muddy clouds had confused him, and the rash which had broken out on the faces of the drivers made him want to rip open the wrists of his gloves to examine his own hands. He could only cycle while he tried to understand, weaving expertly between two side mirrors in fat black plastic housings and kicking another against a Volvo to give himself more room. As the electric window of the Volvo began to hum open he jabbed an open-legs sign at the driver and saw that the spots were crawling over her pudgy pale infuriated face. They were shadows of raindrops on the windscreen, but that didn't help him put any more thoughts together. The lights of the traffic signals at the junction ahead extended from red to amber and then, as if the weight was too much, dropped to green, and Darren veered in front of a Jaguar whose driver was pressing a car phone against the bottom of his turban and jerked the bicycle over the curb onto the smashed pavement. He shook his head until the earphones of his Walkman fell around his neck, but that only let the blurred sounds of the stampede of traffic at him. Then he caught sight of the sign for the probation center and realized he was nearly home.

He couldn't tell whether his forehead was hotter outside or in. The sun looked as though someone was trying to poke the end of a telescope through the clouds in search of him. Surely he'd already been wherever he was supposed to go. He hoisted the Benign Lumps concert into place over his ears and pedalled fast onto the waste ground occupied by workers' cabins, which was the start of the quickest way home through the council estate.

The cabins weren't much narrower than the houses of the estate. Inside were bare metal desks with pens locked up in them, filing cabinets stuffed with paper, graphs on the walls—nothing worth breaking in for. They weren't even a challenge like the new and supposedly unbreakable park benches. A man carrying a clipboard and wearing a pen for a necklace came out of one cabin to watch Darren with an expression like the one all the teachers at secondary school turned on him, especially when they thought he wasn't looking. Darren considered performing a wheelie to spray him with mud, then contented himself with his best spit, which traveled at least twelve feet and spattered the open door of the cabin. A shout of "You dirty little—" was blotted out by the Benign Lumps as he sped off between the backyards, his teeth chattering with mirth.

He could see over the fences by standing on the pedals, but there wasn't much to see except kitchens and back rooms repeating themselves beneath tiny bedroom windows like spyholes for watching out for the police. Where the gutters were clogged with windblown litter, the walls under them looked spongy with January rain. He saw a toddler trying to climb on a car engine covered with a tarpaulin in one yard, a needle and bloody syringe in the next, where the grass straggled like a dosser's beard. A woman toothy with several colors of plastic clothes-pegs glared out of her yard at him as he raced behind Mozart Close, a Doberman snarled at him from behind a fence of Mendelssohn. He spat over the fence and screeched left behind Haydn, feeling as if he'd become the pounding drums and the guitars and singers trying to outshriek one another, and saw several children from his old school blocking the alley ahead.

It wasn't seeing them which made him brake—he would have enjoyed watching them scream and cower against the fence—but in the yard into which they were trooping he'd seen a white rabbit in a green hutch from his last year's classroom. Bugs was the class pet which Mrs. Morris had never let Darren look after during any of the holidays and weekends, though she used to call Darren her little ray of sunshine as if they were sharing a joke, not like any of the multitude of teachers at his new school, none of whom seemed to know or want to know him. He jumped off the mountain bike and ran it into the yard and shook the headphones off. "Eh, whosit, give us a hold of Bugs."

"Don't, Henry. Mam said nobody but us was to."

"Tell your sister to shut her hole, Henry. It's not yours to say who can hold it. Give the bugger here."

The girl sidled behind the two friends she'd brought home. She was twisting a toggle of her duffel coat so hard that moisture oozed out of the cloth. "I'm getting mam."

"You get her," Darren said over the whine and tish of the earphones. "Tell her Darren Fancy's in your yard and all he's after is a hold of Bugs, and see if she wants to get on the wrong side of us."

All he wanted was to stroke the animal, the way Mrs. Morris had let him. His hands were remembering how soft its fur was, except that having to argue was mixing up the sensation with the muffled spiky throbbing at his neck. He ran the bicycle at Henry, and the boy backed away, tripping over the prop of the clothesline which sagged between the corners of the yard. As Henry sprawled on his arse on the concrete and began to howl like a factory siren, his sister dashed out of the gate. "I never touched him," Darren said, not for the first or the dozenth time in his life. "Don't you two be saying I did him when I never. I'm holding Bugs and then you can if you want."

He let the bicycle drop against the fence and stooped to the hutch, tearing open the wrists of his gloves and pulling his hands free. Bugs thumped one paddle-shaped back leg and retreated into the section of the hutch that was boarded up like a derelict house. Henry's howls were making Darren's fingers feel as if he hadn't taken off the gloves. "Shut it, you twat, or I'll stick one in your gob," Darren told him, so savagely that Henry gulped himself silent, and then Darren's fingers were able to turn the wooden catches of the hutch.

As soon as he groped into its nest, the animal fled into the larger compartment. Darren left one hand in the straw sown with hard round turds and reached around with the other to try and stroke the rabbit's ears flat, the way it kept them when it was calm. "Eh, Bugs, you know me. It's Darren from last year."

He'd managed to flatten one ear when the rabbit struggled from under his hand and fled for its nest, then at once dodged aside, having found

Darren there too, and leapt out of the hutch. Darren fell back, banging his knuckles on the wooden underside of the roof. Henry was lying on the concrete as though scared to move until he was told, but he scrabbled backward away from the rabbit, faster when Darren lunged in his direction. Then Darren's hands were around the animal, which was so large that they barely encircled its torso, and lifted it onto his chest.

Its blunt twitching nose pushed under his chin, and he thought it was going to nestle there. Instead it dug its claws into his chest so hard he felt them through his shell suit and hauled itself onto his shoulder. It was going to leap over the fence. "Come here, you dick," Darren growled, squeezing it with all his strength. He felt its ribs crack before it wriggled out of his grasp and sprang over his shoulder, missing the fence and landing on the concrete with a loud slap.

He'd broken it. It lay there shaking with its legs stretched out, and Darren was about to grab the evidence and shove it in the hutch when it grunted. Gathering itself, it performed a tentative hop. As he moved to head it off it hurtled past him, out of the gate.

He couldn't run that fast. He seized his gloves from the top of the hutch and digging his hands into them, swung the bicycle away from the fence and vaulted onto it. Henry had sprinted into the alley, grabbing at his own face in dismay and stretching out his hands and grabbing his face again. One of Darren's handlebars clubbed him in the kidney, knocking him out of the way. Bugs was hesitating at the end of the alley which gave onto one of the patches of grass the planners seemed to have left because they couldn't think what else to do with the ground, and Darren thought it might feel at home on the grass. As he aimed the bicycle to send the rabbit that way so that he could ride around it until it tired, however, it dodged into an alley which led to a road which bordered the estate.

Darren skidded after it, yelling, "Stop, you fucker." He was hoping his shout might bring someone out of a yard to head it off, except people on the estate knew better than to intervene or even to look if they heard anything like that. In seconds Bugs was at the far end of the alley, where it faltered, panting, perhaps confused by the heaps dogs had left on the pavement. But as Darren raced down the alley the rabbit dashed onto the road and froze halfway across. Darren pedalled furiously, having heard the car. He emerged from the alley just in time to see a black Rover traveling at twice the speed it was supposed to on that road. Its right front wheel struck the rabbit, and the thud turned into a muffled pop.

The car was out of sight before Darren bumped over the curb. He made several circuits of the expanded rabbit, which was now more red than white. He was less disturbed by the mess that had spilled out of it than by the color of the innards, a duller red than they ever were in videos. He was fumbling the earphones over his ears when Henry saw him along the alley and ran toward him.

"It's your fault, you selfish little shit," Darren hissed, and rode at Henry, feeling fast and powerful as the Rover. Henry gaped at the rabbit and drew breath for a howl, then read Darren's expression and turned tail. As he fled onto the no man's land of grass Darren was at his heels, and would have ridden him down except that Henry's mother came flustering out of her alley, a glass of what Darren guessed was gin shedding drops over her wristful of tarnished bracelets. The music hammering his ears wanted him to go for Henry anyway. Instead he veered around the boy as Henry and his mother competed to see who could make the highest noise, and sped across the sodden grass and down his alley to the front of Handel Close.

His house was on the corner. Whenever he heard it called the Fancy house it sounded like a joke which everyone but he was afraid to laugh at. Except for having some grass that went around three sides of it, no broader than a hallway along the windowless side, it was much like any house on the estate. He lifted the gate, and the slouching fence with it, so as to open it across the cracked concrete path, and wheeled his bicycle through the mud overgrown with scraps of paper. There was just room for the bicycle among the spare bits of car in the shed. He sneaked to the back door of the house, but as the key turned in the first of the locks one of his uncles had put in, his father's head reared up beyond the window next to the kitchen. By the time Darren finished letting himself in his father was waiting in the hall, scratching the veins of his folded arms with the black crescents of his fingernails and chewing whatever had left wet crumbs in the stubble around his mouth. "Where've you been?"

That meant before the rabbit, Darren guessed. He'd been somewhere for his father. He fumbled with the earphones, which had slipped down his neck, in case they might help him remember. "Eh?" his father shouted.

He'd begun to pinch his eyes with one hand as if to rub them even redder and was pounding the wall rapidly as a pneumatic drill with the side of the other, which was getting ready to punch Darren. "Delivering?" Darren said.

"I know that, you defec. What kept you?"

"Had to wait?"

There was nothing Darren could think of to say that would save him from being knocked down while his father was in this mood. But his father sent his bloodshot glare past him and finished chewing. "Better not do it twice," he muttered, apparently not about him, then stared hard at him. "See anyone we don't know?"

"No?"

After a pause during which Darren felt the music clamping itself to his neck his father said, "Well?"

Darren tensed himself to run as his father's gaze drifted down his body, and then he realized it mightn't be the best place to punch him that his father was looking for. He tore at his wrist and succeeded in dragging off the glove so as to unzip his pocket. "Here, da. It's all here."

"Better fucking be." His father lurched forward so violently that Darren thought he was going to punch him for luck, but only snatched the wad of crumpled grubby notes. He poked between his teeth with one thick finger before using it to leaf through the notes, counting more or less silently. Four hundred and forty, and sixty, and eighty . . . He pinched his eyes harder and went through the notes again while Darren tried to sidle away unnoticed, but then his father finished counting and grimaced, not so much satisfied as frustrated at having no reason to hit anyone. Eventually he said, "Want a tab?"

It occurred to Darren, as it seemed to have quite a few times, that those might be making the hole in his brain where his memory ought to be. "Still got some."

"Suit yourself," his father said, stuffing the notes into the back pocket of his jeans, which he yanked up over his stained Gucci shirt before pulling the belt a notch tighter. "Just stay out. We're talking."

"Where's mam?"

"The old bastard pissed himself again," his father said, turning away as though Darren was no longer there, and let himself into the mutter of male voices in the back room.

Darren retreated to the stairs in case anyone accused him of listening. Lamps which someone, probably one of his parents, must have grabbed for support hung off the walls, exposing their wires. As he hurried upstairs, peeling off his jacket that felt as soaked inside as out, he heard his mother in his grandfather's room. "See what you done, you dirty old sod.

Should be in Bellevue with the rest of the animals." Darren listened outside the door in case there was worse to hear, but the only further sounds were his mother's dramatic groans as she lifted the old man and his grandfather groaning louder as she did, and so Darren crossed the thin rucked carpet to his room.

These days he never knew how large it was going to seem. Today it was bigger, despite the new computer in its box, and the hi-fi and television and video recorder and video game console. He threw his jacket and the Walkman on his unmade bed, and listened to the drip of water sneaking in through some part of the roof, then he tore the box apart to get at the computer which he'd begged when his father and his uncles had had nearly twenty of them in the back room.

Once he'd emptied the box he shoved the screeching polystyrene under the bed with the packing from the other items in his bedroom. He snapped the rubber bands that held various leads, which he pushed into the sockets that appeared to be shaped for them, even if he had to force a couple in. He plugged the computer into the wall socket, which he had to steady with one hand because he'd borrowed one of the screws for some purpose he couldn't remember, and switched on. Though a corner of the keyboard gave him a green light, the screen stayed blank.

He picked up the monitor and shook it hard, then did the same with the keyboard, and jiggled the plugs in their sockets. Nothing helped. At last he picked up the instruction manual, though even the thought of trying to read it made his skull feel squeezed smaller. He flattened the manual on his knees and set about reading the first page, dragging a fingertip under the words. When it became clear to him that he'd spent fifteen minutes in reading how much he was going to enjoy the computer, he flung the manual at the wall and wrenched the leads out of the keyboard and attempted to plug them in different sockets. One plug was determined not to come out, and when he yanked it back and forth to dislodge it he felt a snap as it pulled loose. He'd broken off two of its pins in the socket.

He tried to pretend it didn't matter. He replugged the leads in as many ways as he could think of, but the screen remained blank. The green light winked at him as sweat ran into his eyes. His attempts to pry the pins out of the socket only split his fingernails. Suppose his parents tried to sell the computer if they ran out of money? It wouldn't be the first time they'd taken something from his room when they needed to buy themselves a dose. He switched off the computer and ran to the nearest refuge he could think of—his grandfather's room.

He'd heard his mother go downstairs, and she'd shut the door tight so it would be harder to hear the old man. Darren poked his finger in the hole where the handle used to be and pushed the door open. First he saw the stuff which occupied nearly all the room and kept out most of the light from the slit of a window—rolls of leftover carpet, old photographs covered with broken glass, bulging suitcases with rusty locks, toys Darren had grown out of that weren't worth selling, ornaments nobody wanted, videos nobody watched. When no sound from the bed greeted him he crept into the room.

His grandfather was lolling against the purple plush headboard, his knobbly hands gripping the discolored quilt above his waist as though ensuring that nobody uncovered him. Several buttons were missing from his pajama jacket, which was held shut at his throat by a large safety pin, and Darren thought he saw a new bruise on his chest. Above the cables of the neck, the old man's face looked like an elongated mask of perished whitish rubber, cracking at the forehead and too loose below the ears. Most of his remaining hair sprouted from his nose, and Darren knew without having to venture within reach that his grandfather's breaths would be sucking it in and out. He tiptoed to the end of the bed and squeezed the old man's feet hard.

"Ow, you—" his grandfather wailed, and added something full of syllables, though it was mostly saliva that emerged. One hand groped over his chest and made him wince, then fumbled at the safety pin before eventually locating his eyes, which he flicked open with his nails. The eyes looked drowned. "Who is it?" he mumbled. "Are we there yet?"

For a few seconds Darren only watched, queasily fascinated by what his grandfather might say or do next. When the eyes began to retreat behind their lids he said, "It's Darren, granda."

"Dandy? Thought the Jerries got you."

"Darren." The boy felt as though he was shouting to find himself. "Dee ay ar ee en."

"Oh, Phil's lad." The old man had discovered one of his ears and cupped a hand behind it. He succeeded in focusing on Darren, but not for long. "Sending boys to fight Jerry now, are they? Expendable, that's us, and never even asked who we want to fight for. Sent soldiers to put down the workers, old Two Fingers did. At least Adolf wants to share the money round a bit and take it off them as shouldn't have so much." His eyes narrowed, squeezing trickles of moisture down the channels of his face. "Who did you say you was?"

"Darren," the boy said, and had to repeat it again before his grandfather's suspicion died down. "You don't mind me hearing. You told me about the sergeant. Tell again, go on."

"What bloody sergeant? What are you on about, lad?"

"You know. The one you got killed when he kept picking on you."

"Keep your voice down. You want your head seeing to, saying things like that about a man."

"It's all right, granda, there's only us. You can tell."

The old man rolled his eyes until he identified his surroundings or at least appeared satisfied with them, then began to push the quilt down and kick feebly at it. "Hey up, then. Get in so you can hear."

"I can hear here."

"Hear, hear and yoicks and tally-ho and chin, chin, old chap." What Darren presumed to be his grandfather's caricature of an officer was so savage that the last word turned into a racking cough, at the eventual end of which the old man wiped his cheeks and chin, not very accurately. "Scuttle off and let me try and sleep. I can't remember. It was just a tale."

"It wasn't. You said." Darren felt betrayed. "He picked on you to go first in a minefield, remember, and you got these twigs in your hand."

"Is that a fact? That was cute of me."

"Yes, and it was dark, but you could see better than him, and you crawled along till you saw this mine on your left, then you stuck the twigs in the ground and pretended they was a mine you'd nearly bumped into, and you went along till you were nearly on top of the real mine and he couldn't see it because you were in the way. Tell what happened to him then."

"Aye, I remember him. Eyes like a spaniel when you'd given her a good kicking. Come here first. Losing me voice. Can't speak up."

The coughing did seem to have affected him. Darren didn't need to go too close; he knew all his grandfather's tricks. He took a step forward, clenching his buttocks, and a door crashed open downstairs. "Darren!"

His grandfather dragged the quilt up. "What's that? Who's got in?"

"It's only da. Your son, granda, Phil." Darren was trying to reassure himself too, but it didn't work. "Darren?" his father was yelling. "Where are you, you little fucker? What have you been up to? There's some cunt and her kid hanging round outside."

"I heard him go in your da's room," his mother yelled.

His father pounded up the stairs, and Darren backed into the room until the pile of junk stopped him. He pressed against it rather than edge toward the bed as his father kicked the door wide. "What did you do?"

"Nothing, da."

"Don't give me that."

Darren knew that whatever he might give his father wouldn't save him. As he saw his father stalking at him he felt as if he'd already been punched in the mouth, but managed to make it say, "I only wanted to hold the rabbit."

His father halted long enough to look disgusted and incredulous. "You what?"

The worst thing Darren could do would be to repeat himself, yet he was unable to stop. "I only wanted to hold the—"

The fist caught the side of his mouth and nose and chin. He felt his jaw shudder and his lips burst against his teeth as he fell among the rolls of carpet, drawing his knees up tight against his stomach and covering his head with his arms. "Aw, Phil, don't be doing that all the time," his grandfather croaked. "Spare the lad a bit of loving now and then."

"We know all about your loving, you dirty old sod." For a moment Darren's father seemed to have been infuriated into kicking Darren even harder than he had already planned to, but then he stamped downstairs. "See to the bitch, will you, Marie," he shouted. "I'm talking."

When the old man hitched himself across the bed and reached for Darren while groaning sympathetically, the boy struggled to his feet and stumbled out of the room. His father had shut himself in again, his mother was marching along the hall, and Darren would have gone down to watch except that he wasn't having Henry and the woman see what had been done to his face. He dodged into the bathroom to grab the toilet roll, the mirror showing him his purple lopsided mouth and the column of blood under his nose, and dabbed at himself as he ran into his bedroom, where he turned the computer keyboard on its face and planted the monitor on top of it, and stood on them to spy through the open transom.

Henry's mother was at the fence, pushing her bracelets along her fat wrists as if they were sleeves she was rolling up while she tried to see into the house. Henry was doing his best to look convinced that nobody could touch him so long as he was with her. When the front door banged open, however, he made to flee until his mother caught hold of him. "What are you hanging round here for?" Darren's mother demanded. "Who do you think you are, a social worker?"

"Does Darren Fancy live here?"

"What if he does?" his mother countered, and more loudly, infuriated at having revealed that much, "Think I'd tell you?"

"He just chased our Henry's teacher's rabbit under a car and pushed Henry over where he hurt his spine last year."

"Liar."

"Our Clodagh and her friends all saw him do it."

"Little liars, the lot of them. See, he daren't even look at me."

"You speak up for yourself, Henry. You tell her." Henry's mother gave the boy a shake that jangled her bracelets, and when he twisted his head farther aside, flicked his ear hard with her fingers. "I'm telling you he knocked Henry on his bum where he's already hurt his back being pushed down a slide, and the rabbit his teacher at school said he wasn't to let anyone else have—"

Darren's mother strode to the gate, her red hair flopping about her head as though better to expose the black roots of its parting. "Want some advice?"

"If you think I came here just—"

"Stuff the rabbit up his bum and see if that makes him better. And I'll stuff something up it for you," Darren's mother said, dragging the gate open with a screech of wood on concrete, "if you don't piss off."

Henry's mother had covered his ears during most of this, and now she moved him along the fence with her hands still over them, as though sliding a jug with a woeful face along a shelf. "Everyone knows about you, Marie Fancy," she said at the top of her voice, perhaps in the hope of attracting some support. "No wonder your Darren's like he is."

"You leave our Darren out of it. Don't you try to tell me how to bring him up."

"We'll see what our Henry's school says about what your Darren done," Henry's mother said, and pushed Henry along the pavement. "They know all about him."

She shouldn't have tried to have the last word, Darren thought, although the outcome might have been the same in any case. As soon as she turned away his mother darted out of the gate and thumped her as hard as she could on the back of the neck. Henry's mother collapsed to her knees, and one of her bracelets flew off. "That's just a warning," Darren's mother cried, and flounced back to the house.

She saw Darren at the transom and brandished her fist at him. When the front door shook the house he was afraid she was going to come up and add to the pain in his face. Nevertheless he watched as Henry ran after the rolling bracelet and caught it once it fell over, and fetched it to his mother. She almost pulled him over in the process of hauling herself to her feet, then staggered away, supporting herself with one hand on his shoulder. Once she was out of sight, and Darren's mother had either forgotten or decided not to come after him, Darren climbed down from his perch.

His face felt invaded and too big, as though the pain had been inserted between it and him, but familiar enough. He hung the earphones from his scalp and switched on the Walkman and lay on the bed, having kicked the quilt onto the floor. When he turned the tape up full, the sound seemed to get between him and the pain. He tore off a wad from the toilet roll and laid it beneath his nose to sop up the blood. After a while the bubbling of his nostril became almost pleasurable, and when the tape ended he lay there breathing and listening to the static, and thought there was nothing he enjoyed more. Hearing that stillness felt like being asleep without needing to sleep.

1

VIOLENCE

"Mom, we need to go in now. Everyone is."

"I'm sure we're okay for a few minutes still."

"No, they said it was the last call. What do you think happened to dad?"

"Nothing to look like that about, Marshall. I expect he got held up."

"Or lost."

"That could be Don, true enough. Don't worry, just about everyone in town must know the way here."

"Suppose he had an accident?"

"Don't suppose quite so much, honey. I think his driving's getting pretty near as good as mine. You don't have accidents by being too careful."

Susanne leaned out past the New York Interstate 190 sign and gazed along the street as a car as red as Don's swung around the curve, but it wasn't his—not even a Volvo. "Let's go in, then. They'll send him to us when he shows up," she said, and followed Marshall past a NYPD car.

Beyond it was a yellow school bus, and a line of phone booths next to a 5th Avenue and East 42nd sign overlooked by an illuminated Baskin-Robbins billboard and one for Coca-Cola up which waves of red light were rising. But the phones in the booths were British, as was the rest of the small theme park that belonged to Granada Television, and the interior of the studio building was even more of a jumble of locations. Along a corridor which contained one side of Downing Street, railings and all, the Travises came to a room full of furniture so large that Susanne would have needed help to climb onto a chair. A dressing room crowded with period costumes provoked Marshall's secret smile which tugged his small mouth leftward and half closed his bright blue eyes, an expression which she was never sure whether he'd consciously learned from his father. Ahead was the illuminated plaque of the studio, outside which a young woman with the waist of her long skirt pulled up almost to her breasts was glancing at the Travises over a clipboard. "You'll be . . . ?"

"Not too late, I hope."

"Ah, Mrs. Travis. And son." The studio assistant had apparently gathered all this from Susanne's accent, and inscribed two ticks on her list with a pencil bearing a rubber cat's head. "Some of your students are here, and—yes, well, we'll have you down the front, I think."

"I don't suppose my husband beat us to it?"

"If he's not here he can't be here," the young woman assured her, tapping the name above the pair she'd just checked off. "Why did we want him, did we say?"

"He's a bookseller."

"That wouldn't be it. Unless," the assistant said hopefully, "he's been in trouble with the police?"

"Not even a ticket as of this morning."

"Is he American too?"

"That's for sure."

"Maybe that was it. We'll have to leave a space for him at the back." The assistant steered Marshall past herself, and looked ready to wield Susanne's elbow too. "Travis family. One missing," she told the floor manager who flustered to meet them.

Several wide rows of seats full of people and noise faced an expanse of floor planted with cameras and lights. Quite a few of the people were already red-faced with arguing or with eagerness to do so. Four of Susanne's students were sitting together on the top row, and three of them waved to her—Elaine appeared too embarrassed to acknowledge her as the floor manager indicated seats on the front row with a sweep of his open upturned hands, one of which he then used to rub out some of his frown. Susanne took the seat beside two women in track suits who gave her gray suit and black tights an unimpressed glance each; Marshall shared part of his place with a man who seemed committed to discovering how much space his legs could encompass. As Susanne tugged her skirt over as much of her knees as it covered, a man in a suit which was apparently designed to be a size too big for him strode out from behind the cameras, and the assistant with the clipboard closed the door.

The younger members of the audience whistled and cheered and stamped their feet to celebrate the emergence of the presenter, and their lead was followed by an aggressive theme which sounded almost as though it was being performed by an orchestra as the presenter reappeared, having taken a turn around the cameras and lights. The floor manager wafted the applause higher with the hand that wasn't flattening his forehead, and the younger set went even wilder as the music withdrew in defeat. The floor manager patted the uproar down with both hands, and the presenter turned to the cameras and shot his cuffs. "Violence," he said.

Someone determined to have the last noise or unable to contain it emitted a shrill whistle, but the presenter ignored it. "At this very moment someone in Britain is being raped or mugged or murdered. Last week the whole community was shocked by the case of the nine-year-old whose sister was knocked down by a speeding Ferrari and who went up on a bridge over the Manchester rush hour with some of his friends and dropped a concrete block on the first Ferrari they saw . . ."

"Wasn't that yesterday?" Marshall whispered.

"Not by the time we're transmitted," Susanne said in his ear.

"The Home Office reports that violent criminals are getting younger and younger. Police are resigning because they say they're losing the fight against violence. Are we spending too much time and money trying to understand it? How much of it is caused by what we let people watch? How can we stop it being beamed into the country by satellite? How far should ordinary innocent people be allowed to go in order to protect themselves and their family? What signals should we as a society be sending to criminals? Just some of the questions I'll be discussing with the audience here tonight," the presenter said, and swung around. "So let me start by asking—what are the causes of violence?"

Only his eyes were moving in his round stubble-topped face. Their darting halted as he flung out his right hand. "Yes, there, no, girl at the back."

It was Rachel, one of Susanne's students, for whom a technician was fishing with a microphone. "I don't know what people watching films on satellite has to do with me and my friends being afraid to go out at night," Rachel said. "I should think they'd be home watching them."

"Right, too busy watching to commit violence, lady with her hand up?"

"Ever been raped? You wouldn't say that if you'd been raped."

"I still might if it was true, I hope," Rachel said mildly as another woman shouted, "What about being afraid to stay in? Half the violence is in the home, only they don't want the public knowing."

"Don't all talk at once or we won't hear you. Suppressing evidence of domestic violence. Who are you saying does that?"

"Who do you think? This government that wants the family to be the answer to everything."

"Family answer to everything. Who else believes violence starts at home? Yes, social worker there."

"All the violent criminals I've come in contact with were brutalized at home. In Sweden it's an offense to strike a child, and if we want to break the cycle of violence—"

Uproar greeted this. Susanne made out shouts of "Show me anybody it ever did a bit of harm" and "I'd do more than strike some of them." The presenter ranged back and forth in front of the audience, shouting, "Whoa, whoa" and trying to conceal his delight. "Make punishing children illegal," he said as the noise subsided into incoherence. "Is that the answer, yes, with the mustache?"

"I didn't say—" the social worker protested, but the man called upon to speak was louder. "Anyone who commits violence is a coward. What they need is some violence done to them."

"But then what would that make the doer?"

So said Liu, another student of Susanne's, infuriating the previous speaker. "That's the kind of rubbish that gets police killed on the streets. We should give them all the weapons they need, and teachers while we're at it."

"Arm police and teachers. Yes, no, next to you, T-shirt?"

"If a teacher thumped me I'd just go and thump someone else."

"Yes, you and your friends go in for that, don't you? I'll come back to you, but teachers teaching violence, anyone? Back row, you've had your hand up for a good bit?"

"I hope everyone knows it's being taught as a subject right here in Manchester."

"Violence on the curriculum. Yes, now where is she? Some people would say you're inviting more violence by teaching it."

Though he had been gazing at Susanne for some moments, it had taken her that long to realize he hadn't mistaken her for someone else. "Let's make it clear I teach at the University," she said.

"Yeh-yeh-yeh," the presenter said rapidly, sounding like an imitation of a dog at the end of a run, "but violence."

"Well, I think we need to distinguish between representation and reality. In my course we look at depictions of violence in prose and film."

"Why look at it at all?" shouted the woman who had raised the subject of the course.

"As long as our culture produces images of violence, I think it's important to understand how they're consumed and what they signify."

"That's not culture. That's not what we sent our Elaine to university for."

The presenter held up one hand like a traffic cop toward the woman and bowed at Susanne. "You're saying you don't enjoy it, it's just an academic subject."

"I wouldn't say that academic subjects shouldn't be enjoyable. Sure I enjoy some depictions of violence," she said, raising her voice as a mutter of dissatisfaction from various areas behind her turned into a jeer. "Part of the point of the course is to look at what our enjoyment involves."

"We don't need professors to tell us that," a man yelled.

"Specially not a Yank."

"Are we being expected to pay her wages?" a third wanted to know.

"We want violence stopped and you're making a living out of it," Elaine's mother shouted. "Ban it all and we might get somewhere."

"Don't tell us nobody's proved a connection. It all ought to be banned in case there is."

"If we aren't sure what effects it has," Susanne said, "isn't it possible that trying to suppress something that's so much a part of our culture might be more dangerous?"

"Leave it in case we make it worse. Anyone agree with that? Yes, no, third row, no, you're fourth, yes?"

"Mom, that wasn't what you said."

"Maybe I've said enough," Susanne murmured, failing to catch the response the presenter provoked. "Anyone else?" he urged. "Lady's daughter there?"

"I was just wondering," Elaine said in the somewhat strident voice that meant she'd had to persuade herself to speak up, "if anyone's done any research into the effects of programs like this."

"If we ever do a show on it we'll have you on. Violence, though, any thoughts?"

"That's what I was trying to get at. I can't see what you setting people at each other like this achieves except making them angry, which is on the way to violence, and people watching at home as well."

"I'm the real cause of violence. Well, that's a new one. Any takers? Yes, we haven't been hearing much from that side?"

"You just want to let ordinary folk be heard."

Susanne couldn't decide if that was intended as praise or complaint. "Democracy's the name," the presenter said, and was leaning toward the next speaker when a small woman who looked squashed by her brimless mauve hat and its burden of pins appeared at the end of the front row and stumped toward Susanne. "I'll say this to you in front of all these people," she declared as she came. "You infect our Elaine with any more of that stuff and I'm telling you, I'll split you from gob to navel."

Susanne's instinct was to laugh or to say "That's colorful," but those were only ways of delaying her sense of shock. "Can we keep our seats, please," the presenter said, though failing to direct the microphone away from Susanne and Mrs. Nash, and then Marshall intervened. "You oughtn't to say that. My mom doesn't infect anyone."

"They're just turns of phrase, honey," Susanne assured him, but Mrs. Nash turned on him. "What are you supposed to be doing here? What's any of this got to do with a kiddie of how old?"

"Twelve," Marshall said with injured pride.

"Pull the other one, love." Mrs. Nash peered narrowly at him. "Your mother never lets you watch those films, does she?"

"I'm allowed to see films in America I can't see here."

"That's no answer. All right, keep your hair on, I'm sitting down." Mrs. Nash appeared to be proposing to do so on the floor as she stooped to push her face into Susanne's. "Take yourself and your violence back where you came from," she said, and stumped off.

Susanne was tugging her skirt down again, though the gesture made her feel no less assaulted, and wishing the cameras away when the presenter said to Marshall, "Just clear up a point for me. Who lets you see films in America?"

"The state, I guess. Just because it's rated R doesn't mean you have to be seventeen to see it, but here it's rated eighteen and I'm supposed to wait six years before I can watch it again."

He was talking about an action movie which he'd seen with Don in Florida. "No age restrictions on what you can see and read in America," the presenter interpreted him as having said. "Any comments? Yes, with the glasses, no, the other glasses?"

"Of course there are restrictions," Susanne said, but the microphone had found a woman saying, "All commercial films are an act of male violence. Just look at the titles. They even call cinemas Cannon."

"If we're going to sit here chunnering about films all night," a man on the front row said in a tone as plain and blunt as his face, "I'm off."

Susanne wondered if the assistant with the high waist and the clipboard had eased the studio door open to let him out, but she was inching it shut again, having admitted herself. "Increasing violence," the presenter said. "Any more ideas on why there's so much?"

Susanne had some new ones, but preferred to keep them to herself now that the burning glass of the argument had moved away from her. She gave Marshall a quick grin which wasn't too far removed from how she felt, then realized that the studio assistant was gazing at her and displaying a scrap of paper.

When Susanne made to rise, the assistant gestured her back and held up the paper as a promise of delivery. She was waiting until the attention of the cameras was well away from Susanne, who heard the argument dodge about the audience, retreating from her and then, like a storm, coming back. She found it difficult to be aware of anything except repetitions of the word violence, violence, violence. "They're scared of nothing any more," a man shouted from one end of the back row, "we've got to bring back fear." A pole lifted toward him, and the assistant tiptoed fast across the studio floor, glancing at the cameramen in case they should wave her away.

She placed the folded paper firmly in Susanne's hand and retreated. Had she been ensuring that the paper didn't fall? The pressure of her hand on Susanne's had felt like reassurance. Marshall leaned over to read the message as Susanne unfolded it, and she thought of keeping it from him until she had seen what had been addressed to her, but it was too brief for him not to be able to read it immediately. All it said was YOUR HUSBAND WITH POLICE.

2

MEANING BUSINESS

Just as Don grew convinced that the suburb was so content with its own uniformity that it would repeat itself for as many miles again, he saw a park beyond the low boxy houses which perhaps only the rain, as prevalent in Manchester as he'd heard it was in Seattle, had rendered the color of mud. One of the three-story streets across the park might even be his goal. He pulled over behind a van with a For Sale notice in the rear window, and a lengthily raincoated youth standing restlessly on the street corner stared at him as though he had no right to be there or had better prove he had. "A to Zee," Don mouthed partly for his benefit, and opened the book of street maps on the seat beside him.

It was the only book whose spine he'd ever broken since he could remember, and that was partly from frustration. Not only had some streets been blocked up or restricted to one way or demolished since the compilation of the book, but the reality through which he was driving was out of proportion with the maps, streets ending before they were supposed to or narrowing unexpectedly or curving where they had been shown as straight, so that he kept thinking he had even less sense of where he was. Whenever the streets on the maps grew profuse he was reminded that he needed reading glasses, and now he picked up the magnifying glass from the dashboard.

The glass had come from a drawer in the slipcase of his copy of the *Oxford English Dictionary*, but when he caught sight of himself in the rearview mirror he saw how much it made him resemble some eccentric sleuth in an English detective story, with reddish hair that contradicted any amount of brushing, high forehead whose wrinkles implied it was packed with more thoughts than he presently had, eyebrows trying to meet across the bridge of his long nose, heavy eyelids which lent him a semblance of sleepy watchfulness behind his spectacles, mouth skewed slightly leftward so that even when he wasn't smiling he appeared to be about to do so. His glance had also shown him the youth looking yet more suspicious and perhaps suspected, digging his fists so deep in the pockets of the pallid plastic raincoat that it gaped to reveal he was wearing only a T-shirt and torn jeans. "Do what you want to yourself so long as you keep it to yourself," Don murmured, lowering the glass to lasso the map into focus. There, when he tilted his head until his chin and shoulder squeezed out a pinch of flesh, was the street name he'd been told, and next to it a patch of not much of a shape, identified as a park in larger letters than the streets had room for. He let the glass fall on the open pages and sent the Volvo toward the park.

"Left into traffic," he reminded himself at the end of the street, "learn left, lurch left." An empty swing flew up from a playground in the park to greet him. A boy of about Marshall's age was swinging it to wind the chains tight around the bar, while others smashed the ends of a seesaw against the concrete. Two boys no older than seven, who had apparently been driven out of the playground, were hanging onto the railings and watching the traffic, and Don grimaced sympathetically at them as he passed. The next moment each of them flung an object at the car.

Don almost let go of the wheel in order to protect his face before he realized the missiles had cracked, not the windshield. They were large garden snails, and the impact hadn't killed them. "Hey, come on, guys," Don protested at the boys, who responded with a jeer apiece as they picked up ammunition to await the next car. He might have driven around the park to confront them if he weren't already late for his appointment. He switched on the wipers, then the washers, and gazed ahead, trying to ignore the greenish writhing as he steered into the side road.

This one seemed to have taken the British habit of concealing street names on the walls of houses or front gardens even further. Eventually he located the name, low on an already low garden wall, and figured that Damb Street would have been Dane Street, his destination, until someone had attacked it with a marker pen. He backed the station wagon against the curb in front of a dusty car of indeterminate breed which was either parked or abandoned, and locked all his doors with a single twist of the key before proceeding to the uneven sidewalk.

Unbroken ranks of houses reared up against the white June sky from narrow gardens stuffed with grass gleaming like knives with rain. That had stopped, leaving wet islands to steam as they dwindled on the sidewalk. Don couldn't see into a single room, though more than one curtain blinked. Nor was it easy to find house numbers; those that hadn't been stolen had been spraypainted illegible. He walked several hundred yards before catching sight of a rusty oval plate numbered 66, dangling from its one surviving screw in a position which seemed to turn the digits into frozen sperm. He crossed the cracked backbone of the roadway, and had just determined which of the colorless front doors must be number 73 when a net curtain stirred below it. That would be the basement to which the call from the public call-box had invited him, if invited was the word.

While most of the basements peered through grass, the strip in front of this one was planted with broken bottles. Beside and below the stone steps leading up to the front entrance was an even less painted door, approached by steps scattered with chunks of moss. Don grasped the pockmarked bar of the door knocker and succeeded in raising it about an inch so as to deal its brass plate a timid rap. The brass flap of the letter-box looked capable of issuing more of a summons, and Don was pushing it open, his fingernails catching in its blackened pores, when it said, "I'd not do that."

"Mr. Mevin?"

"Depends. Are you the book feller?"

Don wondered in passing whether the man beyond the door was mispronouncing an old-fashioned S as a bibliographical joke. "Sure am."

"You'll have a name then, will you?"

"Don Travis."

"That's the lad."

A series of noises of bolts and chains descended the edge of the door, which then protested a good deal about opening to disclose a short hall papered with dimness. The tenant, who was so short Don could look down on the three lines of gray hair which linked his ears across his mottled head, swayed backward from foot to foot, retying the cord of his ankle-length tiger-colored dressing-gown. "Step over," he advised.

In place of a welcome mat, Don saw just in time, a line of barbed wire was nailed to the carpet. Barbed wire framed three sides of the front door too, and the inside of the letter-slot, and Don was wary of touching the door to shut it until Mevin laughed at him. "You're fine once you're in.

There's been a few unwelcome sorts have gone hopping away, right enough. Yank, eh?" he said in a tone which suggested he was telling Don what to do, and vanished crabwise into the front room.

Don heeled the door shut and followed. The small room was occupied almost entirely by books, though there was a black and white television with a screen no larger than the spread of Don's hand beneath the window. An announcer was saying, "If you're traveling toward London on the M1—"

"I'm not, you silly prat," Mevin said, and switched him off. "Thought you sounded Yankee on the phone. Something wet?"

"It's a bit early for me."

"Just tea, pal. Always kept me company when I was a watchman. That's where I learned the ropes," Mevin said, indicating barbed wire which surrounded the net-curtained window, and added with a faintly injured air, "It's made."

"In that case, thanks."

"Be having a look at my library. There's a good few Yankee items I brought back when I was on the freighters. You won't have seen some of them too often, I'll wager," Mevin said, and swayed away along the hall.

Don pressed the squeaky brass light-switch down to augment the sunlight which hung from the window, and saw yet more books. Books were piled on the mantelpiece above a fireplace strewn with sooty newspaper tied in knots; they couldn't have been stacked any higher on two of the three infirm chairs without toppling over the chair backs, they surrounded the carpet as though they'd sprouted from the skirting-board below the musty wallpaper. Don sank to his knees to examine the books on the floor, many of which retained their dust wrappers, and the damp he'd been smelling reached up through the carpet for him.

By the time Mevin returned with a plump mug and its leaner relative, Don was squatting in front of a chair piled with books. "You won't find some of those on a church stall," Mevin said.

Don stood up to accept the heavier mug. "I've been surprised by what I've found."

"Not the likes of Henry Miller, though. Bet he's worth a bomb, specially in that kind of nick. Don't worry, they're legal here now. The police won't give you any bother."

Don fed himself a token sip of lukewarm mud. "Unfortunately that's the drawback, that they've been published here."

"Aye, only these were first," Mevin said, screwing up his face as though to wring thoughts out of it. "That's what they pay for in your trade."

"First printings are, but these aren't, you see."

Someone walked past the window, and Mevin ducked to peer at their legs. "Afternoon, Mr. Corcoran. Hope the nags were kind to you today," he muttered, then tilted his face toward Don. "You aren't telling me all these books are common as muck."

"I wouldn't presume to do that, because most of the authors—well, they aren't names I'm overly familiar with."

"Call yourself—" Mevin began, then slurped his tea instead. "The late missus had a lot of time for them," he said with a hint of menace, "and you'll find plenty like her in Manchester."

"I believe you, but I don't know if I see them in my shop."

"You want to advertise more, then. Get yourself a block in the yellow pages. I nearly didn't find you, you're in such piddling little type. You'd think you were ashamed of yourself." Another pair of legs strode by, and Mevin ducked lower. "Afternoon, Mrs. Devine. Got a ladder there. Here, puss, puss, puss," he called, rubbing his thumb and forefinger together, and stared at Don as though to convince him he'd seen nothing of the kind. "I've got to sort my laundry out for the daughter if you want more time."

Don had been surveying the rest of the books while raising the mug to his lips and letting it drop. "If this is the lot I've seen it, thanks."

Mevin drained his mug and spat some tea leaves into it. "So let's be hearing your offer."

Don imagined the amount of space the books would occupy in his shop or in the trays outside it, and saw how much work the basement needed, not that he could justify too significant a contribution. Maybe the condition of the books would indeed help him sell them. "What would you say to two hundred, two hundred and fifty pounds?"

"You wouldn't want to hear it, pal. Double it and double it again and add the number you first thought of and then slope off if that's the best you can do."

"I assure you, Mr. Mevin, I'm trying to be generous."

"Don't bloody strain yourself." Mevin went to the window and gazed up at the deserted street while bumping his mug along the lowest stretch of barbed wire; then he swung around in a crouch, leaving the wire jangling. "The daughter wants me to give the randy books the push before

I move in with her in case the grandchildren get their grubbies on them, and the rest aren't my meat. Come close to a thousand and I'll shake hands with you."

"I'd raise my offer if I could, but honestly—"

"You're not a Jew as well as a Yank, are you?"

Don wasn't, but he couldn't have felt more outraged. "If you're going to put it that way—"

"Better learn how we do business over here, then. I'll be seeing what I get from someone who doesn't mind splashing their money around, in the yellow pages for a start." Mevin seized Don's mug, dunking his fingers in the tea. "Watch where you tread on your way out. I won't be paying your hospital bill."

"Interesting to have met you," Don murmured as he stepped over the barbed wire and groped for the front-door latch, but couldn't prolong his sarcasm when he glanced back out of the sunlight and saw the stooped man watching him along the gloomy hall. "I hope you find someone more amenable," he said, and hurried to the Volvo, wondering what comments Mevin might be addressing to his legs.

Bookselling brought worse encounters, he thought as he pulled on the seatbelt to hush its complaint, and better ones too. Only last week he'd found on a church stall a near fine first of a Conan Doyle novel. A regular client in Georgia had snapped that up before Don had had a chance to list it in his catalog. Any good British finds were assured an American buyer, which was why Don had visited Britain several times, latterly accompanied by Susanne and Marshall, both of whom had grown so fond of it that when Susanne, having been observed by a visiting lecturer at Florida Atlantic, had been offered the opportunity to teach the same course in Manchester—

The sound of high heels interrupted his musing as they halted by the car. A young woman, perhaps not so young once he saw through her makeup, leaned down to gaze at him across the passenger seat. "On business, love?"

"No other word for it. At least I just was. You don't mind if I—" She wasn't wearing much of a skirt, Don noticed, and wondered belatedly if she might after all not be a resident questioning his right to park. He pressed the button to lower the window she was gazing through. "Sorry, what did you ask me?"

He knew as soon as he spoke. She'd said not "On business" but "Want business." Her gaze was losing patience. "Oh, right, got you, yes, no, thanks anyway," Don gabbled, almost knocking his glasses to the floor as he shoved them higher on his nose. "Excuse me," he saw himself repeating in the mirror as he twisted the key twice in the ignition before the Volvo deigned to start. He pulled out without checking for traffic, and for a moment couldn't think whether he was driving on the correct side of the road.

He was, but away from home. Retracing his route past the woman didn't appeal to him, and so he turned right when he could, only to find that the next street which should lead to the park was sentineled by two No Entry signs with terse words added to the horizontal white space on each red disc. He made for the nearest main road, where the three-story houses were split into pairs by gaps not much wider than a man, and a small green bus was chugging from side street to side street as though searching for a bus stop. Brightness was hopping up and down a group of traffic lights half a mile onward, and the route sign which preceded them indicated that he should drive straight on, contrary to his instincts.

The road forked, and he took the rightward curve to be his route. It led to another gathering of traffic lights, before which a black Peugeot was parked on double yellow lines, an orange sticker in its window signifying that the driver was disabled. "Must be some zippy cripple," Don mused, not the kind of comment he would have made if there had been anyone to hear, and hoped that the driver couldn't read lips. Don glanced at him in passing and received such a hostile red-eyed glare that he didn't even consider asking for directions. The lights ahead turned amber, and he trod on the brake. As he did so the driver of the Peugeot jerked a phone away from his face and swung the car out from the curb.

He obviously expected Don to drive through the amber so that he could follow through the red. Don saw the black car rush toward him in the mirror, and pressed his shoulders and the back of his head against the seat-rest and snatched his foot off the brake pedal. His head filled with a stench of burning rubber that seemed to epitomize his panic. Then the Peugeot veered around him, so close he felt the Volvo shake, and slammed to a halt in front of him.

He tramped on the brake again, barely in time. The stench had become a sour taste in his mouth. "You nematode," he called the other driver, which helped his lips not to shake. "You pedicule. You fumarole, you—" He was trawling his mind for further insults when he met the glare of the red eyes in the Peugeot's rear-view mirror.

They were accusing him of having caused the incident, and that was more than he could take. He grabbed the magnifying glass and pretended to scan the registration number of the Peugeot, mouthing it, though in fact the two cars were so close together he couldn't see the plate. He laid the glass beside the book and saw the red eyes bulging with rage in the mirror. The man's shoulders writhed, and his upper body lurched toward the gearshift, though the traffic lights were still against him.

He was going to back his car into the Volvo, Don realized in disbelief. He clutched his own gearshift in order to reverse, just as a green bus bumbled out of the last side street he'd passed and blocked the road behind him. Then a long white police car bearing a tubular crest of unlit lights arrived at the intersection from the right and indicated a right turn. The traffic lights ahead of the Peugeot began to reach for green, and the car roared away along the left-hand road.

Don braked in case the police went after the Peugeot, but the police driver frowned at him. The bus emitted a sound more like a burp than a honk, and Don sent the Volvo across the intersection, almost stalling in his haste. The lights were already changing behind him, and as the bus cruised after him the police car swerved to overtake both it and him.

As its crest brightened he was sure it was about to howl and force him to stop. It sped away, its tube unlit after all, and he saw that only a wedge of sunlight between houses had caused it to appear to be switched on. "Not guilty," he told himself, with a wry grin at needing to be told, and followed the police car around a prolonged curve of the road. Suddenly its crest and its other lights blazed, and it raced into another main road, halting traffic bound for the center of Manchester.

That was the Wilmslow Road, the half a mile of it which was occupied by Indian restaurants and sweetshops and grocery stores, and Don was almost home. Unlike the police, he waited for the traffic lights to give him the signal. Two cars crossed in front of him after they should have, and the red facing him was just sharing its glow with the amber when he saw a black Peugeot approaching far too fast behind him.

Surely it wasn't the same car—surely the driver couldn't have hung back until the police were out of sight. Nevertheless Don took off at speed across the intersection before glancing in the mirror. He saw the Peugeot swing around a turning car with barely inches to spare and rush after him. The sight almost blinded him to the ambulance which was backing out of a hospital entrance ahead of him.

He hadn't time to think or waver. He trod hard on the accelerator pedal, sending the Volvo past the rear of the ambulance, which kept coming. In the mirror he saw it reverse into the path of the Peugeot, and braced himself for the sound of the crash as he steered the Volvo into the nearest side street. But there was no crash. Instead he saw the Peugeot skid around the ambulance, straighten up with a screech of its smoking tires and roar after him.

At that moment all he knew was that he mustn't let himself be followed home. He drove past the turn he would have taken, and the next, and saw the Peugeot hurtle into the road behind him. He was already becoming lost in the maze of balconied three-story houses where quite a few of the streets turned corners only to lead to dead ends. He almost lost control of the car as he swerved into the next side turning—left or right, the meaning of the words had been crowded out of his head. He would have cornered again immediately, except that a cyclist with a wicker basket full of groceries on her handlebars was pedaling leisurely across the junction. She raised her graying eyebrows at him as he put on speed and swung into the middle of the road in his hurry to hide in the next side street, where an old man stripped to the waist was craning with a stick over the wrought-iron railings of his balcony in an attempt to dislodge something from the branches of a sycamore which sprouted from the corner of the sidewalk. There was no Peugeot in the rear-view mirror as he drove as fast as he dared to the corner—no sign of the Peugeot as he braked hard at the sight of a dead end less than a hundred yards ahead.

He needn't feel boxed in by the three-story houses so long as he'd lost his pursuer. He edged the Volvo forward past a parked Daimler so as to have room to turn around. He was easing his car across the middle of the narrow roadway when the Peugeot skidded around the corner and screeched sideways to a halt, blocking the road.

Don was aware of gripping the wheel and poising his foot on the accelerator pedal and awaiting his opponent's next move and feeling so absurd it almost paralyzed him. Did he really propose to try to drive through whatever gap the Peugeot would leave as it came for him? Didn't only stuntmen attempt that kind of trick, even in movies? Then the fumes spurting from the exhaust pipe of the Peugeot faltered, gave a last black belch and died. The driver had switched the engine off.

They were in another kind of movie now, Don thought, the kind where whoever outstared the other at the showdown won. "Do your worst, Red-eye," he murmured, keeping his lips nearly still—and saw the driver fling open the door and climb out of the car.

"You're not disabled," Don said. He felt outraged and yet guilty, as though he'd brought the situation on himself by his earlier sly comment. The man stalked toward the Volvo, scratching his cheeks with nails as blackened as his stubbled chin, dragging at his face to expose more of the veins of his eyes and wrenching his mouth down. He let go of his face, having rendered it sufficiently hideous, as he reached the Volvo and commenced pounding on the roof.

Don stared at the flattened silver skull of the man's belt buckle, at the way his clogged navel winked beneath the ragged hem of his Adidas T-shirt, and waited for the pounding to subside. When he heard the roof begin to give, however, he lowered his window a couple of inches. "Are you likely to get tired of that pretty soon, do you think?"

Eight thick fingers clamped themselves in the gap, and the man's face descended into view. It looked to be suspended from its brush of dyed black hair that was shaved more or less clean below the tops of the ears, the weight of the cheeks having settled around the weak chin, pulling down the lower eyelids, which appeared to be collecting moisture like some kind of pinkish vegetation. The window turned gray with breath like an embodiment of the sluggishly menacing voice. "What you fucking say?"

"I said, would you mind removing your hands and yourself from my car?"

The face jerked closer—close enough to show Don a greenish denizen of the left nostril emerging and withdrawing with each breath, like a snail from a shell. "What you talking in that fucking voice for?"

"I rather fear it's the only one I have. Now if you could—"

"Supposed to make you sound like a hard man, is it? Come out and I'll show you how fucking hard you are."

"I believe I'll take a rain check. I don't like repeating myself, but I really would ask you to—"

The face was almost against the window now, and Don heard the glass creak as the fingers hauled at it. "What you mean taking people's fucking numbers?"

Don was tempted to admit he hadn't, except for feeling that the revelation might lose him some advantage he wasn't even aware of. "What would I mean by it, do you think? If you damage that window—"

"Give it here."

"Not an option, I'm afraid. Now will you please—"

"Give it fucking here."

As much as anything it was the ponderousness of the interruptions which made Don feel trapped, hence increasingly angry and reckless. "I don't suppose it ever occurs to you that you may have a problem with monotonousness of language? This has been fun of a kind, but now if you'll excuse me—"

He'd had enough. He was already late for picking up his family, and now he had to find his way home. A touch of the button would run the glass up against the man's fingers, and when he snatched them out Don would drive away. Then, perhaps having read Don's intention in his eyes, the man shoved himself away from the Volvo so forcefully that Don saw the glass bend inward. "Thank y—" he said, but this time it wasn't the voice that interrupted him. The man had pushed his leather jacket back and snatched an object out of the waistband of his jeans to point at him.

It wasn't a gun, Don tried to think, at least not a real one, not one that was loaded, not here in Britain. But the man's eyes had become as indifferent as the metal hole lined up with Don's face, and with a lurch of awareness which made his head and stomach feel like gaping wounds, Don knew the threat was no pretense. He saw the man slide back the top of the weapon to expose the muzzle and place a bullet in the chamber. "Get your arse out here," the man said, "or I'll blow your fucking head off."

Don's legs were trembling. If he slammed the car into first gear to drive past or even at the man, he was bound to stall the engine. If he didn't try to escape, if he got out of the car—Everything around the black hole of the muzzle appeared to be growing darker and heavier and motionless, paralyzing his ability to think. Then there was movement, though for a dismayingly protracted few seconds he was unable to grasp what it was. The man who had been poking at the sycamore from his balcony had appeared beyond the Peugeot, frowning at it, and now he saw the gun.

Don's hands clenched and unclenched on the wheel. He was struggling not to point out to the gunman that he was being watched, because what might he do to the witness? Yet if he thought he was unobserved— The man with the stick hesitated and fled, almost quietly enough. A single rap of his stick on the sidewalk swung the gunman around just in time to see him.

He aimed the gun with both hands, and the whole of Don's chest seemed to fill with an agonizingly held breath. In a moment the witness was out of sight, but before Don could exhale, the gun was pointing at his forehead. He saw the hands tense on the weapon, and the man narrowing his eyes to focus on the target, and the street appeared to brighten as though to give Don a last look at the world. Then he heard the slam of a front door, and the man jabbed the gun into his belt and lurched toward him. "Don't even fucking dream of giving anyone my fucking number."

He was at the Peugeot in three loping strides. In what seemed to Don to be no time at all the black car bumped one front wheel over the sidewalk and was replaced by a cloud of fumes of its color. Don leaned his forehead against the windshield and closed his eyes. The glass, and the wheel in his fists, and indeed the entire car felt softened and quaking. He swallowed a few times, having remembered to breathe, and fumbled for the button to lower the window before concluding that he was probably not about to be sick. He panted for a while, then raised his head and his wrist to consult his Mexican Rolex. "Got to go," he said indistinctly. "Late."

He groped for the ignition key until he noticed that the engine was still running, and eased the Volvo gingerly around to aim it back the way he'd driven into the trap. He cruised to the bend in the street at no more than ten miles an hour, trying to decide whether to turn left or right at the end. He'd just come in sight of the sycamore when a police car crowned by flashing lights blocked the junction ahead.

"Too late, guys. Could have used you a few minutes ago," Don said, lifting his hands anyway in an appreciative gesture, and was dismayed to see how much they shook. Then all four doors of the police car sprang open and stayed that way, each releasing a policeman. The driver had a megaphone, which he aimed at Don. "Keep your hands where we can see them," it boomed, "and get slowly out of the car."

3

PICTURES

They were showing Marshall himself again. His ears stuck out too far, he thought, and his father's smile kept appearing on his face. Several hairs had sprung up on top of his head to greet the world, and he couldn't believe how often he turned to his mother as though to interrupt her with a question like someone half his age; every time he saw himself do so he felt his face grow hotter. Here came the woman who would threaten to split his mother open, at which point Marshall found that though he'd told Mrs. Lewis he didn't mind her playing the tape for the class, he did.

Why had the program makers left that part in when they'd edited out so much else? Perhaps his face was betraying how he felt, because Mrs. Lewis hit the fast forward button on the control in her hand, so that the mauve-helmeted woman scurried up to his mother and gabbled at her until Marshall squeaked in protest like a mouse in a cartoon, which provoked some titters from the class but which at least was preferable to having his classmates hear what had been said to his mother. The teacher released the button, and Marshall said "—allowed to see movies in America I can't see here."

"Who lets you see films in America?"

The presenter hadn't said that so immediately, nor only that, unless Marshall's memory was rewriting the encounter. "The state, I guess," he watched himself say beneath his wagging sprout of hair. "Just because it's rated R doesn't mean you have to be seventeen to see it, but here it's rated eighteen and I'm supposed to wait six years before I can watch it again."

"No age restrictions on what you can see and read in America. Any comments? Yes, with the glasses, no, the other glasses?"

"You didn't say there were, were, weren't any restrictions," Tom Bold said from his desk next to Marshall's.

"I said more stuff, but—"

"Keep your observations for the end if you will," Mrs. Lewis said in a high quick voice which Marshall gathered was a consequence of being

Welsh. He felt that smile twitch his face, as it did whenever he was embarrassed. "How can we stop it?" the capering presenter said.

"They're scared of nothing any more," a man shouted, his nose appearing to squirm with emotion, thanks to a flaw in the videotape, "we've got to bring back fear."

"You can't have a society without fear," said a woman with an even less stable nose.

"We spend our lives being scared," her friend declared. "It's time they did."

"Kill a few, then they'd be scared."

"Capital punishment. Is that the answer?" the presenter said, the flaw in the tape causing him to perform an impromptu bellydance. "We'll be back after the break." His place was taken by an ad for South African produce accompanied by a rich dark voice. "Cape fruit," it said, "tastes like—freedom," at which point Mrs. Lewis switched off the tape to a chorus of protests from the class. "None of that, now," she said briskly. "Quite enough to talk about there. Who's got something to say? Travis?"

She wasn't trying to discomfort him, she was only doing her job. He suspected she wasn't even aware of looking poised to dart at whomever she spoke to or of the way her greenish eyes flashed in her sharp pale uncooked face, impatient for the next victim. "I was only saying I said more than you saw me say," he said.

"Seemed to me you were given a good chunk of time. Or misrepresentation, is that your complaint?"

"I guess."

"Don't be too ready to credit everything you see on the news or read in the papers either," Mrs. Lewis told the class as though bringing to a close a story with a moral. "Away with Travis's grievance now. Let's just see how many of us have experienced violence or know someone who has."

Marshall folded his arms on the desk-top etched with inky initials, but couldn't prevent his hand being tugged up by the sight of so many raised around him. Mrs. Lewis's head was nodding, pecking at the number of responses. "Nearly the lot of you," she said. "Not you, Lynch? There's lucky. Let's hear from . . . Flynn."

Ben Flynn hunched his shoulders so as not to flinch from her pounce. "Last week in pee ee Mr.—"

"We don't call that violence, anything a teacher does," Mrs. Lewis said with finality. "Travis, you're anxious to talk today. What is it this time?"

Marshall was keeping his hand up only because he still wasn't entirely sure how these things were done in England and hadn't noticed that the other hands had sunk. "Something that happened to you, we want," the teacher insisted.

"Not to me, to my dad."

"Family will do."

"Some guy nearly made him crash his car and then he chased my dad and pulled a gun on him."

"A guy is what we put on a bonfire. I expect your father must have thought he was back in America," Mrs. Lewis said, apparently by way of encouraging Marshall. "He wasn't shot, was he?"

"No, only the—the person with the gun got away before the police came, and when they only found my dad they thought it was him."

"With the gun."

"Right, and when they heard him talk they did."

"How was that, now?"

"Because he talks like me. American."

"I'm sure it couldn't just have been that, Travis, if I know our police. He's not in custody, is he?"

"He might have been, except the person who called them came to tell them it hadn't been my dad."

"Might have been's nothing and nowhere. So have they caught the culprit?"

"They've only just put his description in the paper."

"Fancy that. Now there's a question worth discussing. Haven't the police to make mistakes like everyone else? Shouldn't people be supporting them instead of trying to show them up? Yes, Wisdom? No, you certainly may not. Heathcote?"

"My dad's a security guard and he got put in the hospital by four men in a street full of people because nobody did nothing to help him."

"He must have had plenty of help, then."

"No, nobody did nothing."

"That's what I say. You're telling us he got plenty of help."

"No, miss," Billy Heathcote persisted, and Marshall's frustration with both of them was too much for him to contain. "He means nobody did anything."

The teacher trained her gaze on him. "I'm well aware of that, Travis."

"Then why—"

Her gaze seemed to be poking more words out of him. He manufactured a sneeze to cut them off, but when realism demanded that he bring it to an end she hadn't blinked. Then a bell rang to announce the end of lessons, and he felt as though it was letting him return to his corner at the close of a bout, not that he'd ever been in one. But Mrs. Lewis appeared not to have heard it, and didn't look as if she would take any notice of a referee.

He was saved by the slam of a desk lid. "In a hurry, are we, Manning?"

"Miss, rugby practice."

"You certainly will if you continue to behave like that. And the rest of you will be spending another half an hour in my company unless we have absolute silence. Absolute, Bold, do you understand the word?"

"Yes, mermiss."

Marshall was afraid she would take exception to being called some kind of sea creature, but she was busy darting her gaze about in search of potential movement. "For your homework tonight," she said, "I want you to collect at least six examples of crimes from the paper and write how you would deal with them."

Perhaps she was hoping for groans rather than the few muffled coughs she provoked. "Very well, in rows," she said at last, and scrutinized each as they marched out, so that Marshall didn't quite believe he'd escaped until he was in the corridor.

Tom Bold caught up with him. "Cow. Would you have to purr put up with that in America?"

"Never did have," Marshall said, walking fast to leave the incident behind, past the gymnasium booming with footfalls and down the stone steps into the schoolyard full of boys chasing or pummeling each other or huddling together or swinging their schoolbags or dashing for the gates. Every boy was uniformed, the aspect of British school life Marshall had least expected: white shirt, striped tie that wasn't supposed to be removed or even slackened until you were in your own house, gray trousers and socks which were also required to be gray, black shoes and black blazer which had commenced soaking up the sunlight the moment he emerged from the building. His first sight of all that uniformity had made him feel he'd tricked himself into attending the kind of school George S. would have picked for him, but it was mostly better than that.

Just now, however, Tom Bold mightn't have agreed. "I mean, though, cur cow. Cur keeping us late for no reason and making me miss my burr bus. My mother worries if I'm her home late."

"Can't you ring her?"

"Only got enough to get her home."

"I'll lend you the money," Marshall offered, and had found a twenty-pence piece like a dime with its rim bevelled septagonal when Billy Heathcote strode up, shrugging at the shoulderstraps of his bag to free his brawny arms. "I didn't like that, Travis."

"Yeah, she was pretty—"

"Not her, you. You."

"Anything special about me you want to discuss?"

"My dad says it's people like you and your dad got him beat up."

"Where does he get off saying that when he hasn't met either of us?"

"He wouldn't want to, either. It's like Lewie was saying, people who run down the police."

"Someone tried to run my dad down with a car."

Billy Heathcote stared as if he was doing his best to regard that as an insult, then noticed the coin in Marshall's hand. "What's that for? Paying Bold protection?"

"Just trying to help."

"We don't need your kind of help round here. Another time don't try and do my talking for me. I can talk for myself. I'm not Burr Burr Bold."

Red patches broke out on Tom's face at once. "Less of that," he said, and took a deep breath, "Heathcote."

"What'd you say, Bold? Nobody heard you."

"I sir sir—"

"That's right, you call me sir."

"I didn't sir—"

"Well, if you didn't, Bold, I'll let you off this time."

Tom's face was wholly red with effort and rage now. He shoved Heathcote's chest hard, and Marshall had a sense of being trapped in an invisible tunnel, at the other end of which he'd spoken up for Heathcote in the classroom, or perhaps it led farther back. Where would it end? With Tom going home with a bloody nose and his mother in hysterics? "Wait up, guys," he said, and stepped between them. "Listen, Billy—"

Heathcote punched him in the collarbone, and Bold grabbed him by the upper arms and heaved him out of the way, which hurt more than the punch had. "Hey, that was me, Tom. I thought you needed to make a call."

Heathcote projected a laugh. "I can just see Bold trying to fur fur fur fur—"

Bold ran at him and pushed him over. Heathcote fell as flat on his back on the concrete as his schoolbag would allow, and Marshall heard a crack of plastic in the bag. If that hadn't guaranteed a fight, the gathering circle of boys would have. As Heathcote flung himself upright and dragged at his shoulderstraps Bold shook off his own bag, and Marshall left them to it. He was only just out of the circle when he heard the first thumps and grunts followed by shouts of encouragement from the spectators, and all the sounds continued as he walked fast out of the schoolyard.

He'd reached the end of the railings, opposite a row of houses which resembled a red-brick concertina which had just been squeezed of a note, when he heard a teacher roaring. He thought of going back to explain how the fight had started, but teachers who roared were the same the world over—impervious to explanation. A motorcycle the length of a sports car, with one of his schoolmates perched behind the rider, took off along Bushy Road, snarling like a big cat and leaving a trace of the snarl behind to turn into the protracted drumroll which announced how an airliner was mounting the blue sky, and life was a stream of surprises again, not dammed by the past. Even Mrs. Lewis's homework seemed as though it might be some fun.

The outpouring of monochrome uniforms from Bushy Road was diluted by the crowd on the main road, except where it pooled at bus stops. A wave of it fell back noisily as a half-empty double-decker bus sped past a stop without slowing. Marshall waited for the red stick figures on a set of traffic lights to turn green and adopt a walking stance while peeping like toy birds, and crossed to a newsagent's. Perhaps because they read so many books, his parents only ever bought a Sunday newspaper, and this late in the week the current issue was lost to the recycling bin outside the nearest Safeway store. Marshall bought a local paper once several Indian children had finished disagreeing over which bubble gum to buy, and walked along the Wilmslow Road.

Walking home from school instead of having to be driven miles beside the Everglades felt especially British. He inhaled the aromas of Indian restaurants and grocery stores piled with every color of pepper, and resisted the displays of pink and green Indian fudge and sweets shaped like pretzels, though the sight of them filled his mouth with the memory of syrup. He dodged around a group of Muslim women, their hair concealed by white silk scarves, and into Victoria Park.

Only the stone posts remained of the gates which a book in his father's shop said had barred the lower orders from the Victorian estate after dark, and now they stood at the center of a broad plot of grass surrounded by a circle of houses which the British called a circus. Marshall dumped his schoolbag on a bench facing the posts and a facsimile of an old toll notice, and unfolded the newspaper.

MANCHESTER CUSTOMS SEIZE "BIGGEST COCAINE HAUL EVER." SHOOTING OF THIRTEEN-YEAR-OLD DRUG-RELATED, SAY POLICE. EIGHTY-SEVEN-YEAR-OLD PENSIONER TIED UP IN OWN FLAT THEN RAPED. "PRISON RIOT WAS INEVITABLE"—GOVERNOR. WIFE KILLS HUSBAND AFTER THREE YEARS OF TORTURE. WIDOW WHOSE HUSBAND DIED IN CUSTODY RECEIVES RECORD AWARD FROM POLICE . . . He'd collected enough material right there, Marshall thought, but he continued turning pages until he reached the story he knew.

MANCHESTER BOOKSELLER THREATENED WITH GUN. Mr. Donald Travis, formerly of Florida, was threatened with a handgun in Fallowfield last Friday during an altercation about driving . . . Police have issued the following description of the assailant: about 6 feet tall, heavily built, unshaven, bloodshot eyes, sallow complexion, partly shaven head . . . The drawing of him was even uglier, a cartoon for everyone to hate on sight, glaring at Marshall like an outlaw trapped by a Wanted poster in an Italian Western. Marshall folded the paper so that anyone he met would see it, and ducked one shoulder through a strap of his bag to walk home.

Presumably Victoria Park became Fallowfield where the grounds of houses turned into mere gardens and the houses split amoeba-like into pairs. Trees mopped the sidewalks with shadows as a breeze ruffled the upstanding hairs at the back of his head, reminding him to tame them once he arrived home. He turned right by a house the same colors as his uniform, and right again where a large russet dog of several breeds started to bark as it threw itself against a jangling gate. "Only me, Loper," Marshall said, and patted its smooth head as Mrs. Satterthwaite, who designed costumes for the theater, called the dog into the porch.

Two hundred yards around the corner the street came to a dead end, and one of the white houses which ended it was home. A magpie like a fragment of a piebald house was perched on the second-floor railings, first floor if you were British, but as Marshall approached it clattered into the sky, leaving the street deserted except for several large cars lazing in the sunlight. He unlatched the gate and went up the jigsaw of a path between the flower beds where he and his parents had each put in one new plant, though his seemed determined to keep its flowers to itself. He was resting the newspaper and his schoolbag against the oak door while he inserted the first of his keys when he heard a car door slam behind him. "Hey, lad," a man said, closer to him than the slam had sounded. "Yes, you. Hey, you, lad."

Marshall turned the key in the mortise lock as he looked over his shoulder. A man was gripping the gate with both hands and pressing his stomach against it. Below his red eyes his face was a mass of stubble and spreading flesh. "Can I help you?" Marshall said as he thought his parents would have.

The man jabbed a fist at Marshall and stuck a finger out of it. "What the fuck you think you're doing with that?"

Was he accusing Marshall of having his keys? He sounded drunk, in which case he shouldn't have been driving the black Peugeot which was parked outside the house. Marshall glanced away from him in order to insert the Yale key, and came face to face with the identikit picture which he appeared to be posting on the door. "That's right, take a fucking good look," the man shouted. "Don't you tell me that's me."

The key scraped across the circular plate of the lock and dug into the wood. Surely someone would want to know what was going on, the man was making so much noise and taking so much time about it. "I'll have him for saying I look like that," he shouted ponderously, and Marshall heard the gate clang against the garden wall. "Donald Fucking Travis Booksell. When's he home?"

He wasn't close enough yet to prevent Marshall from unlocking the door if he did so at once. That wasn't his hand on the nape of Marshall's neck, only nerves. Marshall forced himself to slow down for the second it took him to locate the slot in the plate and slide in the key before withdrawing it the fraction of an inch that would allow it to turn without a struggle. It turned, and the newspaper face grimaced with the crumpling of the page as he shoved at the door with it, and felt breath stirring the hairs on the back of his neck. "Get in, lad, don't muck about," the man muttered. "We'll wait for him."

The door yielded less than a foot and stuck, wedged by the day's mail. Marshall could slam it, dodge around the man, cry for help—except that as he pulled the door toward him, fingers dug into his shoulder and a fist like a veined knobbly hammer was thrust into the gap between door and frame. "Don't fuck with me, lad, less you want a kicking," the man said, and used Marshall to shove the door wide.

The vestibule was more spacious than two phone booths, but now it felt small and dark. The impact with his knees and right shoulder seemed to have knocked his mind out of his body, because all he could think was that he was somewhere else, this wasn't happening to him. A line from a movie began to repeat itself in his head: "If you have to defend yourself, make sure there's no comeback." He found himself trying to identify the film as the fingers continued to dig into the junction of his neck and left shoulder. Then the man let go and nudged Marshall forward with his torso and kicked the door behind them before stooping to rummage through the mail. "Leave them alone," Marshall protested in a voice which trailed off in panic.

The man let the envelopes scatter from his thick fingers tipped with grime and raised his head. His gaze stayed low, resting on a famine relief envelope which had remained in his hand. A secretive grin took its time about shaping his mouth, then he stared at Marshall and flung away the envelope. "What's this, a fucking waiting room? Get it open, lad."

All at once Marshall could think again. Opening the inner door would set off the alarm, which could be silenced only by a key on the ring which was still dangling from the outside lock. The man shoved him at the door to bump it open, and the house immediately started to wail.

The man kicked the door so wide the hinges creaked. He glared at the three closed stripped-pine doors, at the staircase with its polished banisters rising from the broad hall. Spit flew out of his mouth instead of the expected word, then, "Kill it, you little—"

Marshall was squeezing the newspaper and the straps of his bag so hard they felt indistinguishable. "You made me leave the keys in the door."

"The fuck I did." The man was shaking his head like an animal as though to rid his ears of the wail of the alarm. He pulled the door open, and Marshall lunged. A hand which smelled of sweat and motor oil closed over his face and threw him back into the house, and he heard the keys being snatched. "Pretty fucking clever, I don't think," the man said, letting go of him.

"I only wanted to switch it off," Marshall pleaded, hating himself and the sound of his voice.

"Aye, and I'm Reverend Chief Constable of Manchester." The man was jerking the keys on the ring as if that would separate the one he needed. Any second now the alarm would go off, a bell outside and a siren to impale the eardrums of anyone in the house. The man would cover his ears, and then Marshall would—

The siren raised its howl, and the man saw the control panel beneath it on the staircase. He stalked at it, apparently intending to wrench the metal box off the wood, though that would only make it impossible to quell the alarm. Then he shook a key forward and jammed it into the slot in the panel.

It was the right key. In a moment the house was filled with a silence almost as deafening as the siren, and the intruder turned on Marshall, who was trying not to betray that he'd been about to flee through the vestibule. "What's so fucking funny?"

"Find out," Marshall yearned to say, or better, "You'll find out if you don't let me go," but his words were as uncontrollable as his mouth. "Nothing," he pleaded.

"I'll give you fucking nothing. Get here." The man dug his fingers into Marshall's collar, fingernails scraping his spine. "You can show us round while we're waiting, give us the tour."

"You're choking me."

"I fucking will less you do as you're told. Drop the bag for a start. What do you think you look like, a burglar with some fucking swag."

Marshall let his schoolbag fall with a thud. Doing so felt like relinquishing a weapon. The man threw open both doors opposite the staircase as he dug a knuckle into Marshall's spine to urge him to the kitchen, and only seizing that doorknob saved Marshall from being used to batter the door open. The man jerked him to a halt in the doorway and sniffed the faint trace of spice in the air. "Your mam a Paki or summat? No wonder you're a wimp if she feeds you muck like them lot eat. You want to get her to give you some roast beef and Yorkshire, that'd build you up."

Marshall saw the extended family of knives offering their points to him from the rack on the wall above the marble chopping block between the fitted oven and the freezer. "If you have to defend yourself . . ." He poised himself to duck out of the man's grasp, just as the man reached past him and slammed the door in his face. "Can't stand that stink. What's in here that's worth anything?"

He marched Marshall into the dining room so fast that the boy felt like an intruder himself. The chandelier jingled, bottles rattled in the wine rack by the oak sideboard; the oval table seemed about to flap its folded wings. "Toffees, eh? Fucking toffos," the man muttered, and stared through the French windows at the lawn stretching to the picnic table beneath the silver birch before he took exception to the bowl of dried flowers Marshall's mother had placed on the veined marble mantelpiece. "Someone die in here?" he snarled, and dragged Marshall to the front room.

For a few seconds he seemed content to play with the dimmer switch, turning the overhead lamp beneath its stained-glass shade up to full and fading it then brightening it again, causing the muscular leather suite and the nest of tables inlaid with minerals and the black shiny tower of the hi-fi to shift stealthily, all of which made Marshall feel as though his eyes were being tweaked in and out of his skull. Then the man twisted the knob, leaving a faint wasteful glow in the bulb, and shoved Marshall to his knees on the thick Oriental carpet while he stooped to grimace at the video recorder. "Pretty flash," he mumbled. "How much, eh?"

A grotesque notion that the man was proposing to make an offer almost tempted Marshall to respond to the illusion of friendship. All he knew was that the machine was the most expensive in the Panasonic range and played both British and American tapes. If he persuaded the intruder he could take it, the man would have to let go of him to do so, and then Marshall could dash out of the room and shut him in and twist the key that was still in the control panel, if the sweat which felt as though it was soaking the carpet beneath his hands didn't cause them to slip, if his legs were able any longer to raise him to his feet . . . He almost sprawled on his face as the man leaned on him so as to crane over and squint at the cassettes which Marshall's mother had been examining. "Hey up, what's these? These aren't toffo films. Into nasties, eh, you sly little twat?"

Being accused of slyness seemed as bad as anything that was happening to Marshall. "My mom teaches them at the University," he blurted.

"The Texan Chaysaw Massarree. Henry, Porter of a Seal Killer. Terrors at the Orepa." The man's voice had ground almost to a halt when he snarled "I've seen some of these. Who are you trying to kid they get taught?"

"My mom," Marshall insisted, outraged almost to the point of forgetting his own situation.

"Peeping Top. The One Two Oh Days of Sod." Without warning the man hauled Marshall upright. "She was on telly."

"I was too."

"My missus saw her. She'll watch any crap. Silly bitch." The man was staring around the room, perhaps in search of a target for his growing anger. "Who's paying her? Where the fuck's the money coming from?"

"Who?"

"Whatever the bitch's name is. Your mam. Whose money are they spending on that crap?"

"You stop calling my mom names."

The man peered at him as if he'd almost forgotten Marshall was there, then aimed him at the doorway. "Let's see more of their little fucking secrets."

Before Marshall could resist he was being forced upstairs, and the key in the control panel was out of reach. Halfway up the first flight he grabbed the banister with both hands and hung on. "No," he said.

"Don't you say fucking no to me. Don't you ever." The man gave him a shove that wrenched Marshall's wrists. "What you hiding up there?" he said, and dug a hard object into his kidney. "That's right, you twat, jump."

It was a gun, no doubt the very one he'd pulled on Marshall's father. It had started such an ache in Marshall's kidney that he couldn't judge whether it was still poking into him or only pointing at him, but he didn't dare glance back. He dragged himself upward, his wet palms slipping on the banisters, and felt as though he was dragging the weight of his captor as well.

When Marshall reached the landing the man jerked him across it to open the nearest door, but spared the Sharon Stone posters and the chair laden with discarded clothes and the bookcase stuffed with Stephen King and books recommended by him no more than a glance. "Don't need to ask whose room that is. You're all the same, you little twats."

Since thumping the next door with Marshall didn't budge it, the man twisted the knob and punched the door open. Brightness shone out from the twin white wardrobes, from the picture of greenery that was the double bed and from the arbor of the wallpaper, but all Marshall could see was the image in the dressing-table mirror of himself helpless in his captor's grip, which tightened on his collar at the sight of someone in the room. Once the man realized it was only a reflection he muttered his favorite word, perhaps at himself, and Marshall felt his collar button dig into his windpipe. Then the man held him at arm's length and blundered him into the room, and Marshall saw there was no gun in his hand.

He must have shoved the weapon into the belt under his jacket. Its concealment only made it more threatening. Anything might provoke the intruder—even, apparently, the hint of perfume which Marshall's mother had left in the bedroom like a reminder that Marshall was alone with the man. "Fucking whorehouse," he said, sniffing, then dragged Marshall around to face him. "Or is it your da wears the scent? Plays with you, does he? Likes your arse?"

His mounting fury was as incomprehensible as it was terrifying. Marshall couldn't speak for being choked, but he didn't have to speak. "If you have to defend yourself . . ." A kick with all his strength in the man's crotch should set him free, and there was perfume on the dressing table to spray in the man's eyes, and his mother's metal comb whose handle tapered to a point. He didn't care about the gun—he'd had enough. He pivoted on his left foot, and heard a car draw up outside the house.

The engine died, and he heard the familiar slam of the door. It was the Volvo. His father had come home. For an instant he was dizzy with relief, and then he remembered the gun, which of course was meant for his father. He threw his weight on his left foot just as the man ground a knuckle into his spine and projected him toward the floor-length windows, in time for him to see over the balcony his father opening the gate.

He tried to call out, but the man twisted his collar so that he couldn't even draw breath. His father was too preoccupied with the small pile of books in his hands to look up. As his approach took him out of sight, the intruder pulled the higher of the bolts which locked the right-hand window, and Marshall was hauled onto his tiptoes as though by a noose. The bolt slid out of its socket, and then the man must have realized that he might be observed on the balcony, because he swung Marshall and himself toward the door of the room.

Marshall's lungs felt like bruises inside his chest. Darkness was starting to grip his eyes. His fingernails scrabbled at the knot of his tie, and then one fingertip probed into it, and it was loose. At once the thread of his collar button snapped, and the button pinged against the dressing-table mirror. He felt the hand at the back of his neck shift to grab him by the scruff, and hurled himself away from it, two more of his shirt buttons springing across the carpet. Then he was free and not quite believing it, and yanking the lower bolt of the window out of its socket, and staggering onto the balcony, where the impact of his stomach with the railings almost drove the breath he'd just drawn out of him. "Dad, don't come in," he screamed. "He's got a gun."

He saw the intruder charge at him, throwing the jacket wide and pawing at the skull-faced belt of the jeans and staring stupidly at it. For a moment he looked as convinced as Marshall had been that he was carrying a gun. Marshall's father appeared, trotting backward on the garden path, the books under one arm, keys wagging in his other hand. "How's that again, son? What did you say?"

The man knocked him aside. The next moment Marshall's father dropped the books, something Marshall would never have expected to see in all his life, and clenched his fists. "If you touch him again—" he warned, and gasped as the intruder grabbed the railings and climbed up on them. "Teach you to fucking say I look like that," he yelled, and launched himself at him.

Marshall's father sidestepped. The man hurtled past him, arms flailing, into the flower bed. His right foot landed on Marshall's plant with a crack so loud that Marshall wondered how such a thin stalk could have made it, until he realized that the rock behind the plant had snapped the man's ankle. A shriek with some syllables in it exploded from the man's lips as he tried to stand up and fell into a low bush. Marshall's father watched him as he began to crawl through the flower bed, tearing plants up by the roots and cursing in a shriek, then gathered the books from the path and ran into the house.

Marshall had to press one hand against the wall, leaving sweaty handprints on the leafy paper, so as to cross the room. He wavered onto the landing and clung to the banister as his father let himself into the house. "Marshall, talk to me, son. Are you all right? Did he—"

"I'm okay. I'm fine," Marshall protested, hoping he wasn't about to be sick down the stairwell. "But catch him. He's escaping. Call the police."

4

A SCREAM

And that was the end of him," said the husband of a history professor.

"So perish all burglars who fancy themselves athletes," said his wife.

"Here's to more criminals dealing with themselves."

"And saving the rest of us a few bob."

"To muggers who beat themselves up."

"And joyriders who can't get out of first gear."

"And gunmen whose weapons fire out of the wrong end."

"And rapists whose—Why, here's the hero of the epic posing as a wine waiter. Some more of the Chardonnay would be welcome, Marshall. How are you this evening? None the worse for your adventure?"

"I'm okay. I'm fine."

"Your mother was just regaling us with your sangfroid in the face of the enemy. What transpired after the ill-advised leap?"

"Did mom tell you he broke his ankle? Dad called the police, and I watched to see where he went."

"You don't have to talk about it if you'd rather not."

"I'm fine, truly, mom. Well, he crawled as far as the gate, and he managed to pull himself up and hold on to the fence so he could hop to his car, except he kind of fell across the sidewalk to it. Then he had to hop around it, and it must have taken him, I think it took him five minutes to climb in, but then he couldn't drive, you know, only having one foot that worked. He kept starting the engine and the car would jump a few inches and stall. Then the police came and dragged him out of it, and they didn't seem to want to know he broke his ankle. I tried to tell them, but they just told me to go in off the balcony so I wouldn't fall, as if I would. Then they threw him in their van, and some of them came to talk to me, and—Sorry, mom, did you want some wine?"

"Quite spellbinding, Marshall," the history professor said. "Only I hope you aren't feeling sorry for this person. He deserved what he did to himself."

"We all do or we wouldn't do it," her husband said.

"I do wish you wouldn't turn Freudian whenever you've had a few drinks. All I was trying to say, Marshall, is that you should forget about him. He's out of your lives now, wouldn't you say, Susanne?"

"I would, Bea," Susanne said, although she was remembering having come home to find Don and Marshall being questioned by the police. For an absurd moment she'd thought that it was her fault—that it was the result of some comment she might have refrained from uttering on the television show. When she'd discovered the actual reason it had seemed progressively less of a relief, even when she'd satisfied herself as far as possible that no harm had come to Marshall. She'd opened all the windows, and she'd felt like scrubbing the whole house, especially her and Don's bedroom. She had been sure she kept smelling a faint stench of male sweat in the house, and she'd felt compelled to take a prolonged shower herself. In bed both she and Don had lain listening in case Marshall had had one of his nightmares, only for Marshall to sleep the soundest of the three of them and to be eager to describe his encounter to his friends. Now she watched him listen to an argument between Film and English until the two lecturers drained their glasses with a simultaneity which looked rehearsed, and then she went to check on the other guests.

Philosophy and spouses were in the dining room, lingering over the salads Don had prepared and the meats she had. A Mancunian crime novelist was demonstrating to members of the English department who'd had her lecture to their students how to play shove-halfpenny on the picnic table beyond the open windows. Some philosophical disagreement was being fueled by the wine in the kitchen, to judge by a line Susanne overheard: "I don't want to harp unfashionably on logic, but I do think it might occasionally be invoked for old time's sake." She made for the next floor, where someone unidentified was expelling random phrases from Wagner in the bathroom while another guest hopped from foot to foot outside. The novelist's husband emerged from the guest room with an English professor's slightly more than teenaged daughter, dabbing at his nostrils with a knuckle and declaring rapidly "Absolutely no question whatsoever in any shape or form at all. Well, except—" and grew red and silent as he saw Susanne. She raised her eyebrows at him as he and his companion hurried snuffling downstairs while she set out to discover what the joke at the top of the house was.

Don was up there in the library, where shelves of books faced shelves of videocassettes, with two professors of law and three of genetics. "But seriously," Barbara Burrows of Law said, wiping her eyes, "all that was his revenge for how you described him to the police."

"Apparently."

"If this was America he'd sue you, like as not," said Wilf Golding, a Law man. "Make an interesting case."

"There's a current case in London," Barbara said, "of someone freed on appeal who's suing all the media that described him as a convicted killer when the original verdict came in. The issue being whether calling him convicted entitles them to claim it wasn't they who were calling him a killer."

"So Don could say," it occurred to Susanne, "he was having to work with the details the identikit gave him."

"I've always thought those things were designed to make the subject look as bad as possible," said Jack Battersby of Genetics. "When did anyone see an identikit picture smile?"

"They're how the criminal looked to the victim," protested another geneticist, Sarah Klein.

"So they mightn't look like that if you met them on the street," Wilf said, poking a copy of *Casablanca* back on the shelf.

"Which rather defeats the object of helping the public spot the bad guy," said a geneticist whose name Susanne's last glass of claret seemed to have washed out of her head.

"Maybe they're meant to tell us bad guys never look like us," Don suggested.

"To make them conform to generic expectations of the bad guy," Susanne said.

"I'll tell you what I think as well," Jack said, draining his glass and holding it up as though that would invoke a bottle. "I think those pictures are a means of undermining the self-image of the subject."

"So's the way the judge describes them and whatever they're supposed to have done," Barbara said, "along with being a kind of hype aimed at the rest of us. The most wicked criminal, the worst crime ever tried in this court, half the time they seem to be."

"I'm not sure what you're saying is wrong with shaking up their self-image," Susanne said.

Jack transferred his attention from the empty glass to her. "Take away someone's image of himself and maybe you leave him with nothing."

"Maybe that's all he deserves."

"Does anyone?"

"Gee," Don said, "and there were Susanne and Marshall and I thinking *we* were the victims. Can we offer anyone besides the thirsty gene another drink?"

"Whenever you're ready to come down from the height. No, you're saved, here comes Marshall. Just an observation," Susanne said lower. "I might forgive the guy for breaking into our house, but not for terrorizing our child and destroying something of his."

She hadn't spoken low enough. "Mom," Marshall protested as he bore the wine into the room, "I don't care about the nuking flower."

She saw that he felt his image was under attack, but before she could speak, Barbara did. "What's your version, Marshall? Did this Fancy man look as bad as his picture in the paper?"

"A name like that," Jack said, half-draining his refilled glass for Marshall to top up, "is a good start for not thinking much of himself."

"Marshall?"

"He looked pretty bad. Like he was on something, maybe a few things."

"Well, quite," Barbara said, and there was a general murmur of agreement which suggested that everyone took his response to confirm what they'd variously said.

"There's just one point I'd like to make about the picture in the paper," Susanne announced.

"Please," Jack said.

"It worked. It caught him."

"There's that," Jack admitted, and the others supplied varieties of murmur. When there was silence Marshall said, "Mom, the head of your department was asking where you were."

"Did you say?"

"He said he'd wait till you could have a talk. Shall I bring drinks?"

"I'll preserve my sobriety in honor of the occasion."

"Kind of late to do that," Don said.

True enough, Susanne found the banister companionable as she descended the stairs. If Clement Daily wanted a private word she could take him up to the study next to the library, perhaps walking off a little of her condition en route. But he was all by himself in the front room, putting compact discs in some new order on the shelves. As Susanne closed the door behind her he straightened up so fast that his rotund form reminded her of an inflated toy bobbing up from underwater. "One thought one would, yes, while one was waiting," he said, producing his pipe from his waistcoat. "Settled in to all appearances, it would seem, hm? Very, yes, really quite impressive."

Susanne gathered from the way he waved the pipe stem that he was referring to the house. She moved his glass of claret from the top of the television to the mantelpiece while he produced a box of matches from another pocket of his waistcoat and carefully extracted a match, which he considered for a pause before replacing it in the box. The story went that nobody had ever seen him smoke the pipe. "Go ahead," Susanne told him, out of frustration almost as much as hospitality. "No prohibitions here, well, within reason."

"Reason, quite. Always worth bearing in mind." Clement gazed at the matchbox, then thumbed it back into its nest and glanced distractedly about in search of his glass. "Settled, however, we were saying. Problems at all? Any that you, yes, you'll recall my telling you when first we spoke, I'm always here."

Even he wasn't usually this staccato. Susanne placed his glass in his hand in case that helped. "We feel as if we've lived here for years," she said.

"My own, entirely, when we moved up from East Anglia. So your criminous encounter hasn't gone any way toward souring you."

"It could have happened anywhere. We certainly aren't blaming here." Susanne was beginning to wish she had let Marshall refill her glass. "Why, do you think we should?"

"If you're so settled I certainly, no. And please don't harbor the impression that I'm in any way, we regard you as an asset to the faculty."

Susanne wasn't sure what he had just contradicted. "I believe you were looking for me."

"Well, yes, or someone very like, if that can ever be said of anyone."

"No, I mean just now. You told Marshall."

"That would be your young, of course. Well, yes, a word." Clement replaced his glass on the television as though that was the only place he would be able to locate it again, and brought the matchbox out with a rattle that suggested he was expecting to find it had somehow emptied itself. "Your, yes, your course."

"Yes?"

"Yes." He stored the matchbox once again and called off the pipe's search for his mouth. "Yes," he said more contemplatively than ever, and Susanne was resisting a compulsion to repeat the word when he said, "Violence in all its forms."

"In which it's portrayed."

"Represented. Representation, yes, one appreciates that's the, yes. Only, now, the, forgive me, question one found it hard to, you understand, was why *violence.*"

"Who was asking?"

"Initially, you mean to, yes." He touched one of his incisors with the pipe stem, and Susanne had the unsettling notion that he was about to play his teeth like a xylophone. "One gathers the Vice-Chancellor rather had mama rumbling in his office."

"Who, sorry?" Susanne's speech seemed increasingly to be acquiring characteristics of his. "Whose?"

"Of a student of yours. Elaine, would it be? Mrs., ah, who threatened you on television, I'm led to, you have it?"

"Nash."

Clement parted his lips as though Susanne had just told him what to do with his teeth. "Concerned about her daughter being exposed to, you'll have gathered as much."

"Her grown-up daughter."

"Age of majority, well, there is that. Not what it was or should be, mama maintains, but that's hardly for us to, appreciated, as I understand the veecee pointed out to her. A view received with a notable lack of enthusiasm, as we might have, yes. Appears to have stung her into vowing to take her complaint further."

"In which direction?"

"Ha," Clement said, not so much a laugh as a description of one he'd heard someone else emit. "To the media was apparently the threat. An idea we may presume she got from, well."

"Do we need to be worried?"

"Well, funding, you understand. Always potentially contentious, and in these frugal times, dear me. Should we really be spending money on and so forth. It might be wise to provide the powers that be with answers they can issue as appropriate."

"About my course."

"Why violence, as I think I, yes."

"Because we're surrounded by it and representations of it. Because people consume it even if they think they don't, and it's our job as educators to equip people to analyze."

"As I recall you told us when you originally, yes. Now, the agreement rather was that a written statement from you would be ideal."

"I don't remember that."

"No, one agreed today with the veecee that it would be useful for issuing if necessary to the media."

"I can do that."

"Capital. We'd expect no less of you. Whenever's convenient within the next few, yes? By Monday would be first rate."

Susanne had the impression that he'd managed to get out of first gear at last and was coming at her faster than she liked. "It's so the University can back me up," she said.

She was seeking confirmation, but perhaps her words didn't sound sufficiently questioning, because he took them for agreement. "Splendid," he said, and dug out the matchbox with a vigor which suggested he was about to celebrate. "Shall we join your other," he said, clamping the pipe stem between his teeth so as to reach for the doorknob.

Susanne had been peripherally aware of some mumbling in the hall. It must have been closer than she'd had a chance to realize, because as Clement opened the door a man fell backward into the room. He recovered himself, but only to receive another push in the chest from Teresa Handley, the crime novelist. "Made sure I won't be invited again, didn't you?" she was saying. "I thought it was only lasses and bum bandits who powdered their noses."

"Let's just remember it was your publisher who gave- —"

"Someone else's fault, is it, like always? Leave me a note if you ever decide to grow up." She gazed at him with a resignation that seemed almost affectionate, then shoved him harder. "I told him I wanted none of it and I told you not to. And what's the tale of you and the prof's big lass?"

"The subject happened to come up and she asked me if I had—"

"Her fault and all, was it? There's a shock. I hope you realize when her father hears about it that'll queer me with his whole department."

"Tess, the only way he'll know is if you carry on—"

"Oh, it's *my* fault! I shouldn't have needed telling, should I? Where do you reckon you're going?"

Each time she gave him a push she stepped back into the doorway. Now he tried to dodge around her as she offered another, and Clement, murmuring, "Do excuse me if you," lurched at the gap on the other side of her. Clement faltered, waving pipe and matchbox with a rattle loud enough to have been emitted by both. "Forgive me, madam, but I think you ought to realize I'm, dear me."

"Not you, you silly old whatever you're supposed to be. I'm talking to the bane of my existence. You scuttle off." She moved out of the doorway to let Clement sidle around her, and her husband made to follow. "Not you!" she roared.

Clement stopped as though she'd collared him, and her husband bumped into him from behind. Don and Marshall and the professors of law and genetics were descending, and came to a halt on seven stairs to watch. Susanne thought it was time to intervene, but before she could Clement swung round, raising his pipe by the stem like a miniature cudgel, a gesture which flung tobacco over his shoulder as though for luck, and squeezing the matchbox in his other fist with a sound of muffled splintering. "I warn you," he said.

"Don't be daft. How old are you? You'd think you were still in the playground," Teresa Handley told him, hauling her spouse away from him. "Just say if you want shut of us and we'll be gone."

This was to Susanne. Presumably the alternative was to leave the couple alone in the room. She was glancing at Don for his opinion when the phone rang in the hall. Clement shoved the crushed matchbox into his pocket and let the bowl of the pipe fall into his other hand. "Shall I, yes?"

"Go ahead," Susanne told him, not least to allow him to save face.

He unhooked the receiver and transferred it to his cheek. "Yes, or rather, Travis residence."

He frowned and seemed about to wave his pipe for silence as the group on the stairs recommenced descending. "I beg your, ah," he said, and his forehead relaxed. "I believe it's for young, yes."

He held out the receiver at arm's length, stretching the coils of the cord taut, as Marshall ran down, having handed Don the bottles. It looked to Susanne as though the receiver would spring out of reach if Marshall didn't catch hold of it in time, but he did. "Hi, it's Marshall. Who's—"

He snatched the receiver away from his face, and Don clutched the bottles to himself. Teresa Handley and her husband backed into the room, and Susanne almost snapped the stem of the wineglass she'd picked up from on top of the television. What came out of the receiver with such force that she could hear the earpiece vibrating was a child's shriek.

She couldn't tell whether it expressed rage or panic or despair. There were words in it, presumably directed at Marshall, but its loudness rendered them incomprehensible. It lasted only a few seconds, which was far more than enough. Then there was a click like the sound of a gun with no bullets, and the receiver began its empty drone, and it and Marshall were isolated by a silence which nobody appeared to want to break.

5

CUSTOMERS

By lunchtime on Saturday Don felt as hungry as Marshall already professed himself to be. They were in Don's shop beneath the Corn Exchange building in the center of Manchester. When Don had taken over the lease from a defunct supplier of military uniforms the basement had smelled of dust and mushrooms, but now it smelled as though he'd imported the exact same odor of old books that had characterized his shop in West Palm Beach. Sometimes that vegetable odor made him feel starved, and now it did. "About time for a pizza, I think you'll agree," he said.

Marshall was perched on the other stool behind the counter, reading a book which Stephen King had been unable to put down. He adopted the crouch which Don knew meant he was going to read at least to the end of a paragraph and probably of a chapter. Don listened to the chimes of the cathedral across the road and the hollow blare of a train in the station beyond the cathedral, and watched the flickering of sunlight shuttered by passing traffic, an effect which made the books nearest the doorway appear to tremble with eagerness to be read. Books occupied the entire height of the interior walls and both sides of three parallel bookcases almost as wide as the shop, but Marshall had found his latest reading in the tray of paperbacks which loitered on the sidewalk. He raced to the end of the chapter and smoothed out a corner which a previous reader had turned down, and inserted a dinosaur bubble-gum card between the pages. "Hut?" he said.

"That's what I figured. Get a small one between us. Remember where Pizza Hut is?"

"Come on, dad, why wouldn't I? Between McDonald's and Burger King."

"See how they're bending over backward to make us feel at home," Don said, only to wish he hadn't when the sole present customer, a man who was leaning backward and raising his spectacles on their cord so as to scan a top shelf, pursed his whitish lips. "How much do you need? Here's two, here's another two. Four quids should cover it."

The customer lowered his head and let the spectacles slide down as far as his enlarged purple nose would allow. "Quid, to be precise, unless you mean tobacco. I don't think the language has been quite so radically revised yet, even slang."

"Just being facetious. Marshall knew that, didn't you, son?"

"Believe it. Don't sell my book, okay?"

"What class of material are the young reading these days? I suppose we should be grateful that they read," the bespectacled customer said, and approached the counter to peer at the cover. "On reflection, perhaps not. What is this kind of thing for?"

"Fun?" Marshall suggested.

"Isn't there enough unpleasantness abroad without imagining this kind of pah?" The customer flipped the book onto its face as though to hide its naked skull and scanned the blurb. "A nightmare from which you'll be afraid to wake. Why on earth give yourself that, child?"

"I don't get nightmares from reading books."

"From where, then?" said the customer with a sharp look over his spectacles at Don.

"Do you want me to go for the pizza, dad?"

"Follow your stomach."

Marshall pocketed the coins and ran up the stone steps, and Don hoped the boy had no reason to brood over the customer's last question. Since leaving the neighborhood bullies behind in West Palm Beach he'd been sleeping more soundly, and even the child's voice on the phone at the party hadn't disturbed Marshall as much as it had affected his parents. Maybe the call hadn't been meant for him—Clement Daily had assumed it was only because of the age of the caller, and hadn't been able to distinguish a single word. The police had advised the Travises to contact them if there was another such call, but why should there be? He felt as though the customer's gaze, bespectacled now, was accusing him of having somehow caused it, except that the man was chastising Marshall's book with a stubby forefinger. "I trust you keep an eye on the ideas your son puts in his head."

"Do my best," Don said, raising his own spectacles and wondering what fool had once declared the customer was always right. "Were you looking for anything special?"

"May I assume we're speaking man to man?" the other said, wetting his lips with his shocking pink tongue, then pirouetted toward the nearest shelf as three people came down the steps.

He thought they were together until he saw one of them was the mailman. Nor did the two men in suits appear to know each other, because they started browsing on opposite sides of the room. The mailman planted on the counter the pile of Jiffy bags and cartons which had hidden his face, and mopped his forehead before trotting streetward. The first customer had been protruding each of his lips in turn as though he found the shop too crowded, and now he hurried to the steps before hoisting his spectacles to gaze through them across the shop at Don. “Don’t think me interfering,” he said, “but I really believe that giving your son access to such material is a form of child abuse.”

“Interfering? How could anyone possibly—” By now Don was addressing either the deserted steps or the remaining browsers, each of whom emitted a reticent cough and shifted his position very slightly. Don quieted himself and turned to the mail.

Here was *And But,* the autobiography of a local poet whose poetry read like the work of a writer too lazy to organize it into prose and whose prose identified itself as the work of a poet by not beginning any sentence with a capital letter and only very intermittently putting dialogue in quotes. Perhaps he was so much in demand as a reader of his own work in pubs because he made his audience feel capable of reaching his standard if not surpassing it, Don thought, and inserted the customer’s order slip between the pages to be phoned about later. Here was a wants list from a dealer in a Scottish village which appeared to be called by a choice of names, Dairsie or Osnaburgh. *Blind Stomachs, The Still Small Loaves, The Rotters of Rotterdam, Eating Earwigs, The Priest Beneath the Bridge, The Slow Teeth, Ten Little Niggers* not *Indians* . . . “Not *Ten Vertically Challenged Members of an Ethnic Minority,”* Don muttered to himself, pushing the list away for later scrutiny, and was unpicking the staples of a Jiffy bag when he smelled the pizza approaching.

Videocassettes spilled out of the bag as Marshall dumped the boxed pizza on the counter. “Who sent you those?”

“Ross at Blockbuster,” Don informed him, having discovered a letter among the cassettes. “Well, will you look at this. All I did was send him a couple of movie books that are only published here, and he’s sent us a bunch of the movies I told him I couldn’t believe were censored in Britain.

Stallone and Arnie and Steven Segal. Some of your favorites, and maybe some for your mother to use with her students."

"Can we watch one tonight?"

"What, a student? That's called voyeurism."

One of the men cleared his throat, and the other coughed as though they were exchanging mating calls, and it occurred to Don that the conversation might be embarrassing either or both. He made space on the counter to open the pizza box and lifted out a slice, tilting it to catch streamers of melted cheese. "How much change was there?"

Marshall disengaged a slice and blushed. "Can I pay you back when we get home?"

"Sure, but in future I'd like you to ask first. You still haven't told me how much."

"Sixty pees."

"It's a good job Mr. Disapproving isn't still around to hear you mauling the language. I hope I get to share the candy."

"I didn't buy any."

"What else does sixty pee buy, or is it a secret?"

"I didn't buy anything, dad."

Don chewed fast and swallowed. "Don't tell me you were robbed."

"No, dad, of course not, truly."

"So are you going to explain the vanishing trick?"

Marshall held up the remains of his slice of pizza in front of his face and lowered his voice. "Dad . . ."

"You'll drip cheese if you're not careful."

"Dad, there was a lady and her baby sitting on the sidewalk outside Pizza Hut with a card saying they were homeless," Marshall said rapidly, and chomped on the slice.

"Okay, Marshall. That's nothing to be ashamed of, for you to be, I mean," Don told him, and realized Marshall was embarrassed by being overheard. "It's all right, son. Nobody's listening but me."

As though to confirm this, the man who'd been pulling books half off the shelves nearest the door approached the counter, lowering his perceptibly unequal eyebrows and opening his large loose mouth. "Have you *Holding Onto My Lamppost* by George Formby?"

Don laid the remains of his slice of pizza on the open lid of the box. "Excuse the lunch. Is that a record?"

"It's his life story told by him."

"I can't say I've come across it. I don't suppose you brought any napkins, Marshall?"

"Sorry, dad."

"How about *Room for a Little One* by Arthur Askey?"

Don used his handkerchief to clear away a strand of cheese which he'd become aware was drying on his chin. "No again, I'm sorry. All the books on theater and film—"

"One Hand on My Fiddle by Ted Ray? *Twenty Years in Knickers and a Dress* by Arthur Lucan?"

"They're British . . . ?"

"Of course they're British."

"I was going to say theater and film are over in that corner, only I don't recall those names."

"Too British?"

If the man wanted books on British comedians, which Don took them to be, why had he been browsing in the criminology section? He didn't even seem particularly interested in the answers to his questions; he kept glancing toward Marshall as though the sight of pizza being eaten held a disagreeable fascination for him. Nevertheless Don said, "Sorry," but was sorry that he had, since the man turned brusquely and headed for the door. "Should be called the Sorry Shop," Don was half convinced he heard him mutter.

"I should bag those videos while we can distinguish them from pizza," Don advised Marshall, and the man went into rewind. He was backing down the steps to make way for a woman preceded by a wheeled tartan basket full of books. He left the shop as she drove the basket to the counter and raised her small flat face beneath its gray thatch to Don. "You don't just sell books, do you?"

"Just sell, no. Sell just, yes. What have you, oh." The lid of the basket had flopped open, exposing a haphazard heap of *Reader's Digest Condensed Books,* which—along with the magazine itself, and car repair manuals, and *By Love Possessed,* and *The Red and the Green,* and almost anything by H. G. Wells which wasn't science fiction and hadn't been filmed, and books which debunked the occult rather than gulping it down—it was his experience that more people wanted to sell than to buy. "Anything besides those?"

"They're improved, those books. They don't take as long to read."

Don had the distinct impression that he wasn't the first bookseller whom she'd found less than enthusiastic. "Some of the authors mightn't feel improved," he said.

"They're paid, aren't they? More than they're worth, most of them, if you ask me. Folk nowadays haven't time to read these big fat things you've got gathering dust."

"You'd be surprised how fat you can be and stay popular." Don saw before he'd completed the sentence that he might have worded it more tactfully, since she wasn't what anyone besides her family was likely to call slim, but he'd been distracted by realizing that the second suited man had at some point slipped out unnoticed by him. "I wonder sometimes if I'll see the day when books are sold by weight."

She could have taken that as some measure of agreement, but she only rocked the basket as though to soothe the books. "You're from the States, aren't you?"

"Could you tell by the pizza?"

"By the accent," she said in a tone which made him feel smaller than Marshall. "So are these books."

"I can only apologize." Most of his mind was on trying to identify whether any stock had vanished with the man. His words having caught up with him, he said, "Have you thought of trying the markets?"

"I've more than thought. Are you not even going to look at them?"

"If they're all in that format . . ." When she only stared he said even more feebly, "I really wish . . ."

"God, I'd like to land you all such a thump." For a moment the woman resembled a bulldog about to leap at him as representative of his profession. Instead she towed the basket as far as the steps before casting a disparaging glance at the pizza. "You'd think you were running a take-away," she said, and left a trail of rubbery bumps behind her all the way to street level.

Marshall finished the last mouthful of his half of the pizza. "Never mind, dad."

"I don't. Fun of a kind, I thought, didn't you?" As that provoked Marshall's version of his grin, Don set about checking the shelves. "Have half that last slice if you want," he said, though the encounters with customers had left him feeling hungrier than ever.

At least no books appeared to have been stolen, and after that the day started to pick up. A young woman with a trace of paint under her fingernails bought more than two hundred pounds' worth of illustrated Victorian books from the display in the locked bookcase, and a researcher from Granada Television bought a rare first of *No Orchids for Miss Blandish* for his producer and a variety of review copies for himself. A reviewer with a hip flask peeking from his back pocket brought in at least a dozen new unread hardcovers, one of which the author of a novel Stephen King had found unputdownable had been unable to relinquish. Marshall finished the book he was reading and took a breath and commenced that one. Don rang the future owner of *And But,* who spent more than half their brief contact in shouting at her dog, then he turned to listing the books he'd bought during the past month but not yet sold.

He was enjoying handling and describing them when Marshall emitted a sound of surprise. No book he read was deemed to be much good unless it earned at least a few audible gasps, and so Don didn't look up until he heard, "Mom, you're early."

"Shall I go away again so you can be men together?" Susanne shaded her face as she descended the steps, and when she took her hand away her long snub-nosed wide-mouthed face seemed to glow with the light in her large eyes. Her hair the color of sunbleached corn swayed forward as she leaned across the counter to kiss Don and then Marshall, who glanced over her shoulder in case anyone saw him. "Good day so far?" she said as Marshall returned to his book.

"Eventful is the word that springs to mind. Are we still on for dinner at the Koreana and a movie at the Cornerhouse, or does the look you aren't quite keeping to yourself forebode a change of plan?"

"I'll go along with you guys. By eventful you don't mean anything I should brace myself for."

"No, only anecdotes to amuse you over dinner. But I'm sensing you have another kind of news."

"Well . . ." She glanced at Marshall, then leaned close to blow softly at his forehead. "Honey."

"Ye," Marshall said as if he hadn't time to choose a final consonant, and crouched over the book.

"Marshall."

"Marshall."

Hearing them both speak made him look up reluctantly. "What?" he said in the tone of someone wakened from a good dream.

"Nothing too terrible. I'm sure it shouldn't be," Susanne said, and dug in her canvas tote bag. "I've written it all down. It won't be for a while yet anyway. Only Marshall, don't mind if you maybe have to see that man again who broke into our house."

6

A TRIAL

Once Marshall was past the security check and upstairs in the waiting area outside the courtrooms, the building reminded him more than ever of an airport terminal. Beneath the high ceiling of the white hall longer than his street the almost floor-length windows might have overlooked runways rather than people pursuing trajectories across a paved square. Next to the windows bunches of six square red armchairs, rows of three stuck back to back, faced one another all the way down the room. An electronic bell sounded two notes, and Marshall wouldn't have been altogether surprised to hear a flight announcement, but a woman's amplified voice said, "PC Pickles please attend Court 13." Nobody in sight took any notice—not the gatherings of bewigged barristers robed like some of Marshall's teachers, nor the people scattered about the armchairs, most of whom appeared in various ways to be trying not to look like criminals—except for a toddler who began to wail, adding to the echoes mating beneath the roof. A man whose head was shaved so close it seemed a metal plate was showing through the skin released the baby from its stroller and bounced it on his knee, and a man with a wig clasping his head as far down as his ears came forward like Dracula to meet the Travises. "Thank you for being so punctual. We shouldn't be kicking our heels long."

He was the barrister who'd visited their house and quizzed him about the intruder, Marshall saw, and heard him say, "Could the young man sit out while we just have a word?"

"Won't you need him as a witness after all?" Marshall's mother said.

"Mom, I want to."

"I would hope there won't be any difficulty at this stage, Mrs. Travis. If we could . . ." the barrister said, flattening one palm to indicate a door beside the entrance to the nearest courtroom. "You can amuse yourself for five minutes, can't you, young man?"

"Sure," Marshall said, feeling his face grow hot and his mouth twitch into a helpless smile, and wishing he'd thought to bring a book. "Sure," he repeated to let his mother hear how unconcerned he was, but she gave him one of the looks she often gave his father, which said that both of them knew the truth, before being ushered by the man into the room.

A statue of a draped woman with no pupils in her eyes was lowering her hands to indicate two armchairs whose foam was exposed by gouges in the plastic. Marshall sat on one of their neighbors, but when he felt its tripe of foam shift uneasily beneath him he stood up to read the notices posted outside each courtroom.

The *Crown vs. Philip Fancy*. So that was the man's full name. It made him feel suddenly present, and Marshall had to suppress a nervous burp as he stared about at all the people who weren't surmounted by a wig. Reading that the case was being tried by Mr. Justice Melon was reapplying that smile to his mouth when he glimpsed movement to his right, beyond the glass doors which led to the stairs. He glanced that way and saw the identikit portrait coming toward him.

It wasn't a portrait, it was the real face rendered flat and colorless by the coating of sunlight on the glass. The doors were shoved aside, and the face split into three and blazed with sunlight and advanced on him.

For a moment which felt like never again being able to breathe Marshall thought they were all somehow the man who'd forced his way into the house, and then he saw none of them was. One was too fat, the others were too young. Nevertheless he wanted to emit the kind of cry which sometimes wakened him from nightmares as, having veered toward the first courtroom and away after a prolonged contemplation of the notice, they converged on him.

He dragged his head around and fixed his stare on the notice. He was surrounded by a smell of new suits and aftershave and deodorant not quite cloaking sweat. The echoes closed around him to drown him, a burp which tasted like too much breakfast rose to his lips, and a voice said almost in his ear, "Here's the fucker."

It wasn't until the trio moved away that Marshall realized the man hadn't been referring to him. A taste of cereal and eggs and English sausage filled his throat, and he floundered between the glass doors and fled down the stairs to the men's room.

The twin of the outer door admitted him with some reluctance to a white room where two cubicles presented Engaged signs to him. In one of them a man was discovering how many different speeds and inflections he could use to moan "Oh God." Marshall stumbled to a washbowl and splashed cold water on his face, and felt his face drip, at which point the pressure within him relocated itself to his bladder. He lifted his head to the mirror and grimaced at the hair peeking over the back of his head, he ran his comb under the faucet and plastered his hair down with water so nearly hot it came as a shock, and then he raced to the nearest urinal and unzipped himself.

He closed his eyes and tried to sense which muscles needed to be used, but the whole of his groin had been overtaken by an ache. He took hold of his penis and wagged it, appreciating how much bigger it was since West Palm Beach, but what good was size if it didn't work? As he shook it hard enough to make it twinge he heard the inner door judder, and saw its tiny misshapen reflection opening on the pipe above the urinal, and a figure bulging through it. "I thought you must be in here," his father said. "They're nearly ready for you."

"I won't be—I'm just—"

"I know the feeling." His father stood at the adjacent urinal and unzipped himself amid the silence which had fallen. "Just let it come, I used to tell myself. Just relax. Try thinking of a stream running down a mountain. Try waving it about a bit," he said as someone else came in.

Marshall's giggle at the thought of that being overheard shifted the dam. He was jetting pleasurably when a second newcomer said close behind him, "Isn't that fucking—"

"Fucking right it is, Ken."

They were both the younger men. Marshall felt as though he was tethered to the bowl by his urine, and sensed that his father couldn't turn either. When a bell went off overhead he jerked so much that his stream almost swayed out of the bowl. "PC Harry please attend Court Four," said the voice which the bell had announced, and the bolt on the door of the non-groaning cubicle slid back to release a policeman in uniform. "Come on, dad," Marshall whispered, and zipped himself up. "You said they were waiting."

"Give a man a chance to micturate." Marshall's father produced a last trickle and shook himself off and packed himself away, and as he turned from the urinal Marshall saw he hadn't realized who was in the room. The policeman was keeping an eye on the room in the mirror while he washed his hands, and seemed more interested in the Travises than in the two men swaggering to the urinals. As his father pushed him out of the men's room Marshall gave a hiccup that tasted stale. "Don't worry," his father said once the twin doors had thumped shut, "they can't touch us."

Until his father had said that Marshall had believed it, and why should it become untrue because it had been said? They were making so much noise in hurrying upstairs he couldn't hear if they were being followed. He felt safer in the long hall planted with barristers, where echoes and his mother came to meet him. "Won't be long now. The lawyer says just tell the truth the way you told it to him and you'll be fine."

It wasn't until Marshall sat down outside the courtroom that he saw he'd walked past the third man with the face, who was watching him from the row of chairs less than ten feet away and breathing so hard Marshall was almost sure he could see the nostrils widen and narrow with each breath. The younger men barged through the glass doors and caught sight of the Travises, and said something to each other which showed their teeth. They stalked forward to sprawl on either side of their relative and stare at Marshall.

He could stare back. He could stare at each of them in turn, except that he felt as though they were paralyzing his eyes in the sockets, around which the skin was beginning to jerk. The men could only stare, and he was with his parents in a place devoted to the law. He swallowed the taste of altogether too much breakfast, and his mother sat forward. "Excuse me, would you mind not staring?"

The six eyes fastened on her, and a virtually identical grin appeared on all three faces. "Fuck off, you silly slag," said the younger man whose name wasn't Ken.

Marshall's father slapped his knees preparatory to standing up, and the speaker and Ken shoved themselves to their feet. "What you going to do about it?" Ken snarled.

Marshall's father sat back and displayed his upturned palms. "I'm open to suggestions."

The man looked as though he might spit on the floor with rage. He took a step forward, clenching his raw fists, and wrenched his arm free as the older man tried to detain him. Surely if he spat someone would intervene—surely they would before he reached Marshall's father, or was everyone too confused by the echoes to notice what was happening? Then the door to the courtroom swished open, and a woman in robes but no wig strode out. "Marshall Travis, please," she called.

A hiccup Marshall had been holding down exploded inside his lips, and he swallowed and stumbled to his feet, raising one hand rather than speak. The young men sniggered, and Marshall's parents turned their backs on them. "Go ahead, Marshall," his father said. "We're behind you."

"That's the boy. This way," the woman urged with an ushering gesture that flapped her robe, and held open the door just long enough for his father to take over the hold before she bustled Marshall through a second door into the courtroom.

The air was full of microphones. More than a dozen of them dangled from a wide sheet of translucent material backed by fluorescent lighting and held up by a lattice set in the high ceiling of the white room. One hung in front of Mr. Justice Melon, a papery-faced old man seated on a dais, who wore robes as red as a streetwalker's dress in a movie and a bib as well as a wig. He watched while Marshall was led to the witness stand, inside which were steps to climb. "Master Travis," he said then, "do you understand the meaning of an oath?"

"Yes, it's swearing." Marshall put his hand over his mouth to straighten his face and keep in a hiccup. "Swearing you'll tell the truth."

"Speak up a little if you would."

Marshall pulled his hand away and leaned closer to his microphone. "Swearing."

"As you say," the judge said after a momentary frown like folds in a sheet of tissue paper, and nodded to the robed woman. "Proceed."

She looked up at Marshall, restricting a smile to her eyes. "Take the book in your right hand and repeat after me . . ."

Marshall groped for the Bible and almost knocked it to the floor of the stand. His parents had sat on the foremost of several benches on the far side of the courtroom from the judge, and the three men had moved directly behind and above them. The men were staring at Marshall as though to tell him they had only to lean forward and—Then the policeman who'd been in the men's room sat behind them, and Marshall almost hiccuped with relief as he echoed the oath.

As the woman returned to her bench he glanced around the courtroom. The jury of two more men than women seated on a pair of benches opposite him looked sympathetic, and the lawyer who'd been to Marshall's house did, while the other lawyer was murmuring to his assistant and not even looking at Marshall. Only where was the gunman, the intruder? Nowhere in sight, which seemed to mean he could be anywhere, especially behind Marshall, who had to swallow as the lawyer who'd already talked to him stood up. "Just tell the court your name," the lawyer said.

The answer was threatening to be a hiccup. Marshall imagined the three men starting to grin beyond the edge of his vision, and his anger cleared his head and his voice. "Marshall Travis."

"And you live . . ."

Marshall told him where, and much else in the way of preamble before they came to the events of the twenty-first of June. He supposed the pace was meant to be helpful, but it gave him more time than he liked to wonder if the gunman would be produced for him to identify. Instead he was shown a photograph which he identified loudly, doing his best to ignore the impression that the face was multiplying at the corner of his right eye, and once he'd done that he didn't mind how much longer they talked; he was quite sorry when they finished. He was stepping back, not to walk down the steps but to shift his position, when the other lawyer said, "Just a few minutes, now."

His hair was almost as white as his wig, Marshall saw as the lawyer strolled toward him, an expression of faint puzzlement on his round plump face. He touched his forehead just below the wig with two fingers pressed together, then raised them as though flicking away whatever question he'd thought of. "So, ah, Marshall. Am I allowed to call you that?"

"It's my name."

"We'll use it then, shall we? We're here for the same reason, to get at the truth. Of course you know that, being under oath. Will you do your best to help me understand a few points?"

"I'll try."

"Good fellow." He glanced at the stenographer, who was typing the transcript onto a prolonged sheet of paper with so little apparent effort that Marshall wondered what each key represented. "So here we have you coming home from school on the day in question. A good day as school days go?"

"It was all right."

"I remember being similarly enthusiastic at your age," said the lawyer in the direction of the jury, most of whom more or less smiled. "So about what time do you arrive home?"

"When?"

"I believe we're discussing the twenty-first of June."

"Sure, but I thought you meant—"

"Yes?"

"Doesn't matter. I was home a bit after four."

"A bit. You wouldn't like to be more precise."

"Between ten and quarter past."

"Well, that's almost a time check. I'm impressed. And do you always take your time?"

"Excuse me?"

"You're let out of school at twenty to four, am I right? Does it always take you over half an hour to walk home?"

"I didn't go straight home."

"Ah, well, at your age . . ." The lawyer might have been contemplating further reminiscence, but asked, "What kept you?"

"I tried to stop a fight in the schoolyard."

"Admirable. Successfully?"

"No, they were too . . ."

"Do please go on."

"You know, they couldn't see anything except wanting to hurt each other."

"Well, we'll leave that. I see it distresses you. So then you hurried home."

Marshall was annoyed both by being described as distressed when he wasn't aware of feeling so and by being made to sound as though he'd fled. "No, I had to buy a paper."

"For your parents, was this? For yourself. Quite the reader. Was there some particular appeal?"

"We were doing crime at school."

"Studying it, that would be, I imagine. And was the paper of some use?"

"Yes, a lot."

"You were pleased to find so much crime in it."

"Well, uh . . ."

"No need to be ashamed. I'm sure we all appreciate that at your age crime can be exciting to read or think about. Do you remember anything specific from the paper?"

The judge cleared his throat dryly and minutely as Marshall said, "It had a picture of the man who pulled a gun on my dad."

Though the judge had seemed about to intervene, he began to leaf through papers on his wide desk. "You must be careful what you say, Marshall," the lawyer said. "Were you present when the alleged incident with the gun took place?"

"No, but my dad told me—"

"You must confine yourself to what you witnessed personally. What were you planning to do when you got home that day?"

"School homework."

"Most conscientious. And after that?"

"I don't know," Marshall said, beginning to grow bored. "Read a book, maybe. Watch a video."

"You have a collection of those."

"My parents do."

"You might watch a film belonging to your parents," the lawyer said with the briefest glance toward them. "But you didn't do any of those things when you got home, did you? Why was that, if you can bear with me?"

Marshall was sure the judge and jury wouldn't want to hear him go through all that again. "The man who—the man in that picture got into the house."

"Which picture are we speaking of?"

"The one in the paper and the photo—" Marshall hadn't realized until then that he didn't know what to call the judge. "The one his lord said I could look at," he said, feeling his mouth twist.

"Just let me understand this," the lawyer said as though to draw attention to the verbal mess Marshall had made. "You arrive home and let yourself into the house."

"Well—"

"I believe that's what you told my learned friend."

"Sure, but he made me. The man in the picture, he made me let him in."

"Help me see this if you'll be so kind. Where was he when you first saw him?"

"At the gate."

"This would be your garden gate. The far side of it, would that be? At which point you were . . ."

"Opening the door."

"And what was your reaction to seeing him? Did you say anything to him?"

"I—" Marshall wished this had come up earlier so that the other lawyer could have helped him deal with it. "I said 'Can I help you?' "

The judge turned over a sheet of paper which Marshall couldn't help thinking had nothing to do with the case and peered across it at him. "Could you speak up a trifle?"

Marshall clenched his fists below the top of the stand in order to control his mouth. " 'Can I help you?' "

"Yes. Thank you." The lawyer let his gaze stray past him. "You told my learned friend you knew who my client was almost as soon as you saw him."

"I did when I'd said that, what I said to him."

"I see. Now he's still at the gate, is that so? About how far away would that be, would you say? As far as from you to the jury?"

That seemed considerably farther than Marshall had been taking for granted. "Yes," he had to say, at once adding, "I could see him fine."

"Very good. So let's see if we can get this clear. You're opening the door, and you believe you recognize the man your father described to you, and there's the width of this courtroom between you. Would you say that represents the situation accurately?"

Why on earth did they need to go over this again? "Yes," Marshall said patiently.

"What made you let him into the house?"

Until that moment Marshall hadn't known that was the question he least wanted to be asked. His parents hadn't put it to him, but he'd demanded it of himself night after night while lying in bed. He'd let the man in to wait for his father, a thought which led to any amount of nightmares of what might have happened next, nightmares which wouldn't let him fall asleep. He was about to say, "I don't know," since he'd sworn to tell the truth, when the lawyer said, "Was he armed?"

For an instant Marshall was tempted to agree, because that seemed capable of making the situation so much simpler. "No," he said.

"Was anybody else about?"

"No."

"You're saying that all the neighboring houses were empty at that time?"

"I don't know," Marshall said, but the lawyer's patient puzzlement wouldn't accept that. "I don't suppose so."

"I think we may assume that some of your neighbors might have been at home, would that be fair? About how many times did you call for help?"

"None."

"I'm sorry, I didn't catch that."

"None."

"Let me understand this. You're alone with someone you have been led to believe threatened your father with violence and yet you don't call for help from any adults who might be within hearing distance. How high is your front garden fence?"

"Huh?"

"I'm sure the court heard the question. How high is your front garden fence?"

"About so high," Marshall said, patting the Bible.

The judge frowned, his eyes shrinking. "Please don't touch that."

The lawyer paused—letting guilt gather on Marshall, it seemed to the boy—and said, "Can you vault that high at school?"

"At school, sure, but there were flowers in the way."

"Please don't anticipate my questions." The lawyer paused again, long enough for Marshall to wonder when the lawyer who was on his side was going to object or intervene or whatever they did in Britain. "Let us move on. You've allowed my client into your parents' house. Quite a large house, you told my learned friend. How many stories has it again?"

The judge cleared his throat, but that was all. "Three," Marshall said.

"Are there places you can hide in it?"

"Some."

"At the top of the building, perhaps?"

"Maybe." Marshall wasn't sure where this was leading, and his uncertainty felt like a potential hiccup. "Not where the videos and books are."

"We'll come to those. Do they occupy the whole of the top floor?"

"No, there's the study and the guest room."

The judge sat forward with a rustle of paper. "Mr. Keen . . ."

"If you'll permit me, my lord, I intend to show the relevance."

Wasn't the judge supposed to say "Please be quick" or "I advise you not to waste the court's time" or declare what he wouldn't allow in his courtroom? But he subsided with only a hint of a frown, and Marshall's hiccups felt more imminent. "Would I be correct in thinking your house is alarmed?" the lawyer said.

Marshall grabbed his mouth to keep in the hiccup, and felt everyone in the court watching him. He must look as if he was trying not to laugh, and so he spoke too soon. "Yug."

"Pardon me, that was . . ."

This time the hiccup and the answer emerged simultaneously. "Yup."

"I assume the alarm was functioning on the day we are discussing."

"Yes," Marshall said, and hiccuped, at which point the judge canted his upper body toward him. "Would you like to excuse yourself for a few minutes?"

Marshall didn't want to delay knowing where the lawyer was trying to lead him any longer than was absolutely necessary. "Could I have a glup, a glass of watup?"

The judge raised his eyebrows at the request, then nodded to the woman who'd ushered Marshall into the courtroom. As she hurried out, Marshall seemed to feel everyone except himself relax. He turned his head on its unexpectedly stiff neck to look at the public gallery. His mother smiled encouragement, his father gave him two thumbs up, but all this was in the shadow of the three faces glaring at him from behind his parents, and he couldn't bring himself to meet any of those eyes. He stared at the Bible, more like a black box than a book, and hiccuped several times before the woman returned with a half-pint glass of water which she handed up to him.

"Thup," Marshall said, and took a not noticeably cool mouthful. He held it in his mouth and felt it fail to work. He swallowed it for fear of spraying the Bible, and breathed in as hard as he could, and filled his mouth from the glass. Almost at once he was aware that the drink would be no match for the approaching hiccup, and restored the mouthful to the glass while the judge watched as though Marshall was botching an unimpressive magic trick. Marshall knew one certain cure for hiccups, but hadn't wanted to perform it in the courtroom; now he appeared to have no choice. He craned forward and began to drink out of the wrong side of the glass.

"Please remove that," the judge said, and Marshall stooped until the glass was almost horizontal, and clung to it so hard he was afraid it might break. Water ran in and out of his mouth, and as he gulped it down he felt the hiccups succumb to his fear of having the glass taken away from him. When the woman reached over the top of the stand he jerked backward and tipped up the glass so as not to spill the last of its contents down himself, and splashed a line of drops like a trail of periods at the end of an unfinished sentence across the Bible which the woman was removing at the behest of the judge, who drew a sharp breath through his nose and expelled it at length before sitting back as if to leave Marshall at the mercy of his interrogator.

The lawyer waited until the woman had carried off the glass, which Marshall nearly dropped in his haste to rid himself of it. "Have you a key to the alarm?"

"Yes," Marshall said, feeling horribly unsure of himself.

"So having admitted my client to the house, you turned off the alarm."

"Yes, but I left the key in it."

"Allow me to move on for a moment. Were you examined afterward?"

"After . . ."

"After the incident which you have alleged took place."

Marshall felt as if something he couldn't identify had been snatched away from beneath him. "Examined, like how? Who by?"

"I understand you live only a few minutes from one of our hospitals. Was it felt necessary to have your injuries looked at by a doctor?"

"Which injuries?" Marshall instantly regretted having said, and interrupted whatever the next question was. "He dragged me all over the house and snapped the buttons off my shirt."

He'd been too ashamed to tell his parents that he'd thought the man's knuckle at his back had been a gun, and how could he admit it in public—worse, in front of three of the man's relatives? The lawyer let him be helplessly quiet for several seconds, and then he said, "In the course of all this dragging, did you by any chance discuss your collection of videocassettes with him?"

"They aren't mine, I said before."

"Quite so. Indeed, I should have realized you would hardly own a copy of *The Texas Chainsaw Massacre* at your age, let alone the Marquis de Sade's—you can perhaps tell me if this is not the correct title—*120 Days of Sodom.*"

The judge lifted his head as though at an unwelcome smell. "Are these films legally available in Britain?"

"Rest assured they aren't, my lord." As the judge nodded an acknowledgment, the lawyer swung toward Marshall. "But these were among the films you showed my client in your house."

Marshall couldn't think for struggling to find a way around the terms of the oath. "I didn't show him, he got hold of them."

"After you had shown him where they were kept."

"They weren't upstairs, they were in the front room."

"I see. Though if that is the kind of material which is left where anyone could see it . . ."

A chair cantered backward, and the lawyer Marshall had thought was supposed to defend him stood up. "My lord, I really must—"

"I share your doubts, Mr. Penman," the judge said, and Marshall wondered if it was part of the ritual that someone else had to raise them on his behalf. "Mr. Keen, I think the time has come for you to indicate where this is leading."

"My lord, my client does not dispute that he gained entry to the house in order to confront Mr. Travis—unarmed, as I believe has been established. But he maintains that he was admitted to the house after expressing interest in the collection of videocassettes which, as you observed, are not legally obtainable in this country."

"How could he have known they were there, Mr. Keen?"

"Because our young witness and his mother who uses them as a teaching aid discussed them on television some weeks ago."

Marshall heard sounds of dissatisfaction from the public gallery, and couldn't look when the judge did. His parents were going to be ejected, and it was his fault for not telling them about Fancy and the videos, an incident which until now hadn't even seemed worth remembering. Apparently the judge's gaze was enough to quell his parents, and perhaps their reaction confirmed what the judge had been led by the lawyer to think, because he said, "You may continue, Mr. Keen."

"Just a few more questions, Marshall, if you can concentrate for me. Would you remind the court where my client was when your father came home?"

Marshall wanted to clarify the business with the videos, but couldn't think how. "In my mom's and dad's room," he said with little patience.

"And just remind us why you'd taken him upstairs."

"Not to look at videos."

"I hear you. Why had you taken him upstairs?"

There seemed to be nothing more to the question than the words of it, yet Marshall was having to rub the palms of his hands on his trousers. "He made me."

"This was a stage of the dragging which you allege took place."

"I guess so."

"It would have to be, wouldn't it? But I still don't understand why he would choose to wait for your father upstairs, or did he expect to find your father up there?"

"No, of course not," Marshall said, wondering why nobody had intervened to prevent him from stating what was only his opinion. As he fought the way his mouth was trying to tug at his face, a memory came to save him. "He wanted to see the rest of the house."

"Wanted to see the rest of the house," the lawyer said, and let his gaze drift past Marshall. Of course there was nothing behind him except the wall, but the gaze was invoking the experience of being pushed upstairs by the intruder: the smell of sweat which must have been partly Marshall's own, his skin crawling as though from the touch of stubble, the presence behind him like a weight on his whole being, the noose of his collar and tie close to throttling him, the hard object digging into his back. "So at any rate," the lawyer said, "we have you in the bedroom. About how long would you say you were there before your father came home?"

"I don't know." The longer Marshall thought about it, the more protracted and oppressive the memory seemed, heavy with undefined fear. "Hardly any, I mean, just a minute."

"You were there for just a minute. Very well, and then . . ."

"I heard my dad's car."

"You heard what precisely?"

"Heard it stop outside and him getting out."

"Help me grasp this if you will. You weren't able to see him."

"I knew who it was, though, and I was right."

"I think you were asked not to anticipate. What did you suppose was likely to happen when your father came into the house?"

"He was going to try and hurt him, the man who'd got in was."

"That was your belief. Acting on that belief, did you attempt to protect your father?"

"Yes, I ran onto the balcony and—"

"I take it that my client could not have been holding you at this point."

"Yes he was, but I got free and—"

"A moment, now. From what exactly did you have to free yourself?"

Marshall rubbed his sweaty palms with his sweaty fingers. "He was holding my shirt collar."

"Is it possible that the buttons which you say were snapped off may have been dislodged as you freed yourself?"

"I guess."

"Mr. Keen . . ."

"I believe I'm leading to my last important point, my lord. So, Marshall, you run onto the balcony and try to warn your father, do you?"

"Right."

"What do you call to him?"

"I . . ." Marshall swallowed and tried to keep his fingers still. "I said . . ."

"A little louder, if you can."

"I said 'Don't come in, he's got a gun.' "

"But you told the court my client was unarmed."

Marshall's right eye twitched, but he couldn't close out the sight of everyone watching him. "Do you wish to change your testimony?" the lawyer said.

The prospect of even more interrogation drove Marshall's voice out of his stiff mouth. "I thought he had a gun, but it was his finger."

There was a chorus of sniggers from the public gallery. Surely now the judge would clear out the intruders, but he only gave them a sharp look. "And what was your father's response to your warning?" the lawyer said as though he was sparing Marshall any number of harder questions.

"He didn't hear what I said."

"In which case you must have believed he was in even greater danger."

"I guess."

"And been prepared to do anything you could to protect him."

"Sure."

"An understandable reaction, given the apparent situation as our young witness saw it," the lawyer told the jury, most of whom were beginning to look as unsure as Marshall felt about where this was leading. "So, Marshall, can you explain to the court how Mr. Fancy came to be hospitalized?"

"He tried to jump on my dad and missed."

"To jump from where?"

"Our balcony."

"A balcony which I think we have established is on the first floor?"

"Second. Well, what you call first, yeah, first."

"We need to be absolutely clear about this. Approximately how far from the ground would you say the top of the balcony railings are?"

"Is," Marshall corrected before he could stop himself, and received a frown from the judge. "I don't know. About . . ."

"In the region of twenty feet, shall we say?"

"About."

"I should inform your lordship I was able to establish that the height is just in excess of twenty feet. Now, Marshall, I would ask you to think carefully before you answer. Are you telling the court that my client jumped from that height in order to catch your father when he could have walked downstairs and confronted him as he let himself into the house?"

"Yes," Marshall responded at once, and heard the answer fall dead. "Well, he did. He jumped like you said."

"Take your time before answering this question. Might you have given him any help?"

"Help?"

"Perhaps the usage is unfamiliar. My client is on the balcony, and you believe he may be preparing to shoot your father, though in fact he is unarmed. Might you have given him a push?"

Marshall saw understanding spread through the jury, and felt it take hold of him. "I didn't," he blurted.

"Let me remind you of the situation as you have described it. You've just freed yourself with enough force to rip buttons off your shirt. Presumably you consider protecting your father more important than, say, stopping a fight in the school playground. Are you saying you wouldn't do everything in your power to protect him and think about the consequences afterward?"

Marshall wished he had indeed behaved like that. Perhaps his wish could be heard in his reply—perhaps he didn't even want the reply to be believed. "No, I didn't," he said.

"No further questions."

"Mr. Penman?"

The opposing lawyer shook his head without bothering to glance at Marshall. "You may stand down," the judge said.

As Marshall turned to the steps the witness stand seemed to quiver, and then the courtroom did. He held onto the edge of the stand as he picked his way down the suddenly rubbery steps. The robed woman took his elbow for a moment to steer him toward the public gallery, and Mr. Penman glanced up from sorting papers long enough to give him a slow blink which Marshall took to express profound disappointment. At least Marshall was trudging to his parents, both of whom only looked relieved. But the youth called Ken leaned sideways behind Marshall's mother and butted the air and opened his mouth. No sound emerged, but his lips around his bared teeth shaped the words unmistakably as he bulged his bloodshot eyes at Marshall. "We'll get you for what you done."

7

A VERDICT

That evening Marshall watched videos with Tom Bold and Ali Syed and Trevor Warris. Tom had brought his girlfriend Pippy, a large girl who, although she was months younger than any of the boys, already had breasts, and who kept calling Tom "Tombola" because her mother did. She ate most of the salad at dinner, while little Trevor devoured several of the burgers on the communal plate which Marshall's father kept replenishing. When the picnic was over Pippy organized the boys in clearing everything into the house and washing up the plates and utensils, and so they were all in the kitchen when Ali said to Marshall, "Show us something we can't see in Britain."

"Just your videos," Marshall's mother said at once.

Trevor, whose older brother apparently talked and read about nothing except videos, turned out to know most about them. In the room at the top of the house he selected a pile tall enough to tuck under his chin, and while Marshall employed the fast forward button he added a commentary to the chorus of pops of the bubble gum Pippy had shared around. "That was cut," he said when Indiana Jones's adversary pulled out a man's living heart, and "So was that" when the screaming man was lowered into a pit of fire. Marshall never enjoyed hearing gum in a movie theater, but now he joined in like the gracious host he was, and had succeeded in producing the loudest pop yet when the phone rang in the hall and upstairs.

There surely wasn't any reason for his palms to begin sweating, and he rubbed them down his pants legs before they could really start. He heard the ringing cease after five repetitions as the machine by the stairs took the call, and then his father picked up the phone in the study. "Hello?"

"Can we hear the music? I like this bit," Pippy said, and so all Marshall heard of the conversation through the microphone on the answering machine was his father's blurred voice and another. As the movie began to rewind Trevor suggested other films to watch—*Robin Hood, Prince of Thieves* was a popular choice—and Marshall heard his mother meet his father as he came downstairs. "Why are you looking like that?" she said.

"It's on the machine. Wait while I play it back."

Marshall sprang himself out of his chair and ran into the hall. "Can I listen?"

His mother made a stern face at him, but his father pondered and said, "Maybe you should."

Marshall wiped his sweat off the remote control he was still holding and entrusted it to Trevor. As he closed the door the answering machine delivered itself of several clicks, and then his father's voice said, "Hello?"

"Don Travis? It's Teresa Handley. I'm the writer who wrecked your party by causing a scene."

"Of course you didn't. How's everything?"

"He can come back if he keeps his nose clean. I used to wonder where you lot across the pond got that phrase from. Meanwhile I'm celebrating publication day all on my own."

"Here's to your book never turning up in my shop."

"I'll drink to that." An interlude of static followed, then, "I just did. How about you and the family? How's the case?"

"The court thing, you mean. Marshall was the star of the show. Kept his head with all the man's relatives watching him."

He mightn't be so confident if he knew what the man in the gallery had mouthed at Marshall. "When are you expecting the verdict?" Teresa Handley said.

"Should be Monday when the bad guy gets justice."

There was a silence which Marshall suspected was occupied by another drink. "Have you thought what to do if he doesn't," the crime novelist said eventually and somewhat indistinctly, "or come to that, if he does?"

"Stay here in either case."

"There's a pioneer. Over there I expect you'd get yourself a gun to be on the safe side."

"We've never owned one."

"Have you not? Me neither, believe me." This time the stretch of static couldn't disguise the clink of glass against teeth. "The point being, at the party I was saying to your wife that when I was researching this last masterpiece of undying literature I got introduced to someone at the supply end of things, so if you ever feel the need I could put you in touch."

"Well, that's very . . ."

"You mustn't think I make a habit of this. Only in the circums, and with you being used to everybody having one that wants one instead of only those who shouldn't like it's getting to be here, and I felt I owe you a favor after wrecking like I said."

"If you want to do us one, send us a signed copy of the new book."

"I will, to all of you and yours for putting up with me. Give my regards to the prof and to junior," she said, and was gone with a clash of glass against the mouthpiece.

"Didn't she realize she was being recorded?" Marshall's mother said as the tape gabbled backward to reset itself. "She mustn't care about technology. She still writes longhand and her husband processes it." Marshall could tell she was clearing this speech out of the way of something else, and as the machine clicked into its listening mode she said, "Frankly, Don . . ."

"Go ahead, be that."

"I don't see why you felt you had to . . ." A nod at Marshall said the rest.

"Marshall's a person too, aren't you, son? I thought we always took his feelings into account."

"I hope we do. Do we, honey? Never hold off saying if you think we aren't."

"So can I stay?"

"I set myself that trap, didn't I?" she said, and had to laugh. "I still wouldn't have minded first chance at hearing the tape, but at least now it's over."

"You don't think we should discuss it."

"Discuss what, Don? Buying a piece?"

"I figured I should hear what you thought at least."

"I think you have to be kidding if you even need to ask. We're talking illegal and dangerous here, the kind of thing that could get us deported. And I have to say I don't like that glint in your eye, Marshall. Guns hurt, and they maim, and generally mess up people's lives if they leave them alive at all. They aren't like they are in the movies, and if you don't know that, maybe you should watch a few less."

"I do know, mom. I've seen the real stuff on television, on the news."

"Of course you know the difference. I'm not attacking you, honey, I'm attacking . . ." She gestured loosely at herself. "And I can't imagine you'd care much for the idea of a gun around the house."

In that case, Marshall reflected, she didn't know him as well as she would like to think, but he also meant it when he said hopefully, "We don't need one, do we?"

"Believe it. Like Don told the lady, we're here and we're staying and we don't need any defenses we haven't already got. Now can I hear an altercation that sounds like it needs you to sort it out, or shall we?"

"I'll get it," Marshall said, though he felt he'd been maneuvered into leaving so that his parents could say things they didn't want to say in front of him.

Pippy was insisting his copy of *Conan the Barbarian* was the one she'd seen on television, and Trevor was maintaining that it couldn't be and, worse, finishing Tom's words for him. Ali was failing to keep the peace by suggesting that the disagreement didn't matter. By the time it had been established that Pippy had watched a satellite broadcast Marshall was dismayed how much anger had been generated to no end. Pippy's mother arrived during the last ten minutes of the film. "Doesn't he ever put his shirt on?" she said of Conan, and "Looks a bit like you, Tombola" and at least half a dozen other comments which everyone tried to ignore. As soon as the credits began to roll she bundled all the visitors out to her milk delivery van, and then there wasn't much to distract Marshall from having to wait all weekend to learn what the judge and jury said.

Meanwhile, as he lay in bed, he kept hearing the threat the man in court had only mouthed. Surely it was the kind of threat you heard in the schoolyard, boys saying they'd smash someone's face to a pulp or break their arms and legs or cut their balls off. Words could be a kind of violence you committed when you hoped not to go any further. The older man had elbowed Ken hard in the ribs when he'd seen him mouthing, and the three had only stared at the Travises as Marshall's parents had led him out. They hadn't been following whenever he'd looked back, and he ought to remember they had no reason to follow. They'd find out as soon as they spoke to their relative—find out that Marshall had done nothing whatsoever to him.

Marshall slept before he expected to, and awoke on Saturday knowing the weekend was planned in advance. That afternoon he went bowling with his friends from school, and later he ate Indian with his parents at the Shere Khan. On Sunday his father took him to Laserquest, where they zapped as many opponents in the dark plasterboard maze as they could without having their own laser guns disabled. After dinner at home they went with Marshall's mother to the ice rink.

It was in a building as large as a barn—too large for the disco music which grew blurred with trying to encompass the rink. Soon Marshall was skating across the ice while clumps of people hobbled around its edge and clung to the low wall. He met his parents in the mist beneath the yellowish arc lights, and then they glided arm in arm away from him, and he thought they were reliving some part of their life together, perhaps from before he'd been born. Suddenly—he didn't know why—the air tasted like tears. He had to give them time with each other, but once he saw them swooping back toward him he wobbled to them, having lost his confidence. "Here he comes," his father cried, stretching out a hand to catch him, but Marshall couldn't feel supported while he was unable to ask whether they already knew what he had only just realized—that his useless performance on the witness stand would set the gunman free.

He tried not to let his mother see him shiver, but she did, and five minutes later the Travises reclaimed their shoes. Outside the night seemed as cold as the rink. As the Volvo swung out of the parking lot onto the main road a pair of headlamp beams hacked through the car, and the outlines of Marshall's parents blazed as if they were exploding. All the way through several suburbs of Manchester he was intensely aware of them, close enough to touch and yet rendered unreal as paper silhouettes by his sense of their vulnerability. A hair sprouted from the top of his father's head, and every oncoming car spotlighted it and the drooping night-heavy flower of his mother's hair. He was still seeing the fragile silhouettes as he fell asleep in bed, afraid to dream. He was still feeling vulnerable on their behalf as he walked to school the next morning.

He'd barely reached the Wilmslow Road when boys from the school, some of whom he hadn't realized he even knew, began to pump him about his day in court. "What did they give him?" "Did they put handcuffs on him?" "Was it like on telly?" "Did you have to swear?" "Did he attack anyone?" "Was it like in the films?" Marshall answered these and many other questions as best he could, wishing he could feel like the celebrity they seemed to take him for. He'd reached the pedestrian crossing nearest Bushy Road when a car even blacker than the July sky squealed to a halt scant inches from him.

As the green guardian of the crossing turned red the car roared away, driven by a brawnier version of Billy Heathcote, presumably the security guard whose job had put him in hospital. Billy stood by Marshall and bumped him negligently with an elbow. "I hope you got him put away for as long as they're allowed to lock him up."

"We don't know yet."

"You know what you did." Heathcote followed him across the road as cars began to bully slowpokes off the crossing. "You know that, I reckon."

"My best."

"I should bloody hope so. If I'd been you I'd have said he did as much as they couldn't prove was wrong and landed him in Strangeways till his hair turned white."

"Or looked a fool when his lawyer kept after you."

"Eh? Half the time I can't tell what you're on about with that accent of yours."

"I thought you and your dad were supposed to believe in the law?"

"Don't you say that about my dad." Heathcote must have felt he'd made clear what he took Marshall to have said, because he went on, "You'd be quick enough to scream for him if you needed him. Or maybe you think you don't need the law, maybe you want the man who nearly shot your dad wandering around loose. I bet you'd rather the police never made up any evidence even if it got scum like him locked up. I bet you'd like the social workers and all the rest of the do-gooders to send him on a holiday to, to Florida."

Marshall had rather lost track of all this, which felt as though a large dog was panting in his face while trying to knock him over. "Why Florida?"

"Never mind bloody laughing about it. That's what they do these days in case you didn't know, send scum to Disneyland because they're so deprived."

"It's Disneyworld in Florida." Marshall was trying to control his mouth, having seen how it aggravated Heathcote's all-embracing anger. "Look, this is crazy. What are we fighting about?"

"I'm not fighting, lad. You'd bloody know if I was."

"Like Tom Bold did," Marshall said, experiencing a sudden urge to throw all his weight behind a punch in Heathcote's face. The ease with which he could be driven to pointless violence dismayed him. Why hadn't he been capable of violence when Fancy had been lying in wait for his father? "I'm not arguing with you any more," he said. "Keep your nose out of my business before it gets hurt."

"Here it is." Heathcote lurched in front of him, poking his own nose almost flat with a forefinger. "What are you going to do about it? Have a go, I dare you, unless you're a queer."

Marshall stepped around him, which brought him in sight of the schoolyard and a teacher. "Is it dark up there?"

Heathcote crowded him as far as the gates and shoved in ahead of him, then turned on him. "Where?"

Marshall walked away before muttering, "Up your ass." Saying it made him feel less satisfied than lazy, no longer taking the trouble to invent a substitute for profanity as his parents did, and not having said it to Heathcote's face smacked of cowardice.

Before long the bell which he imagined earning curses from any night shift workers who lived nearby went off to herd all the boys into line, where they had to stand still and stop talking and then troop class by class into the school. Several hundred of them thundered at the pace of prisoners returning to their cells along the gloomy corridors that smelled of sweat and chalk and floor polish, and into the hall crowded with rows of inseparable folding seats with too little leg room. The last of the boys barely had time to be seated when everyone jumped or reared or lolled or staggered to their feet as Mr. Harbottle strode onto the stage, followed by his staff.

After the morning's token nod to religion the headmaster lectured in his high sharp disappointed voice on bullying and how it must be reported to a member of the staff. "Bullies must learn that being bigger and stronger gives them no advantages in this school." Marshall saw several contradictions in that, but it seemed like the rest of the school day—a dream from which the verdict of the court would awaken him. Classes began with a double dose of French. *Comment t'appelle-toi?* What work does your father do? And your mother? What job will you have when you grow up? Marshall was unable to think that far. "I'd have expected better of you, Travis," the French master said, tapping the desk beside Marshall's exercise book and leaving a chalky fingerprint on the gouged wood etched with fading ink, and strode to the front of the class as a boy peered rodent-like through the glass of the door and knocked timidly on it. "Tingay, isn't it? Yes, Tingay?"

"Mumble mumble bottle," Marshall heard, and "Mumble Travis mumble," and his pen described a squiggle like a lie detector's peak before the teacher hooked a finger at him. "Well, Travis, you've been honored with a summons to the presence."

Marshall banged his knees on the underside of the desk as he stood up, but managed not to stumble as he made for the door, though by the time he reached it he was bearing the weight of the gaze of the entire class on his back. Tingay had fled on another errand, and the corridor the length of the school was deserted. As Marshall trudged along it he heard someone scraping Bach off a cello, the shout of a master echoing over a stampede in the gymnasium, two boys yelling insults at each other in what sounded like a scene from a murder play—Shakespeare, to judge by the odd audible word. All the way along the corridor a charred sky paced Marshall.

Three older boys were waiting haphazardly outside Mr. Harbottle's office—three hindrances to Marshall's learning why he had been sent for. One he'd seen twisting earlobes in the schoolyard to extract lunch money from their owners. All three stared at Marshall as though he had no right to stand near them, and he'd positioned himself diagonally opposite them when the door beside him opened and the headmaster's secretary poked out her head, bristling with bluish curls. "Is Travis here yet?" she demanded, and caught sight of him. "Aren't you Travis?"

"Yes," Marshall said, uncertain whether she was supposed to be a Miss.

"Why are you hiding round there? Come along, step lively. Head's got other people besides you to see," she said in the process of hustling him across her office, and swung her knuckles so close to his head that he thought she meant to rap on it rather than on the inner door. "Travis, Head."

"Send him in."

Marshall didn't have time to breathe before the door was open and then shut behind him. The room resembled a very large oak chest whose interior was decorated with plaques and diplomas, their metal and glass gleaming with electric light. A sharp smell of metal polish snagged his throat. Mr. Harbottle was frowning over a letter and displaying his bald pate, which appeared to have forced its way between the twin leaves of his glossy black hair. As he raised his head with its broad nose and thick pink lips, the light slipped off his scalp like oil. "Ah, Travis," he said as if he either had to remind himself why he'd sent for him or was only now able to put a face to Marshall's name. "How are you finding it?"

His guarded friendliness would have struck Marshall as ponderous in any case, but now it seemed the worst possible omen. "Yes, sir, I am," Marshall stammered. "Fine, thanks."

"I'm led to understand you've found your feet."

This was beginning to seem like a lesson in a foreign language, and Marshall wasn't sure he was expected to answer. "Yes, sir," he said when the silence got to him.

The headmaster passed his right hand over that wing of his hair as though to check he hadn't lost it. "Your performance on television was brought to my notice."

Was that why he'd sent for Marshall? Did he feel that Marshall had somehow let the school down? The disappointed tone had crept into his voice, but then he said, "I'm told you're quite the reader."

"I guess. Sir."

Mr. Harbottle looked askance at him and apparently decided that was sufficiently disapproving. "I suppose that follows from your father's way of life. And does your mother discuss the films you watch with you?"

"She does, sir, and my dad," Marshall said, feeling defensive on behalf of both of them.

"We must hope you are given a suitably critical view of them." The headmaster let his gaze gather on Marshall, who shifted his feet and glanced down to quell them. "As it happens, I was just speaking to your father."

Marshall's nerves dragged at the corner of his mouth. "What about? Sir."

"You and he were both in court, I hear."

"Only because we were witnesses."

"Oh, utterly. It wasn't my intention to suggest you'd been hauled before the beak for watching gruesome twaddle." The headmaster pursed his lips in appreciation of his flight of wit and went on. "Your father sketched the case for me. Most deplorable. Very much the kind of situation I had occasion to refer to at assembly this morning. Or to be more precise, an example of how it develops in adulthood if it goes unchecked. I trust you've suffered nothing of the kind at Bushy Road? No undue hostility to your origins, for instance?"

"No, sir," Marshall blurted, not caring whether that was true. "You said you'd been speaking to my dad."

"That is so," the headmaster said severely, so that Marshall feared he'd provoked a lecture about interrupting. Instead, although after a weighty pause, Mr. Harbottle said, "You will be aware he went to court this morning to hear the verdict."

Marshall couldn't speak, not least because his mouth had gone awry. "You may well smile, Travis," the headmaster said. "Your father asked me to inform you that the miscreant has been found guilty on all counts and sentenced to eighteen months in prison."

Marshall's mouth went slack, but he managed a real smile before his jaw could drop too far. "Gee, thanks, sir."

"Your father tells me that your testimony was instrumental in securing the conviction. I may very well cite your action in the near future as an example of the sort of behavior I was urging earlier."

Though Marshall felt he deserved not nearly so much praise, he didn't mind accepting it amid his euphoria. He walked out of the office feeling as though gravity had been reduced especially for him, and restrained himself from grinning at the three boys in the corridor, who had now become four. All the sounds of the school had acquired a brightness and immediacy which seemed to be addressing him; even the dark sky unspooling beyond the windows appeared as promising as a film yet to be exposed. "Notre ami américain a l'air très heureux," said the French master as Marshall returned to the classroom.

"Bien sûr, monsieur," Marshall said.

Now he was able to think what he wanted to be when he grew up, though he still wasn't sure if he would have time to be both a university librarian and a best-selling author. He settled for librarianship, since he didn't know if the French for "best-selling" was "best-selling." For the rest of the day he knew the answer to every question asked in class. The most gratifying moment, however, was in the dining hall, where everyone who hadn't brought his own lunch was doled out dollops of aggressively nutritious food to be eaten at tables as long as those in just about any prison dining scene Marshall had watched, and where he found a space a few feet away from Billy Heathcote. "Heathcote," he called through the mass of conversations and metallic scraping. "They gave him eighteen months."

"Should have been twice that," Heathcote grumbled, but Marshall saw that his anger was no longer directed at him.

When Marshall arrived home that afternoon just as the sky was beginning to let loose, his mother hugged him and said, "Well done." He accepted this and set about his homework to the sound of rain thumping all the windows, but when his father came home, drenched as he ran from the car to the house, and told him "Well done" as though he and Marshall's mother had rehearsed the phrase, Marshall couldn't take it: not when they'd both watched his performance in court. "I didn't do it," he protested. "I was, I was sewage. You saw."

"We saw you take everything his lawyer threw at you."

"You handled him at least as well as I did," Marshall's father said.

"He still made me say things I oughtn't to have said."

"But that's it, don't you see?" his mother protested, and his father explained, "The judge and the jury could see the lawyer was trying to confuse you because he hadn't any better defense. That's one of the things that went against our gun-toting friend."

Marshall felt unexpectedly exhausted. Perhaps that was an effect of relief, or of his having worried all weekend for no reason. He slogged through his homework and ate dinner, then tried to read a novel whose cover would allegedly stick to his fingers like glue, until his mother brought into the front room a copy of *I Spit on Your Grave*, a rape and revenge movie one of her students had lent her so that Marshall's mother could grade her essay in defense of it. "I don't think you should watch this, Marshall."

That made it sound more interesting, but he was too tired to argue. He went to the bathroom and congratulated himself on the size of his penis, and brushed his teeth until his mouth tasted like a large vanished mint, after which he wandered into his room and sat up in bed and read the same paragraph, and the same paragraph, and the same paragraph. At this point, admitting defeat, he switched off the light and lay watching as the night charcoaled the contents of his room, and listening to the rain around him and the screams downstairs, which seemed to be going on at considerable length, though maybe real rapes did. He found not being able to see the reason for the screams exciting for a while, then irritating, and wakened to find them still continuing, and then he didn't waken.

Soon he wished he'd stayed awake, when a bell began to shrill somewhere near him. Was it inside or outside the house? Was it the alarm? In that case, why wasn't the siren sounding in the hall, and why had nobody responded to it? He unstuck himself from his bed and stumbled out of the room, trying to grasp whether the house was lit by daylight or electric light and, whichever, how dim the slaty glow was. Leaning over the banister, he saw that the key was protruding from the alarm panel, which was turned off. Someone was in the living room; he could see more light beyond the door. He went downstairs faster than he'd known he could, and looked in.

His father was sitting close to the dead television and brushing his hair, repeatedly dragging the brush across the crown of his head in an attempt to tame a tuft which refused to be flattened. At least, that was the reflection Marshall saw on the gray screen, but when he looked at his father he saw that not only was he absolutely still, the brush was lying on the carpet. "Dad," Marshall said.

Perhaps his father couldn't hear him for the bell. Marshall stepped forward and picked up the brush and began to scrape at his father's scalp with it, only to notice that each movement of the brush enlarged a red stain that was pulsing up through his father's hair. "Dad," he pleaded in a voice which seemed to have exploded out of his control, and awoke.

The bell stopped a second later. He heard his father padding heavily downstairs to the hall in the silence. The bedroom was almost dark, and appeared to be in the process of turning into fog. Marshall didn't want to be alone with his dream or without some reassurance that all was well in the house. He flung himself out of bed and hurried to the top of the stairs.

His father was just removing the key from the control panel. It took Marshall a moment to realize that he couldn't have reached the panel to turn off the alarm while he was descending the stairs. Then the doorbell rang again, and his father plodded to the front door and set about unchaining and unlocking it, muttering, "Wrong house. Can't you stop for a minute? Trying to wake the dead?"

Someone was trying to gain entry to the house before the sun came up—before anyone in the building was fully awake. Marshall saw the faces behind his parents in the courtroom, and remembered the words that had been mouthed at him. "Dad," he cried in a voice far too much like the one he'd had to use in his dream. His father blinked over his shoulder at him, surprised to see him, but at the same time pulling the door open, and it was too late.

8

NASTIES

Susanne fell asleep thinking about rape. Had the film really needed to show Buster Keaton's granddaughter being raped by one man and sodomized by another and penetrated with a bottle by a third? It was the only film Susanne had ever felt the need to take a shower after watching, but did that prove the film had shoved the reality of rape in her face? That had been Martha's experience, according to her essay in which she had also cited a study where a group of students had been set the task of constructing a scenario to communicate what gang rape was like for the victim and had found themselves making many of the choices apparent in *I Spit on Your Grave*. Martha had argued her case coherently enough to earn herself a high grade, and Susanne appreciated it was never a bad thing if her own assumptions were given a good shake. Apart from that, she felt so relieved that the court case was over and that Marshall no longer needed to pretend he wasn't anxious, not to mention that she and Don no longer needed to pretend they didn't know he was, she fell asleep almost before Don climbed in beside her and crooked one arm around her midriff.

She had no idea how much later she was roused by an uncomfortable feeling that she ought to awaken. Don's arm was no longer around her, and she had the impression that something had taken him away. She widened her eyes, which persisted in blinking as though the dark was a heavy residue left by the night on their lids. Between the curtains in front of the balcony was a gap which hadn't been there when she'd gone to bed. She heard male voices muttering, several of them somewhere close, and she kicked off the quilt. Planting her feet on the yielding carpet, she padded to the window.

Two cars were outside, their fenders almost touching her car and Don's, and the house had stretched its light along the path to them. The front door was open. The voices weren't in the street but downstairs. Had she heard the doorbell in her sleep? She was holding onto the handles of the windows while a moment of dizziness passed when she saw that the two vehicles boxing in the Travis cars bore police insignia. Everything would be all right—though what was there to be put right? The thought seemed to grab her by the groin and stomach and abruptly dry throat, and she wobbled across the room and unhooked her robe from the back of the door, and struggled into the garment as she wavered onto the landing.

The hall below was lit, and it was crowded. She saw at least eight policemen, their uniforms black around Don, and beyond them a group of people who made her feel she mightn't after all have wakened, or that the family was on "Candid Camera." Then Marshall, who was gripping the wooden bulb which brought a full stop to the last line of banister, looked up at her, and several policemen did. From their expressions she could see that whatever was taking place, it was no joke.

She felt the banisters shake as she swung herself around them, felt the stairs tremble as she ran down faster than she was sure she could control. Everyone was watching her, and from the group of people nearest the front door a movie camera trained its lens on her. She put one hand on Marshall's shoulder so as to sidle past him rather than spend time persuading him to relinquish his white-knuckled grip on the wooden bulb, and the policeman who had been confronting Don took three heavy steps toward her.

He had thin pale lips and a sharp nose with nostrils pinker than the rest of his wide face, and startlingly black eyebrows which appeared to be underlining the wrinkles incised in his forehead. "You are Susanne Travis?"

Being addressed by name gave her a more immediate sense of herself—enough of one that she pinched her robe shut against the gaze of the crowd in the hall and tied the cord tighter, constricting her waist. "Who else would I be?"

His lips parted again, producing a spider-thread of saliva which vanished into their left corner. "I have to inform you that I have just served your husband with a warrant to search these premises."

"You've . . ." It wasn't only the invasion of her house which made her feel backed into a corner and all but undressed by the intruders, it was her being scrutinized by the camera, whose attention felt like the chill of the hour rendered harsher. "Better show it to me."

The policeman unfurled the fingers of one hand toward her, then poked them inside his jacket. "You are involved."

"Damn right I am. We both own this house." Susanne peered at the thick sheet of paper he unfolded in front of her, then she took hold of it in case that helped the mass of legal jargon communicate its sense to her. When he didn't let go of the page she felt as though his blunt grasp was somehow preventing the meaning from reaching her. She glanced at Don, who responded with a dull nod which sent a surge of helpless anger through her. "Would you mind closing that door?" she asked the people nearest to it, and was infuriated by her own politeness. "Who the—who the Gehenna are you anyway?"

Don smiled so wryly it looked as though a stroke had affected one side of his face. "They're filming a documentary about police work."

"What police work?" She heard herself sounding angry with him, and shook her head at him and turned on the policeman with the pressed lips. "What are you supposed to be looking for?"

"I think you know that, Mrs. Travis."

"Then you think a whole lot," she retorted, which didn't sound at all like her intended meaning. "It's a mistake, isn't it, Don? Can they do this? Do we get to make a phone call?"

"I don't know who we'd call this early."

"Of course, sure, that's the way it's meant to work." She became aware of Marshall, and reached to stroke his hand on the banister. "It's okay, honey. They're the police. They aren't going to do anything bad to us, are you?"

The officer in charge gave her a look so blank it was menacing. "We'll start on the ground floor if we may."

That was addressed largely to his forces, who separated into three groups and went into the front room and dining room and kitchen. Maybe they were searching for illegal dinner plates, Susanne thought wildly, or forbidden vintages of wine, or prohibited cutlery, or banned ingredients: maybe you weren't allowed to have a full jar of nutmeg in Britain. Then she knew what they were after, just as one young policeman called "Inspector" from the front room.

As Susanne launched herself in that direction the camera swooped after her, and only grabbing her own wrist prevented her from clapping a hand over the lens. She wasn't going to be made to appear to have something to hide, and they couldn't screen any of this footage without her and Don's permission, could they? She experienced some satisfaction as the pale-lipped inspector collided with the cameraman behind her in the doorway, but then she saw the policeman holding up a videocassette, his plump scrubbed face so triumphant that he might have been imagining the boost he'd just given his career. "I spit on your grave, Inspector."

Susanne hadn't time to laugh at how he sounded. "That belongs—"

"Yes, Mrs. Travis?"

The inspector's question allowed her time to rethink what she'd almost blurted out. "It belongs to a group of films I'm studying with my students."

"I'm afraid that won't help you under the circumstances."

Susanne planted her hands on her hipbones. "What circumstances?"

He turned a look of weary disbelief on her, then his gaze drifted to the policemen who were peering behind furniture and overturning cushions on the chairs. "Nothing else in here, Inspector," one said for all of them.

"Keep hold of that tape, Desmond. You should be aware, Mrs. Travis, that the film has been banned as a video nasty since 1984."

For a moment she heard only the date, which seemed so appropriate that she wondered anew if the entire situation could be someone's idea of an elaborate joke. The other policemen were returning along the hall, followed by Don, who had been keeping an eye on them. "Nothing, Inspector."

"I suspect we'll have more joy at the top of the house."

Susanne felt her mouth open and dry up. Someone who'd been in the building was responsible for the raid—had contacted the police and told them exactly where to look—and the faces of everyone at the party raced in a distorted jumble through her mind. The police were marching upstairs in single file, the camera panning with them, and as Marshall dodged out of their way his eyes met hers. She remembered his saying in court that the cassettes were kept on the top floor, and saw him remember, and went to hug him. "Never mind, honey," she said, feeling awkward and inadequate and more furious than ever with the invasion of the home, and grabbed Don. "What are we supposed to have done?" she whispered. "Clement said he checked it was legal to show those movies as part of a course."

Don shrugged as though trying to heave a burden off his shoulders, and beyond him she saw the director and cameraman exchange glances. They knew. Policemen were opening doors on the floor above while most of the intruders trooped to the top, and she felt them spreading like a mass of blackness through her house. "Go ahead," she urged, pushing Don and Marshall toward the stairs. "We don't want them where we can't see them."

She was trying not to conclude that she and the family were the intruders, strangers in a country where they'd learned the rules too late. Policemen were in her and Don's room and in Marshall's, opening wardrobes and pulling out drawers and groping under beds. She saw Marshall's face go awry, and he ran to his room, then hesitated, unsure whether he was allowed to be there. Her rage at how he was being made to feel could have lashed out in any direction, but she focused her attention on the director, an overweight man in his thirties with nearly all of a mustache and fewer hairs on top of his head than there were purple veins on his round face. "You tell me," she demanded, only inches from him. "What don't we know?"

His eyes flickered, and she saw he was deciding whether answering would help his film. He glanced down at the inspector, who had remained at the foot of the stairs, presumably in case any of the family made a bid for freedom. "One of your students," the director murmured, and seemed about to leave it at that, but instead lowered his voice further, "has been selling copies of banned videos."

"What has that to do with us?"

He blinked slowly at her as though he was squeezing the disbelief out of his eyes, and Susanne thought that if any of the unwelcome visitors gave her one more look she didn't care for—"Read a lot, do you, son?" an avuncular officer was saying, which enraged her too. Then the policeman with the plump scrubbed face leaned over the highest banister. "We've found them, Inspector."

Susanne felt her legs sending her upstairs as if they were thinking for her. The inspector appeared to be in no hurry to climb, and so she had time to tone down her rage at the spectacle of policemen removing dozens of cassettes from the shelves. As soon as he reached the top landing she said, "I want you to know that none of these videos has ever been out of our control."

"Is that so, Mrs. Travis?"

"I'm trying to tell you I've played them on a machine at the University to show them to my students, and on the player downstairs, and that's all."

"I'll note you said so."

"You can't copy these tapes into your British standard from either player. The signal can only be picked up by a suitable monitor, otherwise all you get is garbage."

"Really."

His very expressionlessness was infuriating, and so was the sight of the police pretending not to listen as they denuded the shelves. "Do you intend to leave me any tapes at all?" she said.

He raised his eyebrows slightly, producing another line in his forehead. "Refusing to cooperate won't help your case."

"I'd like to know how you define cooperation," she said, and saw plump Desmond turning a cassette of *Casablanca* over in his hands. "I don't suppose you'll be impounding Bogey, will you? I guess even the British appreciate a weep."

"It doesn't have a British censor's certificate, Inspector."

"Better add it to the pile."

Susanne felt as if darkness was invading the room, clinging to the lightbulb and the inside of her cranium. "You have to be kidding."

"It is illegal to sell or rent or exhibit any videocassette in this country which has not been given a British censor's certificate," the inspector said.

"In that case you may as well save yourselves a whole lot of trouble and take all of them," Susanne said, reflecting that the police would look pretty stupid if they tried to bring *Singin' in the Rain* and all the Astaire-Rogers musicals into court. The notion that a sense of absurdity might catch up with them in time to persuade them to drop the case was beginning to appeal to her when Marshall trailed upstairs after Don and the policeman who had been in Marshall's room. "That's mine," the boy protested.

The policeman whose plumpness and eagerness increasingly reminded Susanne of a schoolboy—the kind of teacher's pet all his classmates would loathe—was examining *Indiana Jones and the Temple of Doom.* "The PG rating on this isn't British, Inspector."

"Good work, Desmond."

Susanne saw Marshall's teeth squeeze his closed lips together as the policeman dropped the cassette on top of the nearest pile. "You call that good work, do you," she demanded, "taking away a child's entertainment?"

"Perhaps he'll turn to something healthier. I don't care what certificate it has," the inspector said, "I wouldn't let my ten-year-old watch that kind of violence."

"I'm twelve," Marshall said, his mouth twisting.

"Ten or twelve, it makes no odds. If there were a few more responsible parents there'd be a few less young thugs for us to have to deal with."

"If we're discussing responsibility," Don said in a thin voice, "maybe you ought to remember my wife uses these tapes to educate people in criticizing what they watch."

"I'm not here to argue with you, Mr. Travis."

"Then I suggest you keep your eructating opinions to yourself."

The inspector's lips stiffened, perhaps because he didn't understand the adjective, and then Marshall intervened. "Never mind, dad, mom. Pippy can tape it for me next time it's on satellite."

The inspector looked as though he might object to that too. Susanne was waiting for him to interfere, and saying, "Don't worry, honey, things can't be as bad as they seem," when a policeman came in from the study. "Inspector, this could be something."

He'd found a printout of the defense of her course which Clement had asked Susanne to write. No doubt her opening sentence had caught his eye: "Recent developments in electronic media have rendered the concept of local film censorship redundant." The inspector seemed pleased as soon as he began reading; she could almost see his face grow heavier. "I should like to take a copy of this, Mrs. Travis."

"Go ahead, take that one. It's meant for dissemination."

He appeared to suspect that of being a dirty word too, and she didn't suppose that, or his feeling patronized by their vocabulary, was going to improve the situation. Her awareness of the film crew jabbed her, and she rounded on them. "Maybe I should read it to the camera."

The cameraman grimaced. She mustn't be reacting as he thought the subject of a police raid should react, or perhaps her movement had undermined the image he was filming. If she could do nothing else for the moment, she could do her best to ensure that he took away no more footage that the director would want to use. She was walking toward the lens, and saying, "Let's consider how an image is constructed" in a voice which she struggled to render conversational, when plump scrubbed Desmond said, "I think that's everything, Inspector."

Susanne stepped closer to the camera so as to block more of its view as she turned her back on it. Every single cassette was piled on the floor. "You aren't kidding," she said, higher and less controllably than ever.

"I'll bring up some boxes, shall I?" another of the mass of policemen said.

"If you're seriously proposing to take all those away," Susanne said, her tone sharper than she would ever have used to a student, "you'll need to store them horizontally. Stacking tapes vertically can ruin the soundtrack."

"Corrupts it, does it?" the inspector said with an air of having proved himself a master of wordplay. "Count them if you would, Desmond, and make out a receipt."

"You'll need to do more than count any you propose to remove," Don said at once. "We'll want them listed by title."

"Don . . ."

"That way there can't be any disagreement about which tapes are ours."

There shouldn't be in any case, since the Travises marked with a T the label of every cassette they bought, and she was about to try again to dissuade him from making unnecessary difficulties when she recalled that *I Spit on Your Grave* wouldn't be so marked. A dormant headache which had apparently been waiting for her to realize this darted twin spikes behind her eyes. She wheeled a chair to the doorway of the study and sat watching while policemen brought cartons which they filled with the cassettes Desmond, resembling a schoolboy kept in after class now, had to list on a sheaf of receipts he rested on Susanne's copy of *How to Read a Film*. She felt emotionless as a camera. The sun was crawling above the roofs by the time the last cassette was stuffed into a carton and the inspector laid the receipts on the study desk. "If you'll read through these and sign them."

The movies were only movies, Susanne told herself, and it was surely inconceivable that most of them wouldn't be returned. Her gaze tumbled down the protracted flights of steps that were the titles, until it snagged painfully on two listings of *Scarface*, both versions of which she'd been planning to run for her students that week. The question of what she could show them began to throb behind her eyes as she signed the receipts. The inspector examined her signature and then, as though some quality of her handwriting had prompted the query, said, "Are you British citizens?"

"That's one aspect of your hospitality we haven't enjoyed."

Several new lines sketched themselves on his forehead, and she wondered if he might seize her passport for the crime of sarcasm, or obstructing the police, or whatever he might call it. He only said, "You aren't planning to leave the country in the near future, are you, Mrs. Travis?"

"What reason could I have?"

He tore off copies of the receipts and spread them like an unbeatable hand of cards across the desk, and stooped so close to her that she could smell his mouthwash and see half an inch of a chest hair poking through the middle buttonhole of his shirt. "Please inform us if you intend to leave the area."

"Am I supposed to get dressed now?"

He looked almost amused, and she clenched her fists. "Am I supposed to accompany you?"

"You'll be hearing from us in due course."

His troops were bearing their cartons of booty downstairs, and he turned to follow them. The cameraman panned from them to the empty shelves and then switched off the camera, and Susanne's anger flew out of her mouth. "You've finished with us, have you? Got everything you wanted?"

"Susanne, I don't think it's their—"

"Their business, were you going to say, Don? Or their problem, how they're going to make us look?" She saw the cameraman's hand creep toward the switch, and lurched at him. "Go ahead, switch it on and I'll give you something real to film."

The inspector was lingering at the top of the stairs. Maybe he would arrest her for threatening behavior, for disturbing the peace in her own house. In that case she would give him a reason, and she opened her fists into claws and went for the cameraman faster than he was backing away. She heard Marshall suck in a breath, and was dismayed by the way her rage had blotted out her awareness of him. "All right," she said, her hands dropping. "That's all, folks. Please leave."

She grabbed a jar of aspirin from the bathroom cabinet and swallowed two with a handful of water as she followed the police and the film crew downstairs. She watched from the front door while the cartons were loaded into the police cars beneath streetlamps which stayed doggedly alight against the brightening sky. Were any of the neighbors observing her from their lit houses or from those which stayed suspiciously dark?

Though the notion made her stance in the doorway feel staged and self-conscious, she didn't move until the cars veered away around the corner of the street, reddening their brake lights. Unsure when he had come to stand beside her, she let go of Don's waist and blundered past him to sit on the stairs with her eyes shut. He closed the door so gently that it almost didn't hurt and said, "I'll make us some coffee, shall I, and then maybe I'll think I'm awake. How about you, Marshall?"

"Can I put on the radio?"

"Well, you see your mother's got a headache. Do you have to?"

"I want to hear if we're on the news."

Susanne pressed one hand against her eyes, adding meaningless light as fierce as a spotlight to the ache. "Can't you bear to miss our fifteen minutes of fame?"

"Mom, I just want to know if they're talking about us."

He wanted to be prepared in case his friends heard about the raid, she thought, and felt ashamed all the way down to the pit of her stomach for having assumed anything else. "I'm sorry, honey, I wasn't thinking. Go ahead, only try not to play it too loud, okay?"

She heard his and Don's footsteps pad in unison to the kitchen, and then a string quartet slashed the air, the volume lessening immediately as Marshall turned it down before racing through the channels, leaping from chunks of pop music to station identification jingles to early-morning voices bright as cartoons. He reached a local station just as the news began.

"—eadlines this morning. Customs officers say heroin discovered in a returning famine relief lorry is the biggest seizure ever. The driver of a vehicle intercepted at the scene dies in a high-speed car chase. Trading Standards officers and police say they have smashed a nationwide ring dealing in horror videos in a series of dawn raids code named Operation Nasty . . ."

Susanne pressed both hands against her eyes. Lights and pains seemed to be exploding throughout her skull. She smelled the sweat of her palms and felt its clamminess on her face. The onslaught of sensations overwhelmed her hearing, shutting out the meaning of the newsreader's unctuous voice. Then a name dug itself into her awareness, and Don shouted, "Susanne, are you hearing this?"

She was now. "Police report that the car overturned when it tried to leave the motorway at a speed in excess of one hundred miles per hour.

The driver James Fancy died before an ambulance could reach him. Police are waiting to question his brother Brad, who was thrown clear of the car and whose condition is described as stable . . ."

"It's them," Don said, "or rather, it's one less of them." He'd come along the hall to her, and she groped for his hand. "At least now they'll have something to take their minds off us," she said, and let the sight of him into her eyes, and glimpsed on his face an expression she wasn't at all sure of. Then it was gone, and she wondered what he'd thought in that instant, and found she didn't want to know.

9

FAMILY

The car with Darren in it was the first to arrive at the Dog & Gun. As soon as Barry had sprawled it across two marked spaces of the pub car park Darren got out, leaving behind the smells of Bernard's cigar and of the perfume his mother had spilled over herself each time she'd gone in the bathroom that morning. He swallowed a breath of air which tasted as stark as the stretch of concrete that surrounded the bungalow of the pub, and thought he mightn't throw up after all. Barry, who had the least hair of any of his relatives and the most spectacular scar on his face, gave Bernard a wink and a handful of notes and said "Buy Jim's bit a few drinks" before speeding off to something more important than the wake. Darren fumbled for his headphones, then remembered the family had ganged up on him to stop him bringing his Walkman to the funeral. He ground his knuckles into his ribs all the way down and glared around him.

The brown cardboardy bungalows, which couldn't be much older than he was, looked squashed by the sky, a blue lid patched with white like the wrong color of paint covering up rust on a car. Their windows poked sunlight in his eyes as he picked at the nails of his right hand with his left, trying to get rid of the sample of graveyard he'd brought away with him.

Two boys about his age were watching him over the sawtoothed fence of a bungalow opposite. They'd less right to be off school today than he had, he thought with a revival of the anger he'd experienced when the teachers had reacted as if Uncle Jim's funeral was just one more excuse he'd made up. He thought of the knife he'd used to scratch the paintwork of as many cars on the road outside the school as he'd suspected might belong to teachers, but he'd dropped it down a grid. He was searching around him for a weapon as he stalked to the wall of the car park. "What's your fucking problem?" he shouted across the road.

Another head appeared next to the boys at once, and started barking and slavering. He'd take the dog out first, he told himself, bare-handed if he had to, and vaulted over the low wall. Then the doors of the rest of the cars began slamming behind him, and his mother cried, "Not now, Darren. Not today. Look what he's doing. Someone stop him."

He heard feet pounding toward him, and turned to see uncles in black swarming like beetles across the concrete. If any of them hit him while the boys were watching, he'd—He climbed back over the wall, carrying more rage with him. "That's right, son," his mother said, and yelled past him "You little sods show some respect. Someone's dead. Shut up that dog."

The door left a hole in the front of the bungalow, and a woman wearing some kind of uniform marched out onto the concrete stub of path. Darren saw his mother getting ready for a fight, and his head, which felt full of one of the cobwebs loaded with rubbish that were appearing in corners all over his house, seemed about to grow clear. Then the woman saw how many people were ready to take her on, and muttered at her children and the dog until they retreated with her into the house.

At least the family had seen her off despite her army uniform, but then Darren realized it had only been Salvation Army, and the weight of his disappointment dragged at the inside of his head. He'd wanted a scene that would remind all the people living around here that this had been his Uncle Jim's favorite pub. He trudged after his mother and the rest of them, feeling sunlight snatch at his ankles as each of his steps pulled up the too-short legs of his only black trousers, under the suddenly shaky sky into the Dog & Gun.

Maybe the previous building had had some reason to be called that, but the brewery had chased the dogs. The interior was someone's idea of a saloon in a Western, with walls and chairs bulging with mauve plush, bare floorboards, a bar and a mirror which both stretched the length of the single room. Rifles were attached to the low beams, and in case anyone still missed the point, the walls were crowded with framed posters of John Wayne and a lot of other old men who Darren supposed must have been in Westerns, not that they meant any more to him than a crumb of a turd stuck on a pimple up his arse. The broad-shouldered box-headed barman in his loud checked shirt and Levi's looked as though he was trying to be in a Western too as he swaggered slowly along the bar, from the glassed-in food counter called The Trough to The Hitching Rail, but his Lancashire accent let him down. "How old's the kid?"

"The Headphone Kid, is that?" said Bill, who never kept a joke to himself.

"The Wanking Kid, I wouldn't be surprised," said his wife, Clara, and made a gesture like shoving a handful of peanuts into her wide sloppy mouth.

"Eh," the barman warned her, and turned his head to survey the party, so slowly that the head reminded Darren of some kind of security device, its large translucent ears sprouting hairs for extra sensitivity. "Who brought him in? Who's he with?"

"Us," Bernard said, showing his teeth behind the reddening remains of his cigar. "Your other feller said he'd be let, seeing as this do's for his uncle."

"The other feller said a lot of things till they found him with his hand in the takings."

"He was a friend to Sharon after she lost Jim," Bernard said, stubbing out his cigar just inside an ashtray a few inches from the barman's fingers.

The two men stared, their heads close enough to crack each other if either moved, while a spark on the back of the barman's hand turned to ash, and then Darren's mother said, "The law says he can come in anyway. He's fourteen."

Darren saw himself in the mirror. He looked older than twelve, at least five years older, maybe ten. He'd never been so proud of the dark under his eyes, dark that resembled bruises on his thin pale face except that they were still there even though his father wasn't around to batter him. His reflection started to twitch and shift, and he pulled his attention away before his face could turn into something else. "I'm nearly fifteen," he said, resenting his mother for not claiming he was older.

Abruptly the barman seemed to lose interest in him, and stepped back to glance under the bar. "What can I get anyone?"

The men set about buying drinks for themselves and their partners. Who was going to buy for Sharon was the subject of an argument. "Don't upset Shar, don't fight on a day like this," the women protested, and Ken took advantage of the lull to declare, "I said I'm buying." Bernard bit the foreskin off another cigar and spat it almost in an ashtray while he waited to buy Darren's mother a large gin, and presented Darren with a faceful of smoke as he turned to him. "What do you want that's soft, lad?"

Darren was speculating what weapon the barman had been checking was under the bar, and heard himself being called a soft lad. Even when the question caught up with him he felt no better. If he'd known he wasn't going to get a proper drink he wouldn't have come to the pub, he'd have stayed home and remembered how Uncle Jim used to take him fishing in the canal, though all they ever caught were condoms and tampons and syringes, and to the arcades where they had lost money until they got thrown out for battering the fruit machines, and to the races where nobody objected twice to anything Jim screamed at his horse or his dog. His eyes felt prickly from remembering Jim or because he was being treated like some wimp who never smoked or drank or took drugs. "Don't give a shit," he mumbled.

The barman swung a finger at him. "If there's any more of that, lad—"

"Just give him whatever kids drink and mind your business," Bernard interrupted. "There's no bugger but us in here."

The barman filled a glass with a drink which the sign on the pump alleged was lemonade but which tasted like water full of gas and sugar to Darren, who felt he was being used by the barman to demonstrate he wasn't scared of any threat Bernard had meant him to hear. He considered spitting the mouthful on the floor, except that some of the women and even some of the men might yell at him. He carried the glass to a table at the edge of the party farthest from Bernard's cigar and scraped his chair closer to the table when his mother gestured angrily toward the empty place next to her and Bernard. Misunderstanding the gesture, Clara brandished her tankard. "Here's to those who aren't with us."

"To Jim," Darren's mother said as if someone had accused her of forgetting him.

"Jim," everyone agreed, and kept agreeing while they clashed glasses with everyone else within reach. When that was completed there was a silence in which Darren sensed the barman watching them. "Phil too," Bernard supplied, "seeing as he can't be with us."

"Phil," everyone repeated, and performed a somewhat less energetic clash of glasses. Darren might have thought the party shared his lack of enthusiasm until Dave said fiercely, "Wouldn't even let him out for his own brother's funeral."

"Must've known we'd have hid him," Bill said.

Ken slammed his tankard down like a hammer. "It was Jim stopped me and Dave doing them Yanks that got Phil put inside."

"We should've fixed them when we found them in the pisser," Dave said.

Ken made an idiot's mouth at him. "That'd've made real fucking sense, that, giving them a kicking in front of the filth."

"We could've waited till the filth went. Or we could've told him we seen the Yank playing with his kid's dick. Six months it took to find a lorry coming back right way with a driver we could trust, and then Jim has to help pick up the stuff 'cos Phil's inside."

His mind must have caught up at last with the possibility that some of this sounded as though he was blaming Ken, whose grip on the handle of his tankard was close to showing its bones. "Don't care," Dave said, never able to stop until all his slow thoughts were out of him. "I still say Brad should have been driving the van even if he was banned for three years. They'd never have found out he was, they'd never have been fast enough to catch him."

"Here's what you do then, Dave. You go and visit fucking Brad in hospital and break the rest of his bones for him for letting Jim drive, that's when you've got past the police."

"I've got nothing against fucking Brad. I reckon it was Jim who wouldn't let him drive."

"Boys," Bernard said, holding up his hands between them and jerking his head to indicate the barman. "Let's have some music."

"*Wet Side Story,*" Dave said. "He were always singing bits of that, Jim."

"And some more drinks," said Ken, swinging himself around his chair toward the bar.

"*Wet Side Story*. Let's have that. It was his favorite."

"It's West Side, Dave," Clara said as Bernard dumped coins for the jukebox in her hand. "It's some place in New York."

"It can rain in New York, can't it? It's a real fucking place, in case you didn't know," Dave said, and even more slowly, "It was his fucking favorite."

Clara headed for the jukebox without speaking as the men swarmed to the bar, leaving Darren with most of the women, their perfume massing beneath their clouds of smoke, the clatter of their bracelets shunting up and down their arms, their browned flesh which bulged out of their black dresses whenever they moved. Sharon was being comforted by the others, who kept patting her or taking her hand and saying "Ah, never mind" or "He was the best" or "Ah, you'll get over it, love" or "There'll never be another like him" or "God love her" or "Aaah, never mind" as she tried to hitch up a smile and dabbed her eyes with an increasingly blackened handkerchief. Darren's embarrassment at all this felt like a new kind of sweat covering the whole of him. Ken brought Sharon another rum and peppermint, and returned with a pint of beer and a large Scotch as a chaser, then shoved the Scotch at Darren. "Here, lad, get that down you before any sod can tell you different."

Darren saw his mother drag a worried look onto her face, but it was turned to Bernard at the bar. Darren gulped half the glassful and clenched his throat to hold down the burning as Dave shouted at the reflection of Clara and the jukebox, "I call it *Wet Side Story*. Put it on."

"It isn't here, Dave. I didn't think it would be."

"Give us a pint and a double vodka and no ice and no lemon," Dave said louder than Bernard, who was ordering, and slapped a note on the bar. "I'll have a look. Tarts can't be trusted to find their own arse half the time. No offense, Bill."

"None taken, lad," Bill said, and dealt Dave's upper arm a punch that could be heard throughout the room.

As Dave showed his teeth Brenda, who was living with him, sprang up and shoved between the two men. "Don't you be upsetting Shar," she muttered, and stared at Dave until he swerved at the jukebox and wrapped his arm around it as if he didn't mean to let go before it gave him what he wanted. By the time he'd finished mouthing the titles of the discs everyone was back at the tables and not looking at him. "It isn't here," he said after a final prolonged glare at the list, "but Shar's kept Jim's record, haven't you? You'd never get rid of your man's favorite."

Sharon lowered her gin and then her face, dabbing her eyes all the time. "It's at home."

"You can get it, can't you? He'd like it. It was his favorite. Or here you are, give us the keys and I will."

"You won't be changing any discs in there," the barman informed him. "It's locked."

"Aye, and which cunt who thinks he's hard has got the key?"

"Don't look at me, pal. The company we rent from has."

The barman's hands were resting above the concealed weapon, and Dave's were groping about the beam above his head. He found the rifle and poked it off some of its hooks as Sharon cried, "Jim used to like the songs on there, the cowboy songs."

Dave closed a fist around the barrel of the rifle. "Weren't his favorite though, were they?"

"He used to listen to them all the time we were in here. He always put them on."

Dave shoved a hand in his pocket, and excitement flared in Darren as though the whiskey in his stomach had caught fire. But the weapon he produced was only a handful of coins which he sent rattling into the jukebox. Darren sagged with disappointment, some of it on Uncle Jim's behalf. The jukebox fed itself a disc, and some woman started singing words that meant nothing to Darren until she told someone to stand by their man, which sounded like a message for him about his dead uncle.

"That was Jim right enough, always stood by you," Bill said.

"Found summat good in everyone," said Clara.

"Always lent you a few bob if you needed it," Darren's mother said, "and never asked for it back."

"Must've known he wouldn't get it."

"Always do anyone a favor," Bernard quickly intervened, "would Jim."

"Couldn't stand anyone being unhappy around him," said a temporary aunt whose name Darren was no longer able to remember.

Perhaps Sharon took that as a criticism, because she forced more of a smile. "You liked going out with him, didn't you, Darren?"

He felt as though a teacher had flung a question at him. "Right," he said, which he could see Sharon and his mother and quite a few others thought wasn't nearly enough. He tried to search his brain, but the unlit empty space of it only grew larger. "He used to tell jokes while he was driving," he remembered suddenly out loud.

Dave shouted a laugh that suggested he'd thought of a prize joke, but he was anticipating. "Tell us one."

The song about standing faded into silence, taking all the conversations with it, and everyone's attention fastened on Darren. "That's right, go on," his mother said as if she thought he hadn't contributed enough to the occasion or was using him to contribute on her behalf. "Remind us."

The hole inside Darren's head was growing darker and deeper—it felt like the earth he hadn't been able to bite out from under his nails. He stared at the jukebox as it retrieved the disc to clear the way for another, but it was taking too long for him to keep quiet until it did. Unless he told one of Jim's jokes he would feel that his uncle had become the empty blackness in his head, and he couldn't think of a single one—and then he remembered a joke he'd heard at school. "This man goes in a chemist and he says have you got some extra large condoms—"

Dave spluttered and wiped his mouth. "I've heard it. It's dead mucky, that."

Sharon had picked up her glass in case she was overcome by memory, but now she put it down, missing the beer mat on which it had been standing. "That was never my Jim."

The weight of attention swung away from Darren to her as the jukebox began to sing about a four-legged friend. Was it telling Darren that unlike the animal, he'd let his uncle down? Sharon seemed to think so, and was leaning hard toward his mother. "He'd never have a paper in the house with tits in it, Jim. What's he trying to do, the little snot? Making out Jim told him some mucky joke."

Darren's mother planted her fists on the table and heaved herself forward with them. "You calling Dar a liar?"

"You saying I am or Jim was?"

One of Jim's jokes sidled into Darren's head, but he thought it was too late to tell it and besides, he didn't want to stop Sharon and his mother from coming to blows—he wanted to see who would win. The song on the jukebox counted four like a referee, and then, to Darren's blazing frustration, Bernard showed his palms to the two women. "Not today, lasses, please. Think of Jim," he said, adding hastily and in a lower voice, "I reckon it's a bad time for both of you, but the family will see you right. We've a few things on the go."

The women subsided against their chairs, looking as though they might otherwise have sprawled across the table, and Dave had to be persuaded not to discuss any of the plans Bernard had hinted at until the jukebox found itself another song. It was about some twat from Laramie who was friendly to everyone he met, which Sharon said was Jim as she blackened her handkerchief further. This was the signal for most of the men to plod at the pace of the music to the bar, where more than one of them ordered drinks in a cowboyish drawl which earned a withering stare from the barman. Darren gulped his latest Scotch in anticipation of one of the family's landing a fist in the middle of the stare, but nobody did. The jukebox raised the disc and lowered another, but had sung only a few lines when Dave lurched at it and began to jab the buttons. "How do you get this off? Shar doesn't want to hear about some cunt being forsaken on his wedding day."

"You let Shar have a good cry if she wants," Brenda shouted.

As Dave stooped to pull the plug he fell against the jukebox, causing the disc to jump. "A cow, a lying coward," it sang as the barman reached down behind the bar. Then Sharon cried, "Leave it, Dave. It was Jim's favorite."

He used the jukebox to haul himself upright before twisting to face her. "Never. *Wet Side Story* was."

"His favorite of these, Dave. He always sang along with it. I can hear him now." Sharon blew her nose, blackening the end of it, as several of the party raised their voices, straggling in pursuit of the lyrics. Dave glared effortfully about as if he suspected he was being made a fool of, then steered his resentment in the general direction of the bar. "I'm fucking famished, me. Where's the grub?"

The barman raised one hand above the bar to point at the sign above The Trough. "Shuts at two, reopens at six."

"Yeah, well, I'm hungry at—" Dave glowered at the clock near the door, apparently suspecting it of trying to confuse him. "Whatever it is past five, past four," he eventually said.

"Can't help you, pal. The girl doesn't come on until six."

The voices floundering after the song fell away one by one, and Ken wrenched his chair and himself around with a screech of wood to confront the barman. "Don't be asking us to wait that long. Why don't you be the girl and thank fuck we're only after grub."

The song dwindled into silence, and the inside of Darren's head began to tingle. He might have been watching one of those films where everything went quiet to make the violence more exciting, only this was better than a film. He drained his glass as the barman reached slowly under the bar and said, "Why don't you all—"

"Have a heart," Bernard interrupted. "The other feller said we'd be able to eat. It isn't a wake without nosh."

Darren was growing hot with the promise of violence. He heard a heavy object rumble against the wood of the bar, and the muscles of the barman's upper arms swelled his checked sleeves as he brought his hands into view. They were empty. "You can have anything you see that's cold, but I'm not cooking," he said. "And while we're on about what you're having, let's have less of the language in front of the lad."

Darren's hands and feet were gathering the suddenly unpleasant warmth of the room. Without warning it rushed up through him. All the talk of food had reminded him he'd eaten nothing since his egg and the last of last night's chips for breakfast, and it seemed that only his lack of awareness of his state had been keeping the Scotch down. The smell of Bernard's cigar turned stale in his nostrils, and he saw the yolk of his breakfast egg surrounded by uncooked white like his grandfather's eyes. He saw his grandfather lying in his unwashed bed that resembled one of the sacks the homeless slept in, the old man's eyes two raw eggs drooling down his cheeks, and then nausea jerked him to his feet and sent him staggering past The Trough to the corridor which led to the toilets and the car park.

A mingled smell of urine and disinfectant jabbed his nostrils as he blundered into the Gents, where he had to hang onto an askew condom dispenser before launching himself at the nearest cubicle. By the time the door rebounded from the tiled wall his head was almost in the stained ceramic pan, and his innards felt as if they were. Words were chanting in his head: "a coward, a lying coward in the grave." That was him, and the grave was his uncle's, and Darren felt as if he'd killed him by being a coward, by not . . . He couldn't think what he'd failed to do, but as soon as he was capable of falling against the cubicle door he bolted it so that nobody would see him. He was holding onto the low cracked cistern and hanging his head over the thoroughly spattered bowl when someone kicked open the door to the Gents. "Darren? You in here, lad?"

It was Ken, by comparison with whom Darren felt more of a coward than ever. He climbed on the bowl to make himself invisible, one foot slipping on the ceramic edge and almost plunging ankle-deep before he leaned on the cistern. He crouched over his mess, feeling like a dog as the jukebox began to croon about Old Shep, and heard Dave say "Must've gone to chuck up in the car park."

"His mam should have said if he can't hold his liquor. Wouldn't like to be her, stuck with Phil's da and a kid and Phil inside."

"Reckon she'll be all right while she can open her legs."

Darren heard two zippers being pulled down and his uncles sighing as their urine struck the porcelain. They thought he was as useless as his grandfather. "Most miserable funeral I've ever been to," Ken eventually said.

"Maybe he's gone to a better place."

"Couldn't be any fucking worse than this." Ken's anger was reviving. "You know, I'll bet Jim swerved so he wouldn't hit someone. I've seen him do it. Soft cunt," he said, his voice veering away as he zipped himself up. "Tell you what, though . . ."

Darren heard his uncles tramp away, and the outer door begin to close with a sound like an animal expiring in a trap, and then "Put your dick away, Dave. Christ, you're like a big kid."

Dave hooted with delighted laughter at himself and did as he was told, blocking the door meanwhile. "What I'm saying, though," Ken said, and the closing door seemed to squeeze his retreating voice smaller. "That Yank's the fucking cause of all this. We haven't finished with him."

Darren felt as if his entire body had stretched into the corridor to catch hold of the words. He rested his hands on the shifting cistern and lowered his feet to the floor as though he was doing gymnastics. He closed his eyes and pressed his forehead against the tiles and leaned on the handle of the cistern. Ken's words had told him what to do so that nobody would call him a lying coward ever again. The rush of water into the toilet reminded him of being sick, but he wasn't going to be again, because he felt too strong, maybe even ready for another drink. Next time he wouldn't just scream down the phone, the way he had when a man had answered. When Darren got him on his own he'd do more than scare the kid who'd sent his father to prison and killed his Uncle Jim.

10

CHARACTERS

It didn't have to be this way."

"You still don't get it, do you? Nobody killed your kid—not yet, anyway. I'd say he still had about half an hour."

"You bastard, tell me where he is or I'll—"

"Go ahead. You can't do anything to me the world hasn't already done."

"Don't harm him. I'm begging you. I'm on my knees. Whatever you think you have to pay back, take it out on me."

"Say, don't you remember? I guess ten years ain't so very much if you're not in jail. The kid won't be inside that long. Half an hour max."

"You want to kill me, kill me. Just let me see him first so I know he's all right."

"Sure you can see him if you get to him. I'm giving you more of a chance than you gave me. Still haven't figured out where he is? Check out the safe."

"I don't believe you. You're trying to make me waste time. Even you wouldn't—Oh Christ, you did it, didn't you? He's dead, you murdering swine. I can't hear him."

"Can't hear much through three inches of steel. He was alive when I put him in, and there was plenty of air. If I were you I wouldn't still be talking, I'd be trying to find the combination. You can make a lot of numbers out of five digits. Don't come any closer or this gun might just go off."

By now Don had grasped all this was intended as some kind of parody—surely no Mancunian would utter such dialogue unless they'd seen far too many movies—but there were reasons why he didn't laugh, one of which was that he was beginning to suspect that any joke might be on him. Teresa Handley had told him to take a book as identification, but he needn't have brought the book she'd signed to Susanne and himself. Indeed, he had barely stepped into the Hangman when he'd begun wishing he had carried anything except a book.

Deciding to call the writer's number had been difficult enough, and she'd proved blunter and less forthcoming now that she was sober. "Don which again?"

"Travis. You came to our party and later we, you and I, spoke on the phone."

"I've got you now. That kind of Don. Sorry, you sounded just like a character I'm writing."

"Thanks very much for the book. Marshall's, you met our son, he's reading it right now."

"Probably more his level than yours. I only sent it because you did ask."

"No, it looks very, it looks great. I saw the reviews of your earlier books on the back."

"Best place to stop."

"We were all delighted, really. We wouldn't have expected it." The prospect of needing to contradict yet more auctorial self-deprecation had made him blurt, "I've been thinking about, I expect you know. What else you said when you called."

"When I'd been making up for having to celebrate alone."

"Sure. I hope you had reason. I mean, I hope the book is doing well."

"Better than some I wish I'd written."

"I guess a lot of writers feel that way. I don't know if you heard how the case came out."

"What case was that? I'm with you, your intruder. I believe he's been treated to a holiday in concrete."

"Eighteen months, he's meant to have gone in for."

"Have to hope he doesn't know the meaning of good behavior. Sighs of relief all round, I bet."

"Yes, except one of his family was killed in a police chase, and I wouldn't like to think it's left them in a mood for more violence."

"So don't."

"Suppose I'm right? I'm beginning to think I might feel happier, well, I won't say happier, safer if I took you up on your suggestion."

"Which was that?"

"Isn't this a good time? Can't you talk?"

"I'm not slurring, am I?"

"No, I mean is there anyone . . ."

"Who?"

"Mr. Handley?"

"Oh, *him*. How's he going to stop me?"

"I only meant in case you'd rather—in case you didn't want—"

"He wouldn't be that kind of problem if he was here, which he's not. He's off spending some of my money on not spending so much of my money. So what were you thinking I could do for you?"

"The suggestion you made, I was wondering if it was still, still extant."

"There's a bookseller. I take it we're talking about what I think we are."

"Arms availability."

He'd heard her shift her grip on the plastic, and had been about to add "Only for defense" or something equally redundant when she'd said, "I don't know if the offer stands. I'll see what I can find out and call you back."

He should have asked her to call him only at the shop, except that the answering machine was awaiting repair. For most of a week he'd pounced on calls before anyone else could reach them, hence had spoken to four of Marshall's friends, and three women who'd called him by name in order to pitch sales to him, and two of Susanne's colleagues offering advice on how to respond to any prosecution after the police raid. Then last night Teresa Handley had found him almost inarticulate with a mouthful of dinner. "Be in the Hangman between noon and one tomorrow and take a book with you and, don't blame me, best I could find, a few hundred," she'd said, and the address.

He'd told Susanne he was going to price a collection of books. Deluding her made him feel untrustworthy, almost unworthy of her, more intensely when he recalled how little he'd done during the raid. He might as well not have been there, any more than he had been when Marshall had been bullied into the house. Maybe it was himself rather than the Fancy threat he'd had enough of, and maybe there'd be more to him once he had a gun.

He hadn't felt like much once he'd entered the bar. The bumbling of conversations had faded, hushed perhaps by the sight of a book, and several men whom he'd found himself unwilling to face had burst out laughing. He'd shoved the novel under his arm and smoothed the hair on top of his head while he bought a bottle of Grolsch, only to notice belatedly that everyone else was drinking draft beer. He didn't give a vermiform appendix what they did, he'd told himself, carrying the lager to an empty table past some snooker players who had seemed ready to trap him with their cues and earning himself a chorus of sniggers by drinking from the bottle and opening the book. He might have sat outside except for the rain pummeling the windows. He'd lowered book and bottle so as to stare at everybody who was watching him. He'd prayed that nobody would approach him unless they were here for him, because otherwise he had only the bottle with which to defend himself. No, he had language, but against how many? Nobody had made for him, however—one by one they'd lost interest in him—and so he'd tried to immerse himself in the book until he was approached, rather than speculate how much of the loud blur of talk around him was about him.

He had to look up whenever anyone entered the bar. Here came a small man dressed in leather trousers and peaked leather cap and jacket zipped up to his dripping chin, who had a word with various people as he strolled about the long low room, the walls and ceiling of which appeared to have absorbed much of the smoke from the cigarettes that smoldered in just about every fist, not to mention the butts which had been trodden out on the torn ashen carpet. Next in was a man as broad as the doorway, his muscles threatening to tear the short sleeves of the wool shirt which was decidedly the fashion in the pub and which made Don in his denim feel even more conspicuous. The man stared at him, aggravating Don's awareness of the three hundred pounds he'd distributed among his pockets, and Don caught himself hoping that if the newcomer was the professional wrestler his build suggested he was, he refrained from setting about people while he was away from the ring. A vicious tickle had lodged in Don's throat from all the smoke, and he sucked on the Grolsch to douse a cough. The bulging man turned and dumped his elbows on the bar, and Don was holding another mouthful of lager in his throat to drown even the possibility of a cough when a man with his head done up in yellow plastic backed into the pub.

He undid the hood, baring his cropped skull, and doffed the yellow cape like a superhero to reveal a scrawny torso bagged in yet another short-sleeved wool shirt, and Don was sure this man was his contact as soon as he hung the cape on a drooping rack beside the door and began to glance around the bar. His attention lingered on the book and Don before drifting onward, and Don felt as though the man was continuing to stare at him as he sidled toward him. Don's hand put the bottle down next to a circular pattern of cigarette burns on the small round table, whose surface had at some stage been repeatedly gouged with a knife, and crept from his left-hand hip pocket to his right and up to his breast pocket to reassure him that the wads of notes were there, describing a pattern which felt like an uncompleted religious symbol. He wondered suddenly if the police were aware of the kind of transaction the pub was used for, and at once was sure they must know—must keep watch on the place. Suppose the scrawny man was a plainclothes detective or an informer? What could Don be arrested for? Conspiracy to commit a crime, intent to buy an illegal weapon . . . Don felt his legs starting to cramp with his struggle not to dodge before the other reached him. Then the man halted between two snooker players and commenced muttering at them, and there came a smell of leather and almost a concert of creaking at Don's back, and a voice in his ear. "Enjoying that, are you?"

The small man had made his way unnoticed to the table behind Don and placed his cap upside down on it as though awaiting a donation. He must be referring to the Grolsch, Don thought, then decided he meant the book, and changed his mind again too late to hold onto his syntax. "What, the this?"

The man's protuberant glossy eyes didn't deign to glance at the bottle Don had hoisted, and Don had had enough of the self he was displaying. "The book," he said shortly. "Yes."

"Enjoying it."

Don had thought he'd answered that question, but the flatness of the man's tone seemed simply to absorb what he'd said. "Sure, in its own terms," he felt compelled to say in Teresa Handley's defense. "It isn't realistic, to put it mildly, but then there's no law that says novels have to be."

"You don't reckon."

"Maybe I don't know all your laws yet, but I'd lay money that isn't one."

The man's expression grew fixed and distant, which Don gathered was meant to indicate he'd given the wrong answer. "Realistic," he said with a laugh at himself. "You mean you think it is."

The man's eyes appeared to be in danger of glazing over. Did he think the laugh had been directed at him? "If you're saying it isn't, I'm agreeing with you," Don said desperately, reflecting that he'd braved the pub only to become involved in an argument—more a forced monologue—about conventions of storytelling. "My point is that it doesn't, well, it matters in some ways, I suppose more to people who feel they're being portrayed or rather not portrayed, but not in purely literary, if that's not stretching it, literary terms."

"Friend of yours, is she."

"Yes, up to a point, yes. More to the, more relevantly, she's a local celebrity just as much as, I don't know, your football team. Support your local writers, that's always my refrain."

"Sent you here."

Don had interposed so much between that and the man's previous comment that it took him some seconds to put them together. "Ah. Yes, she is. Did."

"Told you to bring something."

"Here it is," Don said, and slapped the face of the book. He'd decided at last that there could be no doubt why the man had approached him. "She didn't say hers, you understand, but it seemed like a good sign."

As he lowered his voice the players and the scrawny man moved away along the snooker table, and Don wondered whether everyone in the bar knew why he was there. "Good in the sense of, well, anyway," he said, progressively lower. "And you. I was told you would. Have something. For me."

Each of his pauses was meant to coax out an answer, and each of them emphasized even more of the absence of one as the man's dispirited gaze continued to rest on the book. At last he said, "Hollow, is it?"

"Hollow in the sense of . . ." For a moment Don thought they'd returned to literary analysis. "Oh, you mean as an object. You mean have I brought, yes, of course," he said, patting his three moneyed pockets to demonstrate.

"How much?"

"How much are we discussing?"

"Three hundred. Pounds, in case you're wondering. Take it or leave it. Just be quick."

"I haven't seen it yet."

"You don't expect me to start waving it around in here, do you, you silly bugger? Pay us under the table and it's yours."

Having provoked such a lengthy and expressive speech made Don feel as though he had gained an advantage. "What exactly am I paying for?"

"Automatic with a spare clip. Real little beauty. It'll fit in your fist like your dick."

"If it's that small," Don heard himself saying, and made himself go on, "surely you can give me a glimpse without anyone seeing."

"They see everything, chum, including some I don't want seeing. Give us the price and it's yours."

"Then what? You fetch it?"

"No need. I'll tell you where to go."

"In that case why don't we both go there and then I'll pay you."

Rain slashed at the windows, which were even grayer than the room, and he thought he heard the glass tremble in the frames. The man stared unblinkingly at him as though the protrusion of his eyes was making it impossible to close the lids. "Cough up and I'll show you where to go, or piss off out of it."

All at once Don felt that far more people, perhaps everyone in the bar, were watching him, but when he glanced away from the leathery man nobody appeared to be looking at him. He dug both hands into his hip pockets and brought the notes together, and passed the doubled wad under the table until it met a bunch of clammy fingers which closed on it like an octopus seizing its prey. "That's more than half," he murmured. "I'll give you the rest when we've gone an appreciable way farther."

The man stared as though he was inserting his gaze into Don's eyes so that they couldn't blink. They were beginning to smart by the time he flipped his cap up from the table and caught his head in it as he rose abruptly to his feet. Don followed, feeling as if everyone's awareness of him was a medium thick as deep water through which he was struggling to walk.

The man pulled the door open and dodged into the only corner of the sodden porch which the downpour was leaving untouched. Rain was pounding the parking lot; wherever it struck, a shard flew up like a fragment of the concrete. All the high-rise blocks which loured over the pub had been turned the color of the clogged sky. The man retreated into the shelter, though not far enough to make room for Don. "This is as far as I go, chum. I can see it from here."

Don's glasses were already growing blurred with rain. He unbuttoned his breast pocket and dug the notes out with his streaming fingers and squeezed the wad in his fist. "Where?"

"I won't take them off you if they're stuck together. You won't even be crossing the road, and I'm saying nowt else."

As Don reached out his fist with rain bouncing off the back, the man's fingers dug under it like some kind of secret handshake. They snatched the wad, and Don immediately felt tricked. He didn't quite believe he'd grabbed the man's wrist, but his fingers immediately began to ache with holding on, and he heard himself saying, "Where?"

"Coming the hard feller, are we?" The man's voice rose to a shout Don could feel on his face. Maybe the rain drowned the shout as it doused Don's scalp and his back, because nobody emerged from the pub to outnumber him. The man wrenched himself out of his grasp and said with what sounded like grudging respect, "Look under your car."

"Which one is that?"

"Don't you know, chum?"

Don was questioning how the man had been able to identify it, but his waterlogged lenses were indeed hampering his own efforts to do so. "The same one you got out of," the man said, and before Don could interrogate him further, shouldered him aside and took refuge in the Hangman.

Don was tempted to follow, if only for shelter, except that the rain was dashing the reality of the situation in his face. The mumble of the pub had acquired a mocking quality, but how could he charge in there unarmed to face however many would be ready for him? He ran almost blindly to the spreading red stain that was his car, the downpour drumming on his back. When he fell to his knees, or at least crouched as low as he could without actually kneeling on the swamped concrete, he felt as though the weight of rain was forcing him to abase himself and admit he'd been conned. The dry pale patch of concrete beneath the Volvo was emitting a reflected glow so faint he wasn't convinced he was seeing it until it showed him a package wrapped in black plastic and taped against the rear axle.

It looked like a bomb. Suppose the Fancy family had planted it? Before this irrationality could prevent him he took three squelching paces to the rear of the vehicle and leaning down as if to examine the tires, grasped the far end of the insulating tape and tore it away from the chassis. A heavier package than he was expecting dropped into his free hand, and he felt metal objects knocking together. Then he had both hands around them, and shoved the package down the front of his drenched jacket, and straightened up as if he had been performing a routine check, and fumbled out his keys with his slippery fingers, and made to let himself into the wrong side of the car. He splashed round to the driver's side and twisted the key in the lock and dumped himself on the seat, the crooks of his elbows and knees growing soaked at once, and slammed the door.

The windows had clouded over the moment he'd climbed in. He switched on the heater and the demister, then he picked the buttons of his jacket out of their saturated holes and gazed at the black package resting in his lap. He lifted it gingerly onto the passenger seat and peeled the tape away from the plastic, which tore as he unfolded it, turning it over and over like a spider with a fly. The wrapping revealed itself as a bin bag almost large enough to contain him. He opened its mouth wide to peer into the shiny blackness, and saw a gray angular handgun resting against a clip of bullets. The next moment lights blazed at him through the windshield.

He saw his hand reach for the gun, and felt as though a part of his mind he hadn't known existed was reacting. The lights went out as the car which had swerved into the parking lot drew up facing him, and each front door released a large blurred man, their broad flat heads butting the rain as they advanced toward both sides of Don's car. They cursed at the tops of their voices as they ran into the pub.

Don took hold of the weapon and the clip through the plastic, which he wrapped around and around them before shoving the package under the passenger seat, where it crackled to itself. As soon as a patch of windshield large enough for him to see through had been cleared of condensation he set the wipers to scything the rain off the glass and drove away from the Hangman.

11

VOICES

Mrs. Travis . . ."

"Something else I can help you with, Liu?"

"We just wanted to say . . ."

"Come back in and close the door, Rachel, if it's personal."

"We're speaking for everyone," the student said, but nevertheless closed the door of Susanne's office. "We just wanted to tell you we're sorry, and if we can help . . ."

"Do you two know something I don't? Sorry for . . . ?"

"About what happened."

"The machine breaking down this afternoon, you mean?" A moment after Susanne mistook that for the issue, she knew. "This is about my visit from the police."

Both students nodded, looking so uncomfortable that Susanne said, "It was nothing to do with you, though, was it, surely? You're not telling me it was."

Rachel cleared her throat, then Liu did. "We did know Elaine was selling pirate videos," the Chinese girl said.

"But we never thought anyone could connect them with you."

"We saw some of them, and they weren't like yours. Most of them had Dutch subtitles. Some had Greek."

"So the police ought to be able to see they couldn't have been copied from yours. We were saying, not just us, we'd say so in court if you like."

"That's kind, Rachel, kind of all of you. Maybe they'll have the sense not to push it that far, not with some of the movies they took. Just now I don't know what's in store for us, but thanks."

The two students clearly felt they hadn't said enough. "Was your son upset?" Liu asked.

"He's no fonder of intruders than the rest of us, but he's stopped lying awake waiting for another invasion."

The girls made sympathetic noises, and Rachel said, "How about your husband?"

"He's pretty good at getting a night's sleep."

Rachel seemed to take this answer as a mild rebuff, though Susanne had meant it to lighten the mood. Liu coughed again and said, "We think Elaine went into selling those videos to get back at her mother."

"Her mother's worse at home than she was with you on television, Elaine says."

"I rather gathered as much."

"And Elaine was selling them to make up her grant," said Rachel.

"Only she didn't get the idea from your course, Mrs. Travis."

"So you shouldn't feel responsible because her mother's taken her away."

"I'll try not to," Susanne said. "Was that all? The player should be fixed tomorrow, or I can borrow one from Politics until it is, so let's make the most of our early finish and be ready to startle one another in the morning.

"Thanks for your support," she felt bound to call after them. They seemed to feel they hadn't helped, or not enough. She squared a pile of essays on her desk and transferred them to her briefcase. A police siren went off like a distant alarm as she let herself out of her office and locked the door.

Students were chasing their echoes along the stony corridors. Somewhere outside was a muffled thudding which felt as though it had lodged in the unreachable depths of her ears. She was rubbing the corners of her jaws beneath them, switching her briefcase from hand to hand, when she encountered Clement Daily on the wide stairs near his office. He tilted his head to peer over his cheekbones at her briefcase. "Ah, Susanne. Leaving us?"

"Just for the rest of the day. Technical problems with a player."

"Player of, ah."

"Video recorder."

"Of course, that kind of, obviously. And please don't think for an instant that I was, it goes without saying we'll be seeing you tomorrow. Let me reiterate the department is behind you, and if there's anything we can, within reason, you understand."

"I do," Susanne said, which might sound like a sly joke at the expense of his fractured syntax. "I appreciate it."

"Give my regards to the bibliopole, and your young also."

"I certainly will."

"I hope you'll excuse me if I, a meeting in, dear me, I should be there now."

Susanne couldn't think of a verbal response to that. She gave him a smile with her lips shut and went down to the courtyard where students leaned against trees or cycled across the stone flags. Beyond the red-brick buildings, which were still bleeding with the recent downpour, the thudding sounded like a failing heartbeat. As she reached Oxford Road, which bisected the campus, she saw a man wearing overalls and headphones, or rather protectors to keep out the sound of the pneumatic hammer with which he was smashing the sidewalk. Behind him in the window of a block of small Georgian houses was a sign she hadn't previously noticed, directing customers to a relocated bookshop. That was worth telling Don when he came home, though maybe she'd say only that she knew something he would want to know until he told her whatever he was keeping from her.

She found her way through the maze of vehicles in the parking lot and squeezed between her Honda and its neighbor. She had to steer the Honda back and forth six times before she was able to maneuver it past the vehicles which had been parked too close to its bumpers, and that was quite enough to make her mad at Don for thinking she wasn't aware he had been less than honest about his plans as he'd left the house.

She coasted through a strolling crowd of students and restrained herself from more than touching the horn. The tires emitted a furious screech as she swung at last onto Oxford Road and outdistanced the cars which a pedestrian crossing let fly at her. Once the Indian restaurants began to multiply she turned left into the side streets, which became progressively quieter, so that by the time she drew up alongside the house there were no sounds but hers and those of a breeze scattering raindrops from plants on both sides of her path.

Of the three the family had planted, Don's was putting on the best show by far. She picked a bud and rubbed it between finger and thumb to smell the scent before admitting herself to the house. Marshall wouldn't be home for at least an hour. She listened to the reassuring emptiness and extracted a pair of noonday bills from their dun envelopes, then flattened them on the hall table while the answering machine's tape gibbered backward until it was ready to talk.

"Don Trovis? Jum Peesley hair frum Olster. Cuddn't reese yu at your shoap. I see yu've books by Ostin Forchaild in yure nu cotolog. I wus begunnung tu thonk I was the only follor whu'd hoard of hom. Raid hom yuresolf uf yu're ofter a gud loff. I'd lake yu tu sond me *Daith of a Bodgie* ond *Socks un Rostoronts.* Thonks."

"You're welcome," Susanne murmured, reflecting that she would have to ask Don whether the second book was concerned with socks or sex. The machine held its breath for a couple of seconds before beeping to indicate the end of the message, and then she heard Don's voice. "Hi, Susanne?"

"Hi."

"Are you home?"

"Can't you tell?"

"Are you home yet?"

"I'd say so."

"Pick up the phone if you are."

"Hey, Don, you can tell I'm . . ."

"Sounds like you aren't, huh?"

"If you'd waited maybe just a few minutes . . ."

"I was only going to tell you, well, that's what I'm doing in fact, no, I'll wait until I see you."

"Don, you're really starting to make me itch."

"Let's just say why don't you come to the shop and bring Marshall if he finishes his homework, and we'll eat at the Turkish joint we all liked."

"Are we celebrating something I don't know about? I hope you're going . . ."

"You know, I'm beginning to think we might like to stay in this country for good."

"I take it you're not about to share your reasons. You're not, are you? I don't believe this conversation."

"Call me. I'll wait here until you do."

"I'm glad you at least realize . . ."

"By the way, I love you."

"I should hope so after all that," Susanne retorted, a response which was pierced by the beep. If he'd called a while ago perhaps he might have left a more recent message.

"Don Trovis? Jum Peesley ugon. I shude hov sod the nombors frum yure cotolog. Twonty-sucks and twonty-sovon. Ony chonce I cud hov fofty-sucks as wull, thot's *Sockung the Volcano,* and suxty-tu, *Laife us a Murror?* Thonks os uvor."

"Don't monshon ot," Susanne couldn't resist saying as the beep put an end to him. She waited for Don to come up with an afterthought, but after the beep was only the silence of a caller who'd decided not to speak. Few traits irritated Susanne more, and this particular absence made her anxious to know who might have been there. No doubt she would never know. When the machine beeped again she stopped the tape so that Don would be able to rerun the messages from Jim Paisley of Ulster, and phoned the shop. Had the silent caller bothered her so much that she'd misdialed? Instead of ringing she heard a long lugubrious note like an alarm. She dialed again, and then again before she was convinced the shop phone was out of order.

"Well, that's just fine," she said aloud. How long would it take Don to realize she couldn't return his call? More than once he'd come home hours late, apologetic every time, having lost himself in cataloguing books, and she knew better than to expect a little thing like the silence of the phone to intrude on his concentration. She could be at the shop in half an hour—less if she parked on the street outside. Maybe she should wait for Marshall to arrive home, though on second thought he wouldn't have found her there if her teaching hadn't been cut short. She tramped into the kitchen to brew herself coffee while she attempted to decide what to do, then switched off the lukewarm percolator.

She slid the pencil out of the rings of the pad beside the phone and began to scribble before she was entirely certain what she meant to write. *Gone to the shop. Phone there out of order. Call you as soon as I've spoken to your father.* Wasn't that enough? *Don't worry, everything's fine.* It had to be, the way Don had sounded. She propped the pad against the answering machine and turned on the alarm and locked the house and ran, although there seemed no reason for her to run, to her car.

Vehicles were sniffing one another's tails on both sides of the main road, trying to beat the rush hour. It took Susanne five minutes to nose the Honda across the road and into the cortege heading for Manchester, by which time she'd thought of several new words for the drivers who'd prevented her from crossing sooner. She was able to drive straight for a while, and as steadily as the multitude of traffic lights would allow. But in the city center, where the traffic was heaviest and least accommodating, a series of diversions bullied her off the route she knew.

She spent time in a confusion of back streets rendered even narrower by trucks almost as windowless as the warehouses outside which they were parked. The sight of a main road came as such a relief that she'd driven several miles before the architecture alerted her that she was leaving the city behind. She performed a U-turn at a traffic light, muttering "I'm a crazy foreigner" at the drivers who blared their horns and flashed their headlamps at her, and rubbed one palm and then the other dry on her skirt as she retraced her route.

Just past the intersection where she'd emerged from the back streets she caught sight of an indication of a way to the cathedral. Only when she'd swung across a starting line of cars at yet another traffic light did she realize that the signpost identified a pedestrian route. To add to the frustration which made her scalp feel as though the hair was growing into her head, the street along which she'd turned was one way only. All the paving stones of the right-hand sidewalk were upended and fenced in with orange tapes, and plastic cones lay flattened in the roadway. On the left-hand sidewalk was a line of parking meters, all of them wearing canvas bags over their heads as though awaiting execution. The old brown office buildings on both sides were so dusty from the roadwork that the street looked abandoned, and Susanne was wondering whether to take that as a sign she could park at one of the unwelcoming meters, especially since the road a few hundred yards ahead was barred to cars by two discs on poles, when she saw that the farthest meter had its head bared.

Even if it was jammed, she was going to park in its sketch of a box on the roadway and argue later if she had to. But it was quite prepared to swallow her change and give her credit for it, and over her sneezes at the dust in the air she heard a main road, its blurred sounds underlaid by a clanking of trains and threaded by the whine of a tram, all this not far ahead. Two minutes' walk along the middle of the street brought her a view of the spiny spires of the cathedral. She ran across the main road in stages as various sections of traffic reluctantly acknowledged red lights. She was alongside the cathedral, and striding toward the Corn Exchange, when nervousness started to creep through her like a fever.

At first she couldn't understand what was producing it, which made it worse. Then she saw that around the corner of the Corn Exchange where Don's shop occupied a basement, the air was flickering faintly blue. Maybe a power line had been exposed or someone was using an acetylene torch, except that in either case she would have expected to hear more than an ominous silence. She hurried to the corner, almost tripping over the edge of a flagstone tilted by too many illegally parked vehicles. Three police cars with their roof lights flashing not quite in unison were drawn up alongside the Corn Exchange, the nearest of them outside Don's shop.

An orange police line tied to metal poles roped off a large patch of sidewalk in front of the doorway. Each pole kept sprouting a bunch of faded bluish shadows as the roof lights turned a stain on the patch of sidewalk black and then let it revert to dark red. The dimness beyond the doorway appeared to be pulsing, trying like an injured heart to establish a regular rhythm, but that was all she could distinguish in the shop. She ducked under the line, the blue glare jabbing at her eyes and almost blinding her, and a policeman who was keeping a group of spectators at bay on the opposite side of the roped-off patch swooped toward her. "You mustn't go in there, miss. Stay out, please."

Parts of her felt constricted, not least her brain. "Where mustn't I go?"

"Anywhere inside there." He stooped beneath the tape, and his reddish rather chubby face came up pale with determination. "Please come out, or I'll have to escort you."

At least three policemen were in the shop, one of them leafing through books on the counter. She lurched toward the steps, and the blue pulse brought the doorway flickering forward to meet her. The policeman's hand closed on her upper arm, and she turned on him. "Don't even try to stop me," she said, hating her voice for threatening to shake. "What's going on here? This is my husband's shop."

She felt her legs waver, because all at once the policeman looked as young as he'd been trying not to look. "Inspector?" he called, not quite managing to conceal his dismay at the situation in which he found himself.

Susanne was distantly aware of clamping her free hand over his hand on her arm for support. She saw the three policemen raise their heads and prepare their expressions, and it wasn't until the young man flinched that she realized she'd dug her nails into his hand. Even before a policeman in a dark uniform began to climb the steps, parting his lips the merest fraction as though he wished he needn't speak, she felt darkness rising inexorably toward her from the room where Don should be.

12

FROM THE PAST

Once Don reached the shop he would be safe. He felt as if the rain was helping him conceal his purchase until he could lock it in the drawer behind the counter and maybe leave it there until he'd told Susanne they owned it. But he left the rain behind sooner than the high-rise blocks, and was still at least fifteen minutes from the city center when he had to pull over to the curb of a main road and climb out to brush off the hood the hundreds of beads of rain that were dazzling him.

He'd parked on a double yellow line, he saw, alongside a notice warning him he couldn't park at any time. He imagined a police car drawing up beside him, the policeman writing him a ticket if that was what they did here, and then peering into the car. "What have we got in the package, sir?" He was wiping his hands on his jacket and reaching for the door handle when he caught sight of a notice in the window of one of a block of dingy shops across the road.

ANTIQUES BRIC A
BRAC SECOND
HAND RECORD'S
AND BOOK'S

It looked anything but promising, yet Don knew he wouldn't feel entitled to call himself a bookseller if he passed it up. He drove into the nearest side street, which was blocked after fifty yards or so by a strip of sidewalk planted with pebbledashed bollards. He shoved the black parcel farther under the seat and locked the doors and checked them twice, and gave the Volvo a last backward glance as he waited to cross the main road. Eventually the traffic halted, raindrops trembling on its roofs as the cars vibrated impatiently, and he ran across as the green men started to falter.

The shop was flanked by a butcher's, where the only meat on display was dead flies, and a barber's whose striped pole lay inside like the parent of a brood of empty wine bottles. A curtain or a blanket draped the unwashed window of the shop Don had made for, and was almost enough to discourage him. Nevertheless he went in, though the door was slouching in its frame and reluctant, like quite a few booksellers he'd met, to admit the public.

Beyond the door was one large room. It smelled of stewing tea, which appeared to have lent its color to most of the contents of the place: the sleeves of the old 78s leaning in cartons, the floor and the walls and the music-hall posters tacked to the latter, the spines of nearly all the books packed into a couple of spectacularly homemade bookcases or piled on top, the pages of the tattered magazines stacked on a coltishly unsteady table, the suits of the three men seated on an assortment of chairs around a steaming cylindrical urn. Indeed, their skin looked as though it might have been steeped in tea, though perhaps that was an effect of the dimness that was stagnating in the room. They each gave Don an indifferent glance and returned to slurping tea as they discussed how to make Communism work in Britain, and Don wondered if it was even worth crossing the floor to the books. He misread a title, and felt absurd for going closer to make sure he had, sidling past an oval mirror and a table laid with unfashionable ware. A loose floorboard set a stand of fire irons jangling and nearly tripped him as he reached the bookcase.

He felt as though his anticipation had tripped him, because the spine which had attracted him still said *Beyond the Wall of Sleep*. It must be a reprint, though he'd never heard of one. He inched the book off the splintery shelf, expecting the covers to wobble askew inside the surprisingly intact wrapper or the pages to fall loose. But the binding was tight, and when he turned to the verso of the title page he saw that what he'd thought he was only dreaming was true. This was the first edition of a book of tales by H. P. Lovecraft, his second collection and by far his rarest. It was priced at twenty pence.

He'd glimpsed something else while easing out the volume. He let his gaze stray along the spines, by no means all of which were as faded as they'd looked at first sight: the dimness was bestowing that appearance on them while preserving them. There was the title he hadn't dared believe he'd seen, and it led his gaze to its neighbor, beside which yet another book was waiting to be noticed. *The Outsider and Others. Devil's Tor.*

Stoneground Ghost Tales. Madam Crowl's Ghost. Out of Space and Time. The Eye and the Finger . . . By the time he'd finished unloading the shelves he had more than a dozen books, all of them first editions and as good as unread, and only the weight in his arms convinced him they were real.

He carried them to the grayish counter beside the urn and separated them into two neat piles for fear they might topple, and waited. In his, not Don's, own good time the stoutest of the men, whose shirt was losing a struggle to cover his stomach, remarked, "Bit of reading you've got there."

"Watch out you don't go blind," said the loudest drinker, picking leaves from between his teeth.

"Can I pay someone?"

The man who hadn't yet addressed him commenced rolling his mug of tea between his hands. "Tourist, are you?"

Don suppressed an impulse to declare his profession, and felt instantly guilty. "You could say that."

The mug-roller lost interest, barely glancing at the books Don had selected. "Two pound sixty. Hope you've got the right change."

"Would you happen to know where these came from?"

The proprietor clearly resented having to look, and made his displeasure even more apparent once he had. "Father of a comrade. No wonder he voted Tory all his life with his head in that kind of shite."

"You wouldn't know if there are any more where these came from?"

"Not unless he had them buried with him," the proprietor said with relish.

Don felt in his sodden hip pocket for change. "Could I trouble you for a carrier of some variety?"

The man peered at him for several seconds before producing a crumpled Safeway bag from a pocket of his coat. "That's the best I can do."

"Same here." Don handed him a five-pound note, adding quickly, "Keep the change if you need to."

He'd meant to avoid any argument just in case the proprietor considered not selling him the books, but now the silence seemed to threaten that. He lifted the books into the bag and supported it with both hands, and didn't risk another glance at the three men until he was at the door. "Thanks," he said. "It's been a pleasure."

None of them bothered to look at him, and they started talking as soon as he opened the door. "Must all think they're millionaires, these Yanks."

"My dad always said charity was the sign of a bad conscience."

"A way of not admitting it, more like."

Don no longer felt remotely guilty. He dragged the door shut and strode from one green man to the other, and turned along the side street, where he saw that the windshield of the Volvo had been cracked from top to bottom. The zigzag crack was a trail of rain which had trickled off the roof. He let himself into the car and lowered his prize carefully onto the floor in front of the passenger seat, and sighed luxuriously, and arched his back against the seat and stretched his limbs as far as they would go, and brought his hands and feet slowly to the controls, and sent the car toward Manchester.

He wanted to share his astonishing luck with Susanne, but not by interrupting her at work. She was still teaching her course, for the present examining images of violence in television documentaries and newscasts. He thought it might be easier to tell her about the gun, since if he hadn't gone to buy it he would never have chanced on the books.

A canal like an endlessly unrolling sheet of foil stretched under the road as he approached the center of Manchester. Bridges darkened the road, and a train passed over it with a squeal which could have been emitted by the opening of an enormous metal door. Then the road was gathered into a junction which the British called a roundabout, their word for a carousel. The first time Don had driven into such a junction in Manchester he'd felt as though he'd fallen foul of a white-knuckle ride. Now the sight of three lanes of traffic circling clockwise didn't faze him. He drove past the cathedral and across a wide bridge over skeins of railroad, and cruised into Greengate Arches, a subterranean warehouse that had been turned into a car park.

At the foot of the cobbled ramp he drove along the stony tunnel until he found a space well out of sight of the attendant in the booth, and tried to think what to do with the gun. He didn't want to carry a loaded weapon through the streets, but neither did he like to leave it in the car, just in case someone broke in and stole it, however unlikely that was. He unwrapped the gun and sprang the clip of bullets out of it, and locked both clips in the glove box, then he parcelled the gun again and found room for it in the Safeway bag and lifted the bundle out of the car.

The echoes of the slam of the door sounded like a bass drum and seemed to pound a smell of mold out of the bare walls. Sunlight met him halfway up the ramp and drove back the chill. Three cars ran a red light as he waited to cross the six-lane road, and he thought of pointing the gun at the last offender, and smiled a little uneasily at himself. He tucked the bag under his chin and felt the cold of the metal reach for him through the plastic as he sprinted to an island that was already full of two globular women and a set of traffic lights, and experienced a stopover lasting some minutes before he gained the farther sidewalk.

He carried the bag past the cathedral, outside which several Irish nuns were giggling and drinking on the wall opposite the Mitre Hotel, and hooked his key ring out of his pocket as he came in sight of the Corn Exchange. A bus moved off toward the Arndale Center shopping mall and revealed the hazy apparition of a tram gliding across the gap between two office blocks. The smell of old books greeted him as he unlocked his door and hasped it open and set down his burden on the top step while he untacked the sign that said BACK THIS AFTERNOON—which, now he thought about it, had presumed a good deal—and stuck it between gun and chin so as to bear everything down the steps.

He shut the gun in the drawer behind the counter and spread his other purchases in front of him. His delight with them was going to be feeble compared with the reactions of the customers he planned to contact. He'd write to them before he went home, but first he couldn't resist at least making sure that Susanne was too busy to contact. He dialed the University and had himself put through to her department. "Will Mrs. Travis be teaching just now, can you tell me?"

"Who wants her, please?"

"Is that Alice? This is Don. Mr. Susanne."

"Oh, hello, Mr. Travis." The secretary sounded unsure how to explain her initial wariness. "I think she may have left. I'll check." Alice threw her voice into the distance and received a distant answer. "Yes, she has."

"She wasn't meant to yet, was she? Would you know . . ."

"Just finished early, we think. We believe she was going straight home."

"I'll try her there. And Alice, thanks for making sure I was someone she'd want to know."

He dialed home and heard his own voice. "Susanne, Don and Marshall Travis. Even if any of the family is here we haven't got to the phone yet, so tell us who you are and what you want and your number after this beep."

"Hi, Susanne?" he said once the machine had uttered its cry. "Are you home? Are you home yet? Pick up the phone if you are. Sounds like you aren't, huh? I was only going to tell you, well, that's what I'm doing in fact, no, I'll wait until I see you. Let's just say why don't you come to the shop and bring Marshall if he finishes his homework, and we'll eat at the Turkish joint we all liked. You know, I'm beginning to think we might like to stay in this country for good."

That would need explaining. At once he felt he'd said too much. He wished there was some way he could run the tape back and substitute a less fulsome message. Contradicting it would be worse, and so he said, "Call me. I'll wait here until you do. By the way, I love you," and was aware of loitering with nothing more to say. He cut off his own silence and indulged in another survey of the books on the counter, and then he slapped his open mouth. He'd left Teresa Handley's novel in the Hangman.

It surely couldn't matter. It was inscribed to the Travises, but only by their first names. Most likely it wasn't even there by now, and in any case there was nothing for the author to be connected with. Certainly he shouldn't feel compelled to return to the pub. He'd just finished convincing himself of all this when someone, two men, blocked the sunlight through the doorway and started down the steps.

Before he was able to see their faces, another memory ambushed him. Two men had overheard him enthusing over a parcel of videotapes to Marshall and had then sneaked out of the shop. He'd thought at the time that they might have been thieves, except that he'd never been able to identify any theft. Suppose they'd been police or customs officers who had perhaps already known the contents of the parcel? Suppose the men who were slowly descending the steps were police who'd followed him from the Hangman? Then the foremost said, "Shut the fucking door, Dave," and Don knew why they seemed familiar. "Leave it open, would you, please," he said as loudly and steadily as he could.

"We'll leave you fucking open, pal. Fucking get it, Dave."

The speaker had reached the foot of the steps. His companion started to tramp back up. Don flung out a hand, though for a moment he wasn't sure what he was reaching for. His hand closed on the phone receiver and snatched it to his face. "Either you both leave right now—"

He ought to have shown them the gun. Neither of them faltered—the one who was climbing didn't even glance at him. "Or what?" said the other. "You'll shop us like you did Phil? You won't get the fucking chance."

Don dropped the cordless phone on top of *Out of Space and Time* and fumbled at the drawer with his left hand while he poked the buttons with his right forefinger. He dialed 9 and realized that he was about to follow it with 11, but didn't the British dial 999 in an emergency, or had that been changed? His finger wavered, he glanced at his left hand so as to locate the handle of the drawer, and as he grasped the handle he stabbed a second 9. The man at the foot of the steps crossed the floor in three strides and swept the receiver away with his fist. It flew off the book and smashed against the end of a bookshelf and broke into even more pieces when it struck the floor. "Good one, Ken," shouted the man who was trying to kick the door shut.

"Now what are you going to do, you Yank fuck?"

"What I should have done in the first place," Don said almost evenly, giving silent thanks that the man hadn't damaged any of the first editions, and pulled out the drawer.

He pulled too hard. The drawer shot out of the counter, and its sudden weight was more than his fingers could cope with. It bruised them as it fell, and his other hand clutched at the gun. As the drawer struck the floor with a splintering crash, his thumb and forefinger closed on the butt. The muzzle swung after the drawer, the weight of the gun tugged it out of his grip, and then his other hand caught the muzzle, and he was raising the weapon in both hands toward the man's forehead, his right forefinger hooking the trigger. "Tell Dave you're both leaving, Ken."

Ken let out a snarl which dragged the skin back from his eyes and teeth. "Where'd you fucking get that?"

"Never mind," Don said, lowering his left hand to cover the lack of a clip in the gun. "Just walk."

Ken raised his fists like a furious child, so that Don was afraid he might be stupid enough to lash out at the gun. Instead he nearly screamed, "Dave!"

"I'm fucking closing it. Give us a fucking chance."

"Don't fucking close it, open it."

"You just said—"

"I know what I fucking said. Fucking open it. We're going out. The cunt's got a gun."

"He's fucking never." Dave turned from finally locating the hasp that held the door open and peered down the steps. "Fuck."

"Fuck," Ken seemed to be agreeing, though in a different tone, as he backed to the steps and almost tripped over them. "We'll have the law on you," he yelled at Don, and wiped his chin. "You're not allowed to have guns here."

"Tell that to your relative in prison."

That might be more provocative than they could bear to walk away from. Don wagged the gun at them to speed them on their way, and Ken retreated up the steps, snarling, "Crazy fucker." At the top he collided with Dave, who was still peering down at the gun. "Fucking mind," Ken said through his teeth, and shoved him out onto the sidewalk.

As Don straightened up from leaning across the counter, an ache jabbed the base of his spine. He rubbed the place hard as he crossed the floor, keeping hold of the gun. There was no sign of the two men, but he couldn't assume they'd departed. In a moment he heard the less slow of the two voices mutter, "It isn't over."

"Fucking believe it."

"So where you going, Dave? The cunt's got to come out this way, and he can't call anyone. He's never going to use that on the street, not him."

"Good one."

They didn't know the worst of it, Don realized with a start which jerked his spine. Since Susanne wouldn't be able to return his call, she would almost certainly come to the shop. He had to get rid of them before she arrived or, maybe better, bluff his way past them so as to call her from a public phone. He fished out his keys and held them quiet in his fist as he tiptoed quickly up the steps, and had to take a breath which tasted of old books before he looked out. The two men were only a few paces away, and both of them lurched at him until he swung the muzzle toward them, keeping it low to ensure they couldn't see it wasn't loaded. "I'm coming out," he said urgently. "Stay back."

A movement behind them came to a halt, and there was an outburst of red. A double-decker bus loaded with passengers had been stopped by traffic lights a hundred yards away. The nearness of so many people reassured him more than the weapon in his hand did. He stepped onto the sidewalk and pulled the door shut, and watched the men as he felt with the key for the lock. It found the hole, but wouldn't turn. He saw a dangerous grin twitch both men's lips, and waved the gun at their bellies, and glanced at the key so as to line it up. In that instant Dave strode at him.

Don let go of the key and raised the gun with both hands. Ken tried to hold Dave back, but he kept coming. His clenched red face appeared to have squeezed all sense from his eyes and left nothing but animal fury in them. Don jabbed the muzzle in his direction, and thought at last to pull back the slide. Even then Dave didn't falter, and Don could only retreat a step. He knew instantly that he should have held his ground. Before he could think further, he reacted. His finger closed on the trigger, and the gun emitted a sharp click.

It sounded far louder than was necessary, but mightn't it have been audible only to him? He tried to hold the weapon and his gaze steady as he aimed them at Dave. Then the man shouted, "It isn't fucking loaded." His fury turned gleeful, and he clubbed Don's forearm with both fists clasped together. Don gripped the weapon harder out of pure reflex, and it slammed into his crotch.

The impact felt as though his right testicle had been hammered into his body. The whole of him went into spasm, his knees buckling, his hands clutching at his groin as the gun clattered across the sidewalk, his upper body jackknifing almost horizontal as the agony swelled and forced a scream past the flaring ache of his clenched teeth. The world lurched in sympathy, and then his blurring vision showed him that the traffic lights had changed. The bus was starting toward him. So was Ken, raising one foot too high to be merely running. Don fought to straighten up, but the pain at the center of him was too great. The metal toecap of the heavy boot caught him in the face.

Something broke—it felt like most of the right side of his head. He collapsed to his knees, scraping them across the sidewalk. His head, which had been jerked back like a punch-ball, sagged forward, and he raised a fearful hand toward his face. Before he could make himself touch it, evidence of his injuries appeared on his palm—blood and broken glass.

The remains of his spectacles were still attached to his head. Through the surviving lens he saw the bus approaching. Passengers were pointing at him, and he thought he heard their muted cries of protest or distress. The bus drew alongside, and Don made out that the driver and passengers were less intent on him than on the gun. The bus accelerated, and in response to the signal it had given, Dave kicked him in the head as if to demonstrate to Ken how much better he could do.

Don thought his glasses had been driven into his flesh until he heard them strike the sidewalk. He'd seen the boot rushing toward his right eye, but now that eye saw nothing—less than he could see without his glasses.

Darkness which felt like white-hot chunks was spreading to fill that side of his head, and a wetness which he gathered wasn't only blood was spilling down his cheek. He imagined Susanne and Marshall seeing him like this, and it was the most terrible thought in the world. "Enough," he pleaded, just as a kick smashed his teeth into his mouth.

The sidewalk tipped up to press itself, a cold rough gray blur, against his right cheek. Somewhere his hands were groping about, searching for some part of him to protect. There didn't seem to be much, especially once the boots commenced trampling on him, breaking him like a pile of sticks. At least they were leaving his head alone, he found himself thinking, and when they'd finished someone would take him to hospital, to more than one hospital, first the eye hospital. At least he could no longer see the boots, but then one showed himself to him. It loomed above his head, and as he tried to work his mouth and find words to stop it, it came down. He broke as his skull did, and there was nothing left of him.

13

MESSAGES

"Just ~~explain~~ tell me one thing. I've got to know."

"Sure, now I've ~~got~~ put you where you can't do any more harm."

"The crime in that ~~novel~~ book was perfect. There was no way he could have been caught. I did everything he did, so I shouldn't have been caught either."

"Don't you think the ~~guy who wrote the book~~ author might have known something he didn't put in ~~it~~ the book?"

"So what? You couldn't have asked him. It said he never ~~gave~~ gives interviews."

"This is the only kind ~~of interview~~ he gives. Meet the author."

Marshall hadn't shown any of his stories to his parents, but he thought he might let them see this one, which had earned him an A+ in English once he'd persuaded the teacher that he hadn't copied it from a book or been helped to write it. Perhaps he would wait until he was satisfied with it, since he was still rewriting it in his head. Maybe he could write a bunch of stories or even a novel about Don Marshall Varsit, the writer turned detective who specialized in solving crimes based on books. His father ought to be able to tell him whether any publisher would want to look at his work. Maybe this was Marshall Travis the author who was in the midst of the hundreds of schoolboys crowding along the corridor into the yard, where dark stains on the concrete were the only signs of the afternoon downpour. The crowd dissipated into the sunlight, and Marshall was heading for the gate when someone grabbed him by the shoulder. "Hey up a minute."

Before he looked Marshall knew it was Ali Syed from the hint of spices lingering about his uniform. "I'll bring the tapes my mom borrowed from your dad's shop back later."

"See you then, only here's the one Trevor said you could watch after me. Take it, quick."

"What is it?"

"John Woo's new one. It's amazing. There's one scene where, you know, the one who's always in them shoots nearly thirty people all in the same camera run."

"My mom showed her students one of his. She was really grateful to your dad when he called up to say she could join, by the way."

"She hadn't better show them that one when you aren't supposed to be able to get it. Christ, here comes Dickhead. Don't let him see. I'm off."

The plastic of the supermarket carrier in which the videocassette was wrapped squeaked under Marshall's fingernails as he forced it into the space on top of his English workbook and zippered his bag shut. By the time he turned, Ali was out of the gate. The headmaster was stalking toward Marshall, his bald head gleaming as brightly as its twin wings of black hair.

If he meant to ask what Ali had given him, why did he look embarrassed as his eyes met Marshall's? For most of his approach he seemed to be thinking of turning aside without speaking. He tapped his broad nose and then his thick pink lips with a forefinger, which he wagged to detain Marshall. The boy waited for him to come up, only to have to wait for him to speak. Then the headmaster took him by the shoulder and steered him with unexpected gentleness in the direction of the street. "Just walk out with me, Travis."

As they passed out of the gate, Marshall was aware that everyone in the schoolyard was watching. Some boys were pretending not to, and he imagined they were thinking of fears too secret for him to admit to himself. Once Mr. Harbottle had aimed him at the main road he let go, keeping pace with him. He rubbed his chin as though it was a magic lamp such as figured in the fairy tales Marshall no longer read, and abruptly remarked, "I'm led to believe you're shining in English."

"Doing okay, sir, I guess."

"Doing well, I'm sure you intended to say." The headmaster cocked a frown at him; Marshall couldn't tell whether it was meant to look comical. "May we expect a contribution for the magazine?"

This was so clearly not the subject Mr. Harbottle had been embarrassed to raise that for a moment Marshall was confused enough to think he was being asked for money. "What kind of stuff, sir?"

"I'm glad you asked. Perhaps an essay setting out your impressions of the country in which you are a guest? Something to help banish any less fortunate associations."

He might as well have been talking in code as far as Marshall was concerned. The boy felt small and vulnerable for nodding as though he knew what he was agreeing to. "Mr. Slater is the man to approach when you've produced a suitable piece," the headmaster said, and stopped walking. "Are you for town?"

"I don't think so, sir," Marshall said, and wondered what on earth he was denying. "I mean, am I?"

"Are you bound for the center or home?"

"Home, I think," Marshall said, searching for a reason why he should have been assumed to be going into Manchester. "Sure, home."

"Then there would be little point in my offering you a lift. I hope to continue hearing good reports of you," Mr. Harbottle said, and let himself into the Renault beside which they were standing.

The car winked and swung away from the curb, leaving a taste of its exhaust in Marshall's throat. He hurried after it, anxious to outdistance anyone who might want to know what Mr. Harbottle had wanted, because he was trying to decide that himself. The change in the headmaster's demeanor suggested he believed he had conveyed whatever he'd been embarrassed to say, but had he? Which less fortunate associations had he expected Marshall to recognize? Marshall ran across the road as the green man beckoned him, and made his way to his angular route home through the side streets. Several corners had blocked off the sounds of the main road when he realized what Mr. Harbottle had expected him to remember. The headmaster had proposed to tell the whole school about Marshall's behavior in court, but the police raid had driven that prospect out of Marshall's head. Of course, it was the police raid which had changed the headmaster's mind. Marshall was no longer an example he wanted to hold up to the school.

Marshall didn't care—not on his own behalf. It was the implication that his parents had been found wanting, that it was their fault, he didn't like. When he stopped at the corner before his house to pat Loper's head as the dog bounded up to the costume designer's gate, he was glad nobody would be home for his feelings to be hidden from. He gave the warm hard short-haired scalp a last pat, then crossed the road beneath the emptily blue sky, a rectangle of which had invaded his parents' bedroom. He glanced over his shoulder only twice, as he inserted the first key and as he pushed the front door open. He stepped quickly into the vestibule and pulled the door after him, making sure the lock clicked into place. The inner door swung away from him before he could touch it—the displacement of air had moved it, of course—and set off the alarm.

He dumped his bag at the foot of the stairs and poked his key into the control panel, shutting off the alarm just as the siren raised its howl. He needn't be so nervous of it—it proved that nobody had broken into the house. He was opening the doors of all the downstairs rooms to admit more light and more sense of the house into the hall when he realized that there was a note from his mother on the pad slumped against the answering machine. *Gone to the shop. Phone there out of order. Call you as soon as I've spoken to your father. Don't worry, everything's fine.*

Without that reassurance Marshall might have believed it was, and why shouldn't he still? The note didn't mean to remind him how alone he was in the house. He made to take the key out of the control panel, then left it there in case—in case of nothing in particular. Something which he didn't need to identify stirred in the sideboard as he hurried past the dining room to get himself a Coke from the refrigerator. As he pulled the tab above the sink, the can spat over the window, which he rubbed clean with a kitchen towel. The paper squeaked on the glass, the kitchen bin clattered like a plastic toy with a big dumb mouth as he trod on the pedal. He was heading back along the hall, telling himself not to check the video Ali had given him because he would only end up watching it through before he did his homework, when he saw the pad had obscured the fact that the machine had a message for him.

He twisted the switch and waited while the tape rewound. It appeared to be a long message—long enough to make him uneasy. The tape returned to zero, the mechanism emitted a series of clicks as it rearranged itself, and at last delivered its message. Only there was more than one: an order for books in an Irish accent so thick he thought at first it was meant as a joke, a call from his father which eventually proposed a meal at the Efes Kebab House, a reappearance by the Irishman. Marshall gathered his mother had rewound the tape only to that point so that his father could pick up the order. A beep separated the messages, but whoever had called next hadn't bothered to speak. Another beep, and Marshall wasn't sure if he heard breathing or just static. It might as well have been silence, and it lasted only a few seconds before being ousted by a call the tape had recorded weeks ago.

Marshall stopped the tape and set it to record and picked up his bag, then relinquished it while he dialed the shop in case the phone there had been fixed. A long mournful drone answered him. He carried his bag and the glass of Coke into the dining room and told the rattle in the sideboard to shut up, and spread his homework over the table, and wondered how long ago his mother had gone to the shop. Wondering that would only get mixed up with his math, which they called maths in Britain although it seemed to be the same amount, and he took several deep breaths to clear his head before he wrote down the first equation. He was inscribing an *x* under the ledge of a square root sign when a car door slammed outside the house.

It didn't sound like the Volvo or the Honda, but he thought it was parked directly outside. Maybe somebody had brought one of his parents home. He heard the clash of the gate, and footsteps on the path, heavy footsteps which belonged to neither of his parents. The footsteps halted, and without giving him a chance to think, the doorbell rang.

His chair jerked backward, digging its hind legs into the carpet and almost depositing him on his back as he jumped up. The contents of the sideboard trembled as he let go of the chair and ventured into the hall, as far as the front room. He inched his head around the doorframe until he could see through the window. Standing on the path was a policeman, and another was climbing out of the car beyond the gate.

The man on the path stepped back to survey the front of the house, holding his helmet against his chest, and caught sight of Marshall just as the boy considered dodging back. A number of suppressed expressions almost surfaced on the policeman's face before he raised his eyebrows and hooked a finger several times to indicate that Marshall should let him in. It must be about the videos again, Marshall thought, and instantly felt as though the one in his schoolbag had buried itself in his stomach. They couldn't require him to talk unless there was a lawyer present—unless his parents were. He made himself walk quickly to the vestibule, where he slipped the chain into its socket before opening the front door to the length of the chain.

Both men were just outside, the driver so close behind his colleague that they resembled a double image, especially since they had both removed their helmets. "Is your mother in, son?" the foremost policeman said.

The hair on top of his head was raising itself like turf that had been trodden on. Somehow that made Marshall more uneasy than his sky-blue gaze did—so uneasy that the only answer he could manufacture on the spot was, "I don't know. Why?"

"Come on, son, you know if your mother's in."

"Suppose I do?"

"Just get her for us, will you, there's a good lad."

"She'd want to know what it's about."

The policeman turned his head a fraction toward his colleague while keeping his gaze on Marshall. No communication which Marshall was able to identify had passed between them when the man in front said, "Look, son, don't make this harder than it has to be. Is she here or not?"

"What if she—" Abruptly it occurred to Marshall that besides whatever they wanted her for, there might conceivably be some English law which said he had to be a certain age before he was supposed to be left alone in the house. "How old do you think I am?" he said as nonchalantly as he could.

"Same age as mine, I'd say." For some reason this seemed to bother the policeman. "Now listen, son, do yourself and the rest of us a favor and give me a straight answer. This isn't easy for us."

"Then don't do it. Leave her alone."

The backup policeman leaned forward, narrowing his eyes as though composing his small face around the whisper he aimed in the other man's ear. "Maybe he thinks—you know, Operation Nasty."

The blue-eyed gaze flickered away from Marshall and returned to him. "Look—what's your name, son?"

Something like regret was hiding in his eyes and maybe under his blunt tone of voice. "Marshall Travis," Marshall said.

"Marshall. Well, Marshall, I want you to know we aren't after your mother. I mean, this has nothing to do with any police coming to your house before. We only want to talk to her. We've been to the University, and they told us she'd come home."

"She isn't here now."

"I'm glad we've got that sorted at least. Can you tell us where she is?"

Marshall imagined being left ignorant and even more anxious than now while they went to her. "I'll, I'll phone her and tell her you want her, but I'll need to tell her why."

"It's best if we do that, Marshall. Trust me, son, will you?"

Marshall thought of a way to make his mother sound protected. "She'll be with my dad."

"Whereabouts would that be, son?"

Though the question came from the usual speaker, his awkward gentleness seemed to emanate from both men, and it disturbed Marshall as much as having let himself be maneuvered into a position where he was virtually bound to tell the police what they wanted to know. "I don't know the street names," he lied in a final attempt to maintain some control. "I'd have to take you there."

He sensed the police avoiding looking at each other. "Your mother mightn't want that just now, Marshall," the foremost said.

His colleague touched his elbow. "Shall I—"

The other policeman appeared to have only to glance at him to understand. "Better had."

As the driver hurried to the car the blue-eyed policeman took a step toward Marshall, fingering his lapel badge as though it was a secret sign that would admit him to Marshall's confidence. "Open the door properly, there's a good young feller. We won't come in unless you say."

Marshall saw the driver sit in the car and pick up a microphone from the dashboard. "Who's he calling?"

"Just to find out how things—we'll see."

Marshall felt and heard his own fingers rubbing his sweaty palms. The sensations were distanced from him by the questions which had begun to grind together in his skull and, though he struggled to prevent them, spill out of his mouth. "How do you know what my mother—why do you keep saying—how about my—" He wasn't sure how much of this the policeman heard, but it felt like admitting too much. "I'm going to call them," he blurted.

The policeman reached for him. For a moment Marshall thought he meant to grab him across the chain, but the hand stopped in front of the policeman's chest, fingers spread and almost imperceptibly trembling. "Listen, Marshall, son—I'm sorry. You won't be able to."

That had to be true unless whatever was wrong at the shop had been fixed, but how could the policeman know? "Why?" Marshall said, a question which came out as little more than a breath.

There was a rattle from the police car as the driver replaced the microphone, and the blue-eyed policeman glanced at him. Marshall saw the driver close his eyes and open them as he shook his head from side to side once. The blankness of his small face lent him a resemblance to a crudely animated life-size doll. Marshall's left hand gripped the chain, the links digging into his fingers, the dull ache stinging with sweat. His other hand was rubbing its knuckles against the door as though to convince him something was solid. "Marshall, son, your father's," the blue-eyed policeman said, "been attacked."

Perhaps he hadn't paused between the words, but Marshall felt as if the world had, like a heart stopping. No words seemed likely to be able to struggle out of his stiffening mouth, and he began to fumble at the chain. "That's right, son, we're your friends, we're here to help you," the policeman said.

Marshall wasn't planning to let him in—he was planning to run if, as seemed likely, his emotions became too much for him. The door fell away from him, the chain slipped out of its slot and clanked against the doorframe, and Marshall bruised his shoulder against the door as the policeman placed a hand against it to prevent it from closing. The impact jarred speech out of Marshall as though it had wakened him. "He's not hurt, is he? I mean, not bad? How bad?"

He became aware that his face was jammed in the gap, the frame and the edge of the door trapping his cheeks. He didn't care, he only wanted to know. It didn't matter how old the police thought he was, they had to tell him about his own father. He dragged himself backward with one hand on the vestibule wall and pulled at the door with the other, and the blue-eyed policeman came to him and put an arm around his shoulders. Marshall felt as though he was being held so that he would have to face the driver who was walking inexorably, no more able to halt than a puppet would have been, toward him. "He's not in pain, son. I can promise you that," the driver said.

Words fought their way past Marshall's lips before he could hold them back—hold back the worst from having happened. He didn't know if they were a question or a plea or a denial. "He isn't dead."

The man beside him hugged his shoulders, and Marshall glimpsed him staring a last hope at his colleague. When the driver said, "I'm sorry, son" the arm hugged Marshall tighter, and the boy felt as though it was trying to squeeze him to nothingness. He was still there, still unbearably alive, because he heard his own voice. "No, he isn't. No, he isn't, no," it said with a babyishness that filled him with self-loathing as everything around him grew bright and flat and remote from him.

14

SELF-HELP

"How's your da, Darren?"

"Fucking great."

"Listen to it, will you, Bern. Sounds just like his da. Been to see him, have you, lad?"

"Nah. Says he doesn't want me seeing him with a baldy head."

"How long'd he get, eighteen months? Bet your dick he's out in half that. Is he getting everything he needs?"

"Says you get better dope in there than outside. And he's with lots of his friends, mam says."

"So long as they're not friendly with his arse, eh? Hey up, lad, only joking. No need to get yourself worked up. You don't want to tangle with me even if you are Phil's lad. Where is she, anyway?"

"Out."

"Know where?"

"Never says."

"You want to do something about that as long as you're the man of the house. She knew we was coming, didn't she, Bern?"

"Maybe she forgot. She does. I expect she's out scoring one way or the other. Nobody else in, is there, Darren?"

"Only granda."

"Jesus, is he still around? If I was Phil I'd have taken him up the moors and come back on my tod fucking years ago. He won't say nothing, will he, Bern?"

"Been a long time since he's known what's going on around him."

"Can't think why Phil wants to keep him round the house, costing Christ knows how much and contributing fuck all. Don't you ever get like him, lad. We've got to look after us selves round here, we've no time for cunts who don't muck in. So how much fucking longer are you going to keep us standing on the step?"

"Uncle Bernard didn't say you wanted to come in."

"Aye, well, fucking Uncle Bernard says it now, don't you, Uncle Bernard? And Barry says it too. That's me, in case you forgot."

"I don't forget."

"Look at him, Bern. Just like Phil the time that cunt spilled some ale on his shoe in the pub. You're a credit to your old man, lad. I bet you're a killer when you grow up, only don't come it with me. Want to help us instead?"

"Doing what?"

"That's right, never say yes to any fucker till you know what you're saying yes to. Just go on the pavement and keep an eye out for the filth while we bring some stuff in, will that do you?"

"What sort of stuff?"

"Never mind what sort. You can't tell nobody if you don't know, right? Go on, lad, move your arse."

"If Uncle Bernard says."

"Uncle Bernard wouldn't fucking be here if he didn't, would he? Jesus, tell him, Bern."

"It's all right, Darren. Phil won't mind."

Darren seldom knew what his father would or wouldn't mind from one moment to the next, but at least this time it would have been Bernard who got it wrong. He stepped out of the house as Barry, a wiry man whose gray scalp looked scraped and whose left cheek bore a scar which began near his eye and interrupted the end of his patchy mustache, heaved the garden fence upright so as to drag the gate wider on the concrete. Darren plugged his ears with his headphones and saw Bernard mouthing at him beyond the hiss the tape had come to. He had to pull the headphones down before he realized he was being told to do that and to go across the road to keep watch.

Above him the sky was dark, but behind the low houses was a sediment of blue which made the roofs look razor-edged. Several windows were unsteady with the flickering of televisions, and one was blazing all the colors of disco lights. If anyone was watching as Bernard and Barry unloaded piles of cartons from the back of the old retired Post Office van and hurried in and out of the house like animals stocking a nest, the watchers were staying well out of sight, and Darren was certain they wouldn't dare call the police. He heard a siren racing closer on the main road, but it was an ambulance heading into Manchester. "They'll be sending one for you if you fuck with us," he muttered, glaring at the windows that were dark, seeing the unsteadily illuminated windows shake with fear of him.

He couldn't have been standing on the pavement long, though long enough for his hands and feet to start growing cold as they did whenever he took a trip, when he saw Barry loitering in the doorway of the house, mopping his forehead with the sleeve of his hooded gray shirt. "What's he waiting for, Bern, the filth to come along and ask him what he's up to? Get your arse over here, lad."

It wasn't his house. He wasn't Darren's father. Darren stalked across the road, reaching for his headphones as he passed the van. Only the van wasn't quite the size or shape he'd thought it was, nor was it exactly where it had seemed to be, and he couldn't tell if the road around him was lit or dark. A barking in a yard very close to him sounded like somebody—maybe a policeman—imitating a dog, and the hiss of the headphones was trying to drag him down, to rise above his head and drown him. He'd be all right once he reached the house, but the doorway at the end of the elongated path appeared to be shrinking away from him like a picture on a television which had that moment been switched off. Barry had turned away, and Darren couldn't call to him for help, because the inside of his head had been scooped out, tongue and all. Then the image of the house steadied as if someone had used a remote control, and the prickly lumps of meat in his shoes carried him over the doorstep.

Barry and Bernard seemed not to see anything wrong with him when they bothered to look at him, but he couldn't decide if they were pretending, nor whether it was hot or cold in the house. It must be hot, because Barry was saying, "I could murder a lager now, me."

"Phil keeps some in the fridge sometimes, if the lad or his mam haven't finished it off."

Barry swaggered down the hall and grabbed a can from the refrigerator. He ripped off the metal tab and threw it among the greasy plates in the kitchen sink, and tossed the can and his head back as he made for the front room. "Jesus, lad," he said, wiping his mustache with a thumb and forefinger, "don't you ever turn the telly off?"

"My mam always has it on."

"Don't want to grow up like a tart, do you? Don't want your da coming home to find you in a fucking dress."

"Tell you what, Barry, why don't you take the drink with you while you move the van."

"And what'll you be doing, Bern?"

"I'll hang on till Marie comes home and I can straighten things out with her."

"I hope Phil appreciates what you're doing, pal."

"Reckon he will, pal," Bernard said, and Darren wondered if he was going to punch Barry in the face, a possibility that brought his surroundings into much sharper focus. But the men seemed to have made themselves clear to each other, because Barry slouched down the path to the van, tossing his head to feed himself another drink. "Better at thieving than he is at doing as he's told, that's his trouble," Bernard remarked. "Do us a favor, lad, do you have to have it on that loud?"

He was in the front room now, searching for the remote control among the clothes and bills and free newspapers strewn over and around the chairs which were all that remained of various different suites. "Like a bloody jumble sale, this house. Come ahead, lad, give us the switch and let's have a bit of peace."

Darren saw the control on the black marble mantelpiece above the electric fire into which his mother had stuffed some bills. Barry had said he was the man of the house while his father was inside, which meant he could have the set on as loud as he liked, so why should he let Bernard tell him to turn it down? Then Bernard noticed where he was looking, and grabbed the control and poked at the buttons, switching from police knocking people down with batons to a man making a woman stand on tiptoe with a broken bottle at her throat to a cowboy being shot six times to some soldiers marching past a dead baby, until he located the off button at last. "Don't tell me you were watching any of that," he said, and sat down.

He'd gone for the least cluttered chair, on which Darren's mother had abandoned the cardigan she'd been wearing earlier. As he leaned back Darren felt as if the man was flattening his mother. He groped under his ears to get rid of the hiss that kept merging with Bernard's voice, then remembered he had to switch off the Walkman, and did so. "I wanted to see if Ken and Dave were on again."

"They ought to be soon, right enough. Just remember they're family, lad, not some kind of Yankee thriller."

"I only wanted to see what the telly was saying about them."

"All right, lad, it isn't you I'd like to give a thumping." Bernard reached into his suede jacket and produced an object whose glinting seemed to promise Darren the present of a weapon, but it was only a tin of cigars. "Find us an ashtray, will you? Where's the one you lifted from the Dog & Gun?"

Darren went into the back room where the men of the family met. Whenever he found an excuse to join them, like taking them a packet of cigarettes or food they'd sent him out for, they would discuss him loudly for a few moments and then look at him as though he'd already been told to get out. Now he was able to stand as long as he wanted to, inhaling the memory of cigarette smoke and feeling he owned the room, the built-in bar with hula dancers printed on it, the boxing posters with his father's name inserted on each of them, the loose floorboard hiding the gun which had replaced the one his father had thrown in the canal, the piles of cartons of video cameras which Barry and Bernard had brought in. He didn't know how long he had been standing when Bernard shouted, "Get a move on, lad. I'm gasping."

The only ashtray Darren could see, on the low table whose glass top imprisoned six poker hands with the winner in front of his father's chair, was stuffed with butts and ash. He climbed on a chair and had to thump the narrow transom with both hands until it gave enough for him to empty the ashtray onto the strip of grass alongside the house. He hauled the transom shut and forced the holes in the bar onto the metal struts, and jarred the softness inside his head as he jumped down and walked along the hall into Bernard's stare. "Sweet jogging Jesus, it took you long enough. I thought you were doing a runner."

"Just cleaning this for you."

"Out of the window and out of sight, eh? You take after your mam in some ways right enough." Bernard bit off the end of the cigar jerking in his mouth and spat a fingertip without a nail and some blood which Darren had to tell himself was only stained saliva into the ashtray, and clanked his Zippo open and shut, and puffed out smoke and closed his eyes and leaned his head back like an actor advertising cigars; then he squinted through his cloud at Darren. "How much longer are you going to prowl about, lad? Find something to do for the love of Christ, it's like being in a zoo. Put on the telly if you must, if that'll keep you still."

Darren slung some of his mother's dresses off a chair and hunched his body so that it had to sit down. "You said they won't be on yet."

Bernard eyed him over the flare of red. "Try not to let all this upset you, lad. That bloody Yank's been taken care of good and proper, any road." He clamped his teeth on the cigar, and his anger came out thick as the smoke. "Putting your da in the paper and making him look like that, the bastard got what was coming to him. Pulling a gun on the boys because he couldn't take his medicine and getting them arrested. What were they supposed to do, I'd like to know?" He glared at Darren, who felt held responsible and unable to think of a safe answer, until at last the cigar lit like a bulb outside a studio. "He should have taken himself and his family back where they came from while he had the chance."

"Do you think they'll go back now?"

"They will if they know what's good for them. There's sod all to keep them here. What's it to you anyway, lad?"

Darren saw the newscast so clearly it might still have been on the television instead of just on the end of the tape with the woman and the dog: the pavement outside the bookshop roped off like a boxing ring with the loser's blood splashed over it, the woman and the boy in his posh school uniform, their eyes leaking as though they were acting the kind of scene he would either laugh at or fast-forward in a film. All at once he realized he'd seen what he needed to see. Bernard was staring at him, and Darren was about to dodge out of the room to control his expression in case it betrayed him when he heard a key in the front door. "Here's mam."

"Aye, and a pig on the roof."

By the sound of it she was trying to jiggle the wrong key into the lock. Darren watched Bernard throw his hands about impatiently while the metallic scraping faltered, and keys jangled against the door, and the scraping became more urgent, and at last the door banged open. "What a stink," his mother said at the top of her voice. "Can't he go anywhere without a cigar stuck in his gob? I wouldn't care if it was just a ciggy. When did he go, Darren? Did he want me?"

"No chance, love."

Since Bernard was pushing his lips forward along the cigar, making a face like the gargoyle on the church Darren had broken into last year and not found much except to smash, the response was barely audible. "He's in here, mam," Darren yelled.

"Sneaky sod," his mother said, not low enough, and yelled back, "Tell him to wait. I'm off upstairs."

"She says—"

"Shut it, lad. I'm not deaf, even if you are with those things forever stuck on your head."

Darren told himself he wasn't deaf either, though the world always seemed too quiet when he took off the Walkman. He heard his mother use the toilet in the bathroom, where the door had never shut properly since his father had kicked the bolt off to get to the toilet while Darren was in the shower. He heard his grandfather crying out feebly, "Who's that? They're getting in," and his mother shouting, "It's only me," then having to add "Marie" and "Phil's wife" and "Your son, you useless mong." The toilet flushed, and Darren heard her tapping her way rapidly to her room like two blind men, and then her different footsteps came downstairs. She'd exchanged her high heels for slippers, but was still wearing her short tight red dress and a faceful of makeup. "You look like you've been having a good time," Bernard said.

"You're joking, aren't you? They might as well have locked me up with Phil for all the fun I've had since they put him away."

"I reckon someone had some, any road. I hope you made yourself a good few bob."

"You wouldn't grudge me, would you, Bern? You promised Phil you'd see me right. You don't want him having to bother about that on top of everything else."

Bernard stared away the threat she intended him to hear and dealt the cigar a tap which made its gray head fall off into the ashtray. "Money short, is it, Marie? I don't see why with Phil having his board and lodging paid for him."

"You try running a house by yourself for a while. Maybe you don't realize the gas and the leccy and the rest of them send people like us the final demand when they've not sent the bill in the first place. We're down here and everyone else wants to keep us here with not enough to live on less we go begging to the social. I lie awake at night trying to figure where the money goes."

"I wonder," Bernard said, keeping his gaze on her while he converted half an inch of his cigar to smoke and ash. "So you'll be glad of owt that comes your direction, I reckon."

"Long as it's safe."

"The idea's meant to be you keep it that way. It better had be even with Phil gone," Bernard said, and Darren wondered whom his tone was intended to menace: maybe everyone outside the family. "The latest lot's in the back. Good job the lad was here to take care of us. Me and Barry will be round again once we've got the best deal."

"Darren can let you in if I'm not here."

"Don't you go keeping him off school all the time, Marie. Last thing we want is buggers snooping round any of our houses. Here, give us Phil's keys and I can let myself in whenever I need to."

"Da gave me them," Darren protested.

"Aye, well, he must have forgot to tell you to give them to me. Hand them over, lad, don't piss me about. Your mam'll just have to make sure she's here when you come home from school. My mam always was."

Darren dug a hand into his trousers and clenched his fist around the keys. They felt much solider to him than anything else in the room, and he held onto them until his mother cried, "Give them to your uncle when he tells you. Sometimes I don't know who he thinks he is, Bern. I'll belt him if he doesn't give you them, or you can."

She was trying to make Bernard think Darren did as she said so that he would have a better opinion of her. Darren stood up, his legs jerky with stiffness, and took his fist out of his pocket as he tramped toward Bernard, who withdrew the cigar from his mouth and raised the red-hot end toward him. Darren advanced until his fist was almost in Bernard's face and he could feel the heat stinging the back of his hand, then he opened his fist and let the keys fall on the seat between Bernard's legs. "That was close, lad," Bernard said as Darren backed away.

"When you boys have finished playing," Darren's mother said, and Bernard stared at her while he slowly let out smoke, never blinking. "So we'll see you when we see you," she said as though she hadn't made the previous remark.

Darren saw that Bernard sensed her willing him to leave. As the man replaced the cigar in his mouth so as to adjust his lapels once he'd taken his time about pushing himself to his feet, however, she said, "Are you giving me something to help me be a good mother?"

Bernard emitted a lingering puff that was only a smell by the time he produced his wallet and picked out some twenty-pound notes. "There may be more when we've shifted the merchandise," he said, then lowered the notes out of her reach. "Make sure you spend some of this on the lad."

"God's sake, Bernard, why do you think my hand's never out of my purse? Him and his clothes never being right for him and always wanting to go into town because he can't bear to stay in the house and find something to do. And mam, I want a Big Mac and mam, I want a computer I can play more games on and mam, I want another bike because whatever he gets he breaks. They won't give him a free lunch at school even with Phil where he is. When I was his age I had to make do with clothes other people had grown out of, and glad of it too."

"Those were the days right enough," Bernard said, observing her as she rubbed her arms and jigged her legs until her knees were in danger of banging together. "It's all this watching telly that's to blame for half of what's happening now, if you ask me. Making kids want the earth."

The handful of money was still dangling in front of his crotch. He raised that hand and used it to remove the cigar from his mouth and tap a lump of ash into the ashtray. "Try and keep this place and the lad up a bit more, Marie. Give Phil something to come home to."

"Promise," Darren's mother said, and watched as the hand returned the cigar to his mouth, and held the notes close to the hot end, and then extended them just far enough toward her that she had to take a step to reach them. She stuffed them between her breasts at once, and almost collided with him in the doorway from hurrying to open the front door for him. "Stay out of trouble," she called after him, and shut the door at once. "Nosy twat," she muttered as she almost ran to the back room. "Keep out of here, Darren. And don't you go talking about me to him."

She was in a hurry to get stoned, Darren knew, but the slam of the door made him feel as Barry and Bernard had affected him: shut out, unwanted, no good to anyone. They'd all be surprised. He went into the front room and switched on the television, though he didn't need to watch it to know what to do. If the court didn't let Dave and Ken off for defending themselves against the gunman, then Darren would take it out of the dead man's kid. Surely the Americans wouldn't go home until the trial was over. He knew whereabouts in Manchester they lived, and now he could find the kid's school. The television had shown him the uniform.

15

LIVING

Susanne was wakened by the sun. She was lying on her side of the double bed, her right arm stretched across the other half. The sun filled her closed eyes with light, and its warmth occupied the emptiness next to her. Her fingertips were remembering how they used to feel when she wakened in the night with Don beside her. They would sleepily trace his stomach, which had owned up to its age when he hadn't remembered to hold it in, and then they might trail down to his thigh, the backs of her fingers tingling as they brushed his hairy crotch, or work their way up his ribcage to splay themselves low on his chest. Sometimes he would place a drowsy hand over hers, and sometimes he would murmur incoherently; a few times he'd pronounced a distinct phrase like a code which would recall a dream, though he never remembered saying anything the next day. Once he'd murmured "Happy sky" and pressed her hand against his diaphragm, and for as long as Susanne lay there with her eyes closed she could hear and feel him—could believe he was somewhere. Then the light in her eyes began to go out, and she couldn't avoid noticing that the sheet between her outstretched arm and the mattress felt clammy and stale and crumpled and, instantly, meaningless. As she drew her hand toward her, her fingers closing on nothingness, she felt as though she was letting go of something which she'd failed to grasp and which might have needed her to make it exist. It was an illusion, she told herself, and if she let it remain in her head it would turn into yet another unbearable torment. She dug her fingers into the mattress and pushed herself up against the damp pillow. Her face rose out of the shaft of light between the curtains and grew cold and slack.

It was Saturday, and weekends were bad. At least on weekdays she had plenty to think about since she'd sent herself back to work when Marshall had insisted on going back to school. From dreading meeting anyone who didn't know what had happened to Don she'd progressed to dreading meeting anyone who did, but now she accepted that her colleagues and indeed her students would support her if she broke down, which she nearly had several times. She preferred them to counseling, several weeks of which she'd suffered after Marshall had rejected it outright. Even if it was designed to make her feel better eventually, it had made her feel worse for too long; ultimately it had enraged her almost beyond words that the counselor had taken every attempt she'd made to bring the sessions to an end politely, and then less politely, as evidence that she was really pleading for more. But she couldn't blame counseling for moments like this, when everything around her seemed to die another death: the balcony where she and Don had stood listening to the city on their first night in the house and then taken each other to bed; the twin white wardrobes standing blank-faced as though—she tried again to convince herself how absurd and banal and self-indulgent an idea this was—His and Hers signs had been erased from them; the leafy quilt and matching wallpaper she and Don had chosen together. She found herself thinking the leaves ought to wither, and then starting to watch them with eyes which felt both moist and charred, and that was enough. She pulled her legs from under the quilt and planted her feet on the uncaring carpet. The hem of her nightdress traced her thighs and her knees and the upper part of her calves like a loving hand as she stood up and padded to the door.

She'd left it ajar in case Marshall needed her during the night, though it had been more than a week since she'd heard him cry out while he was asleep. More than once she'd caught herself almost willing him to do so, because at least having to go to him would have distracted her from her agonized helpless thoughts. If he was sleeping soundly at night now, or at least giving her to understand that when she pussyfooted around the subject, then perhaps she needn't feel callous for occasionally doing so despite herself. She tiptoed across the landing and eased open his bedroom door.

He was lying with one ear to the pillow, his hair making the most of his inattention, both his hands outside the quilt and half closed as if they were readying themselves for a fight in a dream. Sharon Stone stood over the head of the bed, the foot of which was guarded by a chair laden with two days' worth of clothes. The only book of Marshall's which he hadn't managed to stuff into one of the shelves was propped within arm's reach against his radio cassette player. If he was able to read himself to sleep—if he enjoyed reading a book at all—surely that was a good sign. Susanne hugged herself and watched him, trying to borrow some of his peacefulness. Then his face moved in his sleep, and she gripped her upper arms until they ached, because he was smiling lopsidedly, exactly like Don. She stayed as the expression wavered, faded, retreated into him, some seconds after which she inched the door shut on his dream and closed herself into the bathroom.

For as long as it took her to hoist her nightdress and hang it on the door she was able to believe that the room hadn't changed significantly; then she remembered why she wished it had. Don's safety razor was still in the bathroom cabinet, because she couldn't bring herself to throw it away. She kept thinking Marshall might want it for his first razor, and would hate her if she didn't leave it for him. Or mightn't he think anything of the kind? It was one of the horde of questions she had yet to ask him. She saw herself in the sliding mirrors of the cabinet, her face which looked closer to the bone, her eyes on their way to being eclipsed by semicircles of darkness, her breasts which no longer had anyone to persuade them they didn't sag even slightly. Her eyes fixed her eyes, and she saw herself considering whether to take out Don's razor and gaze at it until her emotions erupted, just as she would open the wardrobe and gaze at his empty clothes. Instead she dragged herself out of the moment and climbing into the bath, turned on the shower.

The thin plastic curtain billowed at her, the watery tines raked her back as she stooped to open the hot tap further. British showers always felt enfeebled to her, yet this was making her flinch. As its temperature settled she raised her face into the spray. Though it was drenching her hair and drumming on her eyelids, it couldn't scour her voice out of her mind, the words she could only repeat whenever she thought of them, a litany of what she could have said—ought to have said. "You aren't leaving until you tell me what you haven't told me, Don. You aren't getting past me. I'll lock you in unless you tell me where you're really going. You can't leave our house." She ducked and turned the taps full on, and caught the water in her ears until she had to step back, shaking her head. Her left ear popped, then the right one cleared, and she heard Don's voice. "Hi, Susanne?"

The clammy curtain tried to mold itself to her as the water rumbled on the fiberglass of the bath. His voice had sounded real enough to be somewhere beyond the noise and the touch of plastic. Susanne strained her ears for a moment, then she shoved her face into the onslaught of water and rubbed shampoo into her hair, restraining herself from clawing at her scalp. She mustn't start hallucinating, or she would be no good to Marshall. Once she was out of the shower she would dry her hair, following which she could plan next week's teaching in more detail than she already had until Marshall awoke, at which point she would make breakfast for the two of them and find out what he wanted to do with his Saturday, maybe some activity which could involve them both.

She rinsed her hair and turned off the taps. Water trailed down her spine and over the fiberglass as she fought off the curtain and reached for a bath towel and set about rubbing her hair. She stepped onto the mat, and Don said, "We might like to stay in this country for good."

She swallowed a breath and felt her wet hair tugging at her scalp. A drop of water gathered on the upper curve of her left ear before running down to the lobe and falling to the mat with a minute plop. The voice had been lower, and outside the room. She let the towel drop to the floor and used both hands to turn the doorknob and edge the door open. As she did so she heard a muffled gabble of rewinding tape. The noise stopped and became Don's almost inaudible voice. "Hi, Susanne?" Then the cassette player was switched off with a click, and the door creaked as she tried to close it soundlessly so that Marshall wouldn't know she'd heard.

She finished drying herself and went into her bedroom to dress, pulling on faded panties because it no longer seemed to matter what underwear she wore, and jeans and a T-shirt before digging her feet into slippers. When she emerged onto the landing Marshall's door remained shut, and there was silence beyond it. She went down to the kitchen and readied the percolator, and listened to its hissing, a sound which for the moment she could substitute for thoughts. When she heard slow tentative footsteps on the stairs she gazed out at the lawn where a few dead leaves were trying to raise themselves to dance, only to sink back on the grass. She didn't turn when Marshall entered the kitchen; she had no idea how to react or how he would look. At last he said, "Mom?"

"There'll be coffee if you want some."

"Sure. Thanks. Mom?"

She had to turn round then. He was wearing his blue toweling robe, and looked as tousled as he had when she'd seen him asleep. His father's smile was tweaking the left side of his mouth. Though he was gazing a plea at her, she still didn't know what to say—not until he said, "Sorry."

"What do you have to be sorry for, Marshall?"

"For . . ." He raised a hand and lowered his head and waved the hand above it. "I put one of my blank tapes in the machine," he said instead of whatever he'd found himself incapable of saying. "You won't have lost any messages."

"I didn't think so."

She wanted to make it easier for him if she could only think how to, but the best she could produce was, "When did you swap them?"

"The," he said, and looked almost too ashamed to continue. "The same, same day. When you went to lie down."

"It's all right, honey. What's wrong with that?"

"I thought you'd think I should have . . ."

"What?"

"Waited."

"But then someone might have called and . . ." She knew what he meant, she just didn't want to feel it. "I don't blame you at all, I want you to know that. Don't be afraid to say anything you need to say to me. If we can't talk to each other after twelve years together, who can we talk to?"

She might have put it differently if she'd taken time to consider. She didn't know if it was some memory she'd roused which made him say, "Do you want to listen to the tape?"

"Not right now. Maybe . . ." She couldn't imagine listening to Don's last words to her unless she was alone, and perhaps not even then. "But you, you know, you keep it," she said, suddenly afraid of having implied some disapproval in spite of all she'd said.

The percolator was bubbling, diverting her attention to it, which was such a relief she felt herself go limp. She poured him a coffee while it was weak and let hers strengthen itself. That involved more waiting, and another awkward silence, which she was tempted to occupy with some manufactured cheerfulness. Then he said, "Mom?"

"Honey?"

"What's going to happen to Dad's shop?"

"I have to call someone about that."

"Who?"

"A couple of people. Booksellers who Don had some respect for. There's one who has a good reputation round the University."

"Will he keep the shop where it is?"

"She. She'll probably just buy the stock. I hear she has a pretty big place of her own." Susanne watched him dip his face into the steam from his mug and raise his head without having touched the drink. His eyes looked as if the steam had condensed at the corners. "I don't know what else we could do," she said. "Does it matter very much?"

"Do we have to sell the shop because we need the money?"

"We don't just yet. We may in time. I still don't see . . ."

"Couldn't we hire someone to run it for a while?"

"I don't know if there would be anyone who's qualified to do that who doesn't already have work. I mean, it's a possibility, but I'm not getting what the point would be."

"So we could keep it open till I'm old enough to leave school."

"Oh, honey . . ." Susanne experienced such a rush of affection and suppressed grief that she had to busy herself with the percolator. "I thought you wanted to be a librarian."

"I wasn't sure. It's not so different."

"Except they train you to be a librarian. I don't know who . . ." She pretended she hadn't said that, adding hastily, "I think it takes a lot more learning to sell rare books."

"Dad wrote the prices in them."

"I know he did, but once we'd sold those where would we be?"

"Couldn't we see if there's a bookselling course I could take?"

"Alongside your schoolwork? I honestly don't think that would work." She saw his face tighten as he searched for a way to prolong the discussion, and though the question sounded almost unforgivably stupid to her before she asked it, she didn't know how else to reach him. "Why is it so important to you?"

"I asked dad once."

"Asked him . . ."

"If I could help run the shop."

"And what did he say?"

"Yes."

"But you did, didn't you? Won't that be enough?"

"I just feel like when all the books are gone he will be."

Susanne put down her mug, because her fingers were turning red where they held it, and sat opposite Marshall and reached for his hand. "He was more than books though, wasn't he?"

"Sure." Marshall used his free hand to clear his forehead of hair, and knuckled his eyes so quickly that he might be able to believe she hadn't noticed. His other hand flattened itself under hers, and she thought he was about to pull it away, the better to withdraw into himself. She could tell he was remembering Don; maybe they could do that together even if they didn't speak. She was seeing the three of them on a boardwalk in the Everglades at dawn, Don holding Marshall's hand while the seven-year-old craned over the rail to watch a snake twice as thick as his arm and several times as long, when Marshall's hand under hers began to grow lumpy. "Mom?"

"I'm here."

"When they . . . you know, got him ready . . ."

She sensed how important this was to him, and was able to remind herself that he couldn't be seeing what she immediately saw, Don's face no longer resembling a face when she'd had to identify him by his clothes and his wedding ring. "Yes, Marshall, what?"

"They'd have brushed his hair, wouldn't they?"

"I'm certain they must have," Susanne said, trying not to imagine the process, bracing herself for any question Marshall was working toward asking. But his hand relaxed under hers, and he said, "I didn't mind not seeing him as much as granddad and grandmother Travis did."

"I'm glad." That seemed so inadequate that she felt compelled to say "I expect you can see him whenever you want to, can't you?"

"Sometimes." Marshall lowered his face to meet the mug he was raising, and drank, and kept his gaze on the table. All Susanne could see there was pine coated with sunlight, but she didn't like to interrupt whatever he might be seeing. She was thrown when he said, "Do you think they still mind we kept dad here?"

"I think it was mostly the traveling they minded."

"But they keep going on cruises."

"That's called retirement. You can see why they wouldn't like to have to cross the ocean every time they wanted to visit him. They were just trying to keep the family together."

"We're his family too, aren't we? And the last thing he said was he wanted to stay here."

"I know. That's why . . ." As well as that, she'd been unable to face the prospect of flying Don's broken body to America, of herself and Marshall being imprisoned in mid-air for all those hours while he lay among the baggage. "They'll keep sending flowers, they made an arrangement with a florist, but you can see how it isn't the same."

"Are they still mad at him?"

"If they'd been as mad as they made out they wouldn't have come to the funeral." There, she'd said one of the words she had thought she would never be able to force past her lips, and it felt as though it might prove to be the beginning of acceptance. "They're just old, Marshall. That's how people get to be sometimes."

Some didn't get the chance, she reflected, and perhaps he too was thinking that about his father. He turned his head slightly, suggesting that he was listening to the tape upstairs—remembering it, at any rate, because he said, "He meant us also."

"Meant us . . ."

"To stay. That's the very last thing he said, we should stay here for good."

She wondered if Marshall knew how deep he was digging in her—perhaps no deeper than in himself. "Is it what *you* want, honey?"

"I want to see what happens to the guys who killed him."

"What do you want to happen to them?"

"The worst."

She imagined the most violent films he'd watched projecting themselves on the screen of his imagination, and she couldn't blame him. "They don't execute people here, you realize."

"Then those guys ought to be locked up for as long as dad would have lived."

That seemed almost poetic, except that there was no poetry in the situation. "And after we find out what happens to them?"

"Still stay." He closed both hands around his mug, and she was put in mind of someone warming their hands at a very small fire on a very cold night. "How about you, mom? You haven't said."

"I'm with you for waiting for the outcome." She found that gave her thoughts a focus and directness which nothing else did—not the prospect of putting the house on the market, or searching for a post at another university, or packing the contents of the house again and shipping them back to America. All of that felt like running away, and if Marshall was determined not to do that, how could she? She gripped her hands together on the table, fingertips on knuckles, and gazed at him and managed to smile. "And then we can see if we're still of the same mind," she said, and kept to herself what she'd almost added, even though she believed it. "At least there's nothing else they can do to us."

16

LAW

Ladies and gentlemen of the jury, a man has been killed. That is an incontestable fact. Indeed, you have heard my clients admit responsibility for his death. You have heard them describe how they went to Mr. Travis's shop to exact some form of retribution for his having, as they put it, shopped their cousin to the police. You will recall that he did so because in the course of an altercation over driving their cousin threatened him with a gun—a criminal offense in this country, of course, even if the weapon is not meant to be used. That is especially the case if the weapon is unlicensed, even if it is claimed to be used in self-defense.

"You have heard my clients tell how, before they committed any act of violence against Mr. Travis, he produced a gun and threatened them with it. That description of the situation appears to be borne out by the testimony of Mr. Washington, the bus driver who called the police. You will remember that although he saw my clients doing violence to Mr. Travis, he felt it impossible to intervene because he thought he might put himself and his passengers at risk from the gun. You have heard that the police found it not to be loaded, but there is no question that Mr. Travis intended my clients to believe it was. On that basis you must ask yourselves to what extent they were entitled to consider their violence against him to be justified.

"You have heard them admit to the court that they overreacted, but nevertheless they insist that their intention was only to make sure Mr. Travis was incapable of using the gun. They say they were protecting each other in the only way available to them because nobody who was watching was prepared to help. It is a fundamental law of our land that any person has a right to defend himself. If you accept that my clients had reason to believe they were acting in self-defense, ladies and gentlemen of the jury, you must find them not guilty of the charge of murder."

He'd had to say all that, Susanne told herself: it was his job. If he'd met her eyes just once, would he have been able to do it? She hoped he'd avoided them out of embarrassment—that at least he didn't believe what he'd said. His clients had kept glancing in her direction, but they'd been looking at their family which had massed behind her in the public gallery, muttering like spectators at a game until she'd wondered what it would take for the judge to clear them out and relieve her of the sensation which felt like an incessant hot breath encasing the back of her head. The pair in the dock had looked confused and resentful, even betrayed, during much of their lawyer's summation, reactions which had given her some comfort. Maybe he'd got it as wrong as they appeared to think he had. Maybe the jury had been as alienated as Susanne by his speech.

They'd been out for several hours now, and she was sitting on a red plastic armchair in the high white hall outside the courtrooms. Whenever she shifted her weight the chair drew attention to her restlessness by creaking and panting and smacking its clammy plastic where it clung to the backs of her legs. Whenever the glass doors opened at the end of the hall she had to struggle not to remember the sight of Don and Marshall returning through them from the men's room—had to resist wishing to see them each time the doors parted, time having taken pity on her and rescinded everything that had happened since. If Don and Marshall hadn't testified against the gunman . . . if Don hadn't described him to the police . . . if Don hadn't attracted his attention in the first place . . . Turning away from the doors would bring her face to face with the Fancy family, and she wasn't going to be made to feel scared to keep her back to them. She wondered yet again if she could run out to the nearest sandwich shop, because what the British called a sandwich was the most she could imagine forcing down to guard against growing faint with the heat and the waiting and the babble of dislocated voices.

She slapped her knees and pushed herself to her feet. The chair wheezed and puffed out its plastic, and she had taken a step in the direction of the glass doors when all the reporters who'd been in the courtroom crowded toward her. What was the point of besieging her with questions now? She was preparing to dodge them as roughly as necessary when she realized they were heading not for her but for the courtroom. The robed clerk had opened the doors to indicate that the trial was about to reach its conclusion.

Susanne took a breath which felt like thin warm water going the wrong way. She was first through the doors into the empty courtroom, where at least a dozen microphones fished through the ceiling at the air. She took her place in the front row of the public gallery and heard spectators gather behind her with an oppressive rumbling like a storm cloud.

She sensed that the Fancy family was closer to her than the reporters were—she felt as though their eyes were almost touching her neck. Only their muttering, which seemed to be warning the future to do what they wanted, sounded more distant, and she was able to ignore their nearness as the jury trooped into the courtroom.

None of the seven men and five women looked at her, any more than they had througout the trial. She could make nothing of their expressions, which were as good as blank. The two rows of them performed their synchronized routine of filling the jury box, and then there was a silence broken only by the foreman clearing his throat with a sound like a model car failing to start and knuckling his mouth. This might almost have been a signal, because Susanne had counted only two of her uncomfortably palpable heartbeats when the men who'd killed Don were led into the room.

They were wearing suits and ties, as they had throughout the special occasion of the trial. Each of them had a uniformed policeman on his arm, and each raised his handcuffed wrists toward Susanne as he stepped into the dock. She saw from their faces, which seemed to grow momentarily even thinner and sharper, that the defiant gesture was meant for their family, not her. Nevertheless she felt as if a cold heavy object had trapped her lips. Then the court was told that it would rise, and did, and as the judge took his seat on the dais she rubbed her mouth until the sensation of it became more familiar.

The judge was a small squat man with disproportionately broad shoulders which thrust out at severe right angles from his thick neck. During much of the trial he'd seemed intent on the space bounded by his fingers interwoven on the desk in front of him as though in a silent prayer, except when he shot a disapproving look from beneath his wig and over his tethered spectacles at some statement or at any other sound in the courtroom. He'd intervened hardly at all, appearing to take everything he heard as no worse than he expected to hear. Now he nodded at the clerk, the movement shuttering the lenses of his spectacles with light, and she turned to the jury. "Will the foreman rise, please."

The man's fist found his mouth before he did so, but no cough. He bared his mustache and squared his shoulders and seemed about to tug at his lapels, but instead straightened his back as the clerk said, "Have you reached a verdict?"

"We have, your honor."

The convention of address made him visibly unsure whether to look at her or at the judge. He swung toward her as she spoke again. "Do you find the defendant David Francis Fancy guilty or not guilty of murder?"

The foreman opened his mouth and placed the knuckles of his right hand against it to muffle a couple of coughs. He'd been too eager to finish them. A further throat-clearing emerged ahead of his reply, so that Susanne couldn't be certain what he'd said. Seemingly the clerk was, because she said, "Is that the verdict of you all?"

"It is, your honor."

"Do you find the defendant Kenneth Leslie Fancy guilty or not guilty of murder?"

The foreman turned fully to the clerk again. "Not guilty."

He'd already said that once, and this time he said it too clearly for Susanne to be able to delude herself that he'd uttered only one word or to ignore the gleeful murmur of the family behind her. She felt her clenched fists and her legs shaking. "Is that the verdict of you all?" the clerk said, as though a denial could be any consolation.

"It is, your honor."

The judge's eyes appeared to flash like bulbs. His lenses had caught the light again as he leaned forward to beckon the clerk to him. He murmured briefly to her, and Susanne forced her hands to relax, though that admitted more of an ache to the dents her nails had dug in her palms. Perhaps he was refusing to accept the verdict—perhaps he could do that in England. The clerk returned to her position in front of the jury box and said, "Do you find the defendant David Francis Fancy guilty or not guilty of manslaughter?"

"Guilty."

That was the verdict of them all, and they all found Kenneth Leslie Fancy guilty too. Susanne felt as if the family behind her was leaning closer to her at each response, though perhaps it was only that their mutters of resentment were growing louder. The foreman sat down, looking relieved that his job was done, and the judge frowned over his spectacles at Susanne, so sharply that although she realized at once the warning was aimed at the people behind her, some of his disapproval seemed to settle on her. She pressed her knees together with her hands to keep them still and waited for him to speak.

He stared at the jury before turning to the men in the dock. Weary disgust weighed down his eyelids and the corners of his mouth and retarded the turning of his head, a disgust which Susanne was beginning to suspect he felt not only for the case but also for the courtroom, for his profession, for maybe the entire world. Certainly that was how his voice sounded to her as soon as he commenced speaking, the cold stabbing voice of a teacher who hated to teach. She closed her eyes so as not to see the light destroy his whenever he moved his head, only to discover that shutting out one of her senses made it harder to grasp what he was saying; clumps of words got stuck in her brain and shut out whatever he said next. ". . . this deplorable incident . . . all too representative of the growing violence on our streets . . . behavior made to seem acceptable by films and television . . . breakdown of law and order leads inevitably to anarchy . . . duty to rebuild the wall of law against the tide of violence . . . behavior which may be considered acceptable abroad will not be tolerated here . . . people taking the law into their own hands . . ."

Suddenly Susanne wondered how much of this was directed at her or at Don. She snapped her hot eyes open and saw the judge leaning forward between his hands, which were flattened on the desktop. He might as well have had no eyes. "David and Kenneth Fancy, I find you equally culpable in this matter. Whatever provocation you may consider yourselves to have received, you and your kind must be taught that you cannot bring the law of the jungle to this country. Each of you will serve a term in prison of not less than five years."

"Fucking hell," Kenneth Fancy said, and his partner in the dock agreed at once, stressing the second word. They seemed to Susanne not only to be articulating the mutters of protest behind her but also, although she loathed the notion, to be expressing her own outrage, as if they'd stolen her voice and substituted theirs. They continued to object, largely in the same words, as they were dragged away to the cells, kicking some of the courtroom furniture en route, but Susanne was hearing what Marshall had hoped the verdict would be. Five years wouldn't even have let Don see him reach maturity.

The court rose as the judge did, and she held onto the wooden barrier in front of the public gallery as the over-inflated balloon which the resolution of the trial had made of her brain threatened to leave her body to cope for itself. Her lips rubbed together as the judge turned his back on her, presenting her with the sight of the wig draped like a slice of a sheep over his head, and she might have said something aloud if she hadn't had to close her eyes and lean on the barrier to steady herself.

Sounds of the courtroom drained from her head, and a little of the nauseating heat did. When she looked around her she was alone except for a clerk who was approaching her. "Are you all right, miss?"

For a moment Susanne wondered how anyone could make such a cruel joke, and then she realized that the form of address was only a mistake. She pulled her left hand from beneath her right so that her wedding ring glinted dully, and held up that hand to tell him she didn't need his help. The diamond caught the light, which seemed to pierce her eyes and reach into the depths of her. She let go of the barrier and found she was still standing. Since she could stand, she could walk. But when she walked out of the courtroom, everyone who had been sitting behind her was waiting, and all of them stared straight at her.

The reporters were between her and the Fancy contingent, and at first that was some relief. Most of the family, the women in particular, looked ready to go for her; only the eldest, a man with a fat dead cigar poking out of his mouth, was holding them back. He gave her the impression of a teacher barely managing to control a classful of delinquents—at least, that was her sense of him until she saw the naked hatred he was focusing on her. Then the reporters converged on her, veterans and youthful ones alike looking as though they were auditioning for the same role, chorusing for her attention. "Mrs. Travis, what do you—" "Mrs. Travis, will you be—" "What is your—" "How do you—" A lanky pale young woman with microscopic silver barbells in her earlobes and a great deal of red hair caught Susanne with her question. "Mrs. Travis, are you happy with the court's decision?"

Susanne experienced such a rush of disgust that she felt as though more than words might spill out of her mouth. "I've seen better verdicts in bad movies."

"What do you think it should have been?"

"Don't ask. You wouldn't want to print it, or at any rate I hope you wouldn't. You British aren't supposed to go in for that stuff."

"You'd be—" the redhead began, but a man in a stubbly tweed hat interposed his question. "Will you be taking it further, Mrs. Travis?"

"Such as where?"

"The High Court has been known to overturn Crown Court decisions, though of course it could go either way."

"You're saying some judge could let those, those I can't think of a word, out of jail before they've even done five years?"

"I'm not saying that would happen, just that it's possible. I'm not saying it's likely."

"It shouldn't be possible. I used to think we were too hard on our criminals in Florida, but right now I wish I could send those two over there. Back there we call murderers murderers." Maybe she oughtn't to be speaking so freely to the press, but she was distracted before she quite knew why what she had noticed should matter. "Where did they go?"

Most of the reporters looked over their shoulders. "Who, the—" said the redhead. "Oh, *them.*"

She was dismissing the Fancy family as if they no longer mattered, but Susanne was afraid they did. Where had they taken their hatred? Marshall wouldn't be out of school for almost an hour, and she could think of no way they would be able to discover which school that was, but just suppose they did? "Excuse me now, you'll have to excuse me," she said, and had to walk at the reporters to make them let her through.

If the pay phone in the lobby had ever possessed a directory, that had been either stolen or removed so that it couldn't be. She had her address book in her purse, and by the time she reached the phone she'd found the number of the school. The public address system called for a policeman as she fed the coin box and poked the numbers on the keyboard. The receiver at her ear rang twice, and was halfway through a repetition when it was interrupted, and the digital payment display reverted to zero. "Bushy Boys," a woman announced as if challenging whoever heard her to laugh.

"That's Bushy Road School, right. Could I—I should say, I'm just checking one of your boys is there."

"Who would that be?"

"Marshall Travis in the eighth grade, year, I mean. Right now he should be in his Bible, scripture," Susanne said, raising her voice to be heard above another summons to the policeman, "religious education class."

"Then I expect he is, madam. May I ask where you're calling from?"

"Who I am, you mean? I'm his mother. Susanne Travis. Didn't we meet once? You're the girl with the big wooden earrings, yes?"

"We've no girls at Bushy Road. Where are you exactly?"

"At the courts."

"Of course, you would be. Sorry. How did it turn out? Is it over?"

"If it isn't, if . . ." Susanne stared at the zero composed of fragments which seemed about to crumble into the fog of the display. "Yes, it's over. Anyway, you're certain Marshall's there."

"I've no reason to suppose he's not," the secretary said, sounding a little rebuffed. "Was that why you called, or was there a message?"

"No, don't tell him anything," Susanne said so hastily that she almost forgot why she'd called in the first place. "No, wait, why don't you tell him, tell him if by any chance I'm not there when he comes out of school to stay there till I pick him up."

That seemed to cover the situation, and so she thanked the secretary and hurried out into the sunlight, which was far too bright and warm for the way she felt. More reporters crowded toward her, photographers fired at her with their cameras, but she showed them her tight lips as she shoved between them and ran along a street called Dolefield to the car park. She couldn't help realizing how easy it would be for someone to pretend to be her on the phone: they would only need to sound sufficiently American to convince the school secretary, who hadn't asked her to prove who she was. Marshall was too sensible to be in danger from anyone like that—he would want more proof than the secretary had. But as Susanne hurried past shoppers loading purchases into their cars and unlocked her right-hand door, she was seized by apprehension. She wasn't going to him only to reassure herself that he was safe. Sooner or later she would have to tell him what the judge had said.

17

FAME

In the morning Marshall drank his juice and ate his cereal until his mother went out of the kitchen. He didn't feel nauseous, he might even be hungry, but lifting the glass or the spoon to his mouth seemed to call for more effort than he could sell to himself. He trod stealthily on the pedal so as to tip the remains of the cereal into the bin and threw in a length of paper towel to conceal the evidence. Since his mother was still drawing the curtains in the rooms downstairs, he eased the refrigerator open and lifted the carton of juice out of the shelf in the door and emptied his glass into the gaping cardboard beak. He was holding the carton when his mother emerged from the front room and caught sight of him. "Is that dead? Didn't I put another one in the fridge?"

"There's some left, mom. I'm fine, I've had enough," Marshall said, and almost threw the carton in the trash, having confused himself into forgetting what he'd claimed on its behalf. He shut it in the refrigerator and hurried upstairs as his mother brought in the bottle of milk which had been left on the doorstep. He brushed his teeth and threw a handful of water into his eyes and kneaded his face with both hands through a towel, and felt as much like going to school as he was likely to feel. He grabbed his bag from next to his bed and checked that he'd loaded it with all the books he needed on a Friday, and glanced into his parents' bedroom as he headed for the stairs. The pang which he experienced at the thought of not having to say goodbye to two people no longer felt quite so much as though someone was fishing in his guts. "I'll see you tonight, mom," he called.

She came quickly out of the front room, holding a textbook. "Nearly the weekend. Think of something you'd like to do, that maybe we can both do if you like."

"Sure."

"Anything you need right now? I won't know if you don't ask."

"I'm fine, mom, really. Don't worry about me."

"I'll do my best," she said, resting her hands on his shoulders while she planted a kiss on his forehead. For as long as that lasted he couldn't see her eyes, and wondered if she was being reminded of kissing his father. His father's smile tugged at his mouth as her eyes met his again, and he turned away awkwardly, nearly sweeping the answering machine off the hall table as he hefted the strap of his bag onto his shoulder. He blundered out of the front door and along the path through the scent of lavender, and waved to her from beyond the gate. "Be good," she called as if to help him pretend life had returned to normal.

An electric cart was murmuring along the road, slow as a hearse. It stopped with a rattle of bottles whenever the driver arrived at a house where he delivered milk, and Marshall's thoughts matched its speed and intermittence. Did he still want to live here now that the men who'd killed his father were going to jail? Did he maybe want to stay until they were released and see what happened then? He imagined convicts bigger and nastier than they were taking a dislike to them or, better yet, taking a liking they didn't want to be taken, then had to fight to clear his mind of screams and naked hairy struggling flesh.

The sight of the main road, its sidewalks crowded with boys uniformed like him, seemed to help. Some were bound to have heard the verdict, and he wanted to be prepared for whatever they might say, probably things he'd said over and over to himself last night until at last he'd managed to fall asleep. He couldn't see anyone he knew to speak to as he reached the traffic lights by Bushy Road just as the green men gave a last flicker before glaring red. Having thumbed the button to let it know he was there, he glanced around in case any of his friends were nearby, and was confronted by a four-legged placard outside the newspaper shop. VIDEO NASTY PROF SLAMS BRITISH JUSTICE, it said.

For as long as the men on the poles blazed red as branding irons Marshall tried to believe that the description couldn't refer to his mother, or that if it did indeed mean her it didn't matter. The men turned green and mimed hurrying across the road and drilled their mechanical chirping into Marshall's head, and the boy wavered, then shoved through a group of his schoolfellows to march into the shop.

The Indian shopkeeper and his daughter were fully occupied in selling children sweets, or rather the sweets the children decided on second thoughts they wanted or maybe not those either after all. Marshall was able to ease the tabloid from beneath the other newspapers on the counter, far enough for the whole of the front page to be legible. SEND KILLERS TO FLORIDA, SAYS WIDOW. Kenneth Fancy, 23, and David Fancy, 22, were sentenced at Manchester Crown Court yesterday . . . five years each for manslaughter . . . Widow Susanne Travis, a film teacher whose house was raided in Operation Nasty, expressed her outrage at the verdict. "They murdered my husband. It's like a bad movie. If they'd done it in Florida they'd be sent to the gas chamber. I've no faith in British justice anymore."

The tabloid swung away from Marshall as the shopkeeper's daughter looked for the price. "That's thirty pence, lad."

"It isn't worth one pee," Marshall told her, and made for the street before he could vent his anger on her or on the pile of junk about his mother, who could never have sounded like that—like a character in a bad movie. The men on the poles were raw again, so that Marshall had to linger outside the shop. As the crossing released the next waves of pedestrians he stooped and tore the notice off the placard. Several people frowned at him, one woman uttered a breath which quivered her blubbery lips before she plodded vengefully at him, but he dashed across the road, crumpling the notice in his hand.

Once he was part of the uniformed crowd he looked back. Nobody appeared to be following him along the side street, but he wasn't about to care if anyone did. He shoved the notice into his pocket for lack of a bin as he came alongside the schoolyard. Tom and Ali were sharing a joke near the bicycle sheds, Trevor was huddled in a corner with a group of boys around a magazine that was hanging out the tongue of its centerfold, but Marshall didn't want to join them or any of his other friends in case they'd seen the tabloid or, worse, the notices which must be on display wherever the tabloid was sold. He avoided them and looking at anybody else until the bell shrilled at everyone to stand in line, and then he had an excuse not to talk.

In the assembly hall there were Mr. Harbottle's amateur theatricals to distract him, except that the thought of all those notices about his mother infesting the city took over his head. All at once the headmaster's performance was over, and the clatter of folding seats brought Marshall's surroundings back to him, the muggy heat randomly jabbed by the chill from a few open windows, the smells of floor polish and uniforms and feet. The thought still clung to his mind, and loomed between him and his work until he could hardly grasp what he was straining to write, so that when the endless leaden morning was interrupted by a summons to the headmaster, that was almost a relief.

Almost—until he remembered the headmaster sending for him to tell him eventually that his father had called. Wooden tiles stirred beneath his feet as he trudged along the corridor, a whistle sounded on the playing field behind the school as if someone was summoning the police. As he came in sight of the office he poked at the corners of his eyes and dragged his fingertips over any trails that might have appeared on his cheeks. The secretary was patting her bluish curls while holding up a hand mirror; perhaps it was because he'd glimpsed her preening that she gave him an unwelcoming look. "I know you, you're Travis," she said in a tone which could have borne any of several meanings, none of which appealed to Marshall, and darted to the inner door to rap on it. "Travis, Headmaster."

"Yes."

The word was giving nothing else away. The secretary opened the door so fast that Marshall imagined the headmaster unable to dodge it in time and toppling like a skittle. He sidled into the office before the secretary could propel him in. Mr. Harbottle was seated behind his wide desk, his hands resting on the miniature green field of a blotter. He flicked up his right forefinger. "Close the door, Travis."

Marshall took his time, because half a grin was refusing to let go of his mouth. He managed to think of something else besides a skittle with a balding head—the last time he'd been in the office—and felt his mouth tremble instead. "Yes, Travis, is there some hindrance?" the headmaster said.

"No, sir," Marshall said, and turned, to be distracted by a pinkish glimmer in one of the plaques on the wall behind the desk. He tried to fasten his attention on Mr. Harbottle as the man presented his fists sphinx-like to him. "Very well, Travis. Is there anything you wish to say?"

"Like what, sir?"

"Anything you may consider appropriate."

The headmaster opened his hands on the desk and tilted them so that the palms were visible. The glimmer in the plaque shifted, and Marshall saw it was the reflection of the headmaster's shiny pate. "Uh, I guess, I don't believe so, sir."

"I'm sorry to hear that, Travis."

The reflection looked like the ghost of a skittle tipping backward and righting itself, Marshall saw as the headmaster's gaze rested heavily on him. "Do you see some cause for amusement, Travis?"

"No, sir," Marshall said, and rearranged his expression as best he could. "Only I'm not sure what you want me to say. I don't know why you sent for me."

"If that is indeed the case I find it doubly unfortunate." The headmaster changed his tone to incredulity, which he appeared to think was generous of him. "Are you genuinely unable to call anything to mind?"

"Is it about what they did to those two guys, sir?"

"Which two, which two persons?"

Marshall felt entitled to sound incredulous himself. "The guys who killed my dad."

"Ah, I see. Yes, of course." The headmaster touched his forehead and reached beneath the desk before fingering both ends of his collarbone, then rested his fingers on an envelope in the exact center of the blotter. "A very bad business. Deplorable in many ways. I hope it was made clear to you at assembly how much sympathy was felt."

"Sure," Marshall said, though he remembered having felt surrounded by as much embarrassment as outrage when the headmaster had talked about his father's death.

"But you have certainly been present at assembly when I have had occasion to reiterate the principles of the school. I trust you will acknowledge that is the case."

"I guess. I mean, yes, sir."

Mr. Harbottle relinquished one line of his frown. "No guessing need be involved. You will have heard me say more than once that there is behavior which Bushy Road will not tolerate, no matter what the circumstances."

"Three times, sir, I think."

Marshall's attempt to be precise went down less than well. "And yet you would have me believe you are in some doubt as to my reason for having you in."

Wasn't having you in a British term for playing a joke on you? No, that was having you on. "Yes, sir, because I don't," Marshall protested. "I mean, I still haven't figured it out."

"It grieves me to hear you say so," Mr. Harbottle said in a tone which promised Marshall the grief. "Not fifteen minutes ago I had the regrettable duty of speaking to a Mr. . . ." He bent his head to read his scribble on a pad, and the blurred skittle fell and immediately righted itself. "A Mr. Bandapaddhay who had occasion to complain about the behavior of a boy from this school. Given his description and the particulars of the incident, I think there can be no question as to the identity of the boy responsible."

"I don't know anyone called what you said, sir. I mean, if I do I didn't know that was what they were called, and I truly don't think I've done anything—"

"Are you deliberately setting out to try my patience, Travis?"

"No, sir."

Mr. Harbottle examined that answer for concealed impertinence, raising his chin so that the skittle teetered. "Then I can only assume you are deluding yourself that you performed your act of vandalism unnoticed. A very stupid view to take, and not one I would have looked for in a boy of your previous caliber."

"Vandalism, sir?"

"Vandalism. Or has the word fallen out of fashion where you come from?"

"Sure we had vandalism, but I never did any of it. Sir."

"Then get it into your head that it is wholly unacceptable here, whatever reason you may have considered yourself to have."

By now Marshall had grasped what they were supposed to be discussing, but not how to acknowledge that without admitting guilt. "If it's about the notice, sir . . ."

"Ah, so you're not entirely unaware of your own actions after all."

"It was insulting my mom."

The skittle wobbled as the headmaster opened and closed his mouth before speaking. "Granted that the language used to sell some newspapers may err in the direction of simplicity, I must say I encountered the notice in several locations and saw nothing contrary to the truth."

Anger and hilarity at the antics of the skittle were fighting for control of Marshall's mouth. "The paper made my mom say stuff she wouldn't ever have said."

"In that case she should take it up with the editor, although one might then feel bound to query whether she is quite so enthusiastic about freedom of expression as she would have us think. But inaccurate reporting is no excuse for anarchic behavior, Travis, for hooliganism."

He gazed at Marshall, apparently inviting a reply, but Marshall hadn't a word in his head, nothing that would let him shape his mouth. The headmaster picked up the envelope as though Marshall was presuming on his patience. "Please hand this to your mother when you go home."

"What is it, sir?"

The headmaster narrowed his eyes and pushed out his lips. That might have been the whole of the response he felt Marshall was entitled to, except that he then said, "It will invite her to make an appointment to discuss your behavior."

He stood up to thrust the envelope at Marshall, who saw the skittle spring upward as though the mechanism of a bowling alley had had enough of it. He pressed his lips against his teeth with one hand as he took the envelope with the other, but a snort escaped through his nose. Mr. Harbottle glared at him. "I warn you not to take this lightly, Travis."

Marshall rubbed his lips hard and lowered his hand and succeeded in mumbling, "I'm not, sir."

"I rather think you may be persisting in the belief that your action was in some way justified. A very dangerous attitude, and one that will not be tolerated at this school." The headmaster seemed to think he'd asked or at least implied a question, because he raised his eyebrows and prolonged his stare at Marshall. At last he said, "Perhaps you should remind yourself that the men responsible for your tragedy appear to have felt justified too. If they hadn't had the excuse of defending themselves they might not have gone so far."

The envelope in Marshall's hand was cold and thin and hostile. He could twist it like a neck, he thought, or rip it like a face, except that it belonged to his mother, and he wouldn't destroy anything of hers. "Yes, Travis?" said the headmaster. "Is there something you wish to say?"

There was, but Marshall's gritted teeth were shredding it. He moved the burden of his head from side to side until Mr. Harbottle said, "Please make certain that you—"

The lunchtime bell cut through his voice. He was reminding Marshall to deliver the letter. Perhaps he felt he'd broken some rule of his own by referring as he had to Marshall's father; he let Marshall turn his back and walk out of the office without responding. Marshall shoved the letter into his blazer and kept walking, through the flood of boys that was being swollen by each classroom, out of the school and across the crowded yard and through the gates.

The master whose turn it was to police the yard was busy interrogating two boys as to why they wanted to return to the building. He didn't observe Marshall escaping without a lunchtime permit, not that Marshall would have cared if the teacher had. Tom and Ali and Trevor had noticed, but Marshall looked away from them. As he reached the sidewalk Marshall knew where he was going—where he might be able to release the emotions which were knotting themselves into a hard heavy lump in his guts.

He glanced back as he arrived at the main road. Nobody was following him except a boy of his own age a good distance away, who would have been in uniform if he was from the school. A few older boys outside the shops were wearing the uniform, but they couldn't know that Marshall wasn't supposed to go home for lunch. Once he'd left them behind he stared straight ahead, hearing his footsteps become part of his surroundings along with the large aloof houses and the rush of traffic. After a mile or so he dodged into a side street guarded by a bus shelter whose glass had been shattered into an unmelting hailstorm on the sidewalk.

He hadn't located the church spire when the street frayed into three streets which veered away haphazardly, narrowing the sky. A van that sounded rusty headed left past him, jouncing over a roadway patched with tar, and his instincts led him after it, past parked cars with selling prices handwritten on bits of cardboard inside their rear windows, and houses that left little room for the meager sidewalks, and walls sprayed with graffiti such as ROB THE RICH NOT THE POOR in letters bigger than his head. All the downstairs rooms he glanced into reminded him of storerooms, cluttered with stuff which soaked up too much of the light, but in more than one room he saw figures crouched over some kind of work, presumably the only way they had to make the next best thing to a living. Apart from them the sole signs of life in the whole of that street were gunshots which paced him intermittently for several hundred yards, accompanied by so many ricochets that he could tell they were in a Western on half a dozen televisions. The shooting ceased as the street divided, extending one half of itself toward a crossroads boxed in by more houses and the other between fewer of them, its stump of potholed roadway ending at a gate beyond which a bunch of red figures pelted by, yelling at one another. They were footballers, and Marshall remembered seeing such a field over the hedge at the funeral. Before he reached the gate he saw the church beyond the hedge at the opposite side of the field.

He walked around the outside of the field in case there wasn't a gap in the hedge that would admit him to the churchyard. Houses flapped washing above their back fences at him as he followed a cramped path worn down to bare earth between knee-high grass and weeds blossoming with varieties of litter. Ever since passing through the school gates he'd felt as though he was being followed, but the only other person on the path was a boy whose head was carrying a pair of earphones along the hedge toward the last corner Marshall had turned. The sunlight was gathering in the black material of Marshall's blazer and weighing his shoulders down, the narrowness of the path pressed the heat and the unruly greenery against him, but he didn't mind how far he was being forced to walk when it would bring him to his father.

The end of the path was blocked by a supermarket trolley which someone had almost succeeded in bending in half. Marshall lifted it out of the way and walked alongside a high wall holding back a mob of houses, to the gates in the shape of halves of an arch. A wide path wearing a thin coat of moss led him between them and past a silent church.

A fallen ornamental urn lay like an unexploded bomb among the pockmarked monuments. A band of tipsy crosses turning green surrounded a statue of Christ which had sprawled on its back, one hand raised from chest level as though beckoning to passersby to assist it to its feet. The red footballers beyond the hedge had been doubled by players dressed in green, but because of the distance the running clump of them was smaller than ever. The diminution of their shouts struck Marshall as respectful. He was remembering the funeral, to which he and his mother had been accompanied by his father's parents and by everyone from the party except the crime novelist and her husband, and by other people he'd never met before. He'd felt slowed down by the crowd, and unable to release his feelings, but now he was walking slowly because it seemed right and because he was thinking what to say to his father.

"Dad, I've come without mom this time because I wanted to talk. Maybe I can tell you stuff I'd rather not say to her, you know, stuff we'd rather not worry her with. I don't know if you can talk to me. I'll understand if you can't . . ." He was murmuring to himself as he walked the length of an impenetrable rank of bushes which separated the old graves from the new. Maybe he would have to say it all again, but it didn't matter. He came to the end of the bushes, whose foliage was such a dark green it looked shadowed by the open sky, and saw the field of white headstones. He knew exactly where his father's was, and opened his mouth to greet it. But all the memorials were lying on their backs except for his father's stone, which wasn't there at all.

His legs jerked him toward the spot where it should be. He was moving so uncontrollably that he couldn't avoid treading on a beer can, several of which were scattered among the toppled headstones. He heard the metal beginning to uncrumple itself as he stumbled to the row where the newest graves were. His father's memorial had been smashed against another, leaving bits of words on chunks of marble littering the turf. ALD TRAV HUSB FATH MUCH LOV. Worse still, some of the mounds had been kicked apart. One was his father's, which smelled of urine.

"Dad, I'm sorry," he mumbled. "Look what they did." Surely it didn't matter that his words couldn't force open his lips, which felt as swollen as his eyes were growing. "You're okay, though, aren't you? I mean, you're still there?"

A raucous cheer went up from the football field and vanished into the indifferent sky. Marshall thought of the urine seeping down through the earth to his father, and then couldn't bear to think of it. What he was imagining could never have taken place, which had to mean his father wasn't there. He wasn't anywhere. Marshall turned away from the destroyed grave and began to walk very fast toward the other exit from the graveyard, as if he might outrun the memory of what he'd just seen. That route led home eventually, but he didn't know where he was going: certainly not back to the school. Perhaps he would never go back.

18

NOT THERE

Susanne thought she was addressing the question of how to communicate the banality of violence. If she didn't teach the course she had undertaken to teach she would be letting her students down. She'd found she couldn't use commercial movies, at least not yet; the violence in them seemed too cartoonish and stylized—too much of a betrayal of the reality she knew. Even films by Godard and Bergman had struck her as playing at violence, and so she'd borrowed documentaries from Bea in Modern History. Now she was showing footage of riots in Africa: no stunts, no exaggerated sound effects or dramatic makeup, no excitement or even audience involvement with events which had already and unalterably taken place, just the dull squalid spectacle of people injuring one another, unceremoniously falling down when shot or trying to protect themselves from blows with parts of themselves that would only break. Captions ran along the bottom of the screen, and a commentator's voice described the political context in greater detail, but the words were irrelevant to the dismal fascination of the images. This was how life was, this was how people always would be. The film repeated a scene of a man covering his head with his hands as he was clubbed to his knees, this time in slow motion, and then the credits began to crawl off an otherwise blank screen. Susanne watched them all, then sent the tape forward and waited until it rewound to zero, and switched it off, and stood up to face the dozens of students who were gazing at her—somewhat warily, she thought—from their folding chairs lined up across the square white almost featureless room. "Depressing, wasn't it? Not the kind of thing to watch if you're feeling suicidal, right? But that's the way violence should be, on film, I mean. That's what it's like, grubby and mindless and pointless."

She hadn't planned to say any of that when she'd stood up. It was her way of approaching her theme, she told herself. "I'm not saying every film should be like that. Realism in fiction's a convention like any other, we've talked about that, haven't we? Yes. But I'm coming around to wondering how much we should expect anyone who makes a movie to be true to their own experience, which maybe should include watching the kind of material we've just watched . . ." She sensed herself drifting off her chosen theme again, and brought her mind back to it and talked for a while, though she had an odd sensation of not really hearing herself. "Listen, that's enough from me," she said abruptly. "Anybody any thoughts?"

Her students shifted, trying to be unobtrusive. Some of them uncrossed their legs, their bare knees hiding to some extent in holes in their jeans. The class wasn't usually so hard to rouse; what could she say to enliven them? Even Liu was gazing at her hands, crossed in the lap of her ankle-length black dress. She glanced up, and then around her, and parted her lips, but that was all. "Yes, Liu?" Susanne prompted. "You were going to say?"

"Sus—Mrs. Travis?"

"Susanne is fine, but Suse is out," Susanne said, meaning to help. "Sure, go ahead."

"I was only . . ." Liu glanced at her neighbors again. "Well, I only thought that if, let's see, you might want us to, I don't know, watch films by ourselves for a while and write about them, we could."

"Why should I want that, Liu?"

"Well, certainly, if you don't, of course . . ." When Susanne continued gazing at her, unsure if she'd finished, Liu had another try. "It was only an idea, but if you'd rather not watch them . . ."

"Because it makes you feel uncomfortable, you mean?"

"No, it isn't that. That doesn't bother, well, any of us, I shouldn't think."

"I wouldn't say that from your faces. Are you going to let Liu do all the talking? If I've been embarrassing you I'd rather you let me know."

That made most of them look anywhere except at her. "Okay, come on," she said with a roughness that was intended to demonstrate they needn't be reticent. "I know you didn't sign up for me to put you on the spot like this, or to listen to me going through therapy either. I'll try to do my job better if you'll allow me the occasional rant, is that a deal?"

There was an outbreak of uneasy surreptitious movements after which most of the students nodded in agreement—encouragement, even. "We weren't embarrassed," Liu said. "We were just worried about you."

"You've been doing fine," said Pik, the solitary white of the African students. "My father didn't do half so well when the bomb, when we lost my mother."

"You needn't try so hard for us unless you have to for yourself," Rachel said.

Susanne felt her own silence filling her throat. For the moment she was too emotional to speak, especially now she'd belatedly noticed that Liu had been wearing black for weeks. The knock at the door couldn't have been more welcome, and nearly everyone turned gratefully toward it as Alice, the departmental secretary, let herself in. "There's a call for you, Susanne."

"Who is it, do you know?"

"It's from the school."

Susanne experienced a twinge of nervousness which seemed more automatic than meaningful. "What about?"

"She didn't say. The secretary, that is. She'd like you to call her back."

"Do you mind if I call her now?" Susanne said to the class. "I'm sure it can't be anything much, but . . ." They were smiling and shaking their heads and holding out their hands like steppingstones for her. "Thanks for being you," she told them. "See if you can tell me something I don't know about the movie we watched when I get back."

There really was no reason for her to hurry, and so she didn't, not much. It wasn't like the day of the verdict, when she'd felt compelled to race to Marshall, only to realize belatedly that he wouldn't have wanted his friends to see his mother picking him up from school at his age, never mind telling him what she had to tell him. She unlocked her office at the end of the corridor and went to her desk in the room full of books. She glanced at the topmost page of the pile of essays she had to grade, and then she dialed the school. Hurrying herself into a nervous state was one thing, but deliberately taking her time in order to reassure herself there was no urgency didn't quite work. As the phone at the school began to ring she made her hand relax on the scrawny plastic neck of the receiver. This time the secretary allowed the ringing several repetitions before she put a stop to it. "Bushy Boys?"

"Hi, it's Susanne Travis. Marshall's mother."

"Oh yes, Head wanted you to call. He's rather busy at the moment, I'm afraid. Will you hold on for a few minutes, or shall I ask him to ring you when he's free?"

"Can't I have just a quick word? I'm in the middle of teaching a class."

"Teaching." That seemed to alter the situation in Susanne's favor, until the secretary said, "Oh, you mean *students,*" as if she'd been tricked. "I think you're best off waiting till he calls you. He's got some parents in at the present."

"Can you tell me what the problem is at least?"

"I've just told you." After a pause the secretary said, "I get you," and then was silent for too many seconds. "I think that's for Head to say," she said at last.

This time Susanne couldn't relax her grip on the fragile plastic. "Either tell me yourself or put me through to him. You're a mother, aren't you? Even if you aren't you must know how I'm feeling right now."

"The thing is, Mrs. Travis, Marshall . . ." Susanne thought the secretary had decided once again that it wasn't her place to give out the information, until she said, "Bear with me one moment. I think Head's nearly free."

The pause lasted considerably longer than one moment, and was almost more than Susanne could bear. Even when the secretary said, "Putting you through now," that was followed by nothing but static. Suddenly afraid that someone would think she wasn't there and cut her off, Susanne started parroting, "Hello? Hello?" Most of the static ceased, and she heard a man saying, "Thank you for coming in. I wish all our parents were as involved." The hollowness which must have been contained by his hand cupped over the mouthpiece made way for his voice. "Mrs. Travis? Dennis Harbottle here."

"You wanted me to call you about Marshall."

"Thank you for responding so promptly. Mrs. Travis, are you aware of his whereabouts?"

Susanne consulted her watch, having disentangled the strap from the thread which held the button on the cuff of her blouse. It was quarter past three, which meant that school still had twenty-five minutes to run. "Isn't he with you? At school, that's to say?"

"I am very much afraid not. It appears he has not been seen here since the end of the morning session."

Susanne had been standing in an awkward posture which she was scarcely aware of having frozen into, and now she hardly sensed her body lowering itself onto the chair behind the desk. "Did someone—" The idea was so terrible she had to force it out of her mouth. "Did someone take him away?"

"A relative, do you mean?"

"Not a relative, no. We've no relatives in Britain. Someone. Anyone up to no good."

"I think not, Mrs. Travis. I rather fear that Travis was operating under his own steam."

"You're saying he wasn't with anyone."

"I believe those were my words, yes," the headmaster said in a tone which made it clear she wasn't supposed to question his usage. "I have ascertained that Travis was seen by several of his friends leaving the school premises without authorization at the start of the lunch period. Would I be correct in assuming you had not provided him with a letter?"

"Saying he needed to leave, you mean? He'd have handed it in if I had. Are you telling me it's been three hours since he went missing?"

"The teacher who took his first class of the afternoon is only with us for the week, and I regret that Travis's classmates neglected to point out the absence. I assure you they will be dealt with appropriately."

"Their fault, huh," Susanne muttered, and raised her voice. "Did anyone ask them if they know why Marshall did what he did?"

"I think I may have the answer to that, Mrs. Travis. Shortly before he was last seen I had occasion to reprimand Travis. He was to take you my letter inviting you in to discuss his behavior. From his attitude during the interview I would conclude that he may be seeking to avoid doing so."

Last seen at the school, the headmaster meant, she told herself. "What behavior? What are you saying he did?"

"I have to inform you that a member of my staff saw Travis damaging a newsagent's display."

"That doesn't sound like Marshall. What kind of a display?"

"I should hope that as a parent you would agree with me that is irrelevant, Mrs. Travis."

"If it's relevant to why he isn't there I don't agree at all. Did you find out what kind of a display it was?"

"I rather think it referred to the verdict in your most unfortunate court case and your reaction to it."

"Oh, those graffiti, right. I saw them on my way to work. I was hoping Marshall wouldn't come across any of them." Susanne took hold of the receiver with both hands so as to haul it away from her right ear, which had begun to ache with the pressure against it, to the other. "You do realize it would have upset him. It's one more reminder of what those, of what happened to his father."

"Whatever my personal feelings, Mrs. Travis, without rules of behavior not only the school but our whole society would collapse. If I may permit myself an observation—"

"Stop a minute. There's something I don't follow. I'm sure Marshall was upset, and maybe he felt you should have taken that into account, but he'd have come home and told me about it tonight, he wouldn't have run away from that. Was there anything you said to him?"

"Nothing, I assure you, that could justify his leaving here without permission."

"Maybe not justify, but did you say anything to make him?"

She heard a dry sound which might have been the headmaster considering whether to answer her question. At last he said, "It may be possible that one of my comments was open to interpretation."

"Go ahead, let me hear it."

"I believe I commented to the effect that Travis's behavior was as unlawful as the actions of the men who were the subjects of the trial."

"You told Marshall he was like the men who killed his father."

"Steady on, Mrs. Travis. I rather think you must acknowledge that I—"

"That's how it sounded to me, so don't bother saying it couldn't have sounded like that to him. The truth seems to be you upset him more than he was already upset and now you don't know where he is. What do you intend doing about it besides having this conversation?"

"I understood you to imply that Travis was bound to return to you."

"Of course he will, and when he does—" All that mattered was that he would, because what on earth could stop him? "When he does we'll both want to get together with you."

"My office is always open to pupils and their parents. I should appreciate being informed when Travis puts in an appearance. And please allow me to reiterate my sympathy over your difficulties."

She could have done without that, since he was one of them. "Appreciated," she said anyway, and dropped the receiver into its plastic nest before going to the window. A few students were cycling across the quadrangle, scattering sparrows that had gathered about the rind of a sandwich, but there was no sign of Marshall. Maybe he didn't want to risk being upset in anywhere so public as her workplace; maybe he was waiting at home. The sparrows settled like dancing leaves on the remains of the bread, and she hurried to dial the house.

The phone had to ring five times before the answering machine picked up a call. As the fifth pair of rings came to an end she was still hoping it would be Marshall who answered. Instead she heard a click followed by the hiss of the tape carrying her own hollow mechanical voice. "Susanne and Marshall Travis."

That was as much of a message as she had been able to record; she'd been too aware of having erased Don's welcoming voice from the tape. She listened for some hint that Marshall was monitoring her call—another click, or breathing—but all she could hear was her own silence, then and now. After a pause which she shouldn't have allowed to continue for so long when recording the announcement, the machine emitted its beep. "Marshall, are you there?" she said. "If you can hear me, honey, pick up the phone. I'm not mad at you. I just want to know you're safe."

Silence. Even the hiss of the tape had ceased, and the line sounded dead. If she failed to speak for more than a few seconds, the machine would cease recording and switch itself off, and her voice would no longer be audible in the house. "Marshall, please be there," she said, and was reminded of Don's voice wanting her to be there the last time he'd called home. She made herself continue, hoping that would prevent Marshall from being reminded too. "Okay, I'm assuming you aren't. If you get home before I do and hear this, I'll be here at the University till half past four and then I'll come back, so wait there for me, all right? I spoke to your principal and I know what you did, and I know why, so you don't have to worry about telling me. If he didn't understand, I do. The one thing I want is for you to be home when I get there. Nothing else matters, okay?"

She swallowed and held onto the receiver and listened until she heard the click of the machine terminating her call. It wasn't that she couldn't think of anything more to say but rather that she was thinking of too much. If anything happened to Marshall . . . if anything had happened to him . . . Of course there was no reason to suppose that anything apart from playing hooky had. Maybe he would come and find her before she finished for the afternoon, and if not, where else would he go but home? She walked herself out of her office before she could start having second thoughts, and locked the door, and made herself stop listening for the phone to ring, and vowed that by the time she returned to her students she would be ready to teach.

19

IN BROAD DAYLIGHT

When the phone rang Marshall hoped more than anything else that it would be his mother. He'd just been listening to his father's voice, and didn't want to be as alone as that had left him. He ran out of his room and down the stairs, and reached the hall with a double thud of his heels as the answering machine cut in. His hand was an inch away from the receiver when he realized that the call might be from the school. He sat down, a stair digging into the base of his spine, while the faint squeak of the spindle indicated that the machine was announcing itself and holding its breath. Then the speaker emitted a woman's cough, and Marshall was hauling himself to his feet when she said, "Message for Mrs. Travis from Bushy Boys. Will you please call the school as soon as possible," and cut herself off with an abruptness that sounded like a warning not to waste her time.

At least she hadn't spoken to his mother. He rewound the tape so that the next message would erase her, just in case his mother came home before he did, and hurried back to his room. It was almost three o'clock, which meant that she wouldn't return for a couple of hours—far longer than he could bear to stay alone in the house with his raw thoughts. He might have gone to find her at work, but suppose he broke down in public as soon as she asked what was wrong? The desecrated grave was, and the way it had turned his father's last message into nothing more than a recording, the words and pauses and intonations no more meaningful than a pop song he'd played too often. It no longer invoked his father, because the grave had shown him his father was no longer anywhere.

He took off his uniform and laid it on his bed, to be hung up later, and changed into his favorite track suit, whose solitary pocket had room for his handful of change and his keys and handkerchief. He went through the building to close any doors that weren't already shut, and switched on the alarm and locked himself out of the house.

He didn't know what he might say to any neighbors who saw him out of school. When he faced the street, however, it was deserted except for a boy he didn't recognize who was disappearing around the corner. Marshall headed for the gate, but faltered beside the lavender his father had planted. He broke off a sprig and crushed it between finger and thumb as he raised it to his face. It smelled like graves and effeminacy. He threw it into the flower bed before his surge of grief could make him grind it beneath his heel, and slammed the gate behind him.

On the main road he reached a bus stop at the same time as a bus into Manchester. As he clattered upstairs it loitered for the sake of one more passenger. Though the top deck smelled of fish and chips in greasy newspapers and defiant cigarettes, Marshall had it to himself. He sprawled on the left-hand front seat and propped his heels against the metal under the window, and watched the city proceeding in fits and starts toward him.

The Indian restaurants gave way to the University, red bluffs rearing up on both sides of the bus and honeycombed with windows. Marshall leaned across the aisle, closing his fist around a chilly metal pole, to peer between the buildings toward the quadrangle which his mother's office overlooked, and all at once yearned to be with her. Maybe he could stand in the quadrangle until she caught sight of him and came out to him. Then the bus put on speed, and he shoved his heels against the metal and his spine into the worn upholstery until the University was too far behind to tempt him.

When the giant stone skullcap of the public library appeared beyond a pair of trams gliding past each other, Marshall went downstairs, but as soon as he'd walked away from the bus he wondered why he had. What he found he wanted was to go to his father's shop. He hurried down the alley which curved around the library, hearing footsteps very much like his own following him or echoing his, and across the square of which the town hall formed one side, the linked multicolored rings of an Olympic emblem attached like an abandoned plastic toy to its turreted façade. Beyond the square the streets which led in the direction of the bookshop grew narrower and less straightforward, offices and small shops and unexpected churches mixed together in twisted blocks. There were fewer people here, mostly office workers on errands involving bits of paper, and nobody seemed interested in him. Nevertheless he was relieved when a street led him to the Arndale Center, the most crowded area in town.

It consisted of both a shopping mall and a pedestrianized street lined with shops and occupied by ice-cream wagons and hot-potato stalls and bunches of telephone booths. Pigeons marched in disarray past the food stalls while interviewers bearing clipboards, and people selling newspapers devoted to the homeless, tried to single passersby out of the crowds. All this let Marshall feel sufficiently unobtrusive to realize he was very thirsty, and he went into a McDonald's, where the staff repeating "How may I help you?" and "Have a nice day" in Manchester accents brought a grin to his lips. He bought a Coke from a girl with a faint blond mustache like an unwiped trace of lemonade, and sat at the nearest empty table, and tried to relax enough to think.

Though the customers were only talking, the place was in an uproar. Cigarette smoke from the next table seemed determined to find him again whenever he waved it away, and wherever he looked there was at least one small child smearing its face with ketchup and chunks of Big Mac. After a couple of sucks at the Coke he headed for the men's room, not sure if he was going to be sick.

Emptying his bladder relieved most of the pressure which had made him feel that way. When he emerged he saw that a two-seater table had been vacated in the non-smoking area by the window. He grabbed his Coke and took a drink as he hurried to the table. An unexpected object, no doubt a fragment of ice, slid out of the straw and was washed down his throat before it could trouble him. He rested his elbows on the plastic slab and held onto his jaw with his left hand and used the other to raise the cup whenever it occurred to him to drink.

He thought he was taking his time, but maybe he was drinking faster than he should, because after a while he became aware of feeling feverish. The lighting of the restaurant had acquired a glare like the edge of a razor, and the mushy hubbub was spiked with jagged noises—a baby's wail pretending to have finished each time it drew another breath, the clang of utensils in the open kitchen, the scrape of forks on polystyrene. He had the impression that the table had started actively to press itself against his elbows. He felt watched as he had when he'd walked out of the schoolyard, and much less sure of himself. He peered out at the flood of bobbing faces, but couldn't see any that were more than glancing at him. Then he noticed a waitress with a bin on wheels who was edging toward him between the furniture garish as kindergarten toys. He rammed his elbows against the plastic, bruising himself, and lurched out of the restaurant, gripping the cup until he heard it or the ice within it beginning to crack. He was supposed to be going to the bookshop.

The crowd forced him to dodge, and dodge again. He thought he was lost, and the inside of his skull started to crawl. Then a clump of traffic lights reddened and sparked off a trail of brake lights which led his stare toward the cathedral, spiny as a lizard basking in the afternoon sun. He ran past the traffic, ice gnashing inside the cup in his hand with each step, and across the lights, which appeared to be implying he could cross. Now he was by the cathedral, and once he made himself pass a bench displaying a woman with a face like white bread swelling out of her headscarf and pigeons covering her crumby arms, he saw that the brown bulk ahead was indeed the Corn Exchange. His suffocated feet tramped the length of the façade undercut by shops, and there around the corner was the bookshop.

The sign was still above the door. It should have been illuminated, Marshall thought—not just TRAVIS BOOKS in black letters on a white rectangle—but it was too late now. He was trying to grasp what difference illuminating his father's name might have made when he noticed that the door was very slightly open. Was someone deciding whether to buy the stock, or had they broken in? Marshall darted forward stiff-legged and slapped his free hand against the door.

He was ready to charge down the steps, and so when the door didn't yield he felt as if he should be falling. He had to thrust his face close enough to the gap that he smelled old paint and wood before he was able to convince himself that the door was locked, particularly since the line of darkness between it and the frame seemed not quite stable. When at last he raised his head he felt it plunge into the rush of the city, a medium which he sensed threatening to grow more solid.

He had to be sickening for a fever. His hands and feet were sweating, and he had a growing impression that something unpleasant was about to happen inside him or around him, or both. He stepped back, observing how the window looked boarded up with dust and sunlight, and then his gaze dropped to the sidewalk. He was treading on his father's blood.

He recoiled and found himself pressing his back against the wall of the shop, one hand trying to grab a lump out of it. He could no longer distinguish the stain on the flagstones, or could he, very faintly? Had he seen it more clearly before, or had he glimpsed it only because he knew it had once been there? He shouldered himself away from the wall and began to circle the area of sidewalk, trying to find an angle from which the unyielding sunlight wouldn't confuse him. Then a dark spot appeared at his feet, and another.

The spreading drops were too dark for rain. As he jerked backward, a trail of them spattered the sidewalk. They were dripping from the heel of his right hand. He'd broken the cup by gripping it too hard, and cut himself. He fumbled the cup into his other hand and stared at the sticky liquid that was beginning to trickle into his sleeve. Even when he managed to see that it was brown, not red, he had to stop himself searching for a cut, and when he licked the trickle off his palm it didn't taste quite like Coke. His legs scraped together as he ran to the nearest trash bin. Looking up from dumping the cup into the throat choked with garbage, he saw the Arndale Center ahead. Somehow he'd approached his father's shop by as indirect a route as he could find. It didn't matter now, nor did his memory of having seen the inside of the bin gulp as though swallowing the cup, because so many buses stopped alongside the Arndale Center that he was sure of finding one to take him to his mother.

Or should he go home and lie down? He felt indecision thickening around him until he succeeded in grasping that he could decide once he was on the bus. He saw a green man jump and hesitate before commencing a dance to beckon Marshall across the road, along with a random selection of people whose walk he tried to imitate in case any of them noticed he was supposed to be in school or that something was wrong with him.

The roar of the buses hit him in the face. He tried to keep walking toward them, through a square arroyo bridged overhead by the same sandy rock, but the noise was so loud it was dislodging sand from cracks in the bridge—he could see it faintly in the air and feel it gathering on his forehead. Terrified of being crushed by either the bridge or the noise, he ran around the outside of the mall to the street which admitted no traffic.

There was still far too much noise beneath another section of the underbelly of the mall, which he saw lowering itself toward him, absorbing the light as it came. He was surrounded by people who'd taken their faces into the dimness for reasons he didn't want to think about, let alone see happening. He dashed onto the open street and forced himself to slow down, because he was going to have to walk to the University, although by the time he did that, wouldn't his mother have gone home? A woman wheeled a stroller in front of him to show him her doll which looked and sounded almost like a crying two-year-old, but the words on slabs above the shops were reminding Marshall that he'd neglected to deal with the bookshop sign. He ought to go back, except for having to avoid a wagon that was crawling toward him on the brushes on its wheels, poising itself to dodge after him if he dodged. He couldn't tell how fast it was moving or how far away it was. "There's no traffic here," he protested, and heard his voice isolate itself and draw attention to itself—its accent, its aggressive petulance, the way its intonation seemed to mean he was denying the existence of the wagon—and saw inflated heads bob up from collars and nod toward him on the thick strings of their necks. He dodged them and the wagon, then veered away from the hi-fi speakers that were shop doorways, trying to hammer his brain flat with sound. Even if he wouldn't have been able to take down the sign he ought to have written his father's dates on it, or would that attract vandals to smash it like the headstone? Water thick with sunlight began to bulge his eyes, and he was rubbing them clear when he almost tripped over a figure seated against the wall under the window of a clothes shop—a man dressed in a sack or an old coat, which he'd pulled up over his head and draped around a gray dog on his chest. The animal must be dead, because it was gray with dust, and so was the stubble covering much of the man's caved-in face. Were his eyeballs coated with dust, or were his eyes shut? The head fell back, the face began to move, which ought to mean he was alive, except that it appeared to be coming to pieces. Everyone else in the viciously bright street was ignoring him, and Marshall retreated before he would have had to cry out, and found he was facing a telephone booth, one of half a dozen standing back to back to protect one another. He didn't need to phone, he'd been to the shop, his father would tell his mother where he was. He heard what he was thinking, and having thought it frightened him so badly that he ran into the open booth, struggling to dig the University phone number out of his brain. Something came to meet him: a face in the glass of a notice above the phone, a face which was eager for him to see what it looked like and which was bloating through the glass to drag his mind in. As he fell back he saw the sky begin to quiver with the scream that was fighting to burst out of him. The sidewalk exploded into his face, all its eyes gleaming blackly, its gray wings clattering like smashed stone, and he fled into the nearest entrance to the mall.

Or was it a mall? He seemed to have walked into a wardrobe as wide as a main street and full of clothes on either side of him. Maybe it was a street whose two layers of shops were crushed beneath a roof. It was stuffed with voices which couldn't escape because of the roof, some of which Marshall was certain were discussing him. "He isn't fooling me . . ." "Coming in like that . . ." "Who does he think he is?" "About time somebody was told . . ." "I'd break every bone in his . . ." A woman's face was crinkling and losing definition as the air leaked out of it, a man's was so pumped up that Marshall saw moisture drifting over the eyes, the way it did on the surface of a bubble about to burst, and he floundered onto an escalator to leave those sights behind. As he clung to the rubber snakes despite their writhing in his hands, he saw that he was being raised toward tanks brimming with urine on the underside of the roof. He was walking backward fast in case any of the tanks cracked when a voice breathed "Watch it, son" in his ear and a body as plump as the voice pressed itself against him. The tanks were were only full of yellow light, Marshall was almost sure, and he just had a very bad fever and had to get home. He'd give the buses behind the mall another try, he would make himself do that after he returned to the bookshop in order to . . . He faltered while he tried to think, stairs snapping at his heels, and then Plump shoved him away from the top of the escalator. Marshall went staggering toward a block of shops, one of which emitted a series of shrill quick beeps. "Not me, I didn't steal—" he cried, and saw a woman dragging a toddler back into the drugstore and snatching a packet of tampons out of his hand, which meant that Marshall needn't have made himself conspicuous; why couldn't he keep his voice to himself? Because he had a fever, an awful kind of fever, a hideous and loathsome and shameful kind of fever, which was making him taste how it would be if one of the tanks spilled its contents on him. He scraped his tongue against the back of his teeth as he sent himself along the walkway above the exercise yard, praying that none of the prisoners would look up and notice him. Was he heading for the buses? There was a uniformed guard at the end of the walkway, and Marshall only had to prepare his question in advance so that he wouldn't hesitate longer than was normal, or speak too fast, or betray himself by his tone, or his expression, or the way he stood, or how he walked toward the guard. "Can you tell me . . . Sure you can, it's your job . . . I mean, may you, could you tell, I need to know . . ." Then he saw that the guard was sticking out his tongue and farting with his lips, and felt a wild grin wrenching his own mouth open to let out a laugh that might sound more like a scream. But the guard was only doing his best to amuse a woman's second head, a baby that was peeking over her saliva-coated shoulder, and Marshall hurried toward him to apologize for having been about to laugh. The baby waved a hand, the guard stuck a finger in the carnivorous plant it became, and someone took hold of Marshall's arm. "Hey up, Marshall. Where you going?"

Marshall turned his head, feeling the cords of his neck drag at the flesh over his collarbone. The mall zoomed backward to isolate the other and bring him into sharper focus. He looked older than Marshall, maybe because he was an old man shrunken small enough to wear a boy's track suit, and his neck was clamped with a device hissing with electricity. Marshall tried to jerk his arm free, but the other held on, muttering, "Hey, it's all right. You're with me, Marshall."

His voice was undecided whether it was high or low. Marshall recalled that state overtaking his own voice when he was on television, and wondered if he was being filmed now; that would explain the unreality surrounding him. His companion did appear to be a boy, however thin and pale and however cobwebby under the eyes, and his presence was the only reassurance Marshall had. Indeed, he was beginning to look elusively familiar. "Are you in my class?" Marshall said.

The boy's face flickered and rearranged itself. "We aren't all as clever as you, lad. I've seen you round the school. Any road, where do you want to go?"

Would Marshall's mother still be at the University if he went there? He shook his wrist out of his sleeve, feeling the bones shift inside the flesh, and peered in dismay at the nest of swarming bits of blackness under the glass of his digital watch. "What time is it?" he pleaded.

"God," the other boy said incredulously, "give it here."

Marshall was scrabbling at the catch of the metal strap when the boy grabbed his wrist and twisted it so as to look at the watch. "Half four."

Marshall's mother would be through or almost through by now, unless she stopped to talk to anyone, or maybe he could phone her to ask her to wait there for him, though if she had already left he would only be wasting time, and if he couldn't read his watch he mightn't be able to dial either, particularly since he'd forgotten the number of the University and please not his home number as well . . . "I want to go home," he heard himself trying not to wail.

"I'll take you if you want. I know where you live."

Marshall was terrified that if he doubted the claim the boy might abandon him, yet his voice said, "Where?"

"Off Wilmslow Road."

Marshall tensed himself so as not to collapse with relief. "How'll we get there?"

"Howl yourself. On a bus if you can't pay for a taxi."

Marshall groped in his pocket, but seemed unable to insert his entire hand, though he was sure he had before. Had his hand grown or the pocket shrunk? "How much?" he said some of, consonants sticking to his lips.

"It's all right, lad, the bus'll do us. Come on or we'll miss it."

Since the boy appeared to be as anxious to take him home as Marshall was to be there, Marshall's limbs became familiar again and carried him after his savior. He was past the guard and on a street which he needn't remind himself was actually an upper floor when the relief that had flooded through him froze, and cracked, and let a wave of panic overwhelm him. His legs jerked him onward while the rest of him shivered, and he was wondering if everyone in the mall was too disgusted by his appearance to want to acknowledge him, when he saw ahead of him a pillar with a mirror as tall as the ceiling for each of its four sides. The boy he was following slipped out of the nearest mirror, making way for the thing which had reached out of the depths of the phone booth. It was dressed like Marshall, and nearly had his face, except that a doll's head had been substituted for the skull beneath the mottled pink flesh which it was pulling slightly but horribly out of shape. Only the terrified eyes in the sockets cut out of the flesh looked entirely human. He felt the misshapen plastic poking at his face from within. His hands were fumbling up his cheeks toward the raw edges of his eyes when the apparition vanished from the mirror, because the boy had grabbed his arm and tugged him a couple of stumbling steps. "Never mind that. Don't let it fuck your head up. Don't look."

There seemed to be a promise of reassurance in the way the boy had known he must intervene and how, and so Marshall pleaded, "Do you know what's wrong with me?"

"Some bug everybody's getting, it'll be."

The notion that everyone around him felt like him shook Marshall from head to foot, so violently he couldn't tell when the shaking turned into soundless laughter that jabbed at the inside of his chest. "That's it, Ma, have a bit of fun if it helps," the boy said. "Only don't make too much of a show of us."

When he called Marshall his mother the boy meant his name, and when he'd talked about a bug he had meant an infection, but Marshall was afraid that if he didn't laugh aloud he would see an insect pretending to be part of everyone around him, or might laughing make him cough his own bug up? He trailed after the boy, between shops that kept trying to flicker toward him. He mustn't move too fast in case anybody thought he'd stolen from one of the shops, though mightn't they think he had if he moved too slowly? The hairy mound on top of his guide's head escorted him down an escalator, and his panic had begun to subside when he saw he was descending past a cage as high as the mall and fluttering with birds. He clung to the clammy rubber snake and twisted his head round to stare back, attempting to see whether the shops were really cages, until he was unable to swallow or breathe for the dragging at his neck. "We aren't at the zoo, are we?" he gasped.

"Aye, and you're the monkey. Get a grip, lad, there's the bus."

The boy was indicating a sign above the corridor beyond the screeching birds. One of the words on it did appear to be "buses," interpreting a symbol whose incomprehensibility at once spread to the word, which perhaps wasn't "buses" after all. The arrow attached to the word was unable to keep still, but the boy must be confident of its direction, because he led Marshall to the end of the white corridor, where the windows showed darkness outside. How long had Marshall been lost in the mall? "What time is it now?" he cried.

"Five minutes later than last time you asked. Don't make a row less you want us stopped." The boy shoved the glass door between the windows, and Marshall saw that the whole of the wall was composed of black glass. Even though the heavy roar of buses seemed like darkness transformed into sound, the daylight was so welcome that he floundered into it, grabbing a branch wrapped in track suit to steady himself. "Watch who you're handling, lad," the boy warned him, wrenching it away to point across the divided road. "Give us your money, quick. There's the bus."

Marshall dug in his pocket and stepped into the road. A screech of brakes pierced his skull, and an object several times his height overwhelmed him. There was a duet of "Fuck" from the driver and the boy as Marshall staggered sideways, not sure whether the bus had struck him. Apparently not, because he was able to remain standing, though the smell of diesel was slopping back and forth behind his eyes. The driver shouted, "If you want to kill yourself, son, don't make any other bugger do it" as the bus veered around Marshall, squirting fumes at him. Then the boy dragged him back, knocking Marshall's ankles against the curb, the curb. "What you playing at? Get across or we'll miss your bus."

"It's number, number . . ."

"I know which it is. Get your arse across."

Marshall made himself look in the wrong direction, where the traffic on this side of the road was coming from, before dashing to the central barrier. As he clambered over, it dug into his crotch like a huge dull blade poised to saw him in half. The underside of the mall shifted above the road, dislodging a rain of sand which hissed through the mating chorus of the buses, and he was so afraid the bridge was about to fall and crush him that he would have retreated if the boy hadn't bumped him onward with his shoulder. "Get it out, will you. The queue's nearly on."

Marshall understood enough of that to dig out his money as he levered himself onto the sidewalk. Shouldn't he go to the bookshop now that he was almost within sight of it? But the boy pried the money out of his fist and swung himself into the doorway of the bus. Another rush of panic sent Marshall after him, because the number and the destinations on the front of the vehicle were streaming upwards like an image on a dying television, too fast and too distorted for him to read. "Two," the boy said to the driver, and to Marshall, "Up."

Marshall used cold handfuls of the rail to haul himself up the steps, which vibrated with the growling of the bus. He dropped himself on the front seat, which seemed to nod forward and pant in his ear, as the bus unstuck itself from the patch of road and his friend came to find him. The boy threw himself on the seat across the aisle and clanged his heels on the metal windowsill, the bolts on each side of his neck sizzling with power, and Marshall blurted, "Where's the rest of my money?"

"I'm looking after it for you. You don't want to be bothered with it while you're feeling like you're feeling."

"Aren't you? You said everyone."

"I've felt like it, lad, and that's a fact."

The boy stared hard at him as if he was seeing Marshall's face turn into the doll's face. "Evom eht no elpoep," Marshall thought and, in an attempt to rid himself of the tendrils of it which were rooting themselves in his brain, said. What if he'd forgotten how to speak English? Suppose he couldn't understand himself? The bus emerged from beneath the mall, and he heard it grinding its way through the sand that was dimming the light and making his eyes itch, and then he saw the words sailing in the sky. They were the slogan of the bus company, a transfer glued to the outside of the window, but that wasn't at all reassuring; he felt as if everything else had been reversed, including himself. Maybe he'd gone through the looking glass, because he was back in some part of a zoo or a circus, a herd of dusty buses grumbling and roaring around him, crowds of dwarfs dodging boldly in front of them, their little heads held high. The bus emerged from the herd and put on speed toward the stone daggers of the town hall roof. They tore open the sky above the square, and the sun exploded into Marshall's eyes. He felt it blaze all the way through his skull to the back—he could almost see it doing this to the brittle parched bare shell which was the inside of himself. He clapped his hands over his face, crushing his nose until he could hardly breathe, and wedged his soles against the yielding metal. "Can you tell me when we get there?" he pleaded.

"Trust me, Ma."

Marshall persuaded his hands to loosen their grip—his face was throbbing like a wound—and glimpsed darkness toppling toward him. It was the shadow of the town hall, and it was snatched away at once to let the sun at him. When he tried to mask his eyes with his hands held close to them, the stops and starts of the bus kept making him thump himself in the face. Whenever he peered between his fingers the sun knifed his eyes, or he saw sights he couldn't cope with—a railroad train sprouting from the air in front of him, or rooms with people hanging head downward in them being dragged through a canal, or traffic falling into an abyss beside the road. If he kept his eyes covered he saw multicolored cartoon shapes capering toward him, and felt himself turning into a cartoon, so that he didn't dare look at himself. He made his fingers part, only to see clouds come to a complete halt in the sky and shake themselves like sheep and move off. Then the boy pinched his shoulder, and for a moment which seemed to contain all the hope and peace in the world Marshall thought the pinch had wakened him from the nightmare. "Don't go off yet," the boy said. "We're the next stop."

The world spun at two speeds, fast inside the bus and faster outside, as Marshall turned to him and then lunged after him so as not to be left alone with the only other passenger upstairs, a woman's body sitting three seats behind him, holding a carrier bag full of vegetables with a head piled on top. The stairs clanked underfoot like a machine that was running down as he fled, his hooves striking the floor of the horse-box just as the roar of the world cracked open the glass side of it. When the boy stepped through the opening and became a head shorter, Marshall could only leap after him.

The world thumped his heels, and he staggered a few paces while he discovered whether his bruised feet could still walk. The bus shut its driver into his cell and set off in pursuit of the rest of the migration. The shrill hiss of tires pierced the unending thunder with which the road was loaded, and the shrillness transformed the sunlight into lightning which flickered without ever going out. Maybe it was shivering on his behalf, because he had no idea where he was.

It wasn't just another symptom. This wasn't any road he'd seen before. He was standing alongside a block of shops like boxes thrown together in an attic with a few old safes, incomprehensible slogans scrawled across their metal fronts. Even the shops that might be open were crisscrossed with gray mesh. Sections of old signs were visible between some of the signs over the shops, as if the row was about to revert to its previous self. Some of the windows above the signs were broken, and he saw their frames begin to warp and sag as he held out his artificial hands to the boy. "Why did we get off here? You said you knew where we were going."

"Bet your arse I do, Ma. There was a diversion, only you didn't see it for hiding your face. We just have to walk a bit. You can do that, can't you, lad?"

Marshall had to, feeling sweat being squeezed out of his feet and the backs of his knees with each step. He could smell himself, his panic. Red and green cartoons kicked their legs in the air as he followed his keeper across the halves of the road which had gone through the mirror, evom eht no elpoep. Now the boy was leading him along the sidewalk past a strip of turf sown with fragments of newspaper headlines, perhaps about

Marshall or about the murder at the shop he should be going back to, and planted with trees as thin as his arm, their frayed ends wired into the electric sky. The sky was up to its tricks again, grinding to a halt and having to shake itself in order to move off, tweaking the roofs of huddles of low flat-faced houses the color of sodden sand. Marshall had wandered past quite a length of these while he shielded his eyes from the sight of drowned rooms floating by in glass tanks before he realized he was no longer following. The boy had stopped to lift a fence in front of a house to its feet. "Don't go running off, Ma. Don't get lost when you don't know nobody but me."

Marshall stumbled back to him. "Where's this? This isn't where I live."

"No, it's where I do."

There was an aggressiveness, even a threat, in the boy's voice which made Marshall nervous of saying anything wrong, but that was the least of his fears under the jerky old film of the sky. "You said you'd take me home."

"Come in first. I want a drink. You can have one too if you want, a Coke. You like them, don't you?"

How did he know? Maybe he'd seen Marshall drinking Coke at school, or maybe he thought all Americans drank it. He opened the gate, which screeched over the stump of concrete path. "You can lie down if you want, Ma, then you might feel better."

Marshall took a step, feeling his leg haul his foot up and deposit it a few inches forward and somehow take the weight of his leaden body, and then another. "I don't want to stay long. I need to be with my mom."

"You don't want her seeing you looking like that, do you? Get in and I'll give you something you can take."

If he had the antidote to Marshall's condition, Marshall thought he would be mad to hesitate. He mustn't let himself wonder if he was already going mad. He conveyed the burden of himself onto the path between two untended plots of grass without even a headstone to mark them. "Thanks," he pronounced, trying to sound absolutely sincere, and thought of something else it would have been friendly of him to have said much earlier. "What's your name?"

His friend closed the gate, and the fence leaned its points toward Marshall. Now the boy was jabbing a hand at him to urge him toward the house, and slipping a metal glint out of his pocket as his neck whispered to itself. "Darren," he said.

20

UNKNOWING

Susanne had driven out of the car park and was accelerating through a gap in both directions of the traffic when she saw one of her students hurrying toward her along the sidewalk—Pik, his black ponytail wagging. As she swung the Volvo parallel to the sidewalk he waved urgently. She stamped on the brake and switched on her hazard lights and stopped the car close to the curb, even though at this time of day the lane she was in was supposed to be reserved for buses. Her eyes met Pik's, and he smiled, far too fleetingly to be bringing her good news. She pressed the button to lower the passenger window with a finger which had grown clumsy and unsteady. The glass was inching down when Pik hesitated before running past the car. She saw him sprint across the crossing as the invitation to pedestrians began to falter, and seize a girl by the hand and whirl her to face him and set about kissing her on the mouth. He had been waving to her, not to Susanne at all. Of course he had no news of Marshall.

She mustn't worry, certainly not while she was driving. Marshall would be home by now, or on his way home, since he knew she was. She switched off the insect clicking of the hazard lights and steered the car out of the bus lane. "Just be there," she said aloud, and tried to stop remembering the day she'd driven home to find Don's message, but she couldn't forget while she was driving his car. She'd sold hers rather than get rid of his, and by now she'd found everything of his which remained in it—a street map of Manchester annotated in his handwriting, a thin pack of his business cards held by a rubber band which had snapped when she'd extracted one, a dolphin key ring which five-year-old Marshall had bought him for his birthday and which, though broken, he'd stashed in the glove box rather than throw it away. Worst of all had been two clips of bullets which he might have used to save his life and which she wished he had. By now she was able to use the vehicle without having her vision dissolve into a weepy blur, not much of the time anyway. Driving the car felt like being with him, made him seem present in at least a generalized sense, and now the impression appealed to her as a reassurance that she was close to seeing Marshall, since she sensed no ominousness. "We'll look after him," she murmured. She could already see the Indian restaurants ahead, and a minute later she was surrounded by them, and then they shrank into her mirror as she made the first turn. Right, and right again, as the lengths of street grew shorter and narrower. Mrs. Satterthwaite's mongrel lifted its head above the garden gate on the corner and gave a token bark which sounded like a signal as the Travis house came into view. Whatever the bark might have signified, it wasn't that Marshall was waiting outside. No doubt he was in the house.

The scent of lavender rose to meet her as she opened her gate. She parted her lips but didn't speak, and shook the Yale key forward from her bunch of keys and slid it into the lock. It turned easily, but nothing further happened when she pushed at the cold metal plate. The mortise was still locked, and Marshall wasn't home.

She found the mortise key and turned it in the mechanism and palmed the door open. The inner door imitated its movement, and the alarm announced itself. She heeled the front door shut with a vigor that sent her along the hall in time to dig the key into the alarm panel just as its siren raised its shriek. The sound invaded her nerves like a drill finding a tooth, and the silence which followed only left them aching. The answering machine showed one call recorded: her own. At least there was no message about Marshall, but also none from him.

He would have called if he didn't intend to be home any minute. She mustn't let herself start speculating whether he'd thought he would be and had then been prevented somehow, because if that was the case there was no reason to suppose that anything bad had happened to him. She snatched the fistful of keys away from the alarm panel and threw them in her purse, and marched herself to her kitchen, where she raided the freezer for a tinfoil carton of her homemade bolognese sauce, Marshall's favorite of her dinners. She set it down next to the microwave. There was no point in doing any more with it until she knew that Marshall would be home by dinnertime, which obviously he would be, and much earlier if he knew what was good for him. "We'll be having a few words about how not to worry people, young man," she said, and heard the empty house displaying her talking to herself. She tramped back along the hall to grab her case full of essays awaiting grades, but left it on the stairs and made for Marshall's room.

She didn't know what she expected to find. She already knew why he'd abandoned school; what else needed explaining? She turned the doorknob and felt the door pull stealthily away, as it always did as soon as it was opened. She let the knob slip from her grasp, and saw the shelves stuffed with books, as though the room was an extension of Don's shop. The door crept open further and showed her Marshall's school uniform lying on the bed.

Why was the sight of the sloughed clothes dismaying? Because if he had been home she would have expected him to wait for her or, failing that, to leave her a message. Didn't he feel able to tell her what he'd done? Had she lost that much contact with him? No, the lack of a message implied that he'd expected to be home by the time she was, and maybe he was coming up the street right now. She hurried into her room and past the bed that was twice as wide as it needed to be, and gazed over the balcony at the street, which was deserted. She gazed until she became conscious of trying to magic him into sight, and then she made herself go downstairs to work.

She took her case into the front room and moved a low table in front of a chair from which she could see through the window, and lifted the stack of essays out of the case, and tried to concentrate. "Realistic fiction is a contradiction in terms . . ." "There are no such things as violent fiction films, only films pretending to be violent . . ." She wondered if her students had caught a tendency to aphorize from her, and glanced up to see who was strutting down the street, but it was a magpie black and white as Marshall's uniform. "Films showing violence as it really is could never be shown commercially." Her pencil hesitated alongside that until a movement rose above the garden fence—again the magpie, perching on the fence and flying off once Susanne's head jerked up. If she couldn't focus her attention on the essays better than that, perhaps she ought to take them to another room, except she didn't think she could. She drew the essay closer to her and bent her head over it, and the phone rang.

She shoved the pages away, trying not to crumple them, and snatched her feet from beneath the table and jumped up. By now the phone had rung twice, and she was desperate to answer it before it reached the fifth ring and the machine took over, in case Marshall or whoever else was calling thought she wasn't there. It shrilled twice more as she ran into the hall, grabbing so wildly at the receiver that it flew out of her hand. "Hello?" a voice repeated, growing as Susanne clapped the receiver to her ear. "Hello?"

It was a woman, someone she'd spoken to recently—the school secretary? "Yes?" Susanne gasped, feeling and sounding as if she'd just run a race.

"Mrs. Travis?"

"Yes." When that didn't produce an immediate response Susanne added, "Susanne Travis, yes."

"I only ask because the last time I spoke to another American lady. Is it convenient to talk just now?"

The voice seemed to be compensating for Susanne's urgency by slowing itself down, broadening its vowels and pronouncing each syllable almost like a separate word. Perhaps that was why the question sounded ominous. "I—" Susanne said, and made herself ask, "What about?"

"No very significant development, I'm afraid. I wondered if there had been any at your end." The woman laughed, as slowly as she spoke. "Did I forget to identify myself, by the way? My apologies. This is Iris Pendle, the—"

"The bookseller, yes, I know."

"The bookseller, yes," Iris Pendle said, and paused as a further rebuke. "You'll recall we spoke about your late husband's business."

"I do."

"I was wondering whether anyone else in the trade had expressed an interest."

Susanne was imagining Marshall trying to phone her and finding the line busy, and then . . . "A few," she said, and considered not giving too much away, but just now negotiating the best deal hardly seemed to matter. "Not for the whole of the stock like you did."

"That's often the way. I'd still be prepared to make you an overall offer if I get the bank's approval."

"Oh, you need that."

"Most businesses do in these troubled times. I thought if you're agreeable we might meet to discuss a final price."

Susanne could only answer as succinctly as possible. "When?"

"I was thinking tomorrow, when I'll be on an expedition to Manchester. I know you Americans are fond of lunch. Would you be free for a sandwich?"

"Where? What time?"

"I'll do my best to fall in with your day."

"Say, say—" Susanne was wishing the bookseller would. "Twelve under the University clock, the tower, you know, on Oxford Road."

"I'll be in a pale green Nissan estate."

"I'll be looking for you," Susanne said, and was about to thank her for calling when she rang off, leaving Susanne uncertain whether she should have been quite so prepared to meet tomorrow, although why not? The arrangement she'd just made sounded a little like meeting a criminal, a kidnapper, but there was no reason whatsoever for her to begin to think along those lines—sure, some of the Fancy family had waylaid Marshall on his way home and made him change out of his uniform and then kidnapped him. The thought of him made him seem more present, maybe outside the house, steeling himself to face her. She housed the receiver and hurried to open the front door.

Someone moved—ducked out of sight. Why would anyone be hiding from her? She ran to the gate and was about to call "Hello" when Hilda Mattison reappeared beyond the hedge of the house diagonally opposite, wearing overalls even wider than herself and brandishing a pair of garden shears, whose clipping Susanne became aware of having heard for minutes. "All right, love?" her neighbor inquired.

"Pretty much, Hilda. Just looking for Marshall."

"Give a yell if you like, nobody minds round here. I used to do that with our three when they were older than him, and they'd come quick enough."

"Maybe I'll try that," Susanne said, and hoping this was more of a fib "You won't have seen him."

"I've been in and out most of the day."

"You won't have, then."

"Oh yes."

Hilda snipped an inch off a twig of privet as abruptly as she tended to end conversations, and Susanne felt the gate dig into her midriff. "Pardon me, when was he here?"

"As far as I know, not since he said how are you doing to me or whatever it was he said. Well, I never realized that before. That's what some Americans mean when they say howdy, isn't it? Strange, the things you suddenly understand after you've been hearing them for years. Anyway, that was the last I've seen of him, when I was taking in the milk."

"When he was on his way to school."

" 'Fraid so," Hilda admitted with a tinge of defiance. "Don't go running off with the idea we always sleep in that late. Matt and I had a bit of a knees-up at a Conservative Club do last night and couldn't drive home till some of the pop wore off."

Susanne had never been able to work out whether Hilda's husband's first name was Matt or any version of it, and she was angry with herself for being bothered by the question now. She glanced along the street, and then her shoulders drooped. "Savage creatures, those," Hilda said as though agreeing with her, and the magpie darted away around the corner. "I really think they delight in it. I've seen them tear starlings to pieces and leave them after one mouthful."

Susanne was in no mood to be reminded that anything revelled in violence. "Well, watching isn't going to bring him."

"Like the kettle," Hilda said, and not quite so enigmatically. "Do you want me to keep an eye open?"

"You could. To tell you the truth—" Susanne was less than certain that she wanted to, but she could hardly stop now. "Apparently he's been playing hooky. That's why I'm like this."

Perhaps her state wasn't apparent, because Hilda looked bemused; then she said, "It was only us girls who played that when we were at school."

"Only—oh. Not hockey, hooky," Susanne said, though that sounded even more absurd than the misunderstanding. "AWOL. Skiving, I think you may call it. Playing truant. Something at school upset him and he took the afternoon off."

"He must be easily upset still, poor little, well, not so little, but he'll always be your baby, won't he? I know mine are. Shall I march him in if I see him?"

"Just tell him I'm not mad. No, just don't let him go away."

"I didn't mean actually get hold of him. I remember how I used to feel when any of them didn't turn up, Matt included. Like someone was dragging my nerves over sandpaper." Abruptly Hilda seemed to feel she'd said at least enough, and set about pecking at the hedge with the shears.

She meant well. If Susanne didn't feel as bad as Hilda had described, surely that was because she didn't need to feel that way. She retreated into the house, closing the doors and peering at the answering machine in case it showed a call she hadn't heard. Of course she would have heard the phone ring. What time was it? Well past five o'clock, which had to mean she would see Marshall any moment now—he wouldn't want to worry her, not after everything they had been through. She headed for the essays, then made for Marshall's room instead. She ought to have checked if he had taken anything with him—one item in particular.

Three books in various stages of being read were keeping one another company on the floor, one sprawling open on its face, the others protruding bookmarks printed with the name and address of Don's shop. When had Marshall started reading more than one book at a time? She hoped it didn't mean he was losing his ability to concentrate, as she had for a while, but now she'd found what she was looking for: his radio cassette player. Which tape could she see through the plastic window? She lifted the player onto the bed and pushed the play button, and heard a voice saying ". . . *Daith of a Bodgie* ond *Socks un Rostoronts*. Thonks." She had never returned the call or written to the Ulsterman, and now it seemed too late. Never mind, she knew Marshall hadn't taken the tape with him, and she was reaching for the off button, stopping just short of pressing it, when Don said, "Hi, Susanne? Are you home? Are you home yet?"

She shoved the button down so hard she was afraid of having broken her fingernail or the player. Maybe she could listen to that another time, but not while it meant so much. She gazed at the black oblong lying next to the flat empty clothes, each as silent as the other, and then she switched it to the local news; the five-thirty headlines were due. The newsreader's voice drained of most of its accent had nothing to report about Marshall or anybody of his age, only a nine-year-old Asian boy set on fire by three of his white schoolmates, and a policeman beaten up by the drivers of both cars involved in a traffic accident, and a gang who'd gouged out a jeweler's eye to make him tell them the combination of his safe, and a teenager who'd tried to drown his girlfriend's baby in a toilet. She told herself that the way all that affected her had nothing to do with Marshall. Maybe he wasn't even aware of how worried she was growing, maybe he hadn't noticed the time, particularly if he was with one of his friends. She couldn't believe it had only now occurred to her to contact their parents. She ran downstairs to find her address book in her purse.

It opened at the first address she'd ever had for Don. At least that brought her close to one she needed, and by the time she arrived at the phone she'd found the Syeds. She had barely dialed when she was greeted by what sounded like the clangor of a foundry, and thought she'd misdialed until a man said, "Cosmic Video?"

As soon as she identified the noise as the clash of swords it turned into Indian dance music. "Mr. Syed?" she presumed. "Is Ali there?"

"Mrs. Travis, you are? My son is at the mosque."

"Marshall wouldn't have gone there with him, obviously." In case that could be taken as an insult Susanne quickly added, "I mean, there isn't any chance that Marshall's with him, is there, to your knowledge?"

"He seemed not interested in God when I raised the subject with him."

"When was that?"

"Let me see." The pause which this entailed seemed so prolonged that eventually Susanne said, "Today? This afternoon?"

"I suppose it will have been . . ." Only the slightest of intonations suggested this wasn't the end of the sentence. "Four," he let slip as the music worked itself into more of a frenzy, "perhaps five months."

"But not today. That isn't—" Susanne said, and made an effort to grasp her syntax as firmly as she was gripping the receiver. "Today you haven't seen him."

"That is true, Mrs. Travis. Have you not?"

"Sure, this morning, when he went to school. Only now he's late home, quite late, and I'm trying to find out where he is."

"That is boys. I remember not thinking of my mother when I had a game to finish with my friends, and my father—" He cleared his throat so sharply that Susanne heard the mouthpiece vibrate. "I shall ask God to smile upon you, Mrs. Travis."

"That's—" Of course he wasn't implying that he needed to pray for Marshall, he'd just remembered Don. "If Marshall should by any chance come in, could you give me a ring and let him speak to me? I'm just worried, though I expect I shouldn't be. I just want him home."

"It will be my pleasure, Mrs. Travis."

She would have liked to feel as certain as he sounded. Maybe after her next call she could. She dialed the Warris home, where the phone continued ringing for such a long time that she began to imagine the boys engrossed in, as Mr. Syed had suggested, some game. Indeed, one was in rowdy progress when the phone was picked up. "Hell—" was as much of a greeting as the answerer managed before turning away some of his shout. "Shut up while I'm talking on the phone, will you. Shut up or I'll burst you. Shut up, Dick."

The Warrises were a large family, Susanne gathered, and perhaps this was how members of large families addressed one another. "Trevor?"

"Give him that. Give it him now or I'll thump you. Oh," he said, to some extent into the mouthpiece, "it's, I know, hang on, I'll get my dad."

"You'll do, Trevor. I only want—" But he'd dropped the receiver—into her ear, it felt rather like—and presumably had gone to find his father, since the noises off which denoted his intervention in the squabble eventually included progressively receding yells of "Dad!" A male roar came to join the renewed altercation, and seemed to be at some little distance from the phone when there was a clatter of plastic and an immediate question. "Yes?"

"Hi, Mr. Warris. Susanne here, Marshall's mother."

"Yes?"

Surely he was being hostile to the unabated uproar, not to her. "Get out of it, the lot of you. Right out. You too, Trev," he bawled, and had nothing to say to Susanne until the chorus of complaints had receded almost into inaudibility. Then he said, "Yes?"

"Quite a handful you've got there," Susanne said, trying to reach past his continuing hostility, but was confronted by a silence which appeared to imply she'd been more personal than she had intended. "Three boys, isn't it?" she said, and when that provoked no more than a grunt, "I'm sorry to bother you. I only wanted to ask Trevor if Marshall was there with you."

"With me."

"With him. At your house."

"No, he wouldn't be."

"He isn't, then." That was all Susanne needed to know at the moment, but not all she wanted to know. "Why wouldn't he be? I didn't know he and Trevor had fallen out."

"They still see each other at school. Hang around together, knowing Trev." With a resentfulness which struck Susanne as wholly inappropriate he said, "The lassie and me told Trev not to have your lad round for a bit, that's all."

"You won't mind my asking why."

"Come on, lass, I thought you were supposed to be a professor. You don't need it spelling out for you." When she clamped her mouth shut, though she could hear he was resentful because he was embarrassed, he had to go on. "If you think it's on to let your lad watch exactly what he likes then maybe it's not my place to say owt, but we aren't having ours getting mixed up with the law."

"Marshall isn't, except when he was a witness in court."

"Aye, well, we know all about that." Mr. Warris's embarrassment was rendering his words so blunt they sounded as though he was blaming her, especially when he said. "What's up with him, anyway? Trev said he sagged off school this affy. I'd not have thought that was like him."

"It wouldn't be if he wasn't being made to feel a lot of people disapprove of him."

"We disapprove of sagging, right enough. So you won't find him here setting ours a bad example."

Susanne squeezed her eyes shut until the light in them began to pound. "On the remote chance he hasn't realized he's no longer welcome at his friend's house, would it be too much trouble to send him home if he turns up? If you can bear to, you might tell him I'd like to hear his side of what happened at the school."

The distant squabble was returning, eager to invade the room. "I'm coming to sort you lot right now," Mr. Warris yelled, and Susanne thought that would be his excuse to say nothing more to her. Then he said conspiratorially and with audible reluctance, "If he finds his way here I'll put him on the blower and you can tell him yourself."

She was only starting to utter some expression of gratitude when Mr. Warris cut her off. How much time had she wasted in talking to him? Too long to have time to glance at her watch now. She held onto the book while she turned pages with the deftness of a croupier turning cards, then let the book flop shut. She had dialed and was wondering if her haste had garbled the number when Tom Bold said, "Her her—"

A woman's voice which sounded as though it scarcely ever paused for breath commenced gabbling at him. "Who's that, Tom? Is it for me? It's not your Auntie Noddy, is it? Don't you know who it is?"

"Hi, Tom. Have you seen Marshall?"

"Mam, it's Marshall's mermother."

"Which Marshall's that? Is he the one who talks like what's his name when he's at home, the feller with the nose, you know the one I mean, don't be trying to get me all of a tizz, Harvey Kitetail?"

"It's Keitel, mam. I've told you, Mer Mer Marshall doesn't—"

"Tom, I just want to know where Marshall is."

"Hang on, mam. She's asking about her, about him. Hello, Mrs. Travis. Marshall wasn't at sker, at sker—"

"I know he played hoo, took the afternoon off," Susanne interrupted, feeling as if she'd caught some of Tom's stuttering. "But he isn't home. I wondered if you knew where he might be."

"He ser ser—"

"Do you want me to talk to her, son? I'll bet she knows which feller he sounds like. I heard someone just like him in one of the videos you had. Shut my eyes and I'd have sworn it was him. I'll remember what the feller said if you keep quiet for a moment. When you look round I'll be gone, he says at the end, or something like."

"Mam, I'm trer, I'm trying—"

"Did he say anything to you before he walked out, Tom? Anything at all."

"No, Mrs. Travis. I didn't ner, I didn't know he'd gone till we went in. Won't he be all rer—"

"I'm sure he will, Tom. I mean, what are the chances of something bad happening to him? I expect he just doesn't know how to tell me what he did. If he shows up at your house, you'll tell him I only want to know he's safe, won't you? Which he will be, don't you think?"

"I her her—"

"I hope so too," Susanne said, and immediately thought she should apologize for completing his word, except that the apology would make him even more conscious of his problem. She rang off, because Marshall had other friends he sometimes visited, though not as often as the three she'd attempted to contact so far. She was leafing through the address book when the receiver shrilled in her hand.

Surely it was Marshall. The time wasn't far short of six o'clock—dinnertime. He would never keep her guessing past that; he must have at least some sense of how anxious she was. She jabbed the talk button. "Yes, I'm here."

"Susanne Travis?"

How could a voice simply asking if she was herself make her need to sit down on the stairs? Because of its official sound—because its tone was carefully neutral. "This is she," Susanne said, her grip tightening on the receiver.

"Good afternoon, Mrs. Travis. Inspect a drum of Manchester Constabulary."

His vowels were so clipped that for a moment Susanne was able to believe he'd issued that invitation, but it didn't help. She groped with her free hand for the banister to steady herself. "You're the police."

"Right enough, Mrs. Travis. I've been trying to contact you."

"What—" She seemed unable to say much more than that, even when she tried a second time. "What's—"

"We'll need to see you as soon as possible."

Her throat shrank, and her question came out small and pleading. "Why?"

"It isn't as bad as it might be."

She thought he was taking pity on her, which made the next question even more difficult to ask. "How bad?"

"A large fine, Mrs. Travis. Maybe prison. That's how bad it could have been."

The pity had gone from his voice, and there wasn't much patience left either. "I don't—" Susanne said, but didn't feel quite confident enough to finish, not even a question. "What are we talking—"

"The decision has been taken not to prosecute."

"Prosecute whom for what?"

"Under the circumstances, Mrs. Travis, only you."

She was beginning to grasp that the subject might not be Marshall, in which case she saw no point in talking while Marshall could be trying to call her. "For . . ."

"I appreciate you've had a tragedy, but there's a limit to how much we can take that into account, unfortunately. You'll recall our reason for visiting your house."

So that was the point they'd taken all this time to reach. Why couldn't anyone speak plainly to her? Was her uncertainty infecting them? "The videos," she said.

"Precisely. If you'd like to come into the station and sign a waiver that'll be the end of it."

"It isn't too urgent, then."

"I'd like to close the case as soon as possible," he said, more heavily than she felt was required. "Can you come in tomorrow?"

"Tomorrow might be a problem." Surely it wouldn't be, at least not one to do with Marshall, but she found herself wishing she hadn't arranged to meet the bookseller either, not until she was sure . . . "Can I call you tomorrow when my schedule's firmer?"

"I may not be here in the morning."

Though that might have been intended to force her to commit herself, she only waited until he doled out the phone number. "Inspector Drumm," she confirmed, and opened her mouth again, suddenly deciding to tell him about Marshall. But he'd gone, and it was six o'clock, time for the local news. She ran to fetch her radio from the kitchen, and switched it on as she carried it to her vantage point in the front room.

All it had to tell her were more details of the crimes she had already heard headlined. Then came the weather, a cold night for anyone who might be wandering the streets or sleeping on them, and Susanne was reaching for the off switch when the newsreader added, "Some news just in . . ." A hollow tinny sound filled Susanne's ears, and she was afraid both of hearing what he was about to say and of not being able to hear. The information which the local radio had just received, presumably from the police, concerned two men in Balaclavas who had smashed a bank guard's legs with metal bars to make the tellers hand over all the money in the cash drawers. Susanne released a sigh which could have been mistaken for a sob and switched off the radio.

She hadn't written down the addresses and phone numbers of all Marshall's new friends in her book. Some she had to find in the floppy cumbersome directory; more than one surname she had to strain to remember. Most of her calls interrupted families at dinner. She watched the street and saw figures turning the corner, always neighbors coming home, as she spoke into the phone, growing more apologetic and more desperate. It was almost seven o'clock when she exhausted her list of the people she knew Marshall knew, and so she listened to the latest news, which it transpired she had already heard. She opened the front door and gazed along the street, empty of all the people who'd gone into their houses. She closed her door and listened to the silence she was alone with, and then she called the police.

21

MA AND DA

For a while Darren only watched. Marshall had sat down at last, not that it seemed to have done him much good. Darren had given him the channel control and told him he could switch the telly on, but he was too busy trying either to catch sight of things around him in the room or not to see them. Darren watched his eyes dart back and forth as though they were doing their best to jerk themselves out of their sockets, staring at the cardigan which Darren's mother had slung into one corner, and the hair-dryer poking its muzzle out of another, and the bills stuffed through the bars of the electric fire, and the picture above it of some fat women having a bath, Bernard's idea for giving the place a bit of class. Darren had a good idea of how Marshall was feeling, and maybe even what he was seeing; he'd done it to himself often enough. He'd proved he could take it, and if Marshall couldn't, that showed he was as much of a wimp as Ken and Dave had shown his da was. Darren had expected that, but now Marshall's twitching and staring had begun to get on his nerves; he wished he hadn't taken off his Walkman. He hoped his mother or someone else in the family would turn up soon to see what he'd brought them.

Maybe now his mother would stop giving him a hard time about telling the headmaster to fuck off and spitting on his desk. If Darren hadn't been suspended from school he mightn't have been on the spot when Marshall had skived off from his. He'd been hanging around outside the schoolyard in case Marshall went home for lunch, but he couldn't have expected him to make such a present of himself. He would have done him in the graveyard if the footballers hadn't started playing toward that side of the field. He'd crouched behind some bushes near the grave someone had smashed up—he'd felt as though they'd gone for it on his behalf—and watched Marshall's face go red and his mouth pull his chin up and his eyes start to leak. He'd been close enough to thump the back of Marshall's neck when he'd finished sniveling and talking to the grave, a performance which had made Darren have to squash his sniggers behind a hand, but he hadn't been able to think of anything bad enough to do to Marshall for putting his father in jail and killing his favorite uncle. He'd tracked Marshall home, feeling like a camera that was being the eyes of a maniac stalking his prey, only then some bitch who was working in her garden had never gone inside long enough for him to sneak past. He'd seen Marshall come out again, wearing a track suit exactly like one of Darren's, and Darren had dodged ahead until Marshall caught a bus. As Darren had poked around in his pocket for change, he'd found something he'd believed he'd lost, and he'd grinned all the way into Manchester.

It might have been meant just for Marshall. He'd even left his Coke for Darren to slip it into. If anyone had noticed Darren dodging into McDonald's and pretending to pinch a drink, they'd said nothing to him as he'd strolled outside to watch. Marshall had even moved to a window to give him a better view. He'd watched Marshall begin not to know what was wrong, and wander to the shop where Ken and Dave had done for his father, and then around the Arndale Center as the monsters came out to play. He'd intervened only when it had looked as though Marshall might attract the attention of one of the Arndale arseholes who thought wearing a uniform made them somebody. What was going to happen to him had hardly started, and so Darren had brought him home.

Only he was beginning to get tired of him, of his shutting his eyes and popping them open because he couldn't bear to keep them shut for any more hours which in fact had only been seconds, and peering around him in the hope that something he was afraid to see had gone away, and making little kicked puppy noises in his throat. Darren mightn't have been so irritated if he could see what Marshall was seeing, but imagining it was too much trouble and besides, trying made his hair feel as though it was crawling back and forth on his skull. Now Marshall had given over making noises for a bit and was staring at Darren instead. He seemed to be trying to resemble the puppy he'd sounded like, and all that would get him was punched in both eyes if he carried on doing it. Except that was too far to reach unless Darren moved out of his chair, and so he snarled, "What?"

"Darren?"

Marshall might have been asking if that was really his name. Darren wished he hadn't let it out to help Marshall trust him. "Who says?"

"Didn't you?"

"What if I did? What's it to you? Tell you what, you call me Da. What's my name?"

"Da?"

"Bet your arse. Say it again so you know it. Go on, lad, say it a few times."

"Da da."

"It's free, you know. You don't have to fill in a fucking claim form. Really a few, so you'll remember."

"Da da da da da."

"Magic. What's my name?"

"Da."

"You hang onto that, lad. Keep it short so you'll remember it even with all the shit that's happening to you. And your name's Ma. What's your name?"

"Ma?"

A snort of derision escaped from Darren's nose, which he wiped on a bit of one of the newspaper pages strewn about the floor. "Maaa," he said like a sheep he'd once heard, the time a teacher had taken his class at little kids' school up on the moors. The memory took him off guard, and he felt like belting someone, because he was fucked if he was going to let it make him feel sad. Then Marshall said, "Da?"

"What fucking now?"

"You said you'd give me something."

"I will and all, if you don't stop pissing me off." But if he didn't give him something like he'd promised, Marshall might try and leave. "I'll see what we've got," Darren said. "You stay sat in that chair and don't try to get up. You'll be safe if you stay sat in the chair."

He looked back from the hall and turned away quickly, suppressed mirth driving the taste of snot into his mouth. Marshall certainly did as he was told—he was pressing himself into the chair and hanging onto the arms like a tart on a roller coaster. To get him into the house Darren had promised him something that would calm him down, but now he didn't know what he could give him.

He jogged upstairs, letting go of the banister when he felt it grinding its screws in the wall. His grandfather was making a noise like some kind of giant dying insect, in his sleep or out of it, and Darren wondered how the moaning must sound to Marshall. He went into the bathroom and slid back the mirrors speckled with squirts of pus, but there was nothing in the cabinet except bottles and sprays, most of them empty, none of them with tops on. The solitary bottle of pills—aspirins—contained only a spider's cocoon furry with talcum powder. He dug his nails into the dents in the glass and slammed the mirrors shut, and sidled into his parents' room.

The quilt looked as though they'd just been sleeping under it, and not only sleeping. Maybe his mother had had some trade under it while he'd been out hunting Marshall. He lifted it up by one corner while he peered under the bed in case any pills had rolled into the dust there, and one of his fingers sank into the spongy filling through a hole charred by a cigarette. He felt as if it was trying to suck him into what had happened in the bed, and he threw back the quilt and spat on the rumpled grubby sheet which covered part of the mattress, then heaved the quilt over it and glared around the room.

The evening light through the high mingy window looked darkened by the stale smoke the room smelled of, but he could see the wardrobe with one door propping up the other, and the dressing table with bottles and jars of cosmetics staggering against one another where his mother must have shoved them aside to peer at herself in the mirror. The alarm clock which she'd thrown off the bedside table was blinking all its zeros, desperate for attention, and as he showed his teeth at it he saw a half-used tinfoil pack of her pills next to the ashtray snaggletoothed with butts, the kind of pill which her forgetting to take had got her pregnant with Darren, when Bernard wouldn't let her and his father get rid of him. Stealing one of those felt like getting even, though he wasn't sure for what. He pinched the capsule between finger and thumb and ran downstairs. "Get this down you, Ma. It's a stopper."

Marshall hadn't moved. He looked as if he thought he had been staying still for hours, and so grateful for the promise of a cure that Darren wondered if he should give him a bit of one to keep him there. Maybe there was some orange juice in the fridge. Juice is use, he remembered saying over and over to himself once as he'd drunk a liter of it, and after a very long time it had seemed to muffle what was happening to him. But there was no juice in the kitchen anymore, only a carton of milk that smelled as though something had died in it. If the kid was stupid enough to come into the house, he deserved everything he got. Darren grabbed a cracked beer glass from the mass of crockery drowning in the sink and poured most of the gray water out of it to make room for water from the tap, and took it to Marshall along with the pill. "Just stick it in your gob and swallow, lad."

Marshall was watching drips from the bottom of the glass running across the carpet toward him, a trail of drops dark as blood. He snatched the pill and poked it together with all the fingers and thumb of one hand into his mouth, and threw his head back so far that Darren could almost see the pill slipping down the stretched throat. A gulp of water followed, though Marshall would clearly have liked to return that to the glass, which he dropped on the floor, spilling some of its contents. He leaned his head back and closed his eyes, and Darren sat down to watch.

Maybe Marshall wanted to pray; he was trying to fit his fingers between one another. Darren observed him having to look and see what he was holding—the channel control. That led his stare to the television, and he glared at his reflection on the fingermarked screen in such dismay that Darren felt excluded and more irritated than ever. "What's on telly, Ma? Something good?"

A grin of panic dragged at one side of Marshall's mouth and let go. "That isn't me," he pleaded.

"Doesn't baba want to be on it now? Wasn't you once?"

Marshall grabbed at his eyes as though he meant to rip whatever he was seeing out of his head. He held onto them as he twisted awkwardly, drawing his knees up toward his stomach. When he was more or less facing Darren he let go and stared at him, and Darren knew from his look of relief, which was so pitiful it was funny, that he felt as though the horrors were going away. "See," Darren said. "It's working already."

Of course Marshall was just experiencing a lull before the next wave, and when he spoke Darren wondered whether he was too far gone ever to come back. "The police let them into our house."

"Fucking filth," Darren responded automatically, and returned to amusing himself. "Let what in, Ma? If there's summat there you're scared of you won't want to go home."

He was amazed and delighted how easy it was to put ideas into Marshall's head. The kid might think he was better than Darren, or would do if he was able to think straight, but he wouldn't be better in any way by the time Darren had finished with him. He held out his hands to Darren, maybe to plead with him to take the idea back, but visibly didn't like the look of them. "I don't mean now. There's nothing there now."

"Sodded off, have they?"

"They were there, though." Marshall was managing to summon up some resentment at being mocked. "Men with lights, you know, men."

"Fairy lights, was they wearing?"

"You know what I mean. Lights, the kind they hold. Lights and cameras."

"And action, eh, Ma? You was never making a mucky film."

For some reason that made Marshall stare at him as though trying to recognize him. "This is my fucking face all right," Darren said. "Got a problem with it? Want to come here and change it, lad?"

"No," Marshall pleaded, closing his eyes tight. "Only didn't you say that before, about that kind of film?"

Darren hadn't, but wasn't admitting it. "So what if I did?"

"Nothing except I must have told you we weren't in any blue movie. I thought we were on—"

What he said then bewildered Darren, who snarled, "What's a candy camera?"

"Candid, like what's another word, you must know." The grin was flickering in and out of Marshall's mouth, amusement teetering at the edge of panic. He mustn't be able to drive the idea of a candy camera out of his head, and by the look of him it was starting to rot and go soft and taste too sweet, or something at least as gross. "Like truthful or hidden," he said in a rush, and seemed unable to make sense of that himself. "When you're filmed and you don't know you're being."

"They've got them cameras all over outside," Darren lied on impulse, "so stay in if you don't want them coming to take you away. Any road, I thought you said you saw them when the filth let them in your house."

"Sure, when they took all our videos away." He stared hard at Darren. "When did you see us? They oughtn't to have broadcast it when my mom's still waiting to hear what the law's going to do to us."

"You've got a fucking screw loose, lad. The last dick who went around saying I did summat I never, even the dentist couldn't put his teeth back together."

"She hasn't even been to court yet," Marshall insisted, then thrust his legs out clumsily and wavered to his feet. "My mom, she'll be worrying. What time is it now?"

"Fucking hell, don't you ever get sick of asking? There's the clock. The tail's hanging down and the dick's sticking up, which means it's six o'clock. It does here, any road. Maybe you do it different where you come from."

Marshall didn't seem to know. He dropped his head toward his watch, but was obviously unable to decide whether it showed the same time as the clock, which had been stopped for weeks. He only had to glance out of the window to see the time was later, except he was too busy digging his nails into his scalp, maybe trying to persuade himself it wasn't coming loose. "Can I call my mom?"

"If you reckon you can yell that loud. We've got no phone. We're too poor, us. Got one but it doesn't work. They cut us off because my mam can't pay the bill now my da—" Darren shut himself up and glared at Marshall. "I thought you came in to lie down, lad."

"I need to go home if I can't call my mom. She'll be getting upset. She's upset already."

"Why, what's up with her? Won't she let her ickle baba go out by his self?" Fun though this was, it wouldn't keep Marshall in the house. "Listen, I know what," Darren said, moving between Marshall and the door. "You go up on my bed and I'll go and phone."

"What will you say?"

"What do you want saying?"

"Just where I am and I'm all right and she can come and get me. I will be all right once she comes."

Darren wasn't sure whether that was meant to comfort Marshall or himself, not that it mattered. "Straight up then, Ma, and give your pill a chance to work."

"Can I have another?"

"Aye, why not. Do you twice as much good. You get where you're told and don't forget your water and I'll bring you your pill."

Darren stood out of the way, mostly to block Marshall's route to the front door, and followed him upstairs. Maybe Marshall didn't know he was gouging bits out of the wallpaper as he clawed himself along. If Darren's mother even noticed, like as not she would think she'd done it. "Next to the bog," Darren said when Marshall started to prowl back and forth on the landing as though the banisters which Darren's father had shoved him against a few times were a cage. Marshall seemed to have no idea what he meant—maybe they didn't call a toilet that where he came from—and Darren had to catch him by one arm and push him into the bedroom.

Clothes were slung over most of the clutter, including the computer Darren had broken months past; only the television and video were on display. He thought of telling Marshall he could watch a mucky video, because when was the last time he'd had a friend to boast to in his room? Except Marshall wasn't a friend, and Darren didn't need any. "Don't hang about, lie down," he ordered, and went to fetch another pill.

When he came back Marshall had taken off his shoes and pulled the quilt over him, so obedient it made Darren want to heave. At least he wouldn't get far with no shoes on, and he looked as if he mightn't be able to find them again, especially once Darren had kicked them under the bed. "Get your gob open," Darren said, pinching his nose to keep in a snigger at the sight of Marshall poking his head up like some kind of reptile and shutting his eyes and dropping his jaw as far as it would stretch. Darren was tempted to throw in something for Marshall to swallow before he knew what it was, but he couldn't think of anything gross enough that was handy and besides, he was supposed to be keeping Marshall there. He flicked the pill onto Marshall's tongue and watched it go down. "Don't you move while I'm out or I won't phone," he said, and closed the door.

He wasn't going anywhere except downstairs. He could slam the front door a couple of times to convince Marshall he'd gone out and come back. He waited on the landing a few minutes in case Marshall tried to leave the room, but the only sound was his grandfather moaning like a tart in a mucky film. He was heading for the stairs when he heard someone unlocking the front door.

It was his mother, and not by herself. When she said, "This way, love, don't be shy," he knew she'd brought some trade home, and he crouched to watch over the edge of the landing. She came in wearing at least an hour's worth of makeup and her silver dress that clung to all of her arse that it covered, and the man shut the door after them. He was nearly twice as wide as her, with oily black curls and a chin that didn't leave much room for the rest of his face, and a neck that stuck out farther than the chin, and a bald pink chest which showed between the buttons of his white shirt. He plodded toward Darren's mother like a zombie hungry for flesh, his hands making the shape of the tits they were reaching for. "Ooh, you excite me, but give us a tick, love," she said, and raised her voice. "Where are you, Darren? You're in, aren't you?"

The man halted, his neck wobbling. "Who's he? Why do you want him?"

"Don't fret, he's just my little lad. He knows to lock up if he goes out, little bastard. Ooh, I want you so much, but let's just see where he is first. Darren, you answer me right now or I'm telling your Uncle Bernard."

The man poked his face over his bag of neck as if he thought Bernard was about to jump him, and Darren would have liked to carry on watching him and his mother acting stupid, but he couldn't have Marshall coming to see what the row was and letting the man see him. He hauled himself up, letting go of the banisters as they gave. "Here I am, mam."

"Never mind skulking up there and seeing what you can see. This is just a friend of mine I met in the pub. What's your name again, love?"

The man had to think about it, and seemed not to want to. "Dick."

"Ooh, and I'll bet I know why. You come down here and watch telly for a bit, Darren. We won't be long. Or maybe Dick will give you some money to walk to the offy and get yourself something to drink."

"If that's what it takes to get shut of him," said the man whose name was anything but Dick. "How much is he after?"

"You can spare a few quid, can't you? I only brought you home because I thought you was generous."

At any other time Darren would have taken maximum advantage of this. "I'll watch telly in my room, mam."

"You will not. I'm not having you up there. You sod off and get yourself a treat when you're told before I fetch you a few kicks up the backside."

"Fuck off. You aren't my da."

"I'll show you who I am. I'll teach you to tell your own mam to fuck off," she shouted and launched herself at the stairs, then lingered to give the man's arm a hasty stroke. "I'm panting for you, love. Just let me chuck him out," she murmured in the lowest voice she could manage, and flung herself at the stairs again. Darren was wondering where to hide—this was hardly the time to let her find Marshall—when another key scraped into the front-door lock.

His mother twisted round and grabbed her waist with both hands. Alias Dick made a fist and rubbed his mouth with the side of it as though to pretend it wasn't one. The smell of a cigar told Darren who the new arrival was, and he waited for some fun. The door swung open, and Bernard stared at Darren's mother to tell her she should have opened it. "Right, Marie, listen," he began, wagging the cigar at her and scattering ash on the carpet. Then he saw the man, and jammed the cigar between his bared teeth. "Dear bleeding Jesus, not now."

"Bernard, this is—"

"He's Bernard, is he? Got here fast. What kind of setup is this?"

"Who's this? Where's he know me from?"

"He's nobody, Bern. Just someone I met in the pub and, you know, brought home. Darren was winding me up, that's all, and I said I'd get you if he didn't behave."

"Don't know what you think you're playing at sometimes, Marie, letting him see you with the customers. Have a bit of shame or you'll have him growing up with no respect. Chuck him out, any road. I want to talk."

"See, I told you you weren't wanted, Darren. Maybe you'll do as your uncle says."

"Not Darren, you daft bitch. This bugger with a belly for a neck."

The man made a fist to go with the other one. "You want to watch who you're talking about, chum. I've had a few barneys in my time and come off better than the other feller."

"You oughtn't to insult my friends, Bern. I've got to keep the money coming in with Phil being where he is."

"I'll give you plenty if you'll kick this bugger out. Mother of Christ, lass, do him up against the back fence if you have to, just make it quick. He doesn't look like he'll take long."

The man stepped forward, pushing Darren's mother aside. "Listen, matey, I've had just about e—"

Bernard thrust his face into the man's and sucked hard on the cigar. "See this?"

"Aye, it's an ugly mug with a stinker stuck in its mush."

Bernard took the cigar out of his mouth and blew the end redder and poked it in the man's left eye. "Want to carry on seeing?"

Darren hugged himself with delight and admiration. He almost called Marshall to come and see. The man stood his ground for quite a few seconds, and Darren thought he must be too terrified to move when his eye-socket was impaled on the cigar, in which case any moment now he should start dancing on the spot and waving his arms frantically and screaming. Then he retreated beyond Darren's mother, rubbing the eye hard, and Darren saw that the cigar hadn't been nearly as close as it had appeared to him. He felt disappointed and betrayed, and was trying to think of something to tell Bernard to make him go for the intruder when the man said, "No need to be like that. She came on all friendly. I thought I was on."

"You want to thank me, pal. You might have caught something."

Darren's mother grabbed both sides of her waist again, but the man spoke before she could squeeze out a retort. "I wouldn't call it worth four Bacardi and Cokes to find that out."

"Cheap at the price, pal." Bernard bit hard on the cigar and walked fast at him, into his own smoke. When he took hold of the man's collar Darren thought he was going to use the cigar properly this time, but he only pulled a ten-pound note out of his pocket and stuffed it down the man's shirt. "Take that as a souvenir because I'm in a good mood. If I was you I'd get it framed to remind me never to come sniffing round here again. See the door?"

"I'm going, I'm going." The man waddled along the hall, giving Darren the consolation that he was walking as though he'd shat himself. Having opened the front door wide enough to allow him a quick exit, he turned. "You lot against the rest of the world, eh?"

"Couldn't have put it better myself," Bernard said, to Darren's frustration, and slammed the door behind the man. Darren's mother was waiting for her pose to be appreciated, but Bernard held up his hand, pointing the wet end of the cigar at her. "Don't start. Just listen. We've got some real money this time that we'll need to hide for as long as it takes, and I'll see to it there's a cut for you."

"Who's we?"

"Who do you think, with Jim dead and Brad on crutches waiting for his trial and Ken and Dave and Phil inside, all because of those bloody Yanks?"

"That Barry again, is it?"

"That's the feller. Only one I can trust that's left, even if he does get a bit out of hand with any bugger he takes a dislike to. Better have a ride for half an hour, Darren. He's not going to want you seeing what we bring in."

This didn't seem a good time for Darren to announce who was in his room, but he couldn't very well go out and risk Marshall wandering into the midst of the delivery, because Barry might use that as an excuse to stash the loot somewhere else. "There's nowhere to go. You said I was the man of the house. Last time you wanted me to be the lookout."

"All right, lad. May as well get some use out of you. I don't reckon Barry can vote against that."

"I'll just get my Walkman, I mean my cap."

"Sweet sainted Joseph, can't anyone of your age do a thing without one or the other? You'd think you couldn't wipe your bum without listening to that racket you call music and some bloody trademark stuck on your head."

Darren was upstairs by now. He dodged into his room and shut the door and darted to the bed, snatching his baseball cap from the heap of clothes on the computer. Marshall peered between his fingers while he tried to worm his way farther under the quilt. "You stay like that," Darren muttered. "There's someone downstairs you won't want to see. Don't come out till I tell you they've gone."

Marshall looked too scared to do anything else. Darren closed the door and hurried downstairs with a face that said he hadn't been talking. Bernard shoved his phone in his pocket and went into the back room to pull up the loose floorboard and hand Darren's mother the gun to wrap in a cardigan. "Put that somewhere you know where it is. Get across the road, lad. Barry's on his way."

Darren loitered on the doorstep until Bernard snarled at him to get across the road. He went as far as the gate and listened for sounds from the house, Marshall screaming and maybe Darren's mother too, but when there was silence apart from the yelps of an injured dog he made himself walk to the opposite pavement, picking his way between turds on the tire-chewed strip of grass. Soon the old Post Office van with its official words scraped off belched to a halt outside his gate and Barry slid the door open, ignoring him after one glance.

Darren was hoping to see him carry fistfuls of money into the house, to prove that nobody would dare to stop him or report him. Instead Barry lifted out of the rear of the van some bags of pet food, and came back for several plastic bags of straw. All of this might have appeared innocent if it hadn't been for the obvious presence of a lookout, and Barry must have realized that eventually, because he glared at Darren as he slammed the rear doors of the van and jerked his head to indicate the house as though it was his own. That enraged Darren so much that he took all the time he could to cross the road, stopping to tie a shoelace that didn't need tying, although the delay made him itch to be certain that Marshall hadn't ventured out of his room.

Before Darren reached the gate Barry had shut him out of the house. He ran along the path, spitting in as many directions as he could manage, and let himself in. There was nobody in sight, and only a mumble of voices from the back room. He edged that door open, and saw his mother and the two men sitting crouched forward around the hole in the floor, into which Barry was feeding a fat wad of used banknotes from one of the bags of rabbit food. "What the fuck you gawping at?" Barry said.

"He's Phil's lad, he won't snitch. Come in as long as you've seen it, Darren, and shut the door."

Barry was high as a kid on Ecstasy, maybe only with excitement. His metallic shaved scalp was shining with moisture, and the whitish flesh of his scar looked in danger of parting. As soon as Darren had closed the door he demanded, "Got any pets, lad?"

Darren thought of Marshall being kept in his room, but he said, "No."

"Wouldn't want you feeding your rabbit any of this. Here," Barry said, flinging him a bag of food. "Rip out its guts and get to the good stuff."

He watched, rapidly tapping his heels in the air with his toes on the carpet, while Darren tried to poke his fingernails into the knot in the neck of the plastic bag. "Fuck, lad, you'd think you were unbuttoning some tart's dress," he said almost at once. "Just rip it like you'd rip her pants off."

"Uncle Bernard doesn't like mess."

"He puts up with it when it buys him seegars, don't you, Bern? More seegars than one of them Hollywood mongols. What are you, lad, a spastic? Get a move on, we're all falling asleep."

Darren took his time to spite him. He dug a fingernail into the knot and unraveled the plastic and thrust his hand inside the bag, cereal and grains gritting under his nails. He'd just taken hold of a wad of twenty-pound notes which he could barely fit his hand around when Barry straightened like a razor out of his chair and grabbing Darren's wrist, prized the wad loose. "That'll do you. Remember what it felt like and maybe when you're older you'll make somebody's fortune like my dad always said to me. Like he said, let someone else earn it for you, know what I mean?"

For the moment his excitement had veered away from being dangerous. He placed the wad under the floor and started shaking his head, eyes wide and glistening. "Ever smash a crab with a rock, lad?"

"No."

"You want to get your mam to take you to Blackpool. I'm telling you, that's exactly what that guard's knees felt like. You should have heard him screaming at them bank girls to give us the money. Like being on telly and winning the star prize, it was. Don't go away yet, here's another few grand we want you to have so you won't come back next week."

Bernard's fixed look must have told him at last that he was talking too much. He said nothing more as he went for the packages like a dog clawing at bin-bags, scattering the contents across the carpet except for the notes, which he laid to rest under the floor. His expression was pinching itself grimmer, and once the last wad was stored he glared around him. "Don't know why you didn't bring the fucking neighbors in to watch while you was at it, Bern. Listen, lad, this is Barry talking to you. If anyone finds out about this I'll know it was you told them, and I'll do worse to your face than I got when I was your age, see it? Don't bring anyone in here, in the house, understand, till we've shifted all that, and don't even fucking dream of arguing with me. Shut your trap."

Darren already had, and sneered inside himself at Barry for not knowing there was already someone else in the house. Nevertheless he felt nervous as the men headed for the van, Barry turning on his mother: "Every one of them notes is counted, so don't you even look at them." Suppose Barry's voice and the sound of footsteps made Marshall forget he'd been told to stay still? But there was no sound from upstairs as Bernard spoke. "Shouldn't be more than a couple of days," he told Darren's mother, and stopped to light another cigar before ambling after Barry down the path.

"That's right, leave the woman to clear up as usual," she complained, bumping the door shut with her silvery arse, and in the instant before her eyes found him, Darren knew he wasn't going to tell her. Best to get rid of Marshall without anyone knowing. "Stay out while I clear up," she growled, which Darren knew meant she was going to look at the money—maybe more than look. As soon as she closed the door of the back room he ran upstairs.

It ought to be easy. He only had to tell Marshall that the people he wouldn't want to see were downstairs so that he would creep out of the house, and once they were out, with the dark helping to confuse Marshall, Darren could improvise. He dodged into his room and switched on the light. "It's only me. Don't make—"

He felt his free hand lurch to a halt in the air and dig its fingertips into the palm. He dashed to the bed and threw back the quilt, then he flung the wardrobe open before sprawling on the floor to look under the bed, and heaved all the piles of clothes onto the carpet, and jumped on the broken computer so hard he thought it would shatter as he grabbed the window frame. He held on long enough to survey the pavement beneath the few intact streetlamps, but it was no use. There was no more sign of Marshall outside than in the room.

22

INQUIRIES

Now that the police were coming to the house Susanne remembered Don had been there the last time they had, and that brought more memories alive. If only she had realized that he wasn't as opposed to Teresa Handley's offer of a weapon as Susanne . . . if only she had called the woman to tell her what to do with the offer . . . Whenever she thought of the woman Susanne was tempted to call her, but what would be the point? The writer hadn't forced Don to go for the weapon, he had made that choice himself without consulting Susanne, and now she had to wonder what choices Marshall might be making without her.

She went into the front room and peered along the darkening street, where the only movements were of cars returning home. As her knuckles touched the chill glass of the window the first streetlamps lit up, showing her how dark it was. In some parts of the city it must already be darker. She stepped back so as not to frighten Marshall off—in case that could be any kind of possibility—and switched on the light, and hoped the view of the lit room from the far end of the street would act as a beacon. She imagined having to apologize to the police when they arrived, imagined how embarrassed she would be to have to tell them Marshall had beaten them to it, how much more embarrassed he would be, especially at having to apologize to them. She didn't fully realize how these thoughts were sustaining her until a police car as white as a headstone swung into view at the end of the road.

She opened the front door as the car drew up outside the house. The breath she took as the headlamps faded and died felt as cold as the night was threatening to be. The car spread the white wings of its doors, and two men in black rose from it, capping their heads. The simultaneous closing of the doors sounded like a single blow with an enormous blade, and the houses were sending it flatly back when the foremost policeman opened her gate. "Mrs., or is it Professor Travis?"

"Mrs. is fine."

As he strode up the path she saw the scent tug his head the merest fraction toward the lavender plant. His large blue eyes, set widely in his broad round face, gave her the impression of being aware of much that he wasn't looking at directly, which compensated to some extent for his apparent youthfulness. His even more fresh-faced colleague closed the gate, holding the latch between finger and thumb as if it was a piece of evidence, and the blue-eyed policeman pointed both hands at Susanne. "Please. We'll follow."

She mustn't expect them to be bringing her news. They took off their caps as they entered the house, but that only meant they were being polite. She shrugged off a chill which had followed them into the house and watched until both outer doors were shut, then she ushered them into the front room and sat facing the window. You didn't offer British policemen a drink on duty, she knew that much, or if you were supposed to offer one to allow them to refuse she hadn't time for the ritual, nor for making them coffee, nor for anything else that would delay their doing their job. As the blue-eyed policeman sat on the couch to her left she said, "I told you my name but I didn't get yours."

"You told the station, the desk sergeant," he said with an air of gentle reproof which seemed to imply they had better be precise from the outset. "PC Askew and PC Angel."

The initials didn't mean politically correct, she knew, and presumably he'd named himself first, because neither his eyes nor his hands had referred to his colleague, who'd found a seat to her right. Though he pronounced his own name with the accent on the first syllable, the names still sounded like a British comedy duo, and Susanne couldn't help reflecting that although it had taken an inspector and his team to deal with her videos, a couple of constables were apparently considered sufficient for Marshall. So long as they were good at their job, did it matter? They wouldn't be the only ones involved in the investigation. "What do you need me to tell you?" she said.

Blue-eyed Askew produced a notebook and a rudimentary ballpoint without taking his eyes off her. "Your full name, Mrs. Travis, and your date and place of birth."

All her resolution to conduct the interview as swiftly and efficiently as possible collapsed at once. "Do you really need all that at this stage? Can't you take a description of my son first? I only asked you to come here because your sergeant wouldn't let me phone it in."

"I'm sure you can appreciate why, Mrs. Travis. If we started proceedings on the basis of every phone call we receive—"

"Sure, but now you've seen I'm not a crank. I wish I hadn't had to phone at all. Can't you just put out a description before you do the rest of the paperwork? There's too much of that in too many jobs these days."

"So they say," Askew said, making his reluctance more apparent as he placed the pen and notebook next to the heap of essays on the table. "Have you any reason to suppose your son is in danger?"

The question seemed cruelly direct even if it was legitimate. "I should think you'd know the possibilities as well as I do," Susanne said.

"I take your point, but is there anything specific? How long has he been missing?"

That was another question she would have preferred not to consider. "Nearly seven hours."

"Seven hours." It wasn't clear what if any difference rounding up the amount made to Askew. "Can you tell us when he was last sighted to your knowledge?"

"At school. Bushy Road School."

"They had a half-day off, did they?"

"No, he—" Susanne felt as if she was about to be compelled to pick her way through all the thoughts she'd already had. "He had a disagreement with the headmaster, and I'm afraid he walked."

"A disagreement with the headmaster."

"Over something someone had said about me. Don't get the idea he routinely goes AWOL. This is the first time, here or where we came from."

"How long have you been in this country, Mrs. Travis?"

That was Angel, whose long bony face had produced an almost invisible blond mustache once he was in the light. She wished he had remained silent if he was going to slow things down further. "Nine months. Is that relevant?"

"Was your son happy with the move?"

"Yes, very. It was his idea as much as, as anyone's. We wouldn't have done it if he hadn't wanted to."

"You don't think it's possible he might have changed his mind."

"I don't, because he would have told me. We've always talked." Askew's scrutiny was starting to play on her nerves; it felt like her own doubts rendered visible. "What?" she demanded, in the way she'd thought only characters in movies did.

"He's twelve, isn't he, Mrs. Travis? Boys do change around that age."

"I know that. We all do. It doesn't mean—" If she let them they could make her feel she had been willfully unobservant, neglectful, no kind of a parent now that Marshall had only one. "This is crazy," she said. "Why are we even discussing—I'll show you he isn't trying to go back home. He never would without me."

It took her well under a minute to run up to the study and switch on the light and pull out the desk drawer, but that was long enough for her to become unsure what she wanted to find. Just supposing Marshall's passport wasn't there, wouldn't that make him easy to locate when he tried to use it? She turned over the the topmost of the face-down passports, and it fell open at Don's photograph, looking as though being photographed had come as a shock to him. They'd laughed at that every time they'd used the documents, but now her innards tightened, because he looked helplessly shocked by what he saw coming. She shut the passport hastily and grabbed Marshall's from beneath hers. Now her dash seemed pointless, an illusion of activity; worse, it had shown her how much she would have liked to be proved wrong. She ran down even faster to display the evidence. "Here he is. I mean, this is his," she said, furious with losing her grip on language. "He can't have gone far without this."

Askew leafed through the passport with, she thought, unnecessary thoroughness before laying it on the table. He'd already raised his eyes to her. "May I ask if you're a single parent family?"

Other than "media" used as a singular noun, few abuses of language annoyed her more—a person couldn't be a family, yet she'd lost count of the number of people she'd heard making that claim—but this was no occasion for discussing niceties of usage. "My husband's dead," she told him, the words raw in her mouth.

"Would that have been recently, Mrs. Travis?"

"Three months ago. You'd have heard about it," she said, which meant she had to go on. "He was kicked to death outside his bookshop downtown."

"I do recall the case. Wasn't there a gun involved?"

"My husband thought we needed some defense, and what happened shows we did." She wasn't sure how appropriate her flaring anger was; it would hardly help Marshall, and she was about to drop the subject when Askew said, "How did your son feel about it?"

"Bad. How on earth do you imagine he would feel?"

"Do you think that may have any bearing on his absence?"

Susanne had a sudden image, as fleeting and yet lingering as the glare of a flashbulb, of Marshall discovering where the Fancy family lived and going there to extract some revenge for Don's death. "What kind of—what?"

"Has your husband a grave near enough for him to visit?"

"Well—yes." For a moment Susanne was astonished that she'd been so involved in her situation that she had been unable to see that possibility; then her emotions slumped. "He wouldn't be there now. They lock the gates at dusk."

"Where else can you think of he might be?"

"I called all his friends before I called you. He's made plenty of friends, but none of them knew where he is."

"You don't think it's possible any of them were protecting him."

"From what? From me, his mother?"

"I'm just suggesting, Mrs. Travis, that he may be afraid to face you since he, as you say, went AWOL."

"Not seven hours' worth of afraid, no. Not so afraid he wouldn't realize I'd be as worried as I am. Even if he didn't want to face me he'd have left a message on the machine." A bunch of aches made her aware that she was gripping her fist with her other hand. "You have to take my word for it. I know there's more to this," she forced herself to say. "Otherwise he would at least have called by now."

"I'm sorry if we seem unduly thorough. Limited resources, you may have heard." Askew's hand moved in the direction of his notebook, but only as far as his knee. "Can you think of any film your son would have seen that might have suggested a course of action to him?"

"Such as what? He reads more books than he sees movies," Susanne said, trying to fight down her anger. How much did the policemen already know or think they knew about her? "He doesn't imitate anything he reads or watches."

"As long as you're sure of that, Mrs. Travis."

It wasn't Askew's skepticism which infuriated her so much as the slyness of it—his assumption that she couldn't be certain it was there. "If you want to discuss movies with me you'll have to enroll in my class," she said, but that was all the lightness she could summon up. "Maybe I should make this one point clear. You confiscated all our videos, the police did, but you won't be prosecuting. Someone someplace must have seen some sense."

"If you say so, Mrs. Travis."

"Listen," Susanne said, and steadied her lips with a finger. "If either of you feels my son and I deserve what's been happening to us these last few months, if you feel we brought it on ourselves somehow, don't be afraid to share your thoughts with me. Let's at least respect each other."

Angel cleared his throat with two high sharp curt sounds. "Maybe if your husband—"

"We aren't here to express that kind of opinion, Mrs. Travis. I hope you don't think it would affect our handling of your problem."

"I hope I won't have reason to. Maybe if my husband what?"

"Mrs. Travis, we can argue," Askew said, "or we can do our best to find out what's happened to your son."

"Fine, let's do that. I'm convinced I need your help to find him. If I haven't convinced you, just tell me how."

Askew met her stare with his wide-angled gaze. "I still need the details I asked you for."

So it had come to a trade-off. Susanne felt as though she was being given a lesson in communication and human relations, one she would happily have skipped. When he picked up his notebook she could only resolve to answer all his questions. Her full name, her date and place of birth, her nationality—the quicker she told him all these and the same for Marshall, the sooner the police would track down her son. Askew continued writing deliberately for so long after she'd shot him the answers that her determination not to interrupt him was about to collapse when he said, "Have you a better photograph of him?"

"Bigger, you mean. There's the one on the mantel, only it's a year old."

In it Marshall was wearing a tropical shirt and pointing his thumb over his shoulder at three alligators. "Aren't they caged?" Askew said. "They look very close."

"My husband used a telephoto lens. Marshall wasn't in any danger." Far less than he might be in now, she thought, daring Askew even to hint that he believed she was given to exposing him to danger, and then she realized which photograph she could lend. "Wait," she said, and ran into the dining room to fetch the photograph which the Bushy Road school photographer had made.

Askew received it with more approval than she had previously seen him admit. "He'll be wearing this uniform, will he?"

"No." She was so appalled to realize that she hadn't used any of her time to check how he would be dressed that for some seconds she was as dumb as she felt; then her thoughts were too much to contain. "He came home and got changed while I was teaching. That's why I know something's happened. He must have meant to be back by the time I was, or he'd have left me a note."

If Askew challenged that, how much more time might they waste? But he only said, "Are you able to tell us what he will be wearing?"

"I'm sure I can." Upstairs again, her head beginning to pound like her heart, she switched on Marshall's light. His uniform was still laid out on the bed, a sight from which she recoiled to examine his other empty clothes, which felt cold and slack as she sorted through them. Once she'd made herself be thorough she checked the washing basket, but his favorite outfit wasn't there either, and so she raced downstairs. "He'll be in a purple Nike track suit," she panted.

Askew wrote that down. "Shoes?"

She'd noticed without noticing she had. "White Reebok trainers."

"Just like my two," Askew said, presumably referring to children rather than footwear, and made a final note as he stood up. "May I take the photograph?"

"You'll let me have it back, won't you? Marshall was proud of it." She would have corrected the past tense except that might aggravate her nervousness. She watched Marshall disappear as the policeman turned the photograph away from her, and blurted, "If you need to show his picture on television . . ."

"I hope it won't come to that, but if we do?"

"I was only going to say that the police had a movie crew with them when they were here. Assuming they haven't junked the film, since they won't be able to broadcast it now I'm not to be taken to court, they'll have footage of Marshall."

"We'll look into that should it become necessary, but we wouldn't normally use television until a certain period has elapsed."

His taking pity on her only made her feel more apprehensive. He wasn't about to specify the period unless she forced him to, and she told herself that she would never need to know. "So," she said, feeling stupid for asking even before she did, "what do I do now?"

"We'll contact you the moment we have any news. Will you be teaching tomorrow?"

She found she hadn't wanted to be forced to think that far ahead. "I . . . shouldn't think so. I'm not sure."

"I'll take a work number, shall I, just in case."

Giving him the information felt like inviting worse than she wanted to imagine, but what else could she do? She was on the doorstep now, and the two policemen were outside, their blue uniforms rendered black again by the night between the lonely lamps of the deserted street. Askew poised his pen, and she made the numbers come out of her mouth. The last digit had just left her when the phone rang at her back.

It was Marshall. She wouldn't have been able to say how she knew, but she saw the police read her conviction in her face. She dashed into the house, away from their skepticism, and flung out one hand to grab the receiver before the answering machine could beat her to the call. Her fingertips knocked the receiver across the table, but she had it as it toppled over the edge, and brought it to her face. "Yes?" she said breathlessly. "Hello?"

Though the response was faint, it pierced deep into her. It was a squeal lasting less than a second—a strangled cry. She pressed the receiver against her cheek so hard it bruised the bone. "Hello," she pleaded, and heard the noise again, and again, and recognized it as the squeal of the door of a phone booth, opening and closing in a wind. She could hear the wind too, a cold thin sound, and even the creak of the cord from which the receiver in the booth was dangling. Whoever had wanted to speak to her, the night had taken them.

23

NIGHT

Marshall was trying to lie absolutely still. He had to stay like that to give the pills his friend had fed him time to finish working. Waves of heat kept passing through him, starting at his marshmallow feet and oozing the length of his defrosting body until they emerged from the top of his head, but though the sensation of something hatching from his scalp made him shudder, he'd more or less stopped shivering. So long as he held his hands over his face to ward off the stale smells of the bed, he wouldn't have to move. What was happening to him was only like having a nightmare, the worst he'd ever had, and he kept almost wakening from it and believing that this time he might find he was home in bed. He could let himself imagine that, because soon he would be. His friend Darren had gone to phone and tell Marshall's mother where to find him.

Darren had advised him not to move, and Darren's mother was a nurse. So much Marshall had figured out from the way Darren had diagnosed him and been able to provide the right medicine. Marshall was hoping she would come off duty soon and examine him. Meanwhile he could only try to keep his eyes shut as the nightmare rushed him again. He saw himself treading on an anthill like the one he'd overlooked when he was six years old in West Palm Beach, and felt another wave of heat drive the ants out of the holes in his scalp. He had to take a hand away from his face long enough to dig his fingertips into his skull to close as many of the holes as he could locate. Now Max and Vic were forcing his mother to her knees so that George S. could urinate on her, except that as she raised her face into the stream and opened her mouth Marshall saw that the figure standing straddle-legged wasn't George S. but his own father. He smashed a fist into the face that was mirroring his own lopsided grin, and felt his knuckles tingle as his father's head shattered like a wrecked house. He trampled on the eyeballs and ground bits of bone and flesh under his heels, but the lips continued mouthing at him from the mud however much he kicked and stamped on them. "Are you home?" the bruised lips persisted in asking, each question popping a bubble of blood. "Are you home yet?" they asked, until Marshall had to open his eyes so as to stop seeing them—to stop having them inside him.

The room shuddered on his behalf, and as it steadied he was able to hope for a moment that it would prove to be his. No, it was strewn with unfamiliar clothes, even if some of them were the kind he would wear. Could they be clothes he'd forgotten he'd acquired since emigrating to Britain? Maybe he'd forgotten this was now his room. He didn't mind if it was, so long as it kept still—so long as it and all its contents stopped threatening to change.

Even worse than that was feeling the same threat inside himself. All the unbearably shameful dreams he'd just had must be part of him, and they showed him he was someone he couldn't bear to know. Maybe he was the boy the smelly room belonged to, or maybe he would be. He was peering out at the clothes which writhed and resettled themselves against the stained walls when he heard someone running toward him.

He'd been hearing voices ever since his friend had left him, but he'd thought they were on television in the next house. Only the footsteps were outside the bedroom door, and now he realized that the voices had been too. Had they been talking about him—about their plans for him? He used his heels to drag himself farther under the quilt, and clapped his hands over his face, praying that would make him less conspicuous as the door burst open, flinging a gob of pale light off the slab of itself, and launched a figure at him.

It was Darren, who picked up a receptacle in which he must want Marshall to provide a sample and emptied it over his own head. As Marshall saw it was a baseball cap, Darren towered over him and began to gabble in his face words that smelled of teeth. "You stay like that. There's someone downstairs you won't want to see. Don't come out till I tell you they've gone."

Had he called Marshall's mother? Marshall was thumbing his lips open behind his hand to whisper the question so that nobody else would hear when Darren hurried out of the room and slammed the door, which sucked the gob of light back onto itself. His footsteps clattered downstairs, and Marshall felt his own spongy body emitting moisture as it struggled to follow. How could he bear to wait when he didn't know about his mother? Then he heard the mutter of a man's voice which sounded as though it was chewing its way through the floor toward him, and he huddled into his lair. If that was the someone his friend had warned him about, he could hear why. He strained his fluttering ears to hear what the voice was saying—please God, not about him—and heard his friend's footsteps go along the hall and out of the house.

He must be going to phone Marshall's mother. Of course he hadn't had a chance earlier, because the voices had started immediately he'd first left the room, and Marshall had to be as brave as it took now that he was left alone with them. Though now he could hear that one was a woman's, and mustn't she be the nurse? The inkling of hope made the private ward shift, so that he couldn't tell if it was dismayingly enormous or only the size of his head. He eased the quilt off himself, sweating each time he heard it rustle, and lowered himself head first to the floor, testing the boards for creaks with his clammy palms. At last he dared to let his knees touch the wrinkled grubby carpet, and began to crawl toward the door.

He was engrossed in crawling, in the texture of the carpet beneath his increasingly dirty hands, when he heard footsteps heavier than Darren's enter the house. "Back room, is it, burn?" a new man's voice jabbed, catching him in the stomach.

Marshall dragged his knees between his fists and crouched over himself for longer than it took him to be sure the man wasn't talking about this bedroom. He wanted to meet the owner of the voice even less than the one who had been speaking to the woman. Even his impression that the floor was extruding splinters through the carpet into his knuckles was unable to move him. Footsteps marched in and out of the house, and then the front door shook it. The footsteps tramped along the hall, and all the voices were shut in a room.

Marshall lowered himself onto his base, his outstretched legs cracking. He picked at his knuckles with his fingernails, unable to judge whether he was finding any splinters, until it occurred to him that he had to creep out of the house while the people whom he wouldn't want to meet were out of sight—only where were his shoes? Hadn't he left them by the bed?

He scuttled across the floor, forgetting to be silent, and heaved the quilt onto the mattress. There were his trainers, and near them in the dust he saw the dull glint of a seven-sided twenty-pence coin. He would have taken it except that he'd be stealing from his friend, who had only taken Marshall's money to keep it safe. He was dragging both fat white animals by their thin leashes from under the bed when he heard his friend come into the house.

His footsteps stopped some way along the hall, where they were met by the worst of the voices, sounding murderous. He mustn't get into trouble, not when he had a message for Marshall. Marshall crawled fast across the carpet, in time to hear the other man's voice say, "Come in as long as you've seen it, Darren, and shut the door."

He mustn't until he'd given Marshall the message. Marshall staggered to his feet and lurched at the doorknob just as a door slammed downstairs and Darren's voice joined the others in the room. Marshall twisted the knob and pulled the bedroom door open, not least to get rid of the sight of the parody of himself which had come squirming out of the painted surface, and hung onto the frame with both hands. The voices had captured his friend, or could Marshall save him? He sounded as though he didn't want to be saved. Was he trying to distract them so that Marshall could escape?

Marshall pried his fingers loose from the doorframe and sent himself toward the bed. Surely his friend wouldn't mind if he took the twenty pence—it could be deducted from the money Darren was holding. Marshall clawed the coin and some wedges of dust off the carpet, and buried it as deep in his pocket as it would go. He sat on the edge of the bed, which sagged like a rotten branch, and wound the laces round his fingers to coax his trainers to him.

So long as the voices stayed in the room he felt relatively safe. He turned the shoes so that the toes were pointing away from him, and dug his left foot into the shoe on the left, then wrenched it off and tried the other shoe. That seemed to fit better, but not well enough, so that he wondered if he'd commandeered some of Darren's trainers by mistake until he saw he'd poked the tongue into the shoe. He pulled it out, though it wriggled moistly, and pinched the other tongue between finger and thumb while he inserted his right foot into the hot panting mouth. The hardest task remained—tying the laces—at which he fumbled for some time before remembering to use both hands. By the time he'd succeeded in making knots which strangled the laces, killing or at least maiming them enough that they no longer tried to squirm away under the chubby soles, his fingertips felt skinned. He sprang off the bed, only to realize that he'd been so busy taming the shoes that he'd forgotten to listen. The voices had fallen silent—he had no idea when.

He couldn't bear to stay in the room while the door was wide open, but closing it might bring the owners of the savage voices to him. He tiptoed onto the landing and peered down the stairs, which had grown steep and narrow as a ladder. He planted one foot on the top stair, and felt it get ready to give a loud creak. He sat quickly on the landing and stretched his body out until he was flat as a slab, and lowered himself that way, bending his knees, while his heels and elbows caught at the stairs. Long before he reached the hall he was clamping his lips together so that their aching would distract him from the bruising of his elbows and the throbbing of his arms. His shaky breath whistled in his nostrils like some kind of terrified animal's. His heels came to rest in the hall at last, and he sat up and seized his knees and waited for his arms to stop trembling. Then the murderous voice shouted, "Don't know why you didn't bring the fucking neighbors in to watch while you was at it, burn. Listen, lad, this is Barry talking to you."

How long had he known Marshall was there? Shouldn't Marshall go to him rather than infuriating him further by making him shout through the door? Marshall wobbled to his feet, and had taken a step toward the room when he realized the man wasn't addressing him. He would have sneaked out of the house if it weren't for leaving his friend at the mercy of the owner of the voice. He took another step, grabbing one wrist to jerk its hand toward the doorknob, and remembered his friend's warning. Terrified of forgetting to be wary if he stayed in the house, he tiptoed rapidly along the hall crawling with cigarette butts and seized the latch. "Don't even fucking dream," the voice shouted as Marshall squeezed through the gap, unable to figure how to widen it, and pulled the door shut behind him.

The night surrounded him, close and cold as earth. It filled his nostrils, and he had to breathe hard to breathe at all. Now he was out he felt considerably less safe than he'd hoped, but if he kept reminding himself that he was going to phone his mother, maybe he would be able to do what the man had told him—stop himself dreaming. He crept along the stub of path, toward a van that looked flayed raw, and leaned against the gate so as to lift it and the fence. It felt so soft he was afraid that chunks would come off in his hands, and once he was past he stood staring at it, trying to determine whether any had. Then he heard a bus dragging its guts along the main road, and remembered seeing at least one phone booth there.

Much of the sidewalk leading to the road was composed of broken gravestones. He almost fell headlong several times before realizing he no longer had to tiptoe. As he passed one of the hunched brown houses its whole front lit up, and he flinched into the street in case the carnival ride had any more shocks in store for him. Now he was at the main road, along which a box of heads was pulling itself with its lights, past the row of caged shops drowning in the thick orange glow of the bony streetlamps. The exposed nerves of the trees writhed in the air, and at the edge of the poisoned turf whose agony they were expressing stood a phone booth.

He shoved his hand into his pocket to make sure of the coin. It felt thin as tinfoil—felt as though he was rubbing it to nothing as he walked. At least the door of the booth was open wide enough for him to slide in without letting go of the coin. The row of shops was telling him he'd left his father's shop alone in the cold and the dark, but he had to call his mother while he had the chance. He unhooked the orange cartoon of a receiver and its unpleasantly soft shadow, and brought both toward his face.

It was so much colder than it looked that his head snapped away from it, twisting his neck. He tried to hold it just close enough to hear the dial tone, but even when he pressed the earpiece against him it was silent as ice. He stared at it until he was convinced that he wasn't holding it upside down, then he groped for the coin. A sign in front of him said he should wait for the tone before inserting any money, but couldn't the sign be wrong when so many people appeared to have done their best to correct it? He had to hear his mother, had to tell her where he was, but where was he? He fished out the coin, slid as much of it into the icy slot as he could while pinching it between his nails, hung up the receiver and held onto it for a few seconds before lifting it again to his face. It was still dead, and he was losing his grip on the coin, his only coin. He snatched it from the slot and slamming the receiver onto the hook, blundered out of the booth.

There had to be other phones nearby. He hurried past the display of his mother's quivering nerves. He was going to phone, he told her in his head and then outside it, though he wasn't sure how his voice sounded or even, once he'd said it, what he'd said. He was making for the distant city, which should be full of phones—except that the city was on fire, the sky above the charred roofs glaring almost white. No wonder he heard police cars bewailing the situation and ambulances whooping for glee, but where were the fire engines? Maybe they had all burned in the fire; maybe his father's shop had too. The idea felt colder than the night, so that the warmth of the conflagration faded from his chest, leaving him alone. He had to phone his mother to find out whether she was safe. He could ask the women ahead of him the whereabouts of the nearest phone booth.

They were bearing down on him as fast as he was walking toward them, past a bus stop which was composed almost entirely of glass or of none at all. He'd begun to tiptoe on seeing them until he remembered that he needn't—mustn't, in case they realized something was wrong with him. He was beginning to wish he hadn't left the house before the medicine the nurse had given him had finished working, but his friend had said the phone in the house was no use. He set about opening his mouth while he had time to prepare to ask where the phone was, a phone, where he could phone, where was a phone, from, where to phone from . . . A car hurtled by on the wrong side of the road, and he remembered everything had been turned around. His words would come out that way if he didn't control them. "Noph," he pleaded, "rhew noph," not knowing which way around that was or how to turn his sounds into the words that were struggling in his head.

In any case, he didn't think he wanted to speak to the women after all—he wanted to stop seeing how they looked. The orange veils which hung from the streetlamps were collecting on their pouchy faces, dragging them down until he was afraid the flesh was about to slither into the collars of their fur coats, leaving only skulls to bear their crinkly blond wigs. As he saw the skin beneath their eyes growing darker and thinner, preparing to tear, he dodged into the road in front of a car which should have been in front of him, and recoiled onto the sidewalk. He heard the skulls mocking him with a shrill dry giggling which included the clack of their teeth, but he mustn't let them distract him. He'd come abreast of the side road which had produced the furred women. Some indeterminate distance along it, past the remains of streetlamps and several attempts at trees, was another phone booth.

The sound of a plane drove him along the side road. It wasn't the warm lingering rumble he remembered from Florida; it sounded as though the jet was ripping the sky in half. The trees cringed lower, and he ducked so that the end of the rip in the air would pass over him. A house noticed him and flared at him, its vicious light gouging the roadway with the shadow of a tree, but he had to stay on the sidewalk, beneath the meager shelter of the torn foliage, until he reached the booth. He seized the glimmer of a handle in both fists and heaved the door open far enough for him to be able to worm his way in.

The lid thumped shut behind him, silencing the plane. He felt for the coin and held onto it while he waited for the interior of the booth to become sufficiently visible to let him key his number. Now he could see the receiver trying to climb the wall beside a huddle of digits, next to which was a notice he might be able to decipher if he pressed his face against it, though surely he wouldn't have to read it—his eyes were already trembling with the attempt to distinguish what else was in the booth with him. Under the notice was a shelf on which someone had left a Tesco supermarket bag, the contents of which appeared to be poking out a small head.

It must be a doll. He could distinguish one of its hands now, raised above its ear as though it had tried to pull the plastic away from its face to stop it suffocating. Someone had grown tired of their baby doll—maybe they'd outgrown it—and so they'd dumped it in the phone booth. Why would they have bothered putting it in a bag? Maybe it was stolen and they'd had to hide it, and would be coming back for it, in which case he ought to use the phone while he could. He was able to see the digits now, as clearly as the top of the doll's head with a barely visible hint of fine hair on its scalp. Were dolls usually that realistic? Perhaps only when they were so expensive people stole them. All he had to do to prove it was a doll was examine its eyes, and then he would be able to phone. He reached a hand into the cold stagnant dimness, and caught hold of his elbow with his other hand to encourage himself to reach farther, and hooked one finger over the top of the supermarket bag. The back of the first joint of his finger touched something bulbous and unmoving and not quite as firm as it ought to be: an open eye.

He clutched his mouth and staggered back against the door, trying to unhook his finger from the bag. The plastic slithered down the face, exposing the small dead eyes and snub nose and the mouth, gaping toothlessly as though the baby had cried its last inside the bag. He still hadn't freed his finger. As he floundered backward the baby reared at him, waving its raised hand. If it fell on the floor because of him, he wouldn't be able to bear it. He pushed it away from him, and one fingertip dug into its mouth and touched the dry wrinkled fig of its tongue. He heard its head bump against the wall as he fought his way out of the booth, rubbing his hand on his track suit as though he might never be able to stop.

The sidewalk steeped in dimness appeared to be inching away from him in both directions, carrying the ashen shops of the main road into the fire which had spread from the city center, withdrawing some undamaged streetlamps farther down the side road. That couldn't be happening, he tried to convince himself. It was only a nightmare he was somehow having while he was awake. Everything he saw was an image in his head. Perhaps that had been all the baby was.

Though he wanted to believe that, he was walking faster than he meant to in an attempt to leave the idea behind. If everything he saw was only an image, how could he grasp what it really looked like? How could he ever see properly again? He struggled to unthink the idea, because he could feel it parting his brain, digging its point deep between the folds of rubbery flesh. He was running now, jumping over any patch of sidewalk which looked capable of tripping him, dodging into another side road when he caught sight of several teenagers perched on a wall, swinging their robot legs while they waited for someone to stray close enough to kick. All the satellite dishes which sprouted from the manure of the houses were flexing their stems, so that he was afraid they were about to swing in unison to find him. Then he faltered, because dancing toward him along the sidewalk was yet another phone booth.

He had to use the phone, however the booth looked. Only the light of a half-dead streetlamp was making it dance. There couldn't be another baby in it, and if there was he would know it was another of his nightmares, although wouldn't that mean he could trust nothing he saw? He had to speak to his mother so that he would know she was safe from the fire. He forced his hand toward the handle of the block of reddish gelatin beneath the dark crimson tube that kept trying to twitch itself brighter. The gelatin jumped and shuddered as he touched it, and so did he. He peeled the door open, the handle squirming in his grip, and made himself step into the booth.

The soft flap of a door wouldn't quite close. He felt on his back the breaths of the mouth he was in. Every few seconds he saw its pulse, blood suffusing the phone and keypad and the rest of the interior. At least he could see nothing on the shelf, even when he fell to his knees and thrust his face into the alcove. He could use the phone—he wasn't in some carnivorous trap which lifting the receiver would set off. He shoved himself to his feet, trying not to touch anything except himself. He took out the coin with his right hand and used his left to unhook the receiver.

He mustn't mind how soft it was. When he brought it as close to his face as he could bear, he heard the dial tone. He inserted the coin into the raw wound, whose edges reddened and winced as he did so, and poked the numbered squares of gelatin with the tip of his forefinger. The mouth around him took another breath, and a phone began to ring.

It had to be at home. He was almost certain he'd entered the right number, even if he'd felt the keys shift as he found them. In a moment he would hear either his mother or the answering machine—either would reassure him that he was still capable of dialing the right number. One pair of rings which sounded so distant and artificial they were hardly even an image of themselves, two, three, and he was preparing himself to expect the machine when a deafening clatter sprang out of the earpiece at him.

The mouth sucked in a breath which turned it red, and the door wobbled toward him. The trap had been sprung. Only the clatter which the mechanism had made saved him. He dropped the receiver, which fell to the length of its tentacle and swung to catch him. He was already throwing himself backward at the door, baring his teeth at its squeal of frustration. Before the receiver had stopped ranging about in its blind search for him, he was on the sidewalk. He was ready to flee—in which direction didn't matter—when he realized that he had to retrieve his twenty pence.

Blood was pulsing out of the booth onto the surrounding sidewalk. Maybe he'd injured it; the door squealed every time it took a breath. He waited for the receiver to grow tired of its search, but it looked as though it was never going to be still. He grabbed the edge of the quaking door with both hands and wrenched it so wide it screeched in agony. He'd broken its jaw, because it stayed like that as he lurched at the receiver and fumbled it into its socket. He dug his fingers into it and lifted it again and slammed it down. There was still no response—no sound of his coin coming back.

He thumped the coin box with his fist before he had time to wonder what it would feel like. It sounded like metal, and felt almost like it too, but the impact didn't dislodge the coin. The money had to come back, he hadn't made a call. He dug a finger into the return chute, and his fingernail sank into something soft which clung to it. He'd fallen for the trap.

When he snatched his finger out of the hole, part of the booth came with it: a pinkish string which pulsed red as it stretched. Not until he was out of the booth did it snap, leaving several inches dangling from his finger. He dashed along the sidewalk in search of anything he could bear to wipe the finger on—not the bloody pointed teeth of the fences, not a stray newspaper which, when he tried to pick it up, spilled small bones, a baby's bones. By the time he found a streetlamp against which to scrape his fingertip, he'd turned a corner and the booth and the distant main road were gone.

He stopped dragging his fingertip down the stony pole once he thought it hurt enough. He almost sucked the finger until he wondered what he might be putting in his mouth to sneak into his stomach and grow there. He was suddenly afraid that his finger would be too painful for him to be able to place another call, and in any case, how could he when he'd lost his only coin? Maybe if he asked to phone from someone's house, and he peered at all the houses crouching on both sides of him as his rapid mechanical trot carried him along a narrow concrete footpath seared bare by lamps. The oil-flare light was too intense to let him distinguish which sets of curtains were lit from within, and when he took a desperate chance and veered toward one of the houses to which the overhead lines were attached it immediately sprang at him, blazing. He stumbled onward, over the litter which the concrete had begun to extrude to catch his feet, and as soon as he had any control of his movements he sent himself toward another house. When it leapt out of its crouch, glaring at him, he knew that any house he approached would do so. They were lying in wait for him—they were controlled by whatever lived at the center of the overhead web, the thing which grew more aware of him each time he triggered a house. He saw the lines trembling stealthily, and knew it was coming for him. He sprinted for the road at the end of the footpath, beyond which the web mightn't reach. Echoes scuttled in pursuit of him between the fences, or were they above him and not echoes at all? They halted, baulked, as he almost sprawled on the sidewalk beyond the path.

The place looked familiar—familiar enough that he was instinctively aware of some difference. He stared about, feeling his skull shift inside the flesh, and saw to his left a leaning fence supported by its gate. He'd come back to his friend's house, and there was no longer a van outside. It had taken away the people he wouldn't have wanted to meet. He'd turned left from the house, yet here it was on his left, so which way around was he now? All that mattered was that he'd found his way back to where his money was and, better yet, where his friend would be able to give him the message from his mother now that their enemies had gone. He ran to the gate and hauled it open farther, and propped up the fence again before scampering along the path to ring the bell.

24
THE MESSAGE

"You're dead," Darren snarled, staring at his empty room. He should have taken care of Marshall while he had the chance. He ran to the bathroom in case Marshall was hiding in the bath, then to his parents' room. He kicked the bed to scare him out if he was under it, and dragged the sagging door of the wardrobe open far enough to see that it hid nothing but his mother's clothes with not a tit or arse in them. He heard his grandfather moaning. Though he couldn't imagine Marshall in there, he eased open the door to the old man's room.

The smell ought to have been enough to keep Marshall out, though maybe not now Darren had done for his head. Too much junk was piled against the wardrobe for him to have been able to get in there, and so the only place he could be was under the bed, unless the old man had enticed him into it. Darren plugged his nostrils with two fingers and turned his head to take a breath. As he stepped into the room the mound of his grandfather poked up its long white perished head. "Waking a man when he needs his sleep," it complained. "What's all the row? Where's this? Why's the train stopped?"

"They're changing the thingy, the engine."

The cracked eyes peered at Darren over their pinkish lids, which looked so weighed down by liquid they might have been about to peel away from the face. Darren thought the old man wasn't seeing him—was too busy trundling his tongue around his lips as if searching for his teeth—but as Darren took another step, the old man moaned, "I know you, you're Phil's lad. What are you trying to confuse me for?"

"That's right, granda, I'm Darren," Darren said, darting forward to kick up a corner of the quilt. "Has anyone been in except my mam?"

"Not even Phil's cow. Nobody ever. You go to war for them and could've got yourself killed and then they don't want to know. Might as well have died while I was out there, it'd have saved me coming back to this. You're a good lad," he said, patting the quilt beside him with the hand he was trying to use to prop himself up. "Sit with us for a bit and I'll tell you about your da when he was your age."

Darren dodged back, having seen that there was nothing except stains under the bed. "Not now, granda. Not while I'm alive either, you dirty old fucker." He ran downstairs and peered around the kitchen, and thought as he raced along the hall to look in the front room that he should have grabbed a knife. He'd just found nobody when his mother lunged out of the room with the loot in it and dealt him a back-hander, her knuckles missing his face by inches. "What are you trying to do, making all that row when I'm busy?"

"Granda wants his bed changing."

"He can want unless you're going to. I'll set fire to it with him in it one of these days. Where do you reckon you're going now?"

Darren pulled the front door open and let his gaze roam the empty street before answering. "Need some air after being with him."

"What are you making out, I don't look after him? I'd like to see anyone who'd do more than I do. He's your da's da, not mine, not that I'd have that drunken sod in the house after the way he treated my mam." Darren's mother peered out of the front door and grabbed his arm. "You've had your air now. Get in and shut the door."

"I'm going for a ride on my bike."

"You're going nowhere. I want you here where I can see you for a change."

"You and that Dick wanted me out before."

"So you wouldn't go starving now your da's got himself put away." She grabbed Darren's elbow with both hands and flung him along the hall. "You'd think this was a hotel the way you treat it. You'd think I was a landlady stead of your mam."

She'd never gone on like this before. She must be saying things her mother had said to her. Darren kicked up as many cigarette butts as he could while making for the back door. "My da got me that bike. He wouldn't mind me riding it."

His mother rushed into the kitchen and threw him against a flimsy unit, setting knives chattering in the drawer. "You do what you're told, you little shit," she screamed. "I don't want you getting in trouble and bringing the filth back. You keep your arse in this house or I'm telling your Uncle Bernard."

She was scared because there was so much loot in the house—scared she wouldn't get her cut for looking after it. Darren would have told her he had to find Marshall, except then she would go screaming to Bernard. At some point having captured Marshall had begun to seem stupid, more trouble than it was worth, and all Darren knew was he needed to shut Marshall's mouth. "Bernard's not my da and you aren't either. You can't tell me what to do."

"I'll give you who's your da," his mother yelled, and came at him with both fists raised. She must have seen he would kick her in the belly, because she caught hold of the key in the back door instead. Before Darren realized what she meant to do she'd dashed out to his bicycle, which was leaning against the shed, and unscrewed the caps from the tubes to let the air out of both tires. As the tires went flat she threw the caps over the fence. "See how far you get on that, lad."

"I'll fucking kill you for that, you bitch," Darren cried. He could hear the knives clattering around inside his head—it felt as if their points were. He was wasting time, he ought to be chasing Marshall, or mightn't he need to? Surely Marshall wouldn't be able to find his way back to the house or remember more than the first bit of Darren's name. Anyway, what could he tell anyone except that Darren had helped him? Maybe at that very moment he was walking in front of a bus. Darren needn't go out after all.

He wasn't having his mother think she'd won. "I'm getting one of them mucky videos to watch," he said—and then the doorbell rang, a quick dry choked trill followed by a long rattle as though whoever was outside couldn't let go of the push.

"That's you," Darren's mother screamed at him, almost slamming the back door as she rushed into the house. She blocked the slam by flinging out one hand, and turned the key and stalked at him, making her fingers into claws. "Get to that door and say nobody's in," she hissed. "Go and say they'll have to come back."

For a moment he thought she knew more than she did. She was afraid the filth were at the door, and so was he, but not for the same reason. They couldn't prove anything—Marshall hadn't seen what Darren had done to him. All the same, Darren found his footsteps dragging, grinding butts into the carpet as his mother slammed herself into the back room. He wiped her spit off his face and chained the door and clenched his fist around the knob of the latch, and twisted his face as he twisted the knob, then made his face relax into indifference. "My mam's not in," he would say. "I don't know when she'll be back." He was restraining himself from starting to speak until they asked him a question when the door reached the length of its chain, and his mouth sprawled open. Outside on the path was Marshall, all by himself.

One side of Marshall's face twitched, and a smile of relief and gratitude spread across his lips. Darren felt a very similar expression taking hold of his own face as he unchained the door, but his voice came out loud and sharp. "Where've you been?"

Marshall looked embarrassed—so much so that Darren had to nod his head behind the door to hide a snigger. "Trying to phone my mom."

Darren's fist tightened on the latch as though it was the bulge bobbing up and down Marshall's throat as he kept swallowing. "Did you get her?"

"Couldn't. One phone was smashed, and then . . ." Marshall's lips drooped and began to shake while his eyes darted from side to side, and Darren saw with delight that he was in as bad a state as ever. "Get in, lad," he muttered, jerking at the air in front of Marshall with his free hand. "You'll be all right in here."

Once Marshall ventured over the doorstep he had to be pushed out of the way so that Darren could shut the door and set about securing it. "Did you call her?" Marshall pleaded. "You said you would."

"If I did, why'd you go out?"

"Because I thought—I thought those people wouldn't let you come and tell me. I only wanted to know what she said." Maybe Marshall's voice was nearly inaudible from embarrassment, or maybe he was taking his lead from Darren, but then his voice jerked louder. "Is that them?"

"No, it's my mam." They'd heard the thud of her replacing the board over the hiding place in the floor, and Darren thought it was a good job Marshall wasn't the police. "They've gone. They're outside somewhere, so you'd better stay in here where they can't see you."

"Is my mom coming?"

"Not tonight." Darren shot the last of the bolts, which gave him time to think. "She said she'll come tomorrow. Doesn't want you out in the cold while you've got what you've got, she said."

Marshall's lower lip was pulling his chin up. "Was that all she said?"

"She said to tell you she's not worried now she knows where you're at." Darren's head had begun to ache with trying to think what else Marshall might want to hear. Then he knew, and it made him gag. "She said she lugh," he muttered, and covered his mouth, and tried again. "She said she loves you, fucking hell."

"I love her," Marshall immediately responded, and Darren thought that if he didn't at least spit on the floor he would throw up. Before he could do either, however, the door of the back room edged open. "Who was—" his mother demanded, and her voice grew teeth as she saw Marshall. "Who—"

Marshall must have been past hearing her tone. "Are you the nurse?"

As she stared at him, Darren realized she was hearing his accent. "He's never—"

"That's right, mam, you saw him on telly. Get in the front, Ma, and we'll fix you up. The front, lad, the front room."

If Darren was supposed to be the man of the house, everyone had to do as he said. To his amazement and delight, they did—at least, his mother kept quiet while Marshall let himself into the front room. He faltered on the threshold and turned to Darren's mother. "Will you bring me something?"

"She will or I will, Ma. Get in and shut it while I talk to my mam."

Marshall vanished into the room at once. He must think that the quicker he went, the sooner he'd be given some medicine to help him. Darren grimaced at his mother to herd her into the back room, where she hadn't pulled the carpet over the loose board, he saw. She oughtn't even to be in the room with the boxing posters and the bar with dancing girls painted on it—it was supposed to be for men. He closed the door behind him, feeling more in control than he could remember ever having felt, and then he saw that his mother was biding her time, not obeying him at all. She shot out a hand which thumped him on the forehead, and dug her nails into his scalp to throw him on a chair. "What've you been up to? What's he doing here?"

"Hey, don't you fucking—"

"I'll do anything I like to you, anything at all. I'm your mam in case you forgot, for all the thanks I ever get. I wouldn't be if your da hadn't left his Durex off." She dragged a chair in front of the door, the legs grating over spilled pet food, and raked the air within an inch of Darren's face as he made to stand up. "You stay sat there or I'll put you in the hospital. You don't get out of this room till I know what's going on."

His father's gun must be somewhere in the room. Had she put it back under the floor? Just being able to point it at her would make Darren feel in control again, the way he ought to feel after having captured Marshall. "Good one," he mumbled, ducking his head so as to squint about for a sign of the gun. "Go on, let him get away."

"I'll hear if he does anything, don't you fret." She tugged her dress down so that it hid the black lace at her crotch, and squeezed her legs together, and glared at Darren. "Out with it. What are you playing at, letting him in when you was told not to let anyone? He's never really who I thought, is he? What's up with him?"

She couldn't fit her brain around what was happening. Darren could still be the man in charge. "What do you think," he said.

"You never did it to him."

"It was me all right," he said, so proud of himself that at first he didn't react to her raising her voice. "Don't let him hear."

"You did that," she said lower, less like a conspirator than like a dog growling. "After all the bother we've already had with him and his da, you done that to him."

"It's all right, mam. He doesn't know."

"What are you arsing on about? How can't he know?"

"I put it in his drink when he wasn't looking. Didn't even know I was there, and nobody saw me do it."

"I just hope you're right, lad. If anyone comes after you because of him I know nowt about anything." Darren saw her begin to relax, and then she screwed her face up and shook her head as if she was shaking her brain awake. "If he's got no idea like you're trying to say, what's he doing in my house?"

"He doesn't know who we are, mam. He thinks I'm his mate and you're a nurse who'll give him some stuff to make him better. I waited till he was out of his head and went to him like I knew him from his school. Any shit I tell him, he believes it. He thought the bus coming here was taking him home."

"You crafty little sod," Darren's mother said, and Darren knew he'd done right, because for the first time since he could remember he heard her admiring him. That experience lingered until she shook her head again and stared hard at him. "Hang about. When did you bring him?"

"Before," Darren said, and saw that wouldn't be enough. "Before Barry and Bernard come. I was going to tell you, then they come. He was up in my bed thinking he was getting better."

"You're telling me he was here when—You want your sodding brain drilling, you do. You're sitting there on your arse and telling me you'd got him upstairs all the time Bernard and Barry were here, you stupid useless brainless little mong."

"Don't you call me that. He wasn't here all the time. He went to try and call his mam, but he couldn't get her."

"And now he's back, or hadn't you noticed? You're making out he doesn't know where he is when he's come back?"

"He can't know what they were doing in here or he wouldn't have come back, would he? He only came because he thinks we're going to look after him. We've got him and nobody knows where he is, and if he gets away again it'll be your fault."

"Right, we've got him. And what do you reckon we do with him now?"

"Whatever we like, mam, for what he made happen to my da and Uncle Jim."

"Kill him, you reckon? Or torture him first? Cut him open like in one of them videos and make him watch his guts fall out?"

Darren felt apprehensive and queasily excited. "Ooh, God, mam . . ."

His mother stood up to drag her chair away from the door. "Here you go, get a spoon from the kitchen."

"What for?"

"So you can poke one of his eyes out and feed it to him and he'll have to watch. Sound good?"

"God, mam, I don't know."

"Go on then, lad, you tell me what you want to do with him now you've got him."

Darren felt suddenly as useless as she'd said he was, unable to think of a single idea. He'd caught Marshall, and what happened to him ought to be up to the family—and then inspiration came to him. "Put him in bed with my granda and see what granda does to him."

"That's it, is it? That's why you brought him. To get more of the family in trouble than already is."

Darren was sick of her trying to make him feel guilty or stupid or however she wanted to make him feel. "Never mind asking if you don't like it when I say. What are *you* going to do to him?"

His mother flung open the door and craned her head out to check that the front room was still shut. "Not a thing."

"How do you mean, you're just going to . . ."

"I'm not going to nothing. See if you can understand one sodding thing you're told once in your useless little life. I'm going out. I don't know about him, and I don't want to know."

"But what do you—I mean, what'll I—"

"Not interested. Got that? I don't even know he's here. He's nowt to do with me, and don't you dare tell any sod he is. You brought him, you get rid of him. I don't care what you do, but I don't want him in this house when I get back."

She curtseyed in the hall so as to see herself reflected in the kitchen window, and used both hands to pat her hair and tug her skirt down. She stalked to the front door and threw off the chain and slid the bolts back, then she swung toward Darren, who was loitering in the hall. "Get on with it," she said, and slammed the door between them.

"Who's that?" Marshall called, his voice rising and shaking. "Da? Are you there?"

"My mam's gone out. Stay where you're put." Darren felt as though saying that or even thinking it up had exhausted him. If his father had been here he wouldn't have walked out like that, leaving Darren to deal with the situation. He would have known what to do with Marshall—and all at once Darren did too. He'd show his mother he could get rid of Marshall. She mightn't like how he did it, but that would be her fault for telling him to. He listened outside the front room to make sure Marshall was doing as he was told, then he went to find the gun.

25

GAME

Marshall kept having to remember why he needed to stay still: so that the people in the clothes lolling over the chairs wouldn't do what they might do to him. Though he was unable to distinguish many of their words, he knew that their low fierce voices were talking about him. "What's up with him?" he heard one say, and knew it was mocking him, because it must know the answer. He pressed his back and shoulders against the cardigan on the chair to crush anyone who was inside it, and prayed that his movement wouldn't draw the attention of the others to him—that they wouldn't poke their heads out of the collars and close in on him. He must be crushing their voices by leaning back; their snarling was lower than ever, low enough that he wished he couldn't hear the few words that were audible, wished fervently that he was mishearing them. Had one mentioned drilling his brain? He felt sweat pouring out of him as he moved only his eyes in search of something, anything, with which he could defend himself. Now a voice wanted to know what they were going to do with him, and he seemed to hear answers which made him shrink into the womb that was himself. There couldn't actually be people in the clothes—that was just a nightmare—and so he couldn't really be hearing the voices either. No voices could say such things, not outside hell. He squeezed his eyes tight to ward off the threat of a spoon being inserted in the sockets, then opened them so wide he felt them tremble like bubbles about to burst; he couldn't bear to keep them shut while he was surrounded. The shabby walls propped themselves up again, rebuilding the set of a room which felt as cluttered and unstable as the inside of the skull, and then, as if whatever film he might be in had provided the prop, he thought he saw a weapon almost hidden by a pile of newspapers and gloom in one corner. He was wondering whether he dared check that it was what it looked like, or whether knowing it was there if he needed it could be enough, when a woman's voice in the hall said "Get on with it" followed by a slam.

Was she talking to him or to the people hiding around him? "Who's that?" he cried, and realized he'd given himself away. "Da?" he pleaded, feeling abandoned by his friend. "Are you there?"

"My mam's gone out," his friend shouted. "Stay where you're put."

At least the voices had stopped. The people in the clothes must be wary of giving themselves away now that they'd heard there was someone else in the house. Marshall sat and waited for his friend to bring him whatever he was going to bring. But his friend's sounds were moving away, farther and farther, so far it seemed impossible they were still in the house—at least, the one Marshall had thought he was in. He was losing his sense of where he was again, and beginning to fear that even his friend wouldn't be able to keep him safe. "Da?" he called, praying his voice wouldn't rouse the people around him.

There was no response. The other boy's sounds had grown tinny and blurred, a transmission which a radio was no longer able to grasp. Marshall stared around the room in case anything was sneaking toward him, and everything straightened up from starting to creep into another shape. He sucked in a breath which tasted of all the stale smells of the room, tobacco smoke and newspaper and unwashed clothes and some indefinable species of rottenness, and was trying to wait as long as he could bear, even a little longer, before repeating his plea, when he understood why his friend hadn't responded: because Marshall hadn't called him by his proper name. For a moment Marshall was afraid the name had been swallowed by the hole he could feel growing in the midst of his brain, and then he remembered. "Darren," he shouted in panicky triumph.

His friend said a word. Though Marshall couldn't identify it, at least it meant Darren had heard him. The sounds of his activity continued, too distant to be reassuring. He was looking for something; maybe he could use some help. "Darren?"

That brought a rush of footsteps, which sounded as though they were several rooms away an instant before the door was flung open. "*What?*" Darren demanded. "You're worse than some old shit who can't get out of bed."

The idea of illness triggered Marshall's question. "Why did your mom go out?"

When Darren only stared and opened his mouth in a grimace of disbelief, Marshall began answering for him. "I know she's a nurse. Did she have to go to the hospital?"

"What do you think, lad? Don't know why you have to ask."

"I don't suppose I did really, sorry, but did she leave anything?"

"Left a lot of fucking stuff. Nowt you'd want to know about, though."

"I mean, you know what I mean. Anything for me?" Marshall heard his own voice turning harsh. He was desperate not only for an answer but also to shift the expression from Darren's face, which looked as though invisible thumbs were wrenching both corners of his mouth down. "You know, to take?"

"Greedy cunt, aren't you?" Abruptly Darren straightened his mouth. "All right, just stick there and I'll see what she's got."

"Shall I help you look?"

"No chance, lad. You reckon you could find anything the way you are?"

"No," Marshall admitted, and tried to grasp what his friend was feeling which looked like relief. "Only you sounded as if you were looking for something before."

"Aye, well, maybe we won't need it. Up to you. Now just shut the fuck up and do what the fuck you're told," Darren said, his voice growing louder and flatter as if he was shouting at someone beyond Marshall, and stomped out of the room.

Marshall felt unable to move until he comprehended how he had managed to infuriate his friend. At least Darren had left the door open, and the thuds of his feet on the stairs sounded not unbearably far away. Now they were shaking the ceiling above Marshall, and now they were tumbling downstairs so rapidly that Marshall was afraid his friend had fallen until Darren came marching on invisible strings at him. "Swallow this, lad, if it'll stop you whining."

Marshall peered at the object the other boy dropped on the pinkish desert of his hand. Though he couldn't judge its size, dwarfed as it was by the largest dune, it looked familiar. "Didn't I already take two of these?"

"Right, and there's another."

"Doesn't your mom have anything stronger?"

"She said you have to take three before they start to work. Don't look at me like that, lad, I can't do nowt about it. Stick it up your arse for all I care."

"I'm taking it. I mean, thanks for everything you've done for me." Marshall threw back his head to help the pill down his dry throat, and swallowed hard until he could no longer feel it bulging his insides. As he lowered his head, the set of a room raised itself to meet his eyes, and he couldn't keep quiet, even if he sounded more ungrateful than ever. "Will she have something stronger at the hospital?"

"Aren't you satisfied yet? She'll have some stuff where she's gone all right. Maybe you want some of that. That'd do for you, no messing."

Marshall couldn't make sense of the tone of his friend's voice, and hadn't time to try. "Can we go there?"

"That's what you're after, is it? Fucking hell." To Marshall's bewilderment, Darren sounded both disgusted and delighted. "I don't reckon she can say much against it," Darren said, wiping away a snort with the back of his hand. "Fair enough, come on. I'll take you where you can get some."

"Is it far?"

"As far as you'll be going, lad, and no mistake."

"Couldn't you get it for me?"

"What do you think I am, your fucking servant? Got a butler at home to wipe your arse, have you?" Darren visibly controlled himself—Marshall saw his face reform in a series of movements stuck together. "You want to take it as soon as it's got, don't you? Can't do that if I have to bring it back."

His urgency didn't quite override Marshall's doubts. "I know, only . . ."

"What? What's your fucking problem this time?"

"You said my mom said I had to stay in your house till she came."

"Jesus." Darren jerked his fists up and shook them, almost hitting himself in the face. "I know I said that, but you want to get home to her, don't you? You want to talk to her, any road. Can't do that if you stay in the house."

He was making Marshall feel sad behind his eyes and in his chest, but Marshall had to overcome that and think. "I don't need to speak to her now you have. Suppose she comes to fetch me and we aren't here? I mustn't be meant to go outside while it's cold or she'd have come for me by now in the car."

"She's a nurse like my mam, is she?"

"No, but—"

"She knows more about it than a nurse does, you reckon?"

"She's always looked after me. Like you're trying to, Darren," Marshall added in case he was sounding ungrateful. "Only your mom didn't say I should go out either, did she? You'd have said by now if she had."

Incredulity dragged the other boy's mouth down as he shared his stare with the room. Then his attention veered to one corner, and Marshall saw that what he had thought he'd seen before was still there. "Is that real?" he said.

"What do you reckon you can see, lad?"

"That's a gun under those papers, isn't it? A revolver."

"What do you know, I can see it too."

Rather than reassuring Marshall, that confused him, all the more because he couldn't grasp why it did. "Yes, but I mean, is it, you know, really real?"

"That's a song, isn't it?" An uninterpretable smile flickered across Darren's lips, and he seemed to be restraining himself. "I don't know what you're pissing on about."

"You know, real like it can shoot. It only looks real, doesn't it? It's not a real gun that could hurt anyone, it's just a toy. You wouldn't have a real gun in the house in Britain."

"Want to find out?"

"Sure, if—"

That had been all the excuse Darren needed to stop holding himself back. He darted to the corner, kicking aside strewn newspapers and an ashtray full of fractured stubs, and stooped to grab the weapon. As he straightened up he twisted around and levelled the gun at Marshall, who ducked, almost sprawling off the chair, before he saw that Darren's finger wasn't on the trigger. "Don't do that," he protested. "Never point a gun at anyone."

"Not much fucking use having one then, is there? I thought you thought it wasn't real."

Marshall fought off the notion that he'd made it real by being scared of it. "I still don't think it is."

He watched Darren close his free hand around the hand on the butt and hook one finger around the trigger. The gun wasn't quite pointing at him. "How much do you bet?" Darren said.

"I can't bet anything. You have all my change."

The barrel swung toward him, so slowly he saw it catching at the air. "So bet that," Darren said, "and maybe you'll get twice as much back."

That would be twice a few pounds, as far as Marshall could remember. He dug his spine into the chair so as not to dodge while the gun found him, opening its round mouth as it came. Now the mouth was facing him, for the moment emptily, or was it filling with more than darkness? Perhaps his senses had grown so acute that he would be able to glimpse the bullet in the instant before it blew his head open. Apprehension hit him in the stomach, folding him over himself. "I believe you," he almost screamed.

The gun followed him down, and he thought he saw Darren's finger tightening on the trigger. "Bit fucking late, lad."

He hated himself for having let Darren see him panic. He forced himself to sit up straight and gazed at the revolver, which was pointing at his chest. "I didn't bet. You still have to give me my money back."

"Come and get it."

Marshall tensed himself to do so. If he moved slowly there would be no cause for Darren's finger to shift on the trigger. Once Marshall was close enough he could push the gun aside, maybe even take it from him. Darren wouldn't really shoot, he was Marshall's friend, but just suppose he squeezed the trigger without meaning to? How sensitive was it? Marshall couldn't move after all, not while the gun was on him. "I'll let you give it to me," he said, feeling his cheek tug at his mouth.

"That's the idea."

His friend was only playing, Marshall told himself. Only you shouldn't play with guns, and he was suddenly certain that if it was aimed at him much longer it would go off. He wasn't about to plead—he'd humiliated himself enough in front of the other boy—but he had to talk it away from him. "Why do you keep that around the house?"

"Where do you want it kept? In the road?"

The gun wasn't relenting. Maybe Darren thought Marshall's attempt at a conversational tone meant he was planning to grab it. Marshall turned his empty hands up, not too fast, he told himself. "No, I mean why do you have it?"

"Why do you have guns where you come from? To take care of any bugger as shouldn't be in here."

A wave of unexpected grief rose from Marshall's throat to his eyes. "My dad got one," he blurted.

"Got a bugger, did he?"

Darren's voice had turned harsh—because he was embarrassed by Marshall's grief, of course. "No, a gun," Marshall said with a shaky attempt at a laugh. "He shouldn't have without a license, but he thought he needed it."

"Why was that, lad?"

Marshall's ruse wasn't working yet; if anything, Darren's aim looked steadier than ever. "Because some jerk pulled a gun on him in the street over nothing at all," Marshall said, "and when he got sent to jail, this rat sent his family after my dad."

"Good job he had a gun then, eh?"

"No." Another wave of grief was threatening to spill out of Marshall. "He wouldn't have shot anyone. I wish he had. He took the bullets out and tried to make these scum think he hadn't."

Darren flexed his finger and replaced it on the trigger. "He should have got a lesson off my da."

"I wish," Marshall agreed, and tried to think of anything that would stop his eyes from brimming over, then had a thought he couldn't believe he hadn't had sooner. "Are there any in that one?"

"Any bullets? Real bullets, is that? One way to find out, lad."

Darren no longer sounded like a friend. Marshall didn't understand how he could have antagonized him, unless it was any show of emotion Darren couldn't stand. "Sorry," Marshall said, wiping his eyes quickly and hard in the hope the other boy mightn't notice.

"For what?"

"I don't know," Marshall pleaded. "For not trusting you. I mean, I know you aren't going to shoot me. You're my friend."

"You reckon." Darren considered the gun and then Marshall. "Long as I'm your mate, let's play a game. Give you a chance to win some of that money you wanted to win."

"I only wanted my own back."

"Doesn't work like that round here. I thought you were supposed to trust me. You carry on with that and you'll be amazed what you get."

"What kind of game?"

"Bet you guessed. It's been in enough films." Darren pointed the gun at the ceiling and released the cylinder. As he sat down, bullets dropped into his hand. At last, watching them quiver and glisten on the boy's palm, Marshall understood why they were called slugs. When Darren placed the five of them under his chair they crawled about for some moments before subsiding. He swung the cylinder back into place and spun it with the heel of his hand, then sat forward and turned the butt toward Marshall. "Six goes. Three each. You go first."

Marshall's hand hesitated an inch short of the gun. "Have you played before?"

"Course I have, lots of times. And I'm still here, so I don't know what you're shitting your pants for."

"I'm not," Marshall protested, pressing his buttocks together. He glared at his hand to make it stop letting him down, and once it had more or less ceased trembling he took hold of the revolver.

It was larger and heavier than he was prepared for. No wonder Darren had been using both hands. It felt cold and leaden and bulky, and he thought he could smell the metal of it, like the taste of a coin in his mouth. When he extended his finger around the trigger, the presence of the weapon seemed too detailed for him to grasp. The light had grown more artificial, and he saw himself performing on a stage. All the people in the room were watching, no longer a threat to him, just an audience. He turned the gun and pointed it at his forehead.

He felt his wrist twinge and creak. The revolver sagged in his grasp, leaning the trigger against his finger. The mouth of the barrel gaped at him. Its perfect circle seemed capable of hypnotizing him; certainly the aching of his wrist had detached itself from him. He had almost forgotten what he was meant to be doing when Darren lost patience. "Come on, lad," he urged.

The trigger was absurdly stiff. Trying to pull it bruised Marshall's finger, and he felt more of a wimp than ever. To Darren he must look as though he was pretending not to be able to squeeze the trigger. He rested the muzzle against his forehead above his right eye, and closed his free hand around the barrel, and dragged at the trigger with all the strength he could focus.

He felt the lever shift reluctantly, felt the mechanism heaving the hammer back. He was about to reach into himself for one last effort when there was a loud impact which shook both the gun and his head. The hammer had fallen on an empty chamber. He lowered the weapon, grabbing his wrist to steady his shivering hand, and released a breath he hadn't been aware of holding. "Oh, that was—"

"Give us it." Darren lurched forward on his chair and grabbed the barrel, twisted it toward him, jabbed his other thumb behind the guard and pressed the trigger. Marshall heard a click, nothing like as loud as the one he himself had triggered. Darren shoved the butt at him. "You again."

Marshall rubbed his hands on the sleeves of his track suit. Most of the weight of the gun seemed to have remained in the palm of his right hand, bruising it. He used his left to take hold of the barrel, and raised his head so as to rest the muzzle more or less comfortably under his chin. He leaned back, propping the butt low on his chest, and closed his stinging hand around the butt and squeezed the trigger as hard as he could.

It shot up through his jaw, vibrating his teeth—the impact did. The breath he expelled through his nose sounded like a shivery laugh. As he let the barrel fall he had to remind himself to point it well away from his friend, in case the weight of the gun pulled the trigger against his finger. Darren didn't appreciate the gesture, or rather, Marshall told himself, he felt unable to acknowledge it. "Get a move on," he demanded. "I'll be asleep before you're done at this rate."

As soon as Marshall let go of the butt Darren seized it, swung the gun toward his scalp and narrowing his eyes, pulled the trigger. His face was a blank mask, and stayed that way as the revolver emitted a click. He thrust the gun at Marshall. "Here you go. Don't hang about."

The fist which Marshall had clenched on his behalf was opening to accept the gun when Marshall clutched at the wrist to delay it. "Wait a minute, Darren. I know it's only a game, but—"

"Summat up, lad?"

"You didn't really point it at yourself just then. Weren't you aiming past yourself?"

"You reckon, do you? You think you can see what's going on around you in the fucking state you're in?" Darren was blustering, and Marshall saw him realize it was obvious he was. He sneered, showing all his teeth, and opened his mouth wider. "All right then, watch this," he snarled, and stuck the barrel in his mouth.

It was real this time. It was going to happen, and Darren didn't care; his eyes were saying so. Marshall saw the hammer strain itself back. "N—" he moaned, terrified for Darren, and made to throw himself at the other boy and snatch the gun out of his mouth. But the hammer sprang, and he shut his eyes, and felt the sound of the revolver like a nail driven into his skull. "How about that then, lad?" Darren said. "Real enough for you?"

Marshall opened his eyes to get rid of the pounding light, but it only spread into the room. "Too real."

"What's up with you? Like you said, it's only a game. Let's see you do what I just did."

Marshall had to, or he would be letting his friend down—that was the meaning in Darren's eyes now. Marshall stretched out his hand for the weapon, and couldn't understand why he was having difficulty until he realized he was still holding onto the wrist. He made himself relinquish his grip, and closed his hand, which was stinging with sweat, around the butt. A trickle of Darren's saliva glistened on the barrel, and he thought of slugs, the five of them nesting together under the other boy's chair. He wiped the muzzle on his sleeve and pointed the gun at his mouth, supporting the butt with both hands. His teeth were clenched, his tongue was pressed so hard against them he could hear it through his skull. He shoved at his tight lips with the muzzle and prized them apart, and the gun banged against his teeth.

Either they got out of the way or they would ache worse. His jaw dropped, and the barrel nudged his tongue, filling his mouth with the taste of metal. If he had to put up with that for long he would be sick. He took a firmer grip on the butt and poked one thumb inside the guard, and felt the trigger shift to make room. It was less stiff than previously, or perhaps he was more used to handling it. He raised his eyes to meet Darren's, and saw his friend urging him to do as he'd done. The ache which had been growing in his wrist flared through his arm, and the gun jerked out of his mouth as he had a thought. "Darren—"

"What fucking now?"

"We're not playing it right. You're supposed to spin the, you know, the middle bit each time."

"Who says?"

"That's what they do in all the movies," Marshall said, feeling he was in one as he spun the cylinder. When it came to a halt the gun felt subtly changed. It occurred to him that he could sense where the weight of the single bullet was. Before, it had been directly under the hammer, and now it was to one side of it—the left, he was practically certain. So there was no reason for him not to turn the gun on himself. He opened his mouth as wide as he'd ever done for a dentist, and tickled the roof of his mouth with the muzzle, and squeezed the trigger. He'd already heard the click in his mind when it became real. "See, I did it," he said, dropping the gun in his lap.

"If you're going to play like that we'll start again."

"All right." Marshall handed him the revolver. "All right, but let's not play for money."

"What else do you want to play for, a fuck?"

"No, I'm serious. I just thought. I'll do six and you don't have to do any, but if I win you have to let me stay until my mom comes to fetch me."

"Fucking hell."

Darren sounded both frustrated and reluctantly admiring. "So is it a deal?" Marshall persisted.

"We'll see what my mam says when she gets home."

Marshall saw that was the best Darren could offer, and it seemed fine to him; surely no nurse would turn him out of the house while he was ill. "Hand it over, then," he said.

Darren made his incredulous face again as he passed him the revolver. Marshall no longer knew what the expression was meant to communicate, but it didn't matter, any more than the sight of the muzzle homing in on him. He took hold of it and swung the butt into his other hand, and spun the cylinder. He let the gun fall against his chest, the muzzle beneath his chin, and bore down on the trigger.

There was a click, as he'd known there would be. Six consecutive shots were beginning to appear rather more ambitious than they had when he'd proposed them, but he needn't worry, because he would be able to sense if the bullet was under the hammer. In any case, he had only five shots to go. He gazed at Darren, the solitary visible member of the audience, while he lowered the gun to his lap and spun the cylinder. When he raised the gun he was sure he could feel it weighing slightly leftward, where the bullet must be. He lifted the barrel under his chin with his free hand. "Two," he said.

Click, of course. The ache in his weakening wrist seemed far more of a problem than anything the gun would do. They fell, and he dealt the cylinder a spin and hoisted the revolver. Still weighted to the left. "Three."

Click, and the ache found his elbow and dropped his forearm so abruptly that the butt bruised his right thigh. He couldn't falter while Darren was watching, waiting for him to give up. A spin of the cylinder made his fingers throb, and the barrel stung them when he closed them around it. Had he remembered to weigh where the bullet was? Yes, on the left again. "Four."

Click, and he winced as the butt clubbed his thigh. This time he used his knuckles against the cylinder, scraping skin off them. He must be achieving the same amount of spin each time—either that or there was some bias in the cylinder, since the weight was to the left still. He held the barrel in his stinging fist and propped them against his chest. "Five," he said, and the click seemed to penetrate every inch of him, because it had struck him that he mightn't be locating the bullet at all, that the gun might not be quite symmetrical. Was anything? He'd kept hold of the barrel so that the gun couldn't thump him yet again, and now he managed to support the gun in mid-air, though his hand wobbled badly, while he spun the cylinder as hard as he could. It whirred to a stop, and he hefted the revolver.

As far as he was able to judge, its balance hadn't changed. He no longer knew where the bullet was, but he had only one shot to go and then he could stay with his friend. He lifted the gun with both hands and poked himself under the chin. The metal circle, which felt huge, dug into his flesh. He couldn't fire until he'd counted, but his tongue was paralyzed by the nearness of the muzzle. "Sss," he said, and heard how he must sound to Darren. Contempt for himself made him clench his fist, thumbing the trigger down. "Six," he blurted, convinced that he had to say it before the hammer fell, just as it did.

His skull exploded with pain. The room was blotted out. He felt his body retreat from him, driven by the shock. An onslaught of light filled his consciousness, and then his leg jerked as his hand and the revolver struck it. As he managed to grasp that his head was aching with tension, the blinding pain began to dwindle, and after perhaps a few seconds he was able to open his eyes. Darren was watching him expressionlessly. "I did it," Marshall gasped.

"You never counted one, lad."

"I didn't say I would. I said I'd take six shots, and I did. I won." Marshall fumbled for the barrel through the surges of light which threatened to wipe out his surroundings, and flung the weapon away from him. He saw it turn in the air, its muzzle swivelling toward Darren, and was all at once sure that the bullet was lined up with the hammer, so that when the revolver struck the floor—He tried to shove himself out of the chair with his weakened hands, but the thought was already too late. The gun thumped the carpet, and that was all. "Can I get some sleep now?" he said as the light and the pain in his skull continued to throb.

"You can try. Don't bet on it." Darren stared at the gun as though he was thinking of picking it up, then let it lie. "Reckon soon you'll be getting all the rest you need," he muttered.

26

THE CALL

Susanne awoke remembering her search for Marshall. He hadn't been any of the boys who had clustered around the Volvo to offer themselves to her and to anyone else who might be in it, some of them at least as young as Marshall but with faces several times that age. He hadn't been among the children running away from an Indian jewelry store which had been set on fire. She'd thought she recognized him outside an all-night pharmacy until the small figure had turned, catching a neon gleam on the syringe in his arm. Nor had Marshall been the child she'd seen dragged, screaming like an injured animal, into a car which had screeched away before she could read the number-plate. His hadn't been the body sprawled in the middle of a road, the blue pulse of an ambulance insistently blackening its spillage of blood. He hadn't been in any of the piles of newspapers in shop doorways, though each of the piles to which she'd stooped had poked out at least one head, and she hadn't found him among the inhabitants of a gap between the houses of a derelict street, people crowding so closely around a fire that their clothes had begun to smolder.

She hadn't seen that. Though the memories were so vivid and detailed that she was no more able to dislodge them from her mind than to wipe the grubby coating of night from her eyes, she had only dreamed them. That wasn't even slightly comforting, because she could believe in all of them. Worse still, she'd projected them on the screen of her mind instead of trying to find Marshall.

A streetlamp died as she caught sight of it. It was daylight, and Marshall had been out all night, and she had never felt so alone. If she were a character in any of the movies he liked she wouldn't have stayed home, she would have sped from episode to episode of her search, experiencing only a sketch of emotions. If Don were alive one of them could have stayed by the phone while the other searched, but she hadn't felt able to leave the house in case Marshall needed to reach her. Suppose he'd called and she hadn't been there? Hilda Mattison had seen her light on after midnight and had sat with her to make increasingly small talk, not to mention cups of tea, while her husband Matt, a large shy man whose stomach was outgrowing its shirt and purple cardigan, had driven around the streets. He'd looked even more abashed than usual on his eventual return, and quite prepared to start another search although it was past two in the morning. Susanne had been afraid that he might have an accident through drowsiness, and so she'd sent them both home, having had to promise that she would wake them if she needed anything. She'd watched lights climb the inside of their house and go out one by one, and then there had been nothing to do but wait with all her thoughts.

She'd vowed she wouldn't go to sleep. She'd brought in the cordless telephone and held it on her lap, then she'd made herself place it on the table and wondered how to keep herself awake. She'd tried to read the essays, but the first had taken her aback: an unexpectedly bitter piece from Rosemary, a quiet student who required hardly any provocation to blush. Every British film had to have Americans in or behind it, British video stores were really American as far as the films they stocked were concerned and the token World Cinema section was an insult to the rest of the world, all this fostered an addiction to Americanism, just as the tobacco companies were paying to have actors smoke in almost every film . . . Maybe most of this was true, but Susanne hadn't wanted to contemplate it just then; it had made her feel more isolated than ever. She'd attempted to watch television, but the only transmission on any of the four channels had shown her Peter Sellers, whom she'd always thought of as a comedian, trapping a young man's fingers in the lid of a record player and grinding an old man's pet terrapin under his heel. She'd switched off the television and had watched the empty street beneath the unrelenting lamps until sleep had begun to nod her head. She'd jerked it up, she'd pinched her upper arms, she'd staggered to the bathroom to douse her face with cold water. Nevertheless she had slept several times, feeling worse every time she'd wakened. She had slept while Marshall was out somewhere in the dark.

She stumbled to the kitchen in an attempt to shake off the night. Her body felt brittle and stiff and as though she hadn't bathed for days. She made coffee so strong that at the first mouthful a shudder rushed all the way down her and back up to her scalp, then she clutched her portable radio and carried it and the mug to the bathroom, resting an elbow on the banister as she climbed each stair. She dropped her clothes in the washing basket and switched on the radio. She was in the bath, pirouetting like a dancer stuck in treacle through what the British apparently considered to be a powerful shower but which seemed hardly palpable, when a vigorous jingle announced the early breakfast news.

Most of yesterday's atrocities had had their moments of fame, though the police wanted it to be known that they were still looking for the gang who had smashed a bank guard's knees. Susanne twisted the taps shut and fought off the plastic curtain and stepped out of the trough of the bath. A teenage girl who had been thrown into a fire by three youths was described as comfortable in the hospital. A burglar had bitten several householders who'd caught him on their property, and they were being tested for infection. Half a dozen families who were accused of using one another's children, all of them younger than Marshall, for sex had been rounded up in Operation Nursery. Police were appealing for information regarding the whereabouts of Marshall Travis, twelve years old.

Speaks with an American accent, five feet five inches tall, blue eyes, fair hair, slight build, last seen wearing a purple Nike track suit and white Reebok trainers . . . Susanne wasn't sure which dismayed her more, how the description rendered him so present it was as though he had just stepped out of the room and yet so absent that the lack of him felt like an ache as big as the whole of herself, or how the appeal seemed far too generalized to identify him to the public: it hadn't mentioned the way he walked, swinging his arms and rolling a little as though he'd just disembarked from a ship, or his habit of patting the crown of his head to reassure himself that no hair was standing up, or his lopsided smile which was all she had left of his father . . . She didn't realize how fiercely she was toweling herself until her nipples began to sting. She dabbed at them and finished drying herself, and switched off the radio and went into the bedroom, having wakened all her nerves, to get dressed.

She'd forgotten that the curtains were open since she'd slept downstairs. She dodged across the room and hid behind the right-hand curtain so as to pull it across. Then her hands almost yanked it off the rail. A man she'd never seen before was leaning over the wall into her garden.

Susanne dashed into the bathroom and grabbed her robe from the hook beside Marshall's. She struggled into the rough cloth as she padded fast across the landing, and tied the cord, strangling her waist, as she returned to the windows. The man was leaning farther, reaching a hand into the garden, showing her the whole of his naked scalp. She felt as though he was exposing himself to her. She slipped the bolts of the windows and padded onto the balcony, the chill of the stone seizing her feet. When the intruder didn't look up she cleared her throat, forcing out her voice. "What are you doing? What are you leaving there?"

The man raised his head: a broad brow crossed by three ridges of flesh, eyebrows like wads of dust, eyes rather too large for the rest of his face. He drew back his hand before meeting her gaze. "Just admiring your lavender, love."

She wasn't sure if she believed him—not when he stooped to lift something beyond the wall. The pinkish swelling of his scalp confronted her once more as she gripped the railing of the balcony with both cold hands. Then she heard a clink of glass, and realized what he was—didn't need to see the crate of milk bottles which he hoisted into view. "Sorry if I gave you a turn, love," he called. "The other lad's off sick."

Susanne had to clear her throat again as he turned away. "Take a sprig if you like."

"Aye, I will, then." He reached across the wall and broke off a twig, which he inserted in the top buttonhole of his work shirt. "Good bit of gardening you've done. It wasn't here last time I was."

"My—Thanks." She didn't trust herself to mention Don, not when the thought of him was the tip of so much grief, which didn't relate only to him. She watched the milkman trot away, crate jingling, to his wagon at the corner. She ought to have noticed that sooner. She mustn't let her fears blind her, or she would be no use to Marshall. She curtained the street and pulled on enough clothes to make herself feel less shivery, and took the radio and telephone downstairs, telling herself she had to eat breakfast to keep up her strength.

She managed to eat nearly half a bowl of cereal before the question of what, if anything, Marshall might have eaten since she'd last seen him turned the food to soggy cardboard in her mouth. She had to wash the mouthful down with a gulp of coffee so bitter it made her head swim. After that there seemed to be nothing to do except brush her teeth before returning to her chair in the front room.

She tried to grade the essays, setting Rosemary's aside for when she felt able to be objective about it, and waited for the University switchboard to be staffed so that she could call in. The eight o'clock news came first, and she listened to it to reassure herself that the item about Marshall was repeated and nothing new was said about him, though what was reassuring about that? The description was there, again without a headline. That had to mean he soon wouldn't be news, because he would have been found safe. The news gave way to music, to uncommunicative silence as she switched off the radio, and the phone rang.

She snatched it up and pressed the talk button, her hand all at once so slippery that she almost dropped the receiver. "Susanne Travis."

"Susanne, is it? Is that Susanne?"

"That's right, Clement," she told him. "That's what I said."

"I thought it might be your, but I see you're there in the flesh. I hope I haven't called at, if it's inconvenient please do say."

"No no, it's fine," Susanne said, fighting not to let him reach her nerves. "What can I do for you?"

"Well, it's rather what I, what we, you should appreciate. I'm sure I speak for the department, indeed the entire, all of those who've heard the news."

"The"—the word almost blocked her throat—"news."

"About your young, is he not missing? My wife assured me that was what she just, isn't that the case, dear? I was at my ablutions, you understand." His voice, having veered away for five words, came back. "She gathered from the news that your, the name eludes me for the moment, you heard it, dear—"

"Marshall. Yes, he's missing. I'm waiting to hear from the police."

"Ah. Yes. I mustn't interpose myself in the way of, then, no." If anything, Susanne's impatience seemed to be slowing Clement down. "Should we tell your students to expect, or do you plan to stay at home until, ah?"

"I'd rather stay here, Clement. Then if anything urgent," Susanne said, and was unable to continue.

"I quite, yes. Please accept my, indeed our, deepest, shall I advise your colleagues not to attempt to phone you while, until you direct to the contrary?"

"That would be best. I'll let you know as soon as . . ." She'd already wounded him with her impatience, she'd sensed that, and now she sounded as if she was imitating him. "Thanks for calling, Clement. Thanks for your support. It's appreciated."

"If there is any, you know where to reach me."

"I do."

"In that case, let me vacate, goodbye for the present."

"Goodbye, Clement. Thanks again."

It wasn't only that she wanted to convince him of her sincerity—she hadn't realized how much she welcomed talking to another human being. She held the receiver until a click turned him into a drone. Though there were people she needed to call, she supposed it was too early. Cars were deserting the street outside, and she saw a last streetlamp give up the ghost. That only meant daylight was strengthening—had to mean Marshall would be easier to find. A mass of fears was clamoring for her attention, which she tried to divert by keying a number. But the school didn't answer, and the next time the line was busy, and the next, and the time after that too. It was almost nine o'clock before she heard a voice say "Bushy Boys."

"Susanne Travis. I—"

"Oh yes, Mrs. Travis. Head would like a word. He's just about to take assembly. Can he call you back?"

"About what, do you know?"

"I'm afraid I couldn't tell you. That's for Head to say. He shouldn't be more than, oh, twenty minutes at the outside. Will you be at home?"

"Where else would you expect me to be, you stupid—" Susanne persuaded herself that it would be unfair to utter any of that, and all she said was, "Yes."

"I'll just take your number again in case. I'll give Head the message that you called the moment I see him."

Some phrases simply didn't translate across the ocean, Susanne thought. The beginning of a grin tweaked her face awry, but it felt as though Marshall had left her his smile, no longer needing it, perhaps. She wouldn't be able to bear twenty minutes of waiting and wondering. She stood up as the phone in her hand went dead, and ran to the study to find a card on the desk, and poked the keys as she hurried downstairs. The distant phone rang as she dropped herself back in her chair, and then it emitted a long protesting breath, and a woman's voice as fierce demanded, "Yes?"

"Iris Pendle?"

"Yes?"

"Susanne Travis."

"Yes?"

"We're supposed to meet for lunch today."

"To discuss my offer for the bookshop, yes. Yes?"

"I'm sorry, but I need to cancel."

"Excuse me, won't you. I was in the bath." This was apparently meant to explain the bookseller's abruptness, because when she spoke again her tone was softer. "Have you received another offer, Mrs. Travis?"

"Not since we last spoke, no."

"You do realize the figure I mentioned is open to discussion. That was one of the reasons for meeting."

She was giving Susanne the chance to hold out for a better price, but it seemed entirely irrelevant now. "Got you," Susanne said. "It's just that I can't leave the house, at least, I don't know that I'll be able to by lunchtime. My son, he's twelve, he's missing, and I need to be here until, until . . ."

She wished her listener would speak, and after a pause Iris Pendle did. "Would you like me to come to you?"

"I mightn't be competent to discuss business. I hope you understand."

"Fully." The bookseller sounded as though she'd heard meanings Susanne hadn't had in mind. "So we're leaving it that . . ."

"I'll call you as soon as, when all this—I'll call you."

"I plan to be in your vicinity again toward the end of the month."

Susanne couldn't think that far ahead—wasn't afraid to, just couldn't, she told herself. "I'll be in touch," she said, and cleared the phone. She needed to make another call, though had she time before the school rang her back? She'd missed the nine o'clock news, but surely if there had been anything new on it about Marshall she would have been notified first. She found the remote control under her chair and raised television channels rapidly as slides, but any local news was finished. She dropped the control and retrieved the phone, and was searching for the scrap of paper on which she had scribbled the number when the phone went off in her hand.

It creaked in her grip as she jabbed the talk button. "Susanne Travis."

"Bushy Boys, Mrs. Travis. I'll give you Head now."

Susanne felt her mouth start to shape the grin it would wear when she recounted that to Marshall—when he was old enough, when he knew about such things. She composed her face in order to compose her voice as she heard Mr. Harbottle say, "Mrs. Travis."

His tone was more authoritarian than she cared for. "That's right," she said.

"I was told you rang."

"I did." Matching tones with him would get her nowhere, however much of her dislike he was reviving. "I don't suppose Marshall showed up this morning."

"I rather fear that is the case."

"You know he didn't, you mean."

"I believe that is what I said."

"But you wanted to speak to me."

"I can see no objection to that, Mrs. Travis."

"I mean, your secretary told me when I called you wanted to."

"The secretary has instructions to refer all contentious matters to me."

"So you didn't have, you haven't, there haven't been any developments." His tone seemed designed to make her feel like a guilty pupil, and it wasn't helping. "I spoke to all his friends I've met," she said, "but I wanted you to ask if anyone else has seen him since he walked out of the school."

"That has been done, Mrs. Travis. I gather this has now become a matter for the police, and I should like to express the school's—"

"Skip that for the moment. And?"

"Your meaning eludes me, Mrs. Travis."

"For—And what did the other boys say?"

"I very much regret that there appear to have been no sightings of Travis. I think I can fairly claim that my staff and I would be aware if anyone was concealing knowledge of his whereabouts. I take it you have exhausted any possibilities in that area yourself."

Susanne no longer had much sense of what the headmaster was trying to say, nor did it seem worth comprehending. "I don't know where he might have gone," she said, because even the headmaster was somebody to speak to. "I can't imagine what sort of a state he's in to think he can't come home to me. And if it isn't his decision . . ."

She trailed off rather than consider that, but the headmaster took her silence as a cue. "I can assure you, Mrs. Travis, that at Bushy Road we strive to instill self-discipline in all our pupils."

"That's the best kind, but I don't see the relevance."

"Simply that if you were implying Travis has fallen into bad company, I would suggest you ought to look elsewhere than at this school."

"I wasn't." That was ambiguous, but she was too angry to fix it. "Mr. Harbottle, if you're going to call my son by name I'd appreciate it if you'd call him Marshall. His father and I liked it, and that's why we gave it to him."

"Our policy at Bushy Road is that until boys reach the sixth form—"

"Or if you're going to use last names you might put Mister in front of them. That might give your pupils a bit more self-respect, don't you think? You can't have self-discipline without that, it's always seemed to me. I thought it was criminals who got called by their last names and nothing else."

"I'm sorry if our methods are foreign to you, Mrs. Travis. I'm not aware of any other parent finding them objectionable."

Each of the responses she discarded was angrier than the last, and she tried to restrain herself for Marshall's sake. She hadn't spoken when the headmaster said, "Is there anything further I can do for you?"

"Just help me find Marshall. Don't do anything to scare him off. He's done nothing I blame him for."

"I see."

She wanted to end the call—it might be blocking another—but she couldn't ignore the way he'd said that. "What do you see, Mr. Harbottle?"

"I rather fear our attitudes may prove incompatible in the future."

"You don't want Marshall to come back, you mean."

"That would depend on whether we were given sufficient assurance that Travis would abide by the rules."

"You're presuming I still have a son to come back."

That paused the headmaster, but she desperately wished she hadn't said it. Now that she'd heard it, it seemed far worse than just a thought she had been trying not to think. She was searching for a way to break the funereal silence when he said, "I very much hope that is the case. It seems unlikely that the situation is as grave as you imply."

"You would say that," Susanne started, but there was no point in accusing him of being at least partly responsible for it, not until she took Marshall to see him, which she would, she knew she would. "I can't talk any more now," she said, and steadied her voice. "If you need to call and I'm not here there's a machine. Please leave a message, don't just say you called."

"We would scarcely do that, Mrs. Travis."

The secretary already had, when she'd called the University about Marshall's absence, less than twenty-four hours, which seemed like weeks, ago. Everything which Susanne knew or feared had happened since then gathered itself to rush into her mind. "I can't talk any more now," she said, trying to mean only that she hadn't the time, and pressed the button to clear the line. As soon as she'd done so, the phone rang.

Perhaps she had caused it to ring. She couldn't help hoping that, just so she would have a chance to collect herself, not because she was afraid to hear what someone had to tell her. She let the phone ring once while she firmed her grip on it, twice while she sucked in a breath, and then, suddenly afraid that any caller might assume there was nobody home, she bent a fingernail against the button. "Hello? Hello?" she said. "Hello?"

She heard voices and more than one phone ringing. "Bear with me a moment, sorry," a man said in her ear, then spoke away from her. "I think you'll find Inspector Nadler is on that case."

The street beyond the window blazed and sprang at her as though a bomb had exploded, the one which had been detonated in her brain. "Twelve years old, that's right," the man was saying. "Worst case I've ever seen."

Her surroundings seemed to be retreating from her until they were as distant as his voice, and she had to drag them back. "Hello, police," she made herself say. "Speak to me."

"The way I hear it we're well on the way to tracking down the family responsible," the man was saying, no closer. "I wouldn't like to be them once they're inside for doing that to a kid of his age. Let me know if it looks like there's a connection with that bookshop." His voice was approaching; now it was against her ear. "Mrs. Travis. Sorry to have kept you. Are you still there?"

"Yes. What—" She swallowed and tried again. "What were you—"

"Excuse me?"

"What were you talking about just now?"

"Child porn. Particularly nasty case, not that any of them aren't. Nothing to do with my reason for calling you. Sorry if you thought it had."

Why did he think it might have sounded that way? Why was she being called by someone who dealt with such cases? "Why—"

"Yes, Mrs. Travis?"

"What do you want?"

"I was hoping to be of some help." His already flat voice had grown more brusque; perhaps he'd changed his mind. "We spoke yesterday. Drumm."

"About the videos you took."

"The illegal videos we seized, correct. You were coming in to sign the waiver."

If he hadn't said he mightn't be at the police station this morning she would have recognized him sooner. "Yes," she said, struggling to keep her thoughts on track, "but since then—"

"I'm familiar with your situation, Mrs. Travis."

"You are." Surely she hadn't heard more sympathy in his voice than she was afraid to hear. She flexed her tongue in her dry mouth. "What situation?"

"We've got your son down as a missing person, haven't we? Or have things progressed?"

"That's all. That's all, isn't it, as far as you know? I thought you would, being police."

"I'm with you. No progress that I'm aware of, sorry to say. I was calling because we'll have a car in your district sometime before lunch."

Susanne felt as confused as grateful. "Haven't there been any? Searching already, I mean?"

"Not to look for your son. That's another division. I was going to propose that our men could bring the waiver for you to sign if you'll be at home."

Her appreciation of his thoughtfulness almost rushed her into agreeing, but she held back. "What am I signing away?"

"The seizure, Mrs. Travis. I took it you understood that."

"What, all the videos? Not all of them."

"All the American tapes, and I think it's one British tape that's banned. We'll supply you with a breakdown, of course."

"But some of the tapes we brought over are rated PG. You have that here too. Parental Guidance."

"They don't carry a British certificate, Mrs. Travis. That's the view that's being taken. Under all the circumstances I hope you can see it's more than reasonable."

"What's the alternative?"

The policeman sniffed. "To take the matter to court and use up a good deal of time and public money and manpower."

"Quite a few of those tapes belong to my son. Some of his favorite movies. Please don't think I'm being difficult, but I'd have to ask him if he wants to give them up." Signing away Marshall's possessions might feel like signing him away too. "I'll ask him, all right?" she said.

Another phone rang in the police station, and reminded her that someone else might be trying to reach her. She was about to repeat her question when Drumm said, "As you choose, Mrs. Travis. I don't want to insist, given the situation, but I'd appreciate an answer as soon as you have one."

"That's a deal." Yet another phone began to ring—it felt as though it was somewhere deep in her brain. "Thanks, thanks a lot," she said, and silenced the receiver and held it unsteadily, waiting for it to shrill. Suppose the caller she'd sensed failing to reach her had given up? She stared at the phone in case that would rouse it, and released a shaky sigh, and lowered the receiver onto the carpet. The moment she let go of it, it rang.

She grabbed it, grabbed it again as it skittered away under her fingernails, captured it with both hands and hoisted it to her face, awkwardly thumbing the talk button. "Yes. Hello."

"Mrs. Travis?"

She recognized the man's voice, and the sounds of a police station behind it. The voice was unbearably neutral—guarded, she tried not to think. "Ccc," she said rapidly, desperate to get past the exchange of names, and fought off the first attack of stammering she had ever experienced. "Onstable Askew."

"No, this is Angel."

It wasn't the right voice—she must have attached the wrong name to each of the two policemen yesterday—but it was the call she found she had been dreading. She held onto the receiver with both hands and sat up stiffly, gazing straight ahead. "Constable Angel. Yes."

"I'm calling to let you know we'll pick you up in ten minutes."

"Oh." That sounded more like a cry than she'd wanted it to. "Oh, right. Okay. Thanks," she said, and seemed to have nothing left to say except, "Why?"

"Because we believe we may have located someone who saw your son."

27

ALREADY, HOWEVER

He was going to be all right, Marshall kept telling himself. The pills were starting to work. He would be fine if he could sleep just a little. His eyes were stinging with the lack of sleep, and the light of the room felt like dirty liquid which was being poured into them. He'd tried turning off the light, but the darkness showed him his father's face being smashed, coming to bits as metal heels and toecaps were driven into it, then reappearing whole and waiting helplessly with the same lopsided pleading grin. When his father's head appeared on a carnival sideshow stall at which a crowd was hurling bricks, Marshall crashed into the wall in his haste to find the light switch. The light seemed dimmer than it had been, and whenever he shut his eyes the sight of his father's face being burst asunder was waiting. Maybe once he gave the pills a chance to work they would let him sleep. He wished he could ask Darren, but his friend had gone to bed.

Marshall couldn't blame him. He himself was losing patience with his inability to sleep. Darren had nodded off once in his chair, and jerked awake glaring at Marshall and clenching his fists; then he'd grimaced and relaxed, emitting a grunt or a laugh. "What the fuck," he'd said about something that no longer mattered to him. "I'm off up. Do what you want."

"Can I watch television if I feel like it?"

Darren had performed his incredulous gape. "It's there, lad. That's what it's for, watching. There's the channel control. You don't want me to work it for you, do you? Want me to hold your dick for you while you watch a mucky video?"

"You're kidding."

Darren had stared at him as if he couldn't believe they were having this conversation. "Fuck off," he'd snarled, and stomped upstairs.

Marshall still couldn't blame him—not when Marshall had been acting like a little kid, demanding to be found things to do. He felt small and empty, hardly there at all, and dreading any further knowledge of himself. He would have read a book, except that there wasn't a book to be seen, and in any case what were books? All he did with them was stick his ostrich head in them. His skull was filling with sand, and he grabbed the channel control to keep the ants at bay.

A charred picture swam into the tank of the screen, and a face which he was sure he ought to recognize bobbed up. Why, it was Inspector Clouseau, who used to make Marshall and his father laugh together, although what was he doing in monochrome? A salesman's car was stolen and disguised at Clouseau's garage while Marshall waited for the laughs. Maybe he was missing the joke as Clouseau trapped a man's fingers in the lid of a record player, and beat up an old man and trod on his pet terrapin, and went to cut the face of the salesman's wife with some broken glass but punched her in the stomach instead. By now Marshall felt several kinds of betrayed by Clouseau, so that when the salesman caught up with him at last he heard himself yelling "Yay!" But the salesman was beaten up at length before he slammed a car door on Clouseau's hand and smashed his head with a wrench, and then the movie was over.

It wasn't nearly enough, nor was the WCW wrestling that followed. He seemed always to have known that wrestling was mostly stunts and superfitness, but now he saw that some of the wrestlers were life-size plastic figures that were being thrown about the ring. Maybe they all were; the closer he peered, the jerkier their movements grew. The ranting commentary must be intended to convince the viewer they were real. When a figure was flung over the ropes and lay writhing on the concrete, Marshall scoffed aloud and punched the arms of the chair in frustration. He needed something more, and his fists sprang him from the chair. His friend had told him there was something else he could watch.

At first he couldn't find any cassettes in the room. Surely his friend hadn't lied to him. He let out a cry of relief upon discovering a pile of cassettes behind the video recorder, lying flat in the dust. Cassettes should never be stored lying down, and he stood them on end before picking up one to squint at the handwritten label. The scrawled letters, which were of various sizes, wriggled back and forth on the rectangle of paper as he tried to find words in them. Eventually he was almost sure they said *A biTCh ANd heR MATe.* He tugged the cassette out of its cardboard sheath and switched on the video recorder. Having fed the tape into its toothless black mouth he sat down, experiencing a mixture of eagerness and apprehension which made him feel slightly nauseous, to watch.

The image on the screen, an announcement that the next program would follow shortly, remained stubbornly unchanged. It took him a few moments to grasp that the set wasn't tuned to the video channel. He began to press the buttons on the remote control, and had to resist working his way through the digits of his phone number. Maggots of static swarmed hissing out of the television, and then he found a blank screen moaning to itself. Another button, and the screen flared and quivered with the contents of the cassette.

He heard a voice not unlike his mother's saying "Oh, there's a big boy. There's such a big boy" as if those were the only words she could bring to mind, and a dog barking. The sounds were so close that they seemed to be flattening themselves against the inside of the screen, down which a succession of white ropes of static was crawling. Then the ropes sank out of view, leaving a strip of noise lines bunched at the top of the screen, and he saw the woman and the dog.

Their outlines were melting with duplication; their colors leaked. The woman's flesh, of which there appeared to be a generous helping, was bright orange, while the Alsatian's panting head resembled a mask made out of an old rug, and Marshall could almost believe that the part of the animal which was receiving a good deal of attention was a length of dark red plastic pipe. As the woman nodded, mumbling her litany as best she could, her hair trailed back and forth over the dog's pelt, though since they were the same brown Marshall saw the hair reaching out of the animal to pull her head to it. That wasn't the worst, however. The more she tried to pronounce her speech, the more she sounded like his mother talking in her sleep.

He'd once heard his mother murmuring like that to his father, in that tone and maybe in some of those words, when they must have thought Marshall was asleep. Now that his father was gone, what would she do for sex? He'd never thought about that before, and wished he hadn't while the cassette was playing. Her voice was sticking to his ears—the voice of the woman with the dog, which couldn't really be his mother's voice. Nevertheless he was growing desperate to see her face properly, with nothing in its mouth.

Her head gasped up at last, trailing orange streaks. The band of interference hid her eyes like a blindfold. She lifted the dog on top of her and clasped her cartoon legs around it while Marshall stared about, failing to locate a control for the video recorder. He fell on his knees before the television and poked the rewind button of the player. When the stretched black mouth began to utter a sound suggestive of the chewing of tape, he busied himself with the tuning wheel instead. That only spread the band of interference, and so he retreated to his chair.

As though in sympathy with the sections of the participants on which the camera was concentrating, the area of him between his rib-cage and his thighs was growing variously uncomfortable. The action on the screen achieved its point at last, noisily and blurrily, and he very much wanted to look away instead of waiting for the woman's face to make itself clear to him. He couldn't watch once she began to use her tongue, though closing his eyes didn't keep out her moans of apparent pleasure. She looked exactly like his mother now. He didn't know which idea was more loathsome—that it was his mother in the movie or that he was capable of imagining it was. He dug open his eyes with his thumbs in an attempt to escape the self which was trapped in his head, and saw the image on the screen fading into a grayness shot with broken white lines. The movie was finished. He sprang at the machine, though he didn't know if he meant to eject the cassette or rewind it to persuade himself the woman was nobody he knew. Then his mother appeared in front of him.

She was weeping. For a moment in which he felt he was falling apart, he thought that was because she knew he'd recognized her in the movie; then he saw himself weeping beside her. They were at his father's bookshop. A newscaster ousted them from the screen and said "Police—" before giving way to an uneasily blank screen at which Marshall stared, struggling to understand.

The newscast wasn't connected with the movie on the tape—he mustn't let himself imagine it was. His friend must have recorded the newscast out of sympathy for him. Maybe he'd found the tape in the machine when he'd needed to record. Who could have left it there? Of course, the people he'd warned Marshall against. What were such people doing in a nurse's house, and were they likely to return? Marshall's nerves were yearning for at least those answers. He jabbed the control at the television until the screen went blank, and scrambled out of the room.

As he trod on the first stair his foot squashed an insect, gristle turning to pulp. It wasn't an insect, it was one of the cigarette butts which were crawling about the floor. Why would a nurse keep her house in such a state? Maybe because she was overworked, not least by him, or maybe the butts weren't really there, any more than the stairs narrowed as they ascended. He wasn't sure how much of what he had seen on the television was real. Maybe all of this simply proved the pills hadn't worked because he hadn't given them a chance. Since he and his friend were alone in the house, there ought to be a bed he could use. He gasped with relief as he gained the landing, then he recoiled against the banister. A voice had begun to croak at him.

Maybe it was a toy or a talking bird—it sounded repetitive enough. "Who is it? Who is it?" it squawked. He threw himself away from the unfit banister and stopped himself by clutching a doorknob that rattled in its socket. The sound sent the voice into a frenzy. "Who's that? I know you're out there. Come and finish me off if you're going to. Stop your game."

Marshall's hand was turning the doorknob, which he could only hope would come loose. He felt it catch the mechanism, and the yielding of the door rendered him helpless. The knob pulled at his hand, dragging him across the threshold.

For entirely too long he was unable to distinguish any of the contents of the room as its clutter heaped itself up in his skull. Surely the room was the source of all the mess in the house. He had a suffocating impression of countless broken objects piled on the floor and against the walls, blocking off part of the high meager window. Amid all this was a bed in which lay a figure composed of dirty white rubber gone so rotten he could smell it. It was just one more abandoned object, even though it moved, its fleshless knobbly hands plucking at the pajama jacket which hung on its long shrunken arms and mottled torso as its head jerked on the skein of neck and flapped its dangling cheeks. "I know you," it croaked. "Come ahead, don't be frit. You'll see to me, you're a good lad."

So it was a person, and certainly no worse than the other things Marshall had seen during the eternity he'd spent in this state. He wanted to look away from the old man's bulging eyes, in which red cracks were visibly multiplying, but they were brimming over with a plea which his muscles seemed unable to resist. "That's the ticket," the old man wheezed as Marshall took a step toward him. "Only shut us in so they won't hear."

Marshall faltered, his ankles scraping together. "Who?"

"Who do you think, lad. Don't let on you've forgotten. The enemy, that's who."

"The people Darren said I should keep away from, you mean?"

"Darren, aye. Phil's lad. Haven't seen Phil since they took him away."

"Who did?"

"Who are we talking about? Are you trying to confuse me or summat? Get in before they get you too. You'll be safe in here."

Did he mean the room or the bed? His legs appeared to be trying to lift the faded stained quilt, but they kept collapsing, driving out a smell which made Marshall clutch at his face. The boy pulled the door shut and stayed where he was. "What do they do?"

"Nowt if you steer clear of them. They're only ordinary fellers like us and you Yanks. Took the Japs to bring you into it, though, didn't it? They're the worst. If them lot catch you—Here, I'll show you what they do, and worse."

He was kicking the quilt and tugging feebly at it, movements which canceled each other out. "Give us a hand," he whined. "That's how they left me. Can't get it off by meself."

Marshall would have felt cruel if he hadn't approached the bed. He stopped within an arm's length of the side of it, reluctant to see what might have been done to the old man. "Shouldn't I get the nurse?"

"You'll do, lad."

She wasn't in the house. Marshall felt guilty for having offered the old man false hope. "I'm in pain here. You'll be like me one day," the old man complained, and a confusion of emotions—pity, apprehension, panic at the way his mind couldn't be trusted even to remember that the nurse had gone out—took Marshall a step closer. The old eyes swiveled toward him, a gleam appearing through their webs of blood. "That's it, lad, just throw it off."

Marshall breathed through his mouth, which tasted of the stench of the room, and grabbing the quilt by the nearest corner, flung it back. He managed not to recoil, but clapped a hand over the lower half of his face. The old man's pajama jacket was mostly unbuttoned, displaying a mass of purple bruises turning yellow, and his pajama trousers were wide open. Above the sticks of legs, which looked raw with some kind of torture, he was sticking up like the dog in the video. Marshall knew that could happen in bed—he'd wakened more than once to find himself like that—but the sight dismayed him, brought images of the dog and the woman with his mother's voice crowding into his head. He stood swaying, afraid that if he moved he would sprawl across the bed, until the old man sniggered. "You're all right, there's no gas. You don't need a mask."

Marshall drew a deep breath muffled by his fingers and took his hand away from his face. "Shall I cover you up now?"

"No panic. Seen everything you want?"

Marshall felt ashamed of wanting to turn away from the sores and bruises when he'd asked to see them, but they weren't all he yearned to look away from. "Yes," he mumbled. "Sorry. Thanks."

"Maybe you can give us a bit more of a hand."

"How?"

"For a start, help us up a bit."

The request seemed not to tally with the old man's gestures, his hands waving on either side of his groin, unless he wanted Marshall to lift him with one hand behind his back and the other beneath his legs. Marshall was incapable of that, not least because of the concentration of the stench in that area of the mattress. He moved alongside the flaccid grubby pillow and took hold of the old man's shoulders, and hands which felt exactly like bone closed around his wrists. As Marshall lifted him against the sagging headboard, the movement dragged the old man's trousers down his legs. He began to roll his eyes and rub his lips together and poke his moldy tongue between them. "Ooh God, I need—"

"Let go." Marshall tried to pull his wrists free, but the bony grip was tightening spasmodically. "Let go or I won't be able to help."

The old man relinquished one of his wrists so as to grasp the other with both hands. "What are you going to do for me, lad?"

"Can you make it to the bathroom? I mean, can you walk?"

"Do I look as if I can, the way they've treated me?"

"Then where's the bedpan the nurse brings you? Do you know where it is?"

"Not the foggiest."

"I'll look for it. It can't be far. Try and hold on. Not to me. I'll find it if you just let go."

Maybe the old man didn't realize he was digging his long cracked nails into Marshall's wrist. He stared into Marshall's eyes and gave vent to a breath not unrelated to the smell of the bed. "Swear you'll come back?"

"Sure, if you want me to. I swear. I'm your friend."

"Let's see how much you are," the old man declared, digging in his nails so hard that Marshall almost cried out. That was apparently his way of ensuring that Marshall returned, because then he let go. Marshall rubbed his wrist and went down on his knees by the bed, a move which provoked the old man to emit a squeal of what sounded like anticipation. The boy ducked to peer into the clutter of objects blurred by dust under the bed. Directly in front of him was a tin pot, full almost to the brim.

He turned his face aside and breathed hard before taking hold of the icy handle to inch the pot to him. Was the surface of its contents coated with dust? He raised one creaking knee and carefully stood up, cupping his free hand under the tin bottom. As he lifted the pot higher than the bed, the old man's penis started to droop.

It looked like a large worm crawling back into a tuft of dead grass. Marshall saw it wriggling at the edge of his vision as he paced toward the door, where he had to lower the pot to the carpet in order to let himself out of the room. The old man kept repeating a sound between a snarl and a groan while Marshall raised the pot as quickly as he dared and walked with small quick steps to the bathroom. The carpet tiles which presumably had once been arranged so as to cover the floor of the room seemed intent on tripping him up, but he succeeded in reaching the toilet without spilling his burden. He used his foot to align the broken plastic seat with the pan, almost dislodging the lone screw, and as he tipped up the pot he felt as relieved as though he was using the toilet himself. He shook the pot over the bowl and hurried back to the old man, whose penis was draped across one peeling thigh. Marshall placed the pot close to it on the bed and turned away. "Quick, give us a hand, lad," the old man wailed. "Can't do it by meself."

He was attempting to lever himself above the pot with one hand clamped on the edge of the mattress. Marshall leaned awkwardly across the pillow and grabbed his shoulders to swing him toward the receptacle, only just in time. While the stream resounded on the enamel the old man accompanied it with a series of groans and sighs and growls through his teeth. As soon as he'd finished he slumped against the headboard, nearly trapping Marshall's hands. Marshall saved the pot from toppling off the bed and returned to the bathroom to empty it, averting his gaze from the face of the walking doll he had glimpsed in the mirror. A question was trying to drag his mind out of shape. How long had the old man been confined to his room to grow as white as that? If he never left his room—Marshall darted into it, the pot dangling from his fist, and faltered at the sight of the old man wagging his penis with both hands. He still had to ask the question. He dropped the pot with a clang that made the old man clutch at his ears and show his gums and half a dozen teeth the color and texture of wet sand. "Where did you know me from?" Marshall said.

The old man pulled one ear forward by its lobe while his other hand strayed down his body. "Eh?"

"Where did you recognize me from?"

"You're Phil's lad's pal, aren't you? Listen, are you listening? You stick with him. He needs someone like you to help him get away from all the muck he's living in."

The answer was confusing Marshall more than the question had, wiping out the very little sense of himself he had left, and he began to shiver. "Aye, it's parky," the old man said. "Don't hang about till we both catch pneumonia. Climb in and cover us both up."

"I won't, thanks. Thanks, though."

The old man pressed his shoulders against the headboard, which let fly an explosive creak, and jerked his thighs off the mattress, a movement which brandished his penis at Marshall. His hands flew toward it and past it to yank his trousers up. He covered most of his crotch with the discolored flaps, then began to fumble in search of the button and its hole. "I'm lonely, lad. I've had nobody to warm me up in bed since Phil's mam died."

Marshall thought of his own mother lying alone in bed. At least once he'd heard her trying not to let him hear her weeping. He was overcome by a rush of grief which included the old man. He stooped to untie his laces and pull off his trainers before he got into the bed.

Why had he tied the knots so tightly? There seemed not to be a single weak point where he could insert a fingernail. "Just getting these off," he explained as the old man commenced emitting short harsh urgent breaths. If he couldn't unravel the knots, he would just have to wrench the shoes off. He sat on the edge of the bed to do so, and as a bony hand settled on his shoulder and dug its fingers in, a wave of the stench which his sitting had driven out of the mattress reached him.

He hadn't enough pity in him to be able to cope with that. He ducked his shoulder, disengaging himself as gently as he could, and stood up to pull the quilt over the old man. Wasn't there more he could do to stop him looking so disappointed and abandoned? Stepping back, he caught sight of a tray on the floor beyond the bed, biscuit wrappers on a dirty plate beside an overturned chipped mug. "Can I bring you anything to eat?" he suggested.

"Like what, lad? What do you want to stick in my gob?"

"Shall I see what I can find?"

"I've had my rations," the old man said, and tweaked his jacket shut over his bruised chest. "Don't go giving her an excuse."

Marshall was bewildered, but more afraid that the smell of the room was about to make him retch. "I'll be downstairs if you need me, then."

The old man gave a wink that sent a drop of liquid zigzagging down his cheek. "I'll be thinking about you."

"Just call if you need anything," Marshall said, trying not to seem in too much of a hurry to quit the room. He sidled around the door and closed it behind him, and ran down all the stairs he could before having to renew his breath, which was still tinged with the smell of the old man's room. He wasn't sure whether or not he was hungry after the talk of food; his uncertainty dismayed him. He hurried into the kitchen and pulled open the refrigerator, which danced from one foot to the other in its eagerness to please him. He slammed it shut at once, trapping the smell of moldering milk, and retreated to the front room.

He would have left the door ajar to hear if the old man called him, except that the smell of the bedroom seemed to be creeping through the house. He would hear if he was needed, he vowed, but he still felt guilty, both for having left the old man on his own and for indulging even the faintest suspicion of him. The old man had been exposing himself because he was unable to care for himself, that was all. Any other notions were the fault of the video Marshall had watched—of the images he had perhaps only imagined he'd seen. If he could just see what was actually there, surely that would drive them and the shame and self-loathing out of him.

As he squatted to rewind the tape, he felt his groin bulge. He fell back into the chair and watched the digits on the player racing toward zero. Counters wired to bombs did that, and when the digits turned into a line of glowing green holes it took him a while to move; he was afraid of what he might set off.

It appeared that he needn't have worried. Once it settled into visibility, the movie looked so familiar it was comforting. He was growing used to it, and to how much the woman with the dog resembled his mother.

The digits were increasing—counting toward the moment when his mother's face would grow unquestionably recognizable. He watched the melting orange face advance toward that transformation, straining itself into shape. Everything about the movie was reaching for that moment, and he found it hard to breathe. His mother's face came clear at last, weeping for everything she'd had to go through in order to appear to him. Then he was there beside her, but before he could feel that he was, the newsreader did away with them by calling the police and the screen turned nervously blank.

If it had left Marshall and his mother visible for just a moment longer, Marshall was sure he would have felt safe. He crouched in front of the player to rewind the tape no further than the sight of them, but the sound the cassette made scared him into rewinding it entirely. He watched it through again and darted forward to pause it as his mother appeared, but an outburst of noise lines beheaded her, and he released the pause for fear of damaging the tape. He rewound it and watched it again, rested his eyes for as long as he could bear the nightmares which closing them awoke inside and outside him, replayed the tape once more. Each time the orange face turned into hers, he felt a little closer to her. Maybe his watching would bring her to him.

When the colors on the screen began to fade, he thought he'd worn out the tape until he saw that daylight was seeping into the room. It made his surroundings and his situation seem less real. He ran the tape to regain some hold on its reality, and kept replaying it as the light threatened to blot it from the screen and all sense of his mother from his mind. He'd lost count of the times the newsreader had appeared, just too soon for the sight of Marshall's mother to have lasted long enough, when he heard a key at the front door.

The screen became a gray blank disturbed by meaningless flickering, and so did Marshall's mind. Suppose the enemy was here? He'd seen how they'd tortured the old man, and was afraid to think what they might do to him. Footsteps came marching along the hall, away from the slam of the door, and he saw that Darren had left the gun under the chair with the bullets in case Marshall needed to protect himself. Before he could make a grab for the revolver, the door of the room was thrown open. Beyond it was only the nurse.

As soon as she saw him she swung around, her overcoat flapping, and dealt the banisters a thump which set all the uprights rattling. "Darren," she yelled. "Are you in, you little shit? Don't you be hiding from me, you pansy. Come here to me right now."

Marshall heard the old man groaning in protest above him, and was about to draw her attention to that when a door banged open upstairs. "What's up with you?" Darren demanded. "I've got a headache now. I was asleep."

"You'll have worse than a headache if I get hold of you. I told you what to do before I went out. You're worse than useless, you. I should have got rid of you before you were born." She flung herself away from the shaking banisters, and Marshall was afraid she was going to attack his friend, but she stayed in the hall. "You had your chance to fix what you did," she said, so quietly she seemed not to care whether Darren or anyone else could hear. "Now I'll get someone who'll do what needs doing."

28

HAVING SEEN

The car swung off the road between two No Entry signs, twin crimson discs which the sunlight turned raw. As the vehicle coasted along the sidewalk, pedestrians stared at Susanne in the back. She saw that some of them assumed she'd been arrested, but she didn't care what anyone thought; nothing mattered except that she wasn't being led to a false hope. The policemen's heads confronted her with two bulbs of hair cut short above shaved necks, and their silence made her head ache with thoughts. "Where are we meeting him?" she said, to say something.

The large blue eyes of the policeman whom she'd misidentified as Askew found her in the mirror. "He's on duty, Mrs. Travis."

"Oh, right." That was all she could think of to say, and felt rather stupid for having spoken. She gazed between the two policemen while the car crept behind pedestrians who eventually moved aside. She grabbed her purse from beside her on the seat immediately the car showed signs of halting. She had to wait until Askew, whom she'd thought was called Angel, maneuvered the car between a baked-potato stall and a handful of protesters outside a leather store, and then until he switched off the engine and tipped his seat forward so that she could climb out. She unbent on the sidewalk and flexed her shoulders, which were stiff with tension, and met the eyes of spectators as the policemen joined her. She jerked one hand at the nearest entrance to the covered portion of the Arndale Center. "In here?"

"That'll do as well as any, Mrs. Travis," round-faced watchful Angel said.

He and his colleague had to catch up with her as she strode at the doors, one of which slid aside hastily as though sensing her determination. A soft mass composed of dozens of blurred voices and of more than one piece of music which seemed reluctant to identify itself closed around her. At the top of an escalator climbing between two levels of shops she saw a guard in a mostly black uniform. "Is that him?"

It was apparently Askew's turn to answer. "We'll find out right now, Mrs. Travis."

Susanne was on the escalator by the time he finished speaking. She clattered up the moving stairs, because the guard was strolling away into the mall. "Hold on," she cried, clutching at the crawling rubber handrail. "Security. Security."

She subsided once he turned and saw the police, and she let them precede her once they were off the escalator; she didn't want to take over the questioning—she knew she was with them in case the witness said anything that would mean more to her than it did to them. Nevertheless she willed them to be quick as they waited for the guard to approach. "Trevor Tubb?" Angel, not too belatedly if she was going to be fair to him, said.

"I'll get him." The guard planted his feet wide apart and, as Susanne wondered why he wasn't doing as he'd said, reached for his radio. "Trev, they're here for you."

The radio hissed, then hissed louder. "The police, is that?"

"And a lady."

"Send them along. I'm by the birds," the voice said, and was dissolved by a wash of static.

The guard clipped the radio to his belt before pointing along the mall. "Down there, turn right and you'll see the cage by the escalators," he said, and Susanne stopped herself from running, though her stride did require the police to speed up.

At the end of the broad crowded walkway was a cage as tall as the ceiling and fluttering with birds. Beside it stood a guard in conversation with a woman in a checked coat who was holding onto two wheeled baskets. He nodded slowly as he listened to the woman, and tapped his chin with a forefinger whenever it came within reach. Having spared Angel and Askew a nod, he turned his long sharp-nosed face back to the woman. "But you're the guard," she was insisting. "You guard them."

"I'm one of the guards, yes, madam. We patrol the center."

"If you aren't responsible, just you tell me who is."

"I can give you the address of the company that runs the center."

"I'll have that," she said, and leaned on her baskets to stare hard at him. Susanne imposed patience on herself while he unbuttoned his breast pocket and extracted a notebook and laid it open on one large palm so as to write down the information, raising his eyebrows almost imperceptibly higher at each line. He tore out the page and handed it to the woman, who peered suspiciously at it, by which point Susanne had exhausted her capacity for silence. "Mr. Tubb? I'm—"

"Hang about, love, he's not done with me." The woman looked up from aligning the ends of the page so as to fold it precisely in half. She unzipped the top of the left-hand basket and removed a leather wallet into which she inserted the page, then shoved the wallet down among her purchases and secured the basket. "I just want to be sure you know what you're involved in," she told the guard, and pointed at a pair of birds sidestepping together along a branch. "That species shouldn't be kept in these conditions for a start."

Susanne never knew how fiercely she might have interrupted if Angel hadn't. "Excuse me, madam—"

"I'll show you as well. You can be witnesses." The woman lifted both baskets and slammed them down with a thud of rubber tires. "Or did he call you to have me thrown out? I'm not so easy to silence. These poor creatures need someone to speak up for them. They can't speak for themselves."

"I'm sure they'd thank you if they could, madam. Now if you'll excuse us, we're trying to find a lost child."

"Don't you be mocking me," the woman said, and as though she hadn't changed the subject. "Lost child indeed. If you ask me it's some of these children today who want putting in cages, then their parents wouldn't be able to say they don't know where they are."

Susanne felt a sharp breath snag her teeth. She sucked at the ache in them and took a step toward the woman, and Askew intervened. "What's this about the birds, madam?" he said, and moved his head in a gesture at his colleague which was almost as invisible as his mustache. "Show me what you mean."

Angel led the guard and Susanne out of earshot. "Perils of the job," he murmured to the guard.

"You do meet them."

"Don't I know it."

Susanne felt excluded or even, if she let herself, referred to until Angel said, "Anyway, Mr. Tubb, you called us. You think you saw Mrs. Travis's son."

"I won't say one hundred per cent, but yes."

"With another lad."

"Two of them together, that's it."

"What time was this?"

"It'd be about four. More like after it than earlier."

"You'd say that because . . ."

"I wondered if they were skiving off school, the way you automatically do if you see kids on a weekday, specially kids of that age not in uniform. And I thought no, it was too late."

"So you didn't speak to them."

"No reason to." The guard lowered his chin toward his rising forefinger. "No, scrub that. I might have had a word if they hadn't shot off. This lady's lad, if that's who he was, he wasn't looking too champion."

Susanne wished she didn't have to understand. "Too . . ."

"He could have looked happier is what I'm saying." The guard gazed at her as if to judge how much she could take. "Let's be honest, I'd say he was scared. That's why I nearly went after them, except we had an alert just then down the other end."

"Scared." The word came out like an accusation as Susanne tried to steady her voice. "Scared of the boy he was with?"

"No, I'd say definitely not. The way I saw it, the other lad was looking after him. Your lad, if he was yours, he went off with him quick enough, and glad to do it, I'd have said. That's another reason I didn't feel I had to catch them."

Susanne asked the question she would have put sooner if she hadn't been deferring to the police. "What was the other boy like?"

"Like he needed a few good dinners and a week's sleep and all the days out in the sun he could get." To Angel the guard said, "Same height as the other lad, round five three or four, but a lot thinner. Same age too, I'd have to say. Pale complexion, shadows under the eyes. Mousy hair in need of a wash, down over his collar. Green track suit big enough for his pal and I think trainers, I forget what color."

"Anything else? Did you hear him speak?"

"Wish I could say I did."

"Anything you'd like to ask, Mrs. Travis?"

"No." The word felt dismayingly final, and the rest that she had to say didn't help. "I can't think of anything. I don't recognize the description. It isn't anyone I've seen with Marshall."

"There'll be people he knows at school who you've not met, though, won't there?"

"I guess," Susanne said, and heard herself being ungrateful for the hope Angel was offering. "I mean, sure. Of course. Thanks. So you'll . . ."

"We'll contact the school, obviously, and we'll also put out an expanded description. We often find the public remembers having seen more than one person when they couldn't having seen just one."

"That makes sense." She supposed that was so, but nothing else seemed to. Why would Marshall have been frightened and not have phoned her? A blur of voices and insinuating music gathered around her, and she wondered whether it had sounded as meaningless yet ominous to him. She wondered why Angel continued standing where he was, since nothing further could be learned from the guard. He was waiting for Askew, who had helped the woman with the baskets down the escalator and ushered her away from the cage. "Anything?" Askew said when he was close enough to his colleague to be heard.

"Hopeful."

"Yes," Susanne felt she had to say in case that made it so.

"I hope I've been some help," the guard told her. "I'll ask around the shops in case anyone else noticed your lad and his pal."

"Thanks," Susanne responded, unable to imagine what his course of action might achieve. She turned toward a rack of left shoes to hide her dissatisfaction from him, and heard him say, "I'll be in touch if I remember anything, and I'll be keeping my eyes open." His voice was swinging away from her. "They've been having a bad time of it over here recently, these folk."

Susanne glanced at him and saw he was regretting having spoken. "Who?" she said.

"Not you. Not just you, rather. You Americans, I was meaning. There's no connection, I wasn't saying that, don't think that, but a chap from your part of the world, well, he came off worst with a couple of our bad sorts just round the corner from here the other month. Mind you, he was waving a gun about from what I hear."

Susanne gazed at him, unable to speak. Askew emitted a warning cough and folded his arms, and Angel said with heavy gentleness, "That was this lady's husband."

"Good—" The guard turned his body as well as his face toward her. "I'm sorry. I wasn't to know. I wouldn't have—"

"Believed it? I don't blame you. I've difficulty in believing it myself."

Though she didn't mean that to sound sarcastic, she feared it might. "Really, don't feel bad. You did your best for me," she said, moving away into the insubstantial tangled mass of noise, toward dozens of colors too bright for the way she felt. At least there was somewhere else to go—to the school. The other boy must be a pupil there, nothing else made sense. She looked back to see if Angel and Askew were following her, and saw the guard was too, frowning at her. "It's okay, really it is," she said, walking faster, anxious to be at the school.

"Can you spare me one more moment? I was just thinking. I'm just trying to recall."

He'd brought the policemen to a halt. She didn't need them, she could go to the school by herself, but his gaze was holding her—the doubt in it was. "Sorry to keep on like this," he said. "The men who went for your husband. Wasn't that the case where they were relatives of someone he'd put in jail?"

"So?"

"It's coming back to me. There was something about an identikit, wasn't there, that the feller he put away didn't like?"

Susanne shifted her feet, preparing to stride away. "Yes. So."

"I'm trying to picture it in my head. I didn't make the connection till just now. I want to be sure if I can be. You wouldn't have a copy at home by any chance."

"Of what? The picture? You're asking did I keep a picture of the man whose fault it is my husband's dead?" People were turning to stare at her, but her voice and her feelings were out of control. "You think maybe I should have framed it and hung it on the wall?"

Angel raised the splayed fingers of one hand toward her. "Mrs. Travis . . ."

"I didn't think you would have. Kept it, that's to say," the guard said, and to Askew, "Will you have?"

"I doubt it once we caught him."

"That would be right, sure enough," the guard admitted as Susanne, having lost all patience, turned her back. "Madam," he called after her. "Mrs. Travis."

She halted, hunching up her shoulders. "What now?"

"I was just trying not to send you on a false trail. I'm pretty sure I'm right, I'm going to say I am. The more I think about it now, the more I think the other boy, the one with no meat on him, looked like that picture."

As Susanne stumbled to face him, the sounds of the mall drained from her ears while all the colors flared. "How much like?"

"Enough that I'd say he could have been his son."

She was supporting herself with one hand on the window of a boutique. She felt the glass beginning to yield to her weight, as though the world or everything about it which she still took for granted was about to crack. Angel stepped toward her in case she needed support, and she saw that she mustn't panic—mustn't hinder them from following the lead. She straightened up and managed a tight smile to convince Angel she was in control. "What are you going to do?" she said.

"We'll find out where the family lives for a start. We'll have that on record, and then we can track down the boy for questioning."

"Now?"

"We'll call in from the car for the information. Thanks, Mr. Tubb. Solid work."

"Yes. Thanks."

"My pleasure, madam. I only wish—" The guard shook his head as though to erase having said that. "Good luck."

He was wishing he'd remembered sooner, but surely that needn't matter so long as the police acted fast—she mustn't let herself think it did. She hurried along the mall, dodging dozens of people who stared at her or at the police rather than move aside. She thought of the spectators who hadn't intervened to save Don, and told herself that people weren't like that all the time, not most of them. Only the people who had Marshall were important now. She veered around a clot of teenagers and ran down the sluggish escalator. The police clattered after her, the doors parted to let an unexpectedly chill breeze send a shiver through her, and then she had to stand by the police car with Angel while Askew used the radio. Though Angel's alertness seemed to encompass the entire street, she sensed his thoughts were with her, and she avoided looking at him in case he felt bound to offer her more sympathy than she wanted to believe she would need. She stared back at anyone who took her for a spectacle, and tried to hear what Askew's muffled voice was saying. But he had ceased speaking, and there was a protracted pause during which her pulse added itself to the street noise. At last he said a single word, and laid down the microphone, and leaned across the front passenger seat to open the door. "We know the family," he murmured to Angel. "They're all over the area. I had to make sure which address we need."

Susanne wasn't sure how much of that she wanted to understand just now—perhaps only that they had the address. "Are we going there now?"

Askew gazed at her, and she saw doubt in his eyes. "Please," she said. "I have to come with you if Marshall's there. He'll need me."

The policemen glanced at each other, then Askew sat up behind the wheel. Angel walked around her and stooped into the car, and she thought he was ensuring she couldn't climb in, until he levered his seat forward. "All right, Mrs. Travis. We'll go to the address and then we'll decide what's to be done," he said, and Susanne slid in so quickly that she felt suddenly nauseous. She was trying to leave whatever had been left unsaid unconceived as well.

29

GETTING RID

His mother's voice dug into Darren's skull. "You little shit," she was yelling. "You pansy." He was used to that and worse, but as an ache took the place of sleep he began to wonder what she was screeching about, not that he cared. Maybe Marshall had had a last play with the gun, as Darren had gone to sleep hoping he might, except wouldn't the shot have wakened Darren? He kneed the quilt until it sprawled on the floor, and swung his legs off the bed, dragging his shorts up with both hands. He kicked yesterday's track suit across the carpet as he padded to the door and threw it open, snarling through his teeth at his grandfather's moans next door. "What's up with you?" he demanded of his mother. "I've got a headache now. I was asleep."

His mother butted her face at him. "You'll have worse than a headache if I get hold of you," she shouted, grabbing the knob at the end of the banisters as though to hurl it at him. He could see the hem of her coat twitching as her legs wavered with whatever she'd been doing to herself or with someone else. "Try, come ahead, give us a laugh," he scoffed.

"I told you what to do before I went out. You're worse than useless, you. I should have got rid of you before you were born."

"Wish you fucking had."

She shoved herself backward, her gaze drifting away from him. "You had your chance to fix what you did," she muttered. "Now I'll get someone who'll do what needs doing."

That was fine with Darren. He'd had more than enough of Marshall. He was beginning to regret having lured him home, since he'd received no credit for it. Maybe his father would have admired him for it, but his father didn't want to see him. That felt like a good reason not to care what happened to Marshall, and Darren shut himself in his room and grabbed a track suit from the pile on the floor of the wardrobe. He was poking his feet through the legs of the trousers when his mother screamed at him again. "What have you been playing at? You get down here or I'll throw you down."

He stayed sitting on the edge of the bed until he'd brought his head out of the tunnel of the track suit top. He wormed his fists through the sleeves as he strolled to the door. As he emerged onto the landing, his mother pointed the revolver at him. "What's this, you mong? Your da told you never to play with it. That's right, you flinch if you know what's good for you."

Darren's shoulders thumped the wall before he sent himself forward to dare her. "You're fucking mad, you. You want locking up. Go on then, shoot. See if I care."

He wasn't going to be the first to look away. He stared at her and pulled up the track suit top to expose the target of his ribs. He was about to stick his tongue out when Marshall appeared in the doorway of the front room and gazed anxiously at both of them. "Don't hurt him. It was my idea. We were only playing because I couldn't sleep."

Darren's mother gaped at him, then she shook the gun at Darren with the same expression on her face. "Get here now. I want to talk to you. Get in the back."

Marshall stretched out his hands toward the gun. "You won't hurt him, will you?"

"That's up to him and you. You get in there and shut it. Shut it tight. Now."

Marshall obeyed, which was more than enough of a reason for Darren to plod deliberately downstairs, showing his mother he wasn't scared of her. He could see what she was planning to do when he came within reach, and ducked so that the gun barrel missed his head, though he felt the wind of it on his scalp. He dodged into the back room and stood behind a chair in case she had another swing at him, but she wrenched up the floorboard to drop the gun and the bullets on top of the money. She stamped the board down and dragged the carpet over it, then stared at Darren, disgust twisting her lips. "What else have you been up to with him?"

"Not much. He's boring, him."

"God, you're such a liar. I don't know where you get it from. You think I couldn't see the way he was looking at you?"

"He wasn't looking like much I could see. You're seeing things, just like him."

"You can't fool me and don't you think it. I'm your mam." Her mouth twisted again. "He was looking at you like he was in love with you. I'd not have been surprised to find the both of you in bed together."

"Don't you fucking say that to anyone about me. I'd have ripped his balls off if he even touched me, him or anyone else. He thinks I'm his mate, that's all, and you're a nurse." When the shape of her mouth didn't relent he stood it for a few seconds, then he yelled, "What?"

"If he's not your little friend why haven't you got rid of him?"

"I tried, mam. I had him putting the gun in his gob, only it never went off."

"You'd have got his head splashed all over my front room for the police to find, would you? God, I wish your da was here. He'd sort you out and no mistake."

"The filth don't know the little shit's here, mam. Nobody but us does."

"And don't you think they'll come looking for him? Don't you think they might come up with our name after everything him and his family done to us?"

"Better get him moved before they find him here, then."

Her mouth reformed itself, but only into a sneer. "And you still want me to think he means nowt to you."

"He doesn't, either. You just said you didn't want them finding he'd been here."

"So what are you going to do to stop that?"

Had she forgotten she was supposed to be getting someone to deal with Marshall, or was she playing with Darren to see what he would say? "I could stick him on a bus going right out of town," Darren said.

"And do what with him when you get him there?"

"I could take him on the moors where there's nobody about."

"You would too, wouldn't you? There's a bit of your da in you right enough." She tramped across the room to stare more closely at him. "Can I trust you? I can do without getting Barry or Bernard to him. I don't want them knowing he was ever in the house."

She wanted to trust him both to do it and not to tell, and not to make her aware of what they were really talking about either. He said what they always said in films. "You'll have to then, won't you?"

Reaching across the chair, she grabbed his left cheek between finger and thumb and twisted hard. "Don't you bring any more trouble into this house. I've more to put up with already than any woman should."

Darren dug his fingernails into the sides of the chair and met her eyes without blinking. He wasn't going to let her see how much she was hurting him, he was saving it up until he could pass it on to someone else. When at last she let go he clenched his fists so as not to rub his cheek as he shoved past her in his eagerness to get to Marshall. He'd only just reached the hall when Marshall inched open the door of the front room. "What happened to your face?"

"Nowt I know of. You're seeing things still, lad."

"If you say so, Darren." Marshall sounded both relieved for him and nervous for himself. "Your mom didn't hurt you, then. She knows we're only playing."

"Aye, and now we've stopped."

Marshall peered at his wristwatch. "Doesn't this say after nine o'clock? It's on your English time, isn't it? I thought my mom would have been here for me by now."

Darren had wondered if he might be able to grasp what was real by now, but that wouldn't be for some time, if ever. "You get back where you was and I'll find out what's happening," Darren said.

He was making for the front door as Marshall retreated into the room when Darren's mother flounced into the hall. "Where do you think you're sloping off by yourself?"

Darren stepped in front of Marshall, blocking his view. "I'm going to phone his mom," he said with a grimace to tell her what he meant. "Maybe she can't come and get him like she said last time I phoned."

"You won't be long, will you, Darren?"

Darren's mother looked as if she was about to twist his cheek again for having let Marshall know his name. "You bet he won't be."

"I don't want to be any trouble, Mrs. . . ."

"Nurse."

"I hope I'm not being too much trouble, Mrs. Nurse."

She glowered at him until she saw in his eyes that he was genuinely not joking. "You won't be. Just stay where he told you," she said, and watched him shut himself in. "If you know what you're up to, get on with it," she muttered, and glared at Darren as he let himself out of the house.

She might have hurt him worse if Marshall hadn't been there. He didn't want to feel grateful, particularly not to anyone so stupid, but he seemed in danger of feeling that way if he didn't watch himself. Perhaps he would get rid of the feeling once he got rid of Marshall. He needn't decide what to do until he'd taken Marshall where nobody would see them. If he could be certain that Marshall didn't know where he'd been, maybe Darren would only have to leave him somewhere he could never find his way back from. He walked around the block, spitting over the garden fences. As he returned to his gate, a black motorcycle ridden by a figure with a black globe for a head cruised past. He spat after the motorcyclist and dragged the gate and its hem of litter over the concrete, and aimed his key like a knife as he stalked toward the house.

The door beside him wavered open as he kicked the front door shut behind him. "Was she there? Did you get her?" Marshall said through the gap.

"She's there all right. Trouble with her car, though, eh?"

"How do you mean?"

"She's got one, hasn't she, your mam?"

"A car, yes, sure, my dad's, but what did she say about it?"

"She's been after a new one, hasn't she?"

"I don't know. Did she say that?"

Darren was tiring of the game and of the way the other boy was joining in. "I'm just telling you she isn't coming to fetch you in the car."

"Oh." Marshall's gaze sank, then swam up, looking less disappointed. "Well, okay. How is she?"

"Fuck, lad, I don't know. I've never met the—I wouldn't know what she normally sounds like."

"No, I mean how is she coming?"

"She's not." Darren let that hang until he sensed Marshall was about to panic, and said, "You'll have to go to her."

"I don't know if I can. I still don't feel . . ." Marshall backed into the room and sat in the nearest chair, staring at a cardigan before crushing it with his shoulders. "Anyway, you told me she said I wasn't to leave your house until she came."

Darren heard his mother tramping about upstairs, making all the noise she could. He paced toward Marshall, grinding the knuckles of his fists together behind his back so as not to punch Marshall in the face. "That was last night. She only said because it was cold. It's hot out now," Darren said, and forced himself to continue in case it might work. "Warm as being cugh, cuddled by your mam."

It wasn't worth the effort or the disgust which filled his mouth, especially since Marshall looked less comforted by the memory than embarrassed by him. "Didn't you ask if she could come in a taxi?"

"What the fuck else do you want me to do, lad? She's not my mam, or did you forget? What do you think I am, your brother?"

"I know," Marshall said with what sounded like a hint of wistfulness. "I know," he said as a thought struck him. "We can call a taxi and she'll pay for it when I get home."

"No." Darren ground his knuckles together so hard he was sure the other boy must hear them. If they hurt any worse he was going to transfer some of the hurt to Marshall's face—and then he almost grinned with thinking fast. "I said I didn't ask, I didn't say she didn't say. She hasn't enough money for a taxi. We've got to go on a bus."

Marshall frowned hard. "She must have enough money."

"Not at your house, and she'd have to go out to get some, so she wants to wait till you're home." Darren's knuckles were aching as his teeth frequently did, and he knew that if he brought his hands out of hiding he wouldn't be able to control them. He made himself look away from Marshall, to tone down his frustration while he tried to think. He could say his own mother didn't want Marshall in the house because—because she might catch what he had and take it into the hospital. He opened his mouth, and caught sight of a black motorcycle on the road. As the cycle passed, the rider turned the black globe of a head to watch the house.

"Sh—" The rest of the word came out like gas between Darren's clenched teeth. As the motorcycle vanished round the corner of the fence, he knew it would be coming back. Flexing his fingers in front of him as though in search of something to choke, he swung toward Marshall. "Stay there till I talk to my mam."

"You want me to stay now."

Darren twisted the doorknob viciously; it was that or Marshall's throat. "Do what the fuck you want if you don't trust me," he snarled, and slammed the door so hard that the sound seemed to become entangled with his footsteps running upstairs. "Who's that?" his mother cried, throwing her weight against her door as he moved it an inch.

"It's me, mam. There's—"

"Who told you you could come in my room? What are you after seeing, you mucky little sod? I'll have a few things to tell your da when he comes home. You'll be lucky if you just end up in hospital."

"Come out, mam." As Darren pressed his cheek against the door so as to talk low to her, his lips were pulled out of shape, making him sound like an idiot, which added to his rage. "I've got to tell you something you won't want anyone to hear."

"God," she said, a sound not much different from throwing up. He heard her stumping about again, and a clash of hangers in the wardrobe. He was leaning gingerly over the banisters to check that Marshall hadn't sneaked out of the front room when she flung her door open. She was wearing her orange dress which almost covered her knees and which reminded him of an overall, and he wondered if she was trying to look like a nurse. "So what are you bothering me for now?" she demanded. "You know what I want to hear. Have you got rid of your little friend?"

"He's not my friend, I fucking told you." Darren's knuckles ached with clenching, but he mustn't lose his temper when he needed her help. "Not yet, mam. I've seen someone watching the house twice since I went out. I think it's the filth."

"So what are you telling me for?"

"How can I get him out if they're snooping round?"

"How should I know? He's not my problem. I told you, you brought him, you get rid of him. As far as I know he's just one of your friends you had home while I wasn't here and gave him some stuff I didn't know you gave him and don't know where you got it either, and if you tell anyone different I'll have you put in care, and good riddance. I ought to let them have you now and get it over with."

Darren felt as stupid as he'd sounded against the door. "But mam, where can I hide him if they come in?"

"Nowhere I know of. One place you can't, and that's in here." She dug her fingernails into Darren's chest so as to shove him away from her room. "Don't bother sending anyone else up, either. I'll be asleep," she told him, and shut herself in.

Darren spat after her, but the door intervened. He kicked an upright of the banisters and sent it clattering down into the hall, and felt a little better—only it didn't help him get rid of Marshall, and he had no idea what would. Then he heard sounds in the front room, and a grin spread out of his mind onto his face. Not only did the sounds reveal that Marshall was as mucky as anyone else, they'd given Darren an idea.

He crept quickly downstairs and eased the door ajar. Marshall was crouching on the edge of his chair, gripping his knees hard as he watched the woman and the dog. Darren would have liked to spy on him to see what he might do, but there wasn't time. "What about that then?" he said, ignoring the tightening of his own crotch. "Fucking good, eh?"

Marshall began to shake his head from side to side as far as it would reach. "I don't like it."

"Aye, I saw you not liking it just then. Anyway, there's more important things right now than you getting your willy up. Them people I said you wouldn't want to meet, I just saw them watching the house."

"Can they stop me going to my mom?"

Marshall sounded doubtful, dangerously close to rebellion. Darren switched off the panting video to command all his attention. "They can do what they want round here. I'd stay out of their way, I'm telling you."

"I heard them making you and your mom do something last night, didn't I?"

"That's nowt to what they'd do to someone they don't know. If I'm scared of them you'd better be, lad."

"Did they make you have that video?"

"Aye, and worse ones, and they said if my mam gives them any trouble they'll make her be in one." The idea of his mother going with the dog both amused and excited Darren, and he had to put the distraction of it out of his mind. "If they find you, that's what they'll make you do, and I won't be able to save you."

Marshall shuddered and pressed the back of one hand against his mouth. "Where do you want me to hide?"

"Upstairs again. Only—"

"What?"

Darren had glanced out of the window to check there was no sign of the motorcyclist, an action which revived Marshall's panic. "They may have seen there's someone in the house they don't know," Darren said.

Marshall crouched over himself as though he'd been kicked in the stomach. "Hey up, no need to shit yourself," Darren said, furious in case he'd terrified Marshall so much that the boy wouldn't be able to move. "You'll just have to make them think it's not you if they come looking."

"How? How?"

"Bark."

Marshall raised his head, staying in his crouch. "You mean—"

"I mean fucking bark like a dog."

The left side of Marshall's face twitched into a grin, and that eye narrowed toward a wink. While Darren didn't know if the expression was the product of nervousness or disbelief, his fingers were writhing with an urge to twist it off Marshall's face. Then Marshall squeezed his eyes shut and nodded his torso a few times, apparently to pump some breath into himself. He jerked up his face and bared his teeth and forced out two embarrassed sounds. "Uff uff," he said, and peered pleadingly at Darren.

"Pathetic. Get ready for them to pull your pants down if that's the best you can manage."

"Wuff." Marshall growled through his teeth in an attempt to sound fiercer. "Wuff wuff wuff."

"What's that supposed to be, a fucking steam engine?"

Darren glanced toward the window as a movement caught his eye, and the black helmet turned to confront him. "Bastard," he spat, and leaned his face into Marshall's. "They're coming for you. Better get it right while there's time. Christ, can't you even be a dog?"

Marshall sprang out of the chair, almost knocking Darren over backwards. Darren thought he was making a break for freedom, and darted between him and the door, only to see Marshall drop to all fours and claw at the carpet and begin to yap. "Raf raf," he cried, so fiercely that spit flew between his teeth. "Raf raf raf raf raf."

"Not bad. I reckon it'll do." As Darren swung away from him to check that the motorcycle was out of sight, he could believe there was a vicious mongrel in the room. The road was deserted. "Best place for you is under my bed," he told Marshall, "and if you hear anyone come in the room—"

He hadn't realized how tense his own nerves were. For a moment he thought he heard someone battering the front door in, and then he realized it was somebody pounding down the stairs—his mother, who threw open the door of the room, splintering the plastic handle against the wall. "What are you playing at now?" she screeched. "What's all the sodding noise?"

"He's going to hide and pretend he's not him. He knows there's people looking for him he doesn't want finding him." Surely that would be clear enough to anybody except a cretin, but his mother was staring at Marshall on the floor as if she either didn't understand or didn't want to. So long as she didn't interfere, she didn't matter. If she got in the way now, having told Darren to solve the problem, he didn't know what he would do. He risked another glance out of the window to reassure himself there was time to spare, and pain flared in his knuckles as he clenched his fists. A police car was drawing up outside the house.

30

MADE IN AMERICA

For just a few seconds, as the wheels of the police car pulverized a stray chunk of brick and squealed faintly against the curb, Susanne wished British police were armed; then Angel dragged at the parking brake, and she told herself she mustn't wish. She'd had enough of guns to last her the rest of her life, and there surely wouldn't be any in the house on the corner of Handel Close, since none had been found there when the man who'd threatened Don had been arrested. Where there were guns there could be crossfire, and the thought of Marshall in the midst of that made her stomach jerk. She clutched at it and rubbed it to help herself relax as much as possible, because otherwise she would be less use to Marshall and the police. She was preparing to duck past Askew's seat once he tilted it forward when Angel craned around his headrest to encompass her with his wide gaze. "I think it might be best if you stay in the car for the moment, Mrs. Travis."

"You mustn't ask me to do that." Susanne heard herself pleading, and sharpened her voice, the way she'd very occasionally had to use it on Marshall. "We already established I can help. You can see I'm in control. All we want is to find my son safe, and you don't imagine I'd do anything to jeopardize that."

Angel gazed at her for several of her heartbeats, and she gave him back the same and held herself still. She saw him change his mind before he spoke, and in that instant she became fully aware that he and his partner were years younger than she was. That didn't matter, only their professional training did, but she couldn't avoid feeling that Marshall's safety might have been entrusted to people less experienced than she would have chosen. Oughtn't they to call for backup, just in case? But they were climbing out of the car, having exchanged glances, and Askew levered his seat forward to release her. "We'd appreciate it if you'd leave the talking to us to begin with, Mrs. Travis," Angel said.

"Fine. Whatever achieves what we're here for."

Askew straightened the fence in front of the house in order to open the gate, which bumped over the broken concrete path with a screech of wood. Now anyone in the house must know there were intruders, and Susanne considered sprinting to the back, since both policemen were heading for the front. She hurried after them, between twin patches of littered marshy garden which smelled like an untended enclosure in a zoo, toward the last of the row of boxy flat brown houses whose upper windows put her far too much in mind of gun holes in a bunker. She didn't think she had ever seen homes she disliked so much—ghetto architecture, she found herself thinking, houses designed for secrecy or for caging their occupants. In almost any other circumstances she would have felt sympathy for whoever had to live here, but now she experienced a mixture of loathing and raw fury as Angel thumbed the doorbell.

She didn't like the noise it made—more like a rattle than a trill. Like a snake, she thought, the only comparison she wanted to admit to her mind as the rattle died away and Askew kept his thumb raised an inch from the bellpush as though he was giving her an optimistic sign. She saw him prepare to ring again just as footsteps rushed downstairs beyond the door. Someone was running for it, and she poised herself to chase around the side of the house. But the footsteps approached the door, and chains and bolts sounded through it, and then it swung wide open. Beyond it was a boy about as old as Marshall, and at once she could see nothing else.

He wore a dark green track suit slightly too big for him. His thin pale face was aged in a way she would never want Marshall's to look. She had the impression that he was doing his best to resemble the identikit picture of his father even more than he did. He'd thrown open the door with a swagger, and managed to appear to be standing with one too. As his gaze trailed over Susanne as though she wasn't there, she saw him pretending not to care that she was. He'd only been expecting the police, she realized. She willed them to take advantage of that, because if they didn't, she should. But Angel said, "Is your mother in, son?"

"Who wants to know?"

Askew's foot shot out, and Susanne thought he meant to kick the boy into the house—thought she might look away from anything that helped find Marshall. The toecap met the door with a gentleness which suggested that the men were restraining themselves as much as she was. "Life's tough enough, son," Askew said. "Fancy, isn't it? Just tell her we're here, Fancy. You don't want to be alone with us."

The boy gave him a blink which scarcely bothered looking contemptuous, and stepped rapidly backward. He threw his head back, jerking his ragged hair over his forehead and ears and brandishing the cords of his neck. "Mam, there's two filth and some woman," he yelled, staring at them down his face.

"Charming," Askew muttered with what sounded like genuine offense, and Susanne wondered uneasily how inexperienced he was. She kept her stinging gaze on the boy in case, despite his street wisdom, he betrayed anything. When he returned her stare she pressed her palms against her hipbones so as not to shove between the policemen and go for him. He kept staring at her, though it made his reddened old man's eyes bulge, while he strained his head back further to yell, "Mam, they want you. Mam."

He was playing a trick. He was alone in the house, but he was going to pretend he had to fetch his mother, and escape. Susanne grabbed both policemen by the arm before she knew she meant to, just as a door struck a wall upstairs. "What's wrong with you, you little shit? I told you—"

The voice stopped as the woman tramped down enough stairs to be able to see out the front door. Her orange dress, the kind of garment one might wear around the house when there was no likelihood of visitors, bulged and crinkled and gaped between her lower thighs at each step. Susanne saw bruises on the pudgy mottled pinkish arms, and what looked like the remains of several days' worth of makeup beneath the current layer on the heavy swollen immature face, and thought that if the woman cared so little for herself, how much less might she care about anyone else? Then the woman glared at her as if the police weren't there. "What do *you* want?"

"My son," Susanne almost blurted, except that the woman's defiant look was choking her—the look which she could imagine meaning that the woman already knew. The woman stepped two stairs closer as if to demonstrate she couldn't be touched, and Susanne pressed her hands against herself. "Mrs. Marie Fancy?" Angel said.

"What are you going to do about it?"

"And this is your son Darren, is it?"

"No other sod would have him. What's he done now?"

"Shouldn't he be at school, Mrs. Fancy?"

"You tell his headmaster that," Mrs. Fancy said, and shook off the banisters as her heels thumped the floor of the hall.

"You're saying he's suspended."

"Wish he was, by his balls. Might teach him how to behave."

Susanne saw the boy's eyes and mouth tighten. He looked ready to be even more unhelpful, and she felt her nails scrape her hips. "How long has he been off, Mrs. Fancy?" Angel said.

"All his life, if you ask me."

Askew leaned his head around the doorframe and spoke into her face, which she'd brought close enough for him to touch. "Off school."

"What's it to you? You're not the truant man."

"We can find out from the school if we have to," Angel said.

Did they know which school? How long were they going to stand out here playing the Fancy game? The boy had retreated and was watching from beyond his mother, who abruptly shrugged. "This week. Let's see that do you any good."

"We'd like to ask him a few questions."

"Do what you want with him."

Susanne imagined her saying that to someone else, about someone else, and had to overcome a sudden queasiness. "Perhaps we could talk inside, Mrs. Fancy," Angel said.

"Why not, your pal's already got his boot in. Wouldn't have much chance against you two, would I. I'm only a woman, it isn't even like I own the house. Don't blame me for the state it's in, I've only just come back."

Though Susanne had the impression that at least some of this was aimed at her, she didn't let it reach her. Even before she followed the police into the hall she could see that the condition of the house had taken years to achieve—the carpets gray with spilled ash and decorated with trampled cigarette ends, the wallpaper blotched with blurry handprints, the smell of trapped stale sweat and worse. When she closed the door behind her, cutting out most of the sunlight, she felt as though she had entered a cell. Mrs. Fancy picked up a post which had fallen out of the banisters, and used it to prod open the door of the front room. "Get in there."

Susanne wasn't certain she was addressing her son, but he was the first to respond. Angel gestured Mrs. Fancy and then Susanne to follow the boy. There were only three chairs, all of them unmatched, and the Fancys each dumped themselves in a chair once Mrs. Fancy had kicked a caseless videocassette behind the player. Angel bowed slightly to indicate that Susanne should take the third chair, on which a cardigan sprawled as though to reserve Mrs. Fancy another place, and then he leaned against the mantelpiece, beside an electric fire stuffed with paper, as Askew shouldered the door closed. Angel gazed at Darren for some seconds without admitting to any expression, and was opening his mouth when Mrs. Fancy demanded, "So what's she, a social worker?"

"This is Mrs. Travis, Mrs. Fancy," Angel said.

"Why say her name like that? Supposed to mean something?"

"It ought to. Her late husband had an encounter with yours and then with some of your relatives."

"Don't try to blame me for any of that. I'm not their mam."

This denial of responsibility was too much for Susanne. "But you're this boy's mother," she said, and faltered. She was almost certain she'd heard movement overhead.

Perhaps Mrs. Fancy was raising her voice to blot it out. "Don't you think I know that? I've had to put up with it for thirteen years."

"Twelve, mam."

"All right, lad, if you're so clever you do all the talking."

"Thank you, Mrs. Fancy." Angel shifted his weight only minutely, but it seemed as if he'd brought it all to bear on Darren. "Now, son, just you give me direct answers and we'll get this over quick. Where were you yesterday afternoon?"

"I was here, wasn't I, mam?"

"Don't look at me."

"That's not the way we hear it, son."

"Who's been fucking lying? I was here all day and nobody can say different."

"Someone does."

"Then they're a fucking liar. Who?"

"Who do you think it might be?"

"Mr. Shit out of your arse."

"Not too clever, Darren. Try again. Try telling the truth."

"I fucking am. I did. I was here all yesterday, never went out."

"You're asking us to believe that a lively young feller like you stays home all day when he isn't at school."

"I was—" Darren's voice trailed off, and his gaze drifted upward as though in search of inspiration. This time everyone in the room must have heard the creak of floorboards overhead. Susanne glanced at Askew to reassure herself that he was blocking any escape from the room. Darren was lowering his head to Angel, and looked more defiant than ever, but that had to be a last bluff. "You were what, son?" Angel said with a gentleness close to parental.

"I had to look after my granda. Didn't I, mam?"

"If you say so."

"I did. You know I did. I couldn't go out because you was."

His mother stared at him, pressing her lips thin and pale as though he'd shown her up. Angel let her do so for some seconds before he asked, "Where would the gentleman in question be?"

"Up in bed where he always is." Darren jerked a thumb at the ceiling. "That's him."

The boards had creaked again. Susanne felt her stiff body go limp. She shouldn't have imagined Marshall was in the house—it was surely the least logical place for the other boy to have taken him. Angel's voice seemed to have retreated some distance from her. "Your grandfather will confirm you were here, will he?"

"He doesn't know who I am half the time, him."

"Not much of a witness compared to our man. I want to give you one more chance, son. Tell us the truth and we'll go as easy as we can on you. You know why we're here, so help us."

Darren's head turned almost imperceptibly toward his mother as though he was appealing for advice. The woman didn't speak or otherwise acknowledge him. Susanne's chest began to ache from holding her breath. She tried to admit air into her lungs without making any sound that might divert his attention from what Angel had said. Then Mrs. Fancy scoffed, "What man?"

"Mrs. Fancy, if you can just—"

"I don't believe there's any man or you'd have said by now who he is. The fact is you're here because this bitch has got it in for us. You don't know what they're on about any more than I do, lad, because they don't know nothing. They're just fishing, so don't get taken for a fool."

Angel didn't try to interrupt again. He kept Darren at the center of his gaze, and when Mrs. Fancy sprawled back in her chair to indicate she'd finished, he clapped his hands softly once before he spoke. "I wouldn't count on any of that, son. You were seen by a guard at the Arndale."

"So where is he? Why didn't you bring him?"

That was Mrs. Fancy. Susanne told herself that if she tried to shut the woman up she would only be adding to the distractions. She trapped her hands under her armpits to make herself feel restrained, just as Darren said, "It's all right, mam. He did."

His mother swung her staring face toward him and then decisively away, as if the wall deserved her attention more than he did. "Carry on, son," Angel said.

"I was at the Arndale, so he wasn't lying after all."

"That's the way. Feels better when you tell the truth, doesn't it? Now tell us the rest of it. Take your time."

"That's all."

"I don't think so, son. When were you there?"

"Afternoon."

"That's our information. Who were you with?"

"Myself."

"You would be, and who else?"

"No bugger."

"Now, son, that's not how the guard tells it. You don't want to go calling him a liar again after you were saying he was right."

"He was wrong if he says I was with anyone, and that's not all he's wrong about."

"What are you trying to tell us now, son?"

"He saw me the day before yesterday, that's when I was there. He couldn't have seen me yesterday because I told you, I was home all day with my granda."

"Is that true, Mrs. Fancy?"

"You don't expect me to call my kid a liar. He already told you I was out."

Her face was blank with defiance. She looked exactly like an overgrown child refusing to own up, Susanne thought, and gripped her hands harder with her arms, because if they pulled free she no longer knew what she might be capable of. Angel rested his gaze on the Fancys, then straightened himself away from the mantelpiece. "I think it's time we spoke to the gentleman upstairs."

"I can't stop you, I suppose. There's only one of me, and you're the police."

This was a kind of defiance too. She knew everything, Susanne was certain, otherwise there were any number of questions she would have asked by now. Askew opened the door and stepped into the hall, and Susanne followed quickly to make it harder for the Fancys to hide anything, although what could there be for them to hide? He was halfway up the stairs, and she was close behind him, when Mrs. Fancy tramped after them in a fit of anger. "Third one along," she shouted.

At the top of the stairs a bathroom gaped; along the right-hand wall were three closed doors. Askew leaned into the bathroom and surveyed it, then strode along the narrow landing as Angel arrived at the foot of the stairs, trapping Darren and his mother on them. Askew closed his hand around the last doorknob and was turning it before Mrs. Fancy started yelling, "Third one, I said, you. That's my room."

"Oh, third door. I thought you meant third bedroom." Askew opened the door as he spoke, and Susanne edged along the shaky banister so that she could see in. Had the woman tried to direct him away from the room simply because she was ashamed to have him see how she lived? Even from across the landing Susanne could smell the staleness, a mixture of cigarettes and perfume and unwashed sheets. Askew picked his way among the clothes littering the carpet and held onto one door of the wardrobe while he persuaded the other to wobble along its grooves. Having peered within, he squatted to glance under the bed, where Susanne could see there was nothing worth seeing. He gave the room a thorough scan and came out to face Mrs. Fancy, who was standing on the top stair with her legs so wide apart that the lowest surviving button on her dress was losing its grip on its hole. "This one, you mean," Askew said, moving to the next door.

"That's what I said and you know it."

Darren's head rose over the edge of the landing as he crept up one more stair. Now he would be able to see into the room, and Susanne saw him set blankness on his face. He was nervous, she was almost certain, and she felt her body grow brittle as Askew raised his fist to rap on the door. "Mr. Fancy, is it?" he said to Darren's mother.

"I wouldn't have him for my da, I'll tell you that."

Askew knuckled the flimsy panel, which looked coated with colored oil. "Mr. Fancy? Can we speak to you?"

A series of noises responded. At first they were groans, rising in pitch, and then they formed into a word, still rising. "What? What?" they protested as Askew pushed open the door.

The smell of the room filled Susanne's throat, and she had to plant her feet more firmly in order not to sway against the banister. For a dismaying few moments the smell affected her vision, so that she was unable to distinguish the contents of the room. It resembled a long-abandoned attic more than a bedroom, and a rubbish tip more than either, but in the midst of the clutter an old man lay in a bed. His long white half-melted candle of a head wavered up to peer at the intruders, his chin bumping against his collarbone, as he wrapped his thin arms about himself. The quilt was sagging off the foot of the bed, uncovering him as far as his navel. "Come to see how I'm doing, have you?" he growled at Askew. "All the same, you bloody officers. Never there when there's fighting and then you come sniffing round to find out who's been hurt."

"It's the police, Mr. Fancy."

The old man tried to lift his head further, but his chin was already on his chest. "I've done nowt. Touched nobody. Who's been putting it round that I have?"

"This isn't about you, sir. We just want to ask you some questions. Do you know where you are?"

"What's that you want to know?"

"I'm asking you if you can tell me where this is."

"Where what is? It's like a bloody court-martial, this. Worse than being captured by the Japs, going up in front of an officer."

"I just want you to tell me where you're living now, where this house is."

"Handel Close." What Susanne took at first to be a wriggle of delight passed through the old man's undernourished frame, but he was easing himself worm-like up the creaking bed to rest his shoulders against the pillow and let his head fall back. "Ask me another. Do I get a fiver if I get them all right?"

Askew gave him a fleeting almost straight-lipped smile. "I don't mean this rudely, but would you mind telling me what day this is?"

"That's as easy as wiping your bum, that. The day after yesterday," the old man croaked, adding a cackle which turned into a cough. This was the signal—or rather, Susanne thought, the excuse—for Mrs. Fancy to intervene, hurrying along the landing to shove past Askew. "Granda, you'll be catching something undressed like that. Let's do you up."

Susanne wouldn't have allowed her in the room. Suppose she murmured to the old man what to say or silently menaced him into it? At least Askew had followed the woman, though he stopped short of the bed. She hauled the old man's pajama jacket around his chest while he flapped his arms like a dying chicken's wings, then she seized the edge of the quilt. "Let's have this up over you. You don't want everyone looking at you in your nightie."

The quilt shifted an inch, and then something caught at it from under the foot of the bed. As she gave another tug the quilt was pinned down more firmly from beneath, and the cause of that began yapping. "Leave it, mam," Darren called over the edge of the landing, "or the dog'll get out."

Her gaze drifted toward him, passing over Askew and Susanne. "Right enough, it will," she said slowly as the yapping grew louder and more vicious. "It bites, so don't you all come crowding in here. It goes for anyone it doesn't know."

Askew retreated softly out of the door. Susanne was considering taking his place when Angel tapped Darren on the shoulder. "Just go along to your grandfather's room where he can see you. No need to talk."

He paced after Darren, not quite treading on his heels. The yapping sounded as though it was tearing the animal's throat raw. The noise—the meaninglessness of it—felt like hooks in Susanne's brain, and she couldn't help being grateful to Darren when he intervened from the doorway. "It's all right, boy. I'm here. It's Darren. Quiet now. You'll be fine."

His voice had grown progressively gentler. As he fell silent, so did the yapping. If he cared so much for an animal, Susanne thought, perhaps he wouldn't have been able to bring himself to do anything very bad to Marshall. "Mr. Fancy?" Angel said.

"Another bugger. How many more of you is there out there? Come cheaper by the dozen, do you? Trot them all on and let's have a gander."

"I'm PC Angel, Mr. Fancy, and this is PC Askew. We're—"

"They've got Phil's lad." The old man thumped the mattress with his knuckles in an attempt to raise himself. "Look, Marie, they've got Darren. You sods lay off him. Pick on someone your own size for a change."

"It's Darren we want to ask you about," Angel said.

"Ask away. Here I am, not going nowhere. He's a good lad, sits with his old granda. Never saw him do nobody no harm. Needs a bit more loving, that's all. You can see he does. Just look at his face."

"Sits with you, you said. But he wasn't doing that yesterday, was he?"

"What, was you in here watching? I don't reckon so, pal. Him and me knows he was here, don't us, Darren?"

"Ah, but which part of the day, Mr. Fancy?"

"Eh?"

The old man dug his elbows into the pillow and succeeded in cupping his hands behind his ears. Angel took a heavy step forward, and the quilt at the end of the bed stirred where it touched the floor. "Which part of the day?" Angel repeated, separating each word.

"Hard to tell in here. Haven't seen proper daylight for years, seems like."

"I see what you mean. So you'd have to say you don't know—"

"Hang on, pal. Let a man get his breath to answer. I'm saying nowt like that. Which part, every part. The lad was sitting with me all day yesterday until after it got dark."

"Excuse me for suggesting this, but I wonder if you can be sure—"

"I'm sure what bloody day it is and don't you be saying different, and I'm sure we're talking about yesterday before you ask. He was in here soon as he'd got up and had his bath because I asked him to come in, and he listened to his old granda telling tales all day about the war. He only went down for five minutes to get me a drink and a bit of bread."

"You're absolutely certain."

"Absobloodylutely. Certain as I am that I'm due for a piss if someone brings me the jerry and if they don't too."

Mrs. Fancy stooped, more deftly than might have been expected from her bulk, and slid a tin pot from under the bed, and stared at Susanne and the policemen. "Satisfied? Or do you want to watch?"

"We're finished for the moment, thank you," Angel said, and pulled the door shut, setting off an outburst of muttering from the woman and groans from the old man, succeeded by a metallic resonance falling in pitch. Neither policeman looked at Susanne; she couldn't tell whether they were embarrassed by the sound or by their lack of progress. She was alone with something far worse than embarrassment—the thought that the security guard had been mistaken. He'd jumped to a conclusion, just as she had, and she was further than ever from finding Marshall.

The noise trailed away, and a few seconds later Mrs. Fancy opened the door. "Empty that for us, lad." She could have been addressing anyone except Susanne, at whom she gazed defiantly, and Darren didn't take the pot until she shook it at him. He stalked to the bathroom and sloshed its contents down the toilet and yanked the handle, every one of the sounds and movements plucking at Susanne's nerves. His mother accepted the pot he thrust at her, and placed it next to the bed. "Stay there," she murmured to the creature underneath, and marched out of the room and shut the door. "Seen enough?"

"This'll be your room, will it, son?" Angel said, opening the door of the last bedroom.

Darren darted after him, and Susanne moved in pursuit, thinking as she did so that there was nothing suspicious about the boy's swiftness—he simply didn't want a stranger invading his room. No wonder when it was such a mess, almost as cluttered as his grandfather's, though with newer stuff. It made her yearn for the untidiness of Marshall's room—the sight of clothes on the floor did. A purple track-suit top like Marshall's was hanging out of the bottom of a wardrobe; for an instant it made her see him lying still on the floor, and then it seemed to render his absence visible, as though he'd been snatched out of the purple top, leaving it to mime his bid for escape. It was very like his track suit—so like that the words she was suddenly desperate to speak felt solid in her throat. "That's—"

Renewed blankness clamped itself to Darren's face. "What is it, Mrs. Travis?" Angel prompted.

"That's my son's. It's Marshall's."

"The item of clothing, you mean? How can you—"

"It's his, I'm sure it is." She wouldn't have been except for the way Darren had reacted as soon as she'd begun to speak. "I'd know it anywhere. It's his favorite. He wouldn't wear anything else on the plane over though we told him he'd be too hot. He'd wear it to school if they let him."

Darren's mother flounced along the landing and stopped just short of knocking Susanne aside. "What's the bitch saying now?"

"Mrs. Travis says that's her son's track suit, Mrs. Fancy."

"Then she wants her eyes examined, or her head. The lad bought himself that in the market. Them suits is all he ever wears."

Susanne knew she was lying. Defiance, an aura of hot staleness, seemed to surround the woman. Angel paced into the bedroom and hunkered down on an uncluttered patch of carpet to scrutinize the purple garment. Susanne was wondering what he expected to establish, and how quickly the mother or the boy could be made to admit the truth, when Askew sidled past Susanne and what felt like two captors keeping her away from Marshall. "Maybe there's a way to sort this out," Askew said.

"Be my guest," said his partner as Askew squatted beside him, blocking Susanne's view of the track-suit top. She saw him reach for it and do something to it, and Angel craned over to examine whatever he was indicating before both men turned their heads toward her. Their faces were unreadable. "You say your son was wearing it on the flight over," Angel said.

"He definitely was, yes."

"Which means he would have bought it . . ."

"His father bought it for one of his birthday presents last November."

"I see. I'm sorry if this is painful for you, but can I ask where?"

"In our local mall in West Palm Beach. I know you see people over here wearing the same style, but believe me, that's his."

The policemen didn't quite look at each other as both of them rose to their feet. Askew had the track-suit top, its empty arms waving helplessly. "You'd better look for yourself, Mrs. Travis."

He'd turned the headless neck toward her to expose a rectangular tag. That couldn't identify it unless the other woman had sewn her son's name tag in it overnight, in which case what had Angel just been talking about? Susanne stepped forward, her legs not as steady as they should be, and read the words printed on the tag, a set of standard instructions from the manufacturer. "What am I supposed to be seeing?" she said with more patience than she felt. "What do you want me to see?"

Askew pinched the tag between finger and thumb so that the garment dangled from it. Now the words were the right way up for her to read, but his thumb covered the first lines. "I can't . . ." she said, then wondered if he was indicating whatever he imagined was significant. His thumbnail, which had recently been clipped almost to the quick, was digging into the tag directly above one word, at which she narrowed her eyes in case that might squeeze some extra meaning out of it. It was "color," and if he could make that signify more than it did to her—It was "color," except that it wasn't spelled quite like that, it was spelled—As Askew watched her realize, regret glistened in his eyes. "I'm sorry, Mrs. Travis, but it can't be your son's, can it? It's British."

She saw him fold the garment in half twice and plant it on top of the pile in the wardrobe. She caught herself looking for another purple garment which might be Marshall's, and was appalled by her own desperation. Angel eased himself past her to the doorway. "I'm sorry, Mrs. Fancy," he said briskly, only just apologetic. "I'm sure you appreciate we have to be thorough when a boy of your son's age is missing."

"No excuse for picking on us." Mrs. Fancy shoved Darren to clear space outside the room. "Have you done in there yet? Anywhere else you want to snoop around? Want to take the floors up?"

"We'll get out of your way now," Angel said, but Susanne thought he was allowing his gaze to linger on the room in the hope of noticing some overlooked clue until he murmured, "Mrs. Travis?"

"What?" She felt inert, drained of energy by her lack of sleep and by her mistake. All she'd done was delay the police from searching elsewhere and give them reason to distrust any further ideas she might have, not that she had any. Once she grasped that he'd asked her to quit the room she did so, followed by Askew, after whom Mrs. Fancy slammed the door. The old man groaned a protest from the next room, and his companion recommenced yapping as Mrs. Fancy stomped downstairs and threw the front door open with a rattle of its bolts. "Goodbye," she snapped, adding "Good riddance" as she flung it shut as soon as Susanne and the police were through it. "Shut that bastard of a dog up," Susanne heard her yell, and then there was silence from the house.

"We'll run you home, Mrs. Travis," Angel said, taking her arm.

"Yes," Susanne said, and once she'd thought to say it, "Thanks." It wouldn't be home until Marshall was there. She was aware that Angel held her arm lightly all the way to the car and handed her into it while his partner dealt with the gate. They must be afraid that she might try to get into the Fancy house again, but she had to admit when she was wrong. She wouldn't be able to help Marshall otherwise, though she felt as if she no longer could. As Angel started the car she turned her head away from the Fancy house. It weighed down the edge of her vision, reminding her how she'd tricked herself, just as the guard at the mall had been too eager to be right. When at last the house sailed out of sight, she experienced only relief.

31

LAST CHANCE

"Shut that bastard of a dog up," Darren's mother yelled, and Marshall stopped yapping at once. Darren heard the gate screech on the path, and two car doors slam, and the car engine start and then shrink around the corner. His mother tramped into the front room and stared out of the window, then turned on him. "So what are you hanging round for? You needn't think you're keeping him up there."

"Just making sure they've gone."

"They've gone all right. They've never coming back here, not for him, anyway. Maybe for you if you don't get rid of him quick."

"I'm going to. I said I would." Darren shoved a hand in his pocket and wondered where Marshall's money was. In the pocket of the track suit Darren had worn yesterday, of course, and it could stay there—it wasn't much for all the trouble he'd been through. "Give us some bus fare."

"Do you reckon I've nowt to do with my money except spend it on you?" his mother demanded, and even more angrily, "How much are you after?"

"Enough to get both of us as far as the bus goes and one of us back."

"Don't you go thinking I heard that," she warned him, lowering her voice as he had, and peered up the stairs. "Good job for you he does as he's told. You want your head examining, telling him to be a dog."

It was a good job for her too, Darren thought. Something like admiration had crept into her voice, perhaps without her knowledge, but not for long. "And what did you think you were playing at, hiding him in your granda's room?"

"I didn't, mam. I put him under my bed."

"Dirty little sod, him." She rubbed her lips together in a grimace of disgust and marched so fast into the hall that Darren thought she meant to knock him down, but she was heading for the back room. "Sooner he's out of here the better. Christ knows what he was up to up there," she muttered, and kicked the carpet away from the loose floorboard. She squatted to prize up the board, and there was a screech of wood.

It wasn't the board, it was the garden gate. Whoever had closed it must have left the fence about to topple over. Darren made for the front room to peek through the window. He was still in the hall when he heard footsteps tramping rapidly along the path. Before he could react, the doorbell began rattling in an attempt to ring, and a fist pounded on the front door.

"You've done it now, you little shit," his mother shrieked, slinging herself into the hall to glare at him with a kind of disgusted triumph. "Go on then, open it. Get it over with."

He didn't have to do as she said—he wasn't Marshall. He could run out of the back of the house, except that she moved between him and the stairs, cutting off any escape unless he wanted to fight her. The bell rattled again, and the fist shook the door. The sounds filled his head, leaving him no room to think, so that the only way of releasing himself from them was to open the door. He managed to fit his stiffening fingers around the knob of the latch, and twisted it, and pulled. Outside the door—only just outside—was the motorcyclist with a black helmet encasing his head.

The helmet nodded toward Darren, who saw his face caught in the bowl, floating there like a dead fish. He thought the helmet was going to butt him, and retreated into the hall, treading on one shoelace, which brought him lurching to a halt. The cyclist came after him, throwing out a black-gloved fist which bruised Darren's collarbone and sent him staggering against his mother as the cyclist slammed the door with a boot heel. "Get off me," Darren's mother screamed, heaving Darren at the wall, and backed away from the intruder. "What do you want? You get out of here or I'll call . . ."

Darren almost laughed. She didn't know who to call because she didn't know who the cyclist was. He straightened up, rubbing his shoulder where it had struck the wall. If he shoved past her he could get the gun. Then Marshall began yapping upstairs, presumably having heard the panic in her voice, and Darren wondered if she might threaten to set the dog on the cyclist, who was chaining and bolting the door. From inside the helmet a hollow muffled voice said, "Who'll you fucking call?"

It was his father, Darren thought. Nobody else would behave like that. He must have escaped from prison and been watching the house until he decided it was safe to approach. At last there was someone who would appreciate how Darren had got the better of Marshall and everyone who was looking for him. "Da," he said happily, as he seemed to remember he used to once.

The cyclist turned, and the black gloves cupped themselves around the helmet. It inched upward, exposing his father's neck, his unshaven chin, his sneering mouth. A livid scar appeared to climb the stubbled cheek as the helmet rose farther and the mouth spoke. "I'm not your da, thank fuck," Barry said, thrusting the helmet at him to put somewhere, and immediately ignored him. "What's going on, Marie? Bernard better be grateful I'm a suspicious prick. I was keeping an eye on things and I saw you had the filth round."

"They weren't anything to do with you."

"Everything that happens is to do with me while you've got my fucking money in the house." Barry popped the studs at his wrists and tugged off the gloves to dump them in the helmet Darren was still holding, and rubbed his hands over his skinny scalp, and flexed his fingers as though he was contemplating how to use them on Darren's mother. "Let's hear it, Marie, quick. They weren't looking for the loot or they'd have found it," he said, and then his hands began to turn into fists. "It's where I stashed it, isn't it?"

"Where else would it be? If you don't believe me, go and look."

"Don't think I won't." Barry's fists were still closing. "What did they want, then? Were they after this little dick?"

"I'm saying nowt," she said, and stared between them. "Your turn, lad. Speak up."

Marshall had stopped yapping as Barry removed his helmet. The silence was bullying Darren into opening his mouth. At least the helmet gave him an excuse to move away, to drop it on a chair in the front room—maybe even time to think what he could say that might save him from a kicking. However much he loathed Barry for acting as though he owned the house, mightn't Barry appreciate what he'd done to Marshall? "You know the bastard who got my da in jail," Darren said.

"Rest in fucking peace."

"That's him. You remember, my da never even touched him and he got him put away for eighteen months."

"Reckon Dave and Ken gave the dick who did that eighteen months' worth." Barry shook his head like a fighter in a video, summoning his strength to rip his opponent to bits. "So what are we talking about him for?"

"It wasn't fair, was it? Dave and Ken only went after him because of what he did to my da, and it was him who pulled a gun on them, and now they've got five years each."

"The world's not fucking fair. That's why anyone like us has to even it up for ourselves, haven't you figured that out yet?" Barry clenched his right fist and brought it toward his face. "So what's your point?" he muttered at his knuckles.

Darren was afraid he'd lost that himself. Barry's comments were cluttering his head, pushing his thoughts out of shape. It took him several seconds to recall his theme, by which time Barry was swaying in and out of the front-room doorway on his left arm, threatening to lunge at him. "It wasn't just the bastard with the gun who got them all in trouble, was it?" Darren blurted. "It was his kid."

"Go find him and kick him senseless if you want to. You're not asking me to waste time on a kid."

"No, that's right. That's what I did, only I gave him better than a kicking."

"Fuck." Barry jerked his eyebrows up and twisted his mouth sideways in appreciation. "You're Phil's lad all right. So that's why the filth were sniffing round," he said almost to himself; then his voice and his eyes sharpened. "Didn't they find you? They'll be coming back."

"They won't. My granda made them think it wasn't me."

"Good on him for once. That's what family's for."

"I was here too, you know," Darren's mother complained.

"I should hope you was, Marie. Wouldn't want to think you went out while you've got my loot in the house." Barry was swinging his arms and dancing in the doorway without moving his feet. "So tell us all about it, lad. What did you do to him?"

"Found him in McDonald's in the Arndale and slipped some acid in his Coke when nobody was looking."

"Listen to that, Marie. He's a prize, your lad. Maybe he'll be giving us ideas before he's much older. You'll be one of us when you grow up if you carry on like that, Darren. Did you hang round to see what happened?"

"Watched him not know where he was and run round the Arndale seeing things."

"Wish I'd been there. Where'd he end up, or didn't you see?"

"Fucking did. I followed him and stopped him going to this guard. Pretended I was his mate. He thought he knew me from his school."

"Your lad's got some nous, Marie, I'm telling you. You'll have to tell his da what he done next time you see him. Took him somewhere, did you, Darren? Make sure nobody saw?"

"The filth'd still be here if anybody seen me, wouldn't they? It was just his mam brought them because she wanted it to be us."

Darren saw his mother not looking at him from behind Barry. She was right to keep her mouth shut—she would be making trouble for herself otherwise. "Where'd you take him?" Barry said, widening his eyes eagerly. "What'd you do?"

There seemed to be no way to tell it except straight. "Brought him home. Doesn't matter. He'll never be able to find his way back."

Except, Darren thought, he already had once. His mother was making more of an issue of not looking at him. "What are you getting at, lad?" Barry demanded. "Suppose he can recognize you? Where did you leave him?"

"He'll never, and even if he could it wouldn't matter, would it? He thinks I'm his mate who was looking after him."

"Yeah, and if he says how he felt the filth will know what someone did to him, and who are they going to think it was if it wasn't you?"

"I didn't think of that."

"Fucking good job there's someone here to do the thinking then, isn't it? You should have finished him while you had the chance. Never leave anyone you don't want to identify you, and there's only one way to be sure."

"Okay, I will."

"How are you going to do that, lad? Did you put him somewhere he can't get out of?"

"Yes."

"Go on then, tell us. I'm impressed so far."

"Even the filth couldn't find him."

"You mean they looked? You saw them looking? This is a treat, this. Where?"

Darren's mother turned her head and stared at Darren. Whatever her fierceness was supposed to communicate, it couldn't alter the only reply he had left. "Here. Upstairs."

Barry rubbed his scalp hard, rucking the skin, then made a fist which he held ready. "You're not trying to tell me he's still here."

"Didn't you hear the dog when you came in?"

"Don't try any shit on me, lad, or your mam won't be able to protect you. We aren't talking about no dog."

"That was him."

Barry scraped his knuckles against his chin and shook his fist, but thoughtfully. "Is this the best bit coming now? Spit it out, lad."

"He thinks he's hiding from some people that are after him. He thought the filth was them. I got him to pretend to be a dog if he heard anyone coming."

"You're never telling me you got him barking at the filth."

"He did that," Darren's mother said.

"You're a star, lad. I can't give you a kicking for being such a sly bugger." Barry knuckled his eyes as an indication that he could have laughed until he wept, then opened his fist. "All the same, you can't be sure nobody saw you with him. The filth might come back. I'm getting my loot out of here before they do, Marie, and while I'm at it I'll take care of him upstairs."

"The kid, you mean."

"I wouldn't be talking about Phil's da, would I? What's the face for? Got a problem with me finishing the kid?"

"No, only—"

"If it's your cut you're worried about it's coming out of Bernard's half. It's between you and him, nowt to do with me."

"That's all right, then."

"You fucking bet it is. You still don't look too pleased. Makes me nervous, people having secrets round me, and there's a few could tell you what happens then."

"I'm just looking at Darren. It's him that doesn't seem too happy."

That caught Darren off guard. He was certain his mother was simply trying to divert Barry's attention away from her, but he was still in the process of ensuring his face was blank when Barry swung around to him. "What's your beef? Don't want to keep him for a pet, do you?"

"If you ask me they're a bit too sweet on each other."

"You're never turning into one of them, lad. If there's one thing makes me sick it's them mucky sods who stick themselves up each other."

"I don't reckon they had chance to do that, Barry, but I saw the way they were looking at each other."

"When did you do that, mam? Seeing as you was—"

Before Darren could let Barry know she'd been out all night, Barry shoved himself out of the doorway and punched his collarbone again. "Don't you be getting up to that shit because your da's not here. Maybe I should give you that kicking after all. I know Phil would."

"You fuck off. You're not my da."

"Don't you fucking tell me to fuck off, you little fucker."

As Darren attempted to dodge, the end of an arm of the chair against which he'd been thrown trapped his leg. The next moment Barry jammed one hand between Darren's legs and grasped his genitals and twisted them. "Know what this is for? To stick up tarts or in your own fist and nowhere else. You're not a fucking animal that doesn't know no better."

Through the pain which turned his vision gray Darren saw his mother shaking her head, at him or Barry or herself for not intervening. He sprawled into the chair, but the pain only exploded, because Barry hadn't let go. Then he did, and marched out of the room. "You want to keep an eye on him if he's going that road, Marie. Right now just keep an eye on the other little sod. I'll be back as soon as I've got the van and then you can help me take him out."

The front door slammed, shaking the house. The gate screeched, the motorcycle coughed, then roared away. Darren was bent double over an ache which felt like a hole torn out of him. He didn't look up when his mother stood over him. "Come on, you're not hurt that bad," she told him. "And if you are you shouldn't have been messing round like that. We can do without one of them in the family. Come on, will you, get up and do what you're supposed to be doing before Barry comes back."

He ought to have used the gun on the motorcyclist when he hadn't known who it was, Darren was thinking. He would have stuck the muzzle under the chin beneath the helmet, blowing it open like a goldfish bowl full of blood that would have covered every surface in the hall, leaving Barry standing with no head. The image made the agony between his legs a shade more bearable. If he couldn't see it happen, some other violence might suffice. "He's going to do it to him," he said through his teeth.

"I don't want that. He'll get me mixed up in it if you don't do what you said. You know Barry, he might do it here if he loses his temper. I want it kept away from the house, and you ought to and all. You don't want me locked up like your da."

Just now Darren didn't care who was locked up, except he wished Barry had been. He was entirely preoccupied with unbending by painful fractions of an inch as a preliminary to sitting up. He became aware that his mother was rummaging through her handbag, an activity which seemed irrelevant until she dropped two five-pound notes in his lap. Even so little weight made him crouch over himself again. "Ow, fuck, mam . . ."

"Stop putting it on, will you. Be glad Barry only gave you a warning. Stop wasting time and get your little friend out of here before he comes back."

Darren groped gingerly for the notes and stuffed them into his pocket. "You stop calling him my what you're calling him."

"You want Barry getting hold of him then, do you?"

Darren told himself he didn't care, but as the pain gave another sickening throb he realized that he hated Barry even more than he hated Marshall. If he sneaked Marshall out, not only would that be a way of getting back at Barry—he would be leaving his mother to face him. Serve her right for the triumphant smirk which showed she thought he'd betrayed his real feelings about Marshall. He clutched the arms of the chair and eased himself to his feet and set about the task of hobbling across the room. His mother folded her arms to let him know she wouldn't help him and watched in disbelief as he began to haul himself upstairs with the aid of the banister. "You're worse than your granda, you. Thank Christ your da's not here to see."

It was Marshall's fault he wasn't there—Marshall's fault that Darren's crotch was a swelling bruise. Suddenly Darren wanted to deal with him after all, if only to get him alone, far from any chance of being rescued, and watch his face when Darren revealed who he was. What Marshall would say, and what might happen then, were prospects which made Darren's suffering seem almost worthwhile as he heaved himself onto the landing and limped to his grandfather's room.

The old man was asleep, his head lolling sideways on the pillow, a trail of moisture glistening through the stubble on his chin as though a snail had crawled into his open mouth. The end of the quilt hid the lair under the bed. Darren hung onto the doorframe while he tried to stay out of reach of most of the smell of the room. "Marshall," he called. "They've gone. We're getting out before they come back."

A snore caught in the old man's throat, and the dangling quilt shifted, but only because his legs had. Then Marshall's muffled voice said, "Who's that?"

"Who do you think?"

"Is it Darren?"

"No bugger else."

A hand appeared from under the bed and pulled Marshall's head after it. "I thought you might be one of them pretending."

"Even they can't make me into owt I'm not, lad. Come out of there before you wake my granda."

Marshall sidled out on his stomach and shoved himself back on his haunches, and glanced along the bed, apparently hoping the old man would be awake. "Thanks," he said wistfully as he wobbled to his feet, and tiptoed toward the door.

As Darren moved aside, pain stabbed his crotch. "Fuck," he gasped.

"What's wrong?"

Darren's hands strayed toward the pain, but rubbing it might make it worse. "What does it look like?"

"Did they do that to you?"

"Aye, because I wouldn't tell them where you was. I mean, they didn't know it was you, but they thought I was hiding someone. They nearly found you, lad."

"They came in here. I made them think I was a dog."

"You can thank me for thinking that up. Shut the door and let's get moving. Didn't you hear me tell you they're coming back?"

Marshall's face seemed to narrow with panic. He darted out of the room and closed the door and hurried down the stairs. When he saw Darren holding onto the banister and lowering himself step by step, however, he returned to him and put an arm around his waist. "Here, lean on me."

The support was too welcome for Darren to fight it off, though it made him feel uncomfortable with himself. He winced as stepping down renewed all the pain in his crotch, and Marshall helped him more carefully onto the next stair. Their awkward progress had taken them halfway downstairs when Marshall said, "Maybe . . ."

"Maybe all sorts of shit, lad. What?"

"I was thinking if these people may try and stop us, maybe we should take your gun with us."

"You take it if you want. I'm not."

"Where is it?"

The pain was getting in the way of Darren's thoughts. He eased one foot onto the next stair, and the ache opened like a wound. The gun might come in useful once they were away from any witnesses, especially if only Marshall's fingerprints were to be found on it. "Under the floor in the back," he said.

"Can you manage while I get it?" Marshall said, just as Darren's mother came out of the back room. She planted her clawed hands on her hips and stared in incredulous disgust at the boys. "God, what do you look like. What are you playing at now."

"We're going out, mam. We're going straight out. Never mind what you were after, lad." Darren had realized just in time that if Marshall found the gun he would see the loot, and then how could he be argued onto a bus when there was so much money for a taxi? Besides, Darren's mother would hardly let them take the gun. Marshall was hesitating, not quite dissuaded, and Darren stepped down faster, grinding his teeth. He'd be passing on the pain and more to Marshall once he got him by himself. "Move," he snarled.

His mother flounced to the front door to open it for them. Marshall's hold on his waist loosened as they trod on the hall floor, and Darren forced himself to put an arm around the other boy's shoulders to stop him making for the back room. That action and his pain were greeted by a series of nearby sounds: the halting of an engine, a sliding and a slam of metal. His mother grabbed the latch and threw open the door as if she hadn't heard, and Darren limped forward as Marshall took a step. But there was a van at the end of the path, and as the gate screeched over the concrete, Barry stalked toward the house.

32

THE LOOK

You fool, Susanne was still thinking. You idiot. Imbecile. Cretin. Incompetent. Blunderer. Useless bitch. Perhaps when she'd finished calling herself everything she felt she was she would once more be able to think. Worse than wasting police time with her mistake about the track suit, she'd wasted Marshall's, and her sense of having done that walled her off from the world. She was dully aware that only a few minutes' driving through unfamiliar side streets had brought the police car to an area she knew, the Wilmslow Road. Angel braked at the end of the side street as an ambulance wailed past, its blue light pounding. She became conscious that it was lunchtime: the Indian takeaways were crowded with patrons, quite a few of whom were boys uniformed like mourners. The car swung onto the main road as a munching group of them prepared to step off the corner of the sidewalk, and she heard herself speak for the first time since she'd climbed into the vehicle outside the Fancy house. "They're from my son's school."

Angel steered the car into the street which led to hers. "We may want to interview some of his friends."

"Shall I come with you?"

"Just give us their names, Mrs. Travis. I should try and get some rest if I were you."

No doubt he meant that sympathetically, and she appreciated that it was good advice, but it made her feel criticized and excluded, not least because she couldn't blame him for doing either. Being able to rest was another matter entirely, depending on whether she was too exhausted or only too exhausted to stay awake. The passing street made her eyes smart as though it was physically catching at her vision, but she had to keep looking, to assure herself there was nothing she needed to see while she told Askew all the names of Marshall's friends she could recall. She saw a mailman hitching his bag over his shoulder as he went back to close a garden gate, but otherwise the sidewalks were deserted all the way to her house.

As soon as the car drew up outside, one front tire momentarily brushing the curb, she planted her hands on the seat on either side of her, ready to send her toward the house. She'd had a sudden intuition that while she and the police had been searching, Marshall had come home. She could hardly tell that to the police. "I'd better see if there are any messages," she said.

Askew's seat crouched forward to release her, and both men climbed out of the car. "We'll wait in case there are," Angel said.

"Come and listen," Susanne said, intent on finding her keys as she ducked onto the sidewalk. Askew opened the gate for her, and they followed her along the path. Shutters of sunlight slid up the windows, revealing her uninhabited front room, and she wondered if Marshall had just dodged out of it, having seen the police. "Let me go in first," she said. "I need to switch off the alarm."

She slipped her key into the Yale lock, and twisted it, and pushed. The door was unmoved. She reached for the doorbell in case Marshall had bolted himself in for some reason, and sensed the policemen watching her, and felt absurdly guilty—so much so that she withdrew the key in order to try the mortise lock rather than have them realize she'd been less than honest with them about her expectations. The mortise was indeed locked, but then, she told herself, Marshall could have done that from within if he wasn't feeling safe. She turned the key, and then the Yale, and pushed the door open. The inner door imitated its movement, and set off the warning drone of the alarm, the cry of an empty house.

Susanne strode in like a robot, protruding another piece of metal which she thrust into its slot. The alarm fell silent before its siren could tear at her ears, but the silence was as painful, and more difficult to bring to an end. She'd already glimpsed the illuminated numeral on the answering machine, and when she made herself confront it, it was still a zero, a red rim as raw as her eyes. She swung her leaden body toward the policemen who were standing in the irrelevant sunlight just beyond the gaping doors. "Nothing," she said.

Angel gave two blinks which seemed designed to rid her of a little of his constant scrutiny, and Askew offered her a minute shake of his head. "So," she heard herself say dully, "what happens now?"

"We'll continue the investigation, rest assured, Mrs. Travis," Angel said. "And of course you appreciate it isn't just the two of us who are looking for your lad."

"Do you want to call in while you're here in case anyone, anyone made any progress?"

"I'm sure they would have contacted us in the car if there'd been any developments."

"I imagine." Susanne felt as though her mind and her body had come to a complete stop. It took the sensation of something like cold liquid trickling down her wrist—a key dangling from the ring in her raised fist—to start her up. "I'm keeping you," she said. "I've got in your way long enough."

"We'll be in touch the moment there's anything. Is there someone who can sit with you?"

"If I need them." She let go of the banister, which she had become aware of clutching, and gestured the policemen away. When the keys jangled she realized she was waving her fists as if to mime triumph, and let them drop. "Go ahead, please go," she said. "I'll be all right."

Perhaps she would be once she felt she wasn't delaying the police. She stood by the phone while they returned to their car, which left a grayness in the air as it swung away. The smell of the fumes reached her just as the rear lights reddened at the corner of the street. The hint of a metallic taste coupled with the sight of red made her feel faint. Then the car was gone, the grayness fading along with its smell, and she saw Hilda Mattison emerge from the house diagonally opposite.

Perhaps Susanne could use company, but she only watched as Hilda stepped onto the sidewalk. Hilda looked at her and advanced another step, and when Susanne didn't countermand that, kept coming. Susanne pushed herself away from the banister, which somehow she had once more taken hold of, and into the front room to sit quickly. She landed on the seat facing the table piled with essays as Hilda arrived on the doorstep. "Susanne? Shall I come in?"

"If you—" Susanne said in virtually no voice, and breathed one in. "I'm through here."

"Shall I shut these?"

"May as well."

The two doors were closed with a respectful gentleness which served only to make Susanne feel that worse had happened than she knew, and then Hilda ventured into the room. Her broad face beneath the flat cap of her auburn hair was trying to decide whether to smile. She took some seconds to lower herself into an armchair which barely contained her, and hitched herself forward, hands on her overalled knees. "So did they . . ." she said, and turned up her hands.

"Not yet, Hilda, no."

"Ah dear." Hilda seemed not to know where to put her hands now that there was nothing to receive. "Ah dear," she repeated as if that might lend the words more sense, and sat back with a sigh which the chair emulated. "Us neither. I'm so sorry."

"I'm sure you did all you could."

"Hopefully."

"That would be the way to do it."

"I expect so." Hilda gave a small puzzled frown, and Susanne felt ashamed of having corrected her even so lightly. "Half a dozen of us from the street have been looking," Hilda said. "What you'd call a posse, wouldn't you? Everyone who's at home and knows your lad."

"Tell them thanks for me, Hilda, if I don't see them myself."

"You'd rather not have them come in."

Susanne supposed she had meant that, however ungrateful it sounded. Company wasn't reassuring her as she'd hoped it might, because she had an impression, so slight it could well be illusory, that talking was preventing her from grasping some important detail. A movement beyond Hilda caught her attention, but she had to focus her mind in order to distinguish that the figure ambling toward her house was the mailman, and then a further effort was needed to remind her that she hadn't answered Hilda. "Maybe not right now," she said.

"I understand. You don't want crowds all over you. You know where we are, anyway, love. Any time at all you don't want to be by yourself."

"I know. I appreciate it. I'm grateful. Thanks." Susanne saw Hilda planting her hands on the arms of the chair to hoist herself out of it, and felt compelled to explain whatever attitude she had been conveying. "I'm sorry, Hilda. Maybe if I can just sit and think I'll be able to straighten out my head. Right now I'm wishing I'd left the police alone to do their job. All I did was lead them wrong."

"How was that, Susanne?"

From the tone of the question it was clear that Hilda aimed to try to coax her out of that view, and Susanne regretted having mentioned it. "We went looking for the son of the guy who pulled the gun on my husband in the first place," she said.

"You thought he might have wanted some kind of revenge for his father being in prison."

"I didn't, no. Well, yes, I suppose I may have thought that, but that wasn't why we went to his house. A guard at your Arndale Center thought he saw him with Marshall."

"When?"

"Late yesterday afternoon."

"But that sounds . . . You'd think . . ."

"Except that the boy and his family swear he was home all yesterday."

"They would though, wouldn't they, if . . ."

"And the guard only remembered seeing Marshall with another boy until he realized who I was, and then he remembered the picture of the father in the papers and started saying the other boy had looked like him."

"That doesn't mean he was wrong though, does it?" Hilda sounded close to angry with Susanne for arguing against her. "And even if he was wrong about that, there's still this other boy."

"If there was one."

"They'll be able to check, won't they? They'll have the security video."

"I suppose," Susanne admitted before the idea caught up with her. "I hadn't thought of that. You think the police will have?"

"I'm positive they will."

"They won't want me ringing them up to tell them their job." More to the point, Susanne was certain this wasn't the issue she'd overlooked, and that convinced her there was one. The mailman was advancing, helping to distract her. "They'll have had enough of me," she said.

"I'm sure they wouldn't have taken you if they didn't want you there, and I can't believe you were any hindrance."

"You would if you'd been there." Susanne wanted to leave it at that, and then she knew she had to explain, because that might recall whatever she'd forgotten. "I found a track suit I thought was Marshall's in the other boy's room. It looked exactly like."

"I don't want to upset you all over again, Susanne, but how can you . . ."

"Because it was made in England, maybe a fake that they sell in your markets, and Marshall's was made in America. One letter on the tag showed me I was wrong, but only after I nearly convinced the police."

"They'll have understood, love. They must know how you feel."

Susanne no longer knew that herself. There was something she ought just to have realized which the sight of the mailman was driving out of her mind. He was coming up the path and removing from his bag a package too bulky to fit through the slot in the door. She had a sudden dreadful suspicion that the contents might relate to Marshall in some way she wouldn't be able to bear, and yet it rushed her to the front door to head off the shrilling of the bell. She wasn't quite in time, and only her pulling open the door caused the mailman to take his finger off the button. She grabbed the package from him as he raised his eyebrows cheerfully, and then she saw the house number on the label. "This isn't mine."

"Didn't I see Mrs. Mattison come in here?"

"I know what it is, Susanne," Hilda called, and plodded into the hall. "He'll be bringing me my seeds."

Susanne supposed she ought to be reassured because the package wasn't anything she'd been afraid to define to herself. She handed it to Hilda as the mailman strolled away, whistling in search of a tune. "Do you mind if I see about rousing the old man now?" Hilda said.

Susanne managed a tweak of a smile at that. "Go on before he wonders where you've vanished to," she said, wincing inwardly at her choice of words. She closed the door after Hilda to conceal the dismay that might have brought her neighbor back. Her mind was dulling again. Since she'd been wrong about the package as well as the track suit, how could she persist in believing she had almost noticed some detail which nobody else had found significant? It seemed to be only her lack of any sense of purpose which was lifting her feet and planting them on each stair up to Marshall's room.

She pushed the door and watched it fall away from her, and gazed into the room. There appeared to be nothing that meant more to her than the last time she had looked. Movie posters; as many books as the shelves could hold; Marshall's bed and his school uniform lying on it, their emptiness multiplied by the dressing-table mirror. A few clothes slept on the floor, reminding her until she recoiled from any such comparison of the boy's bedroom in the Fancy house. Did she secretly believe that leaving the clothes where they were might conjure Marshall back to her? The idea sent her into the room as though she was fleeing her own irrationality. She was remembering another instance of that—her behavior in the Fancy boy's room. As she cringed at the recollection it touched off another memory, and she became absolutely still.

She'd been wrong to think the track suit was Marshall's, and she'd been suffering the mistake ever since. She'd let it gather in her mind until she couldn't see past it. She remembered saying "That's—" and the boy's face turning blank as Angel asked her what she'd noticed. Why would the boy have assumed that lack of an expression unless he'd known not only what she'd seen but the meaning it would have for her?

He knew what Marshall had been wearing yesterday, and she was certain how he knew. The room around her seemed to grow clear and bright and even emptier. The next moment she was running downstairs to the phone, and then she knew she had no time to try to convince the police. Where had she put her keys? She dodged into the front room and saw them huddled on top of the essays, and selected the key for the alarm as she snatched them up.

All at once her nerves were working for her, her brittle sleeplessness concentrating her actions. She turned the key in the control panel, and was immediately through the inner door, closing it behind her, and locking the house. She let herself into the Volvo, which started the first time, and reached the speed limit almost as soon as the car swung away from the curb.

The police might well not have believed her. They might have pointed out that the Fancy boy could have learned from the appeals on the radio what Marshall was wearing. But they hadn't seen how the boy had arranged his face—they hadn't glimpsed the realization which he had almost succeeded in hiding. It would take far too long to persuade them of all this. She had to reach his house before he left it. He knew where Marshall was, she had seen he did, and he was going to lead her to him.

She braked at the corners and more decisively at the Wilmslow Road. A car flashed its headlamps to invite her into the rush of traffic, and it wasn't until brakes screeched as she accelerated out of the side street that she understood it had been sunlight making the lamps flare. The driver leaned on his horn and thrust his grimace close to the windshield, but she was across the road now, just ahead of a bus, so near that a sample of it filled her mirror. She swerved left into the first side street. That was the direction for the Fancy house.

It wasn't the precise route the police had used to bring her home. The narrow roads were breaking out in old cobblestones which made the car and her head jounce. Blocks of small shops alternated with blocks of houses as flat-faced. All the shops appeared to sell secondhand goods, some of which loitered outside them. She was driving as fast as the law allowed—indeed, unless she kept glancing at the dial, somewhat faster. Her senses were trawling everything she passed. The blank screens of a dozen televisions piled in a window turned from gray to blinding white as sunlight trailed over them, a cat lying on top of a refrigerator between two armchairs on the sidewalk stretched its black and white body like a movie projected through the wrong lens, and Susanne was wondering if the immediacy of details such as these had caused her to lose her way—she was wishing she'd thought to ascertain the name of the main road nearest the Fancy house so that she could ask for directions, although just now there was nobody in sight to ask—when the street curved, and at the end of it she saw the very road, the saplings tottering on crutches in front of the low brown boxy houses on the far side of the concrete strip which divided it. She drove to it only as fast as the limit, and braked at the intersection, and looked left. No traffic was coming. She trod on the gas pedal and spun the wheel right, and was speeding toward two lanes of traffic which raced headlong at her.

There was nowhere to go. The concrete which split the road in half was surmounted by a metal railing. She clutched at the gearshift and slammed it into reverse. The gears shrieked, the car juddered, and then it was veering backward at speed, not quite along the same curve it had just described. She felt one rear wheel mount the curb, and a lamppost hurtled toward her in the mirror.

It scraped her rear bumper as the car bucked to a halt. The traffic flashed past the intersection without slackening its pace, and blared at her like trumpets of doom. She leaned her forehead against the windshield and tried to breathe and swallow. If she could see she could drive, which was all that mattered. When the mirror showed her several people hurrying out of a shop toward the car she took a deep breath and turned left onto the main road, scraping her bumper again. She was almost in sight of the Fancy house.

As she indicated right to turn across an intersection controlled by lights, she saw the people from the shop still watching her. Maybe they would call the police. Fine, if that brought police to the Fancy house, so long as they didn't prevent her from finding Marshall. A green arrow sprang into being above her, urging her to cross the intersection. As soon as she was beyond the double yellow lines which trailed along the side road into which her turn had brought her, she pulled over to the curb. Any farther and she might be visible from the house around the corner.

She withdrew the keys from the ignition as she stooped onto the sidewalk. She eased the door shut, and felt absurdly overcautious; surely a slam couldn't alert anyone at the house. She let go of the handle and heard, like an impossible echo of the noise she had avoided making, a sharp flat sound, somewhere close.

It must have been a car backfiring, whatever it had felt like to her nerves. This was England, and guns weren't common here, not yet. The boxy houses stood unmoving beneath the translucently blue sky, reassuring her that nothing significant had just taken place. She dropped her keys into her purse and began to walk fast toward the house. Her legs were almost steady; she told herself there was no cause for them not to be. She had taken several steps before the screams began.

33

THE KILLER

It was stopping, Marshall told himself. It was going to stop. He didn't really think he was a dog, even though he smelled like one—even though when he'd heard Darren calling to him under the bed he'd been afraid that he wouldn't be able to speak. That had only been because his throat ached from yapping, not because all he was able to do was yap. Now he was standing up like a person and talking like one, and he could stay like that so long as he didn't panic. He wouldn't have time to panic while he was helping his friend.

The people who had almost found him in his hiding place had hurt Darren. It had been Darren's idea for him to hide, but if Marshall had been with him they mightn't have hurt him. That made Marshall feel guilty, grubby inside himself, not least for hiding under the old man's bed rather than Darren's, where he'd been told to go. He'd only thought he would be safest where there was a witness who might have prevented them from hurting him, but it seemed as though he hadn't trusted Darren sufficiently to let him know where he would be. He took a firmer grip on his friend's waist as they performed another lingering step down the littered stairs toward the littered hall, but didn't feel he was caring nearly enough for his friend. "Maybe . . ."

Darren's voice was screwed tight by pain. "Maybe all sorts of shit, lad. What?"

Marshall heard himself suggesting they take the gun. His words were coming from somewhere outside him, and that brought him closer to panic. Everything was standing back so as not to be infected by whatever was still wrong with him: even Darren, whom he sensed pulling almost imperceptibly away from him; even his own voice. The slowness of each step he took alongside Darren seemed to threaten that some part of his surroundings or of himself was about to change for the worse. Now the voices, his and Darren's, had established that the gun was under the floor in the back; presumably that meant the back room. That gave him an excuse, not to leave Darren—he wouldn't dream of wanting to abandon his friend—but to move more quickly for a little while, perhaps long enough to let him feel in control of his body. "Can you manage while I get it?" he said, trying to reclaim his voice from the instability all around him.

The instability fought back. Before Darren could even have drawn a breath, it sent his mother out of the room where the gun was. She perched two spiders that were her hands on her hips and stared up. "God, what do you look like. What are you playing at now."

Did she mean Marshall, for walking as though he was as injured as her son? Surely as a nurse she ought to realize he was trying to help, unless she didn't realize Darren was hurt. Marshall hoped that was true, because otherwise it would mean she had been powerless to shield him. At least Darren appeared to be undisturbed by her attitude, and so perhaps it was all right in some way Marshall failed to understand. "We're going out, mam. We're going straight out," Darren said, and to Marshall, "Never mind what you were after, lad."

Was he saying that only because he couldn't see how Marshall would get the weapon past his mother? Marshall hesitated, trying to locate the solution in the slippery brittle hollow of his mind, until Darren stepped down quicker, pulling Marshall with him. "Move," he snarled through his teeth.

It must be important to move fast, or he wouldn't be hurting himself. His mother raced them to the front door as they reached the hall. Marshall relaxed his hand on Darren's waist, but Darren put an arm around his shoulders. Marshall couldn't go for the gun without shaking him off, and he assumed his friend most needed him to be close. At least their haste should mean that Marshall would be home sooner. Darren's mother pulled at the door, which seemed to be making several more noises than a door really should, and threw it open. But the noises continued with a screech of wood on concrete, and beyond them the end of the path was blocked by a lump of raw red. It was the van which belonged to the people he'd hidden from, and here came one of them, wearing motorcycle gear apart from the helmet. He felt his friend stiffen, and the next moment he saw something worse than Darren could know. The figure stalking toward them was the man who'd pulled a gun on Marshall's father and bullied Marshall into their house.

The face jerked closer above the creaking of the leather body, and Marshall saw he was mistaken. It wasn't the same man, although the lower half of the pale face jagged with bone and displaying a scar to show where it was fitted together looked like him, especially the sneer. His wasn't the only face which would turn into the gunman's if Marshall let it: he'd had to keep his friend's from doing so. Even if this wasn't the other man, he was just as dangerous, because Darren was falling back into the house, dragging Marshall with him. "That's right, you little twat," the man said with gleeful contempt on the edge of becoming more dangerous. "Limp off while you can still limp."

"Leave my friend alone," Marshall heard himself protest, but nobody else could have heard him. He was shrinking into a hollow at the center of himself. Darren's mother retreated crabwise into the front room as the boys stumbled backward as far as the stairs, and the man planted his feet in the house with such force that the floor quaked under the rucked torn carpet. For a moment Marshall felt exactly as he had when the other man had forced his way into his house. The man in motorcycle leather raised one boot, and Marshall felt Darren flinch, but instead of kicking either of them the intruder thrust his heel against the door to slam it, shaking the floorboards again. The action sent him forward a heavy step, and the cramped hall filled with the smells of sweat and leather. "What's your game," he demanded of Darren's mother, "besides the one you're on?"

"I don't know what you mean, Barry."

"Even you aren't that stupid, and don't you fucking think I am. What do you reckon, I've got no eyes? I didn't see you letting him get away?"

"I didn't want anything happening—"

"Never mind what you want. You do what the fuck you're told. Who do you think you are, messing with me? I ought to give you a kicking you won't get up from."

All this was coming too fast and too loud for Marshall, but he deduced that the man called Barry had put Darren's mother on the street. No wonder they were afraid of him. He'd told her to keep either Marshall or her son in the house, and she'd been trying to save them when he came back too soon. Suddenly Marshall's fear for her was greater than his fear of the man. "She didn't do anything wrong," he blurted. "She's been looking after me."

Barry's eyes grew redder as they swiveled to take him in. The man's mouth had become a slit full of teeth, but now it turned into a sneer which was almost a grin. "Been good to you, has she?"

"She has, hasn't she, Darren?"

"Didn't know you did them that young, Marie. Whatever brings the loot in, eh?"

Marshall couldn't decide if the man was mocking him or genuinely mistaken, and Darren's face wasn't telling him—indeed, Darren had moved away from him as though he was an embarrassment. "No, I mean I was ill and she took care of me," Marshall insisted. "Darren brought me home because he knew she would."

Was that entirely true? Marshall's memories weren't quite fitting together, and Barry jabbed another question at him before he had time to think. "What kind of ill was that, lad?"

Barry's eyes and grin were wider, and Marshall could only ignore them. "I don't know exactly. Some kind of fever, what you call a bug. Mrs., Darren's mom will know."

"I bet she does. Mrs. who, lad?"

Barry's expression might have disturbed Marshall more if it hadn't looked so stupid. "Don't you know?"

"Don't get fucking clever with me." Barry's lips shifted, then reverted to the grin. "Shall I tell him, Marie?"

"Bit late to start asking my permission when you're behaving like you own the house."

"As far as you're concerned I do, bitch, while it's got my loot in it." Barry stamped a pace toward her, and Marshall threw out his hands. They came nowhere near touching Barry—it had been just a panic reaction—but the man gaped at him. "What's up? Don't you want to see the bitch get what she's asking for?"

"She isn't what you said." All at once Marshall's words rushed out of control. "You leave her alone, or—"

"This is fucking unbelievable, this is. Or what, you little dick?"

Marshall hadn't prevented any violence, he'd simply focused it on himself. He stood at the foot of the stairs, unable to dodge out of reach, his hands still raised, trembling in front of him. Even if he made them into fists they wouldn't be any use. Without warning Barry darted at him, and Marshall felt the lowest banister bludgeon his spine as he retreated. But the man hardly bothered to sneer at him before turning his back on him. "I'm bored of this," he muttered, and thrust a hand at Darren's mother. "Give us your keys."

"What for?"

"Never mind what fucking for, Mrs. F." Barry hooked at the air with his fingers as if that should bring the keys. "Give them here before I rip that rag off you to see where you've stuffed them."

"If you ruin my things you can buy me some more."

"I'll ruin your things for you all right," Barry said, and bore down on her. Marshall saw her face quiver as Barry turned his hooked hand over and fitted it to her left breast. "Last tart that said no to me couldn't bear anyone touching her for months."

Darren's mother managed to stiffen her face, unless fear was doing that. "Go on. I dare you. See what Phil does to you when he comes home."

"Fuck all at his age if he knows what's good for him. Maybe he won't be interested in you anymore. Depends who he's had up his arse, eh?" Barry was closing his fingers and thumb very slowly while he peered into her face, and Marshall saw her eyes begin to dart from side to side as if they were trying to escape what was being done to her. They found a stick lying on the floor of the front room—part of the banisters, it looked like. Barry glanced at it and gave her breast a vicious tweak before opening his hand. "Want a fight? Go on then, fetch. I'll even give you first crack, and then it'll be my turn."

Darren's mother clenched her fists in front of her breast, apparently rather than let him see her rubbing it, but didn't move otherwise. Barry pointed one shoulder at Marshall and gazed sidelong over it. "What do you reckon, lad? Think Mrs. F should have a go? Better make a run for it if you can't cope."

Of course he was mocking him—Marshall was only unsure how much. Nobody since George S. had treated him quite like that, and he felt his mind shrinking back to that last day in the woods behind the house in West Palm Beach. He'd run away then, but he wouldn't now, because his presence might inhibit Barry from doing anything too dreadful. "Don't keep calling her that," he blurted.

"Mrs. F, are we talking about? What's your problem with that, lad?"

His mockery infuriated Marshall. "I know what it's supposed to mean. You shouldn't call anyone that."

"Is that right. You know what F stands for, eh. Maybe you know where you are and all, do you?"

"In my friend's house."

"You reckon."

Marshall rummaged in his brain for something else to say, however outrageous, that would hold his attention, because Darren's mother had dodged aside behind Barry and was wincing, rubbing her breast. If he could distract Barry for just a few more seconds she'd have time to grab the piece of wood. "In Darren's mom's house," he said, but that certainly wasn't enough. "She isn't what you said, you are. You're Mr. Fuck."

He'd never said that word in his life. It felt even odder out of his mouth than in; it seemed to hover just before his face, an invisible lump which he hadn't known he had in him. He didn't care, because Darren's mother had managed to stoop. She straightened up, lifting not the pole from the banisters but her purse, which she snapped open to produce a bunch of keys. "Here, have them. Do what you want. Only don't go trying to make out it was anything to do with me."

Barry was grinning with wide-eyed delight at Marshall, but as he turned to her his face dulled as though he couldn't be bothered to maintain the expression. He snatched the keys and stalked to the back door, and stuck the largest key in it to confirm it was locked. At once he was returning, glaring along the hall to see that nobody had dared move, and his glare settled on Marshall. "Get in the front, you. Get your arse on a chair and shut your gob, and don't fucking move till I tell you. I'll give you Mr. Fuck."

Marshall seemed to have no choice but to obey, since the only adult there hadn't dared stand up to Barry. If he tried to run, Barry would be on him before he reached the door. Maybe nothing very bad would happen so long as he did as he was told, he thought; maybe Darren wouldn't be hurt worse—and then he saw he was abandoning his friend. "I'll go if Darren comes with me."

"I reckon I was right about these two, Marie. Do you want some of what I gave your boyfriend, lad?"

"Leave him alone." Marshall had said it aloud at last. "He didn't do anything to you. He's got to come in with me where you won't be able to touch him."

"You think I won't while you're watching? Watch this."

Darren had been gazing away from Marshall, but now he turned a look full of accusation and disgust on him. Marshall saw Barry lurching at the other boy, one hand swooping toward Darren's crotch. "Don't," he cried as Darren limped backward. "I'll go in. I'm going now. Please don't hurt him."

Darren's mother shoved him out of her way as he blundered into the front room. If anyone had been visible through the window he might have cried for help, but there was nothing to be seen beyond the wreck of a garden except the flayed van. At least Darren's mother was in the hall now, between Barry and her son, and Marshall was alone with the banister post. Couldn't he grab it while Barry wasn't looking? Mightn't one blow with all his strength to Barry's head at least disable the man for long enough to let them escape? Could he steel himself to injure Barry worse for Darren's sake—to smash the man's testicles or poke the wood into his eyes? He glanced at Darren while Barry couldn't see any communication that passed between them, but Darren was again not looking at him. He saw the boy and his mother retreat a step as Barry came to glare into the room, and then it was too late. "I fucking said sit down," Barry said, and watched Marshall have to do so, and jerked his head at the others. "You two can give me a hand in the back."

Marshall sprang out of the chair. Perhaps he could dodge around Barry while the man wasn't looking at him. But Barry's head swung like a snake's toward him, and Barry threw out his arms, clenching his hands on the doorframe so that Marshall wasn't sure if it was only leather he heard creaking or the frame as well. "I left something in there," he said almost faster than he could think. "Just let me get it, okay?"

Beyond Barry, Darren goggled at him as though he'd just said the stupidest thing possible. Didn't Darren realize that if Barry was first into the back room he might find the gun? That couldn't have occurred to him, or surely he would be taking the chance to head Barry off. "You know, Darren," Marshall pleaded. "What I left in there before. You know, what I left under—you know."

Darren's face withdrew its expression into itself. If he understood, he wasn't admitting it. Much worse, he was making no move. Perhaps he felt bound to side with his mother, who had started to protest in a voice that grew increasingly wheedling. "He's talking crap, Barry. I don't know what he's on about. He was never in the back. You know I'd never have let him."

Barry's head snaked to face her as he let go of the hinged side of the frame. There might just be space for Marshall to dart through unnoticed for at least a second, just a few seconds. He dropped into a crouch that would help him dart under the outstretched arm. The movement caught Barry's attention, and he grinned so fiercely his scar turned white. "Fair enough, lad," he said, moving toward the front door, out of Marshall's way. "Get whatever you're whining for."

"Honest, Barry, he never—"

"Shut the fuck up, Marie, or I'll rip both them lumps off you. You do like you're told, lad, before I fetch you one up the arse."

Marshall was already sidling out of the doorway. He looked at Darren, and the other boy met his gaze, but his eyes were as blank as his face. Marshall was certain they meant to tell him something, only what? Darren's mother threw up her hands, distorting them into claws as though she intended to scratch Marshall with them, then let them drop as he dodged past. Barry was striding after him, so that he would have at most a few seconds unobserved in the back room. He grabbed the doorknob with both slippery inflated hands and wrung it, and followed the door across the threshold, and halted in panic.

He didn't know whether the room had expanded in his first moment of seeing it or he himself had shrunk. Either way, his fever had been lying in wait for him. He seemed to be in a deserted barroom, or perhaps an attic in which a few shabby chairs had been stored together with a homemade bar and a low table preserving hands of cards beneath its surface. The side of the bar was covered with garish hula dancers, all of them twitching like a cartoon stuck in a projector and about to burst into movement when the film pulled free of the obstruction. Several boxing posters drooped on the wall next to the bar, and the name on each of them was trying to form into the name of the man who'd pulled a gun on his father. Not now, he pleaded with his uncontrollably alien mind, any time but now. The floor was growing shifty, shaken by the footsteps which were coming for him. He stared desperately around the room, unable to determine how much he was seeing was real.

Under the window gray as thick smoke was a wrinkle in the carpet where it might have been lifted; against the foot of the bar an edge of the carpet was turned back like the inside of an old man's eyelid. The quivering of the floor seized his body as a creaking of leather arrived behind him. "Grab your chance, lad," Barry said in his ear.

Marshall floundered forward through the dim stale light which smelled and felt like ash. He was aiming to kneel, but his momentum sent him sprawling against the bar in a helpless crouch. He dragged his knees backwards, one hand flattening a restless cartoon dancer, and peeled the edge of the carpet away from the floor. Beneath the carpet was ragged brown linoleum which splintered when he tried to pull it up, and beneath that was a board which was clearly not loose, since part of it was trapped under the bar. He retreated several inches on his knees to be able to reach the next board, his shoulders flinching from the possibility that Barry was behind him, poised to capture him. But when Barry spoke, his voice came from across the room. "This what you're after?"

He was in the corner farthest from the door. As Marshall swiveled on his aching knees, Barry brandished one hand at him to let him see it take hold of the corner of the carpet and lift a wide strip away from the wall, and dig its fingers under the end of the exposed floorboard. The board tilted up, and Barry's creaking arm thrust into the gap, and reappeared with the gun in his fist. "Want it, lad?"

Marshall couldn't speak, nor could he judge how visibly he was shaking his head. As he raised one knee and gripped it with both hands, Barry jabbed the revolver at him. "Here it comes," he said in delight as wild as his grin, and snatched a cushion from the nearest chair.

"Don't, Barry, Christ, not here," Darren's mother screamed. If that had any effect, it was to encourage him. He shoved the muzzle into the cushion and lined them up with Marshall's face less than a yard away, and pulled the trigger.

There was a muffled sound—a click. "Lucky twat," Barry muttered, "and now your luck's run out," and squeezed the trigger again. This click sounded yet more muffled, almost apologetic. He stared at the gun for a moment, then flung it and the cushion onto the chair. "Fucking useless," he snarled, kicking the loose carpet against the dislodged board, and turned on Darren's mother, who was loitering in the hall. "Right, so when was he in here?"

"I told you, Barry—"

"I'll tell you what you fucking tell me. You tell me the fucking truth." Barry crossed the room in three strides which vibrated boards against Marshall's knees. Darren's mother pivoted like a weathercock caught by a gale, then she dashed for the kitchen. "Stop your boyfriend going anywhere or you won't even be able to limp," Barry snarled at Darren, and stalked after her.

The moment Barry was through the door, Marshall lunged for the revolver. He bumped into the chair, and the gun slid off the cushion, onto the floor. He clutched at the barrel before it could fall, and swung the butt into his hand, and closed the other hand around it, and hooked the trigger with his finger. The gun felt lighter than he remembered, but surely there must still be a bullet in it. He tiptoed swiftly into the hall, just as Darren came to find him.

As Darren saw the revolver, what might have been a secret grin passed over his face before it reverted to blankness. His attention strayed along the hall, toward the source of a jangling crash. His mother had pulled out a kitchen drawer, presumably in search of a knife, so hastily that the broken drawer and all its knives were scattered across the linoleum. "Come ahead, Marie, give us a fight," Barry jeered as she tried to grab a knife but sent it skittering under the table. "Only if I get it off you, think where I'll be sticking it." Then his lowered head rose slowly, and turned even slower, and Marshall saw his own reflection which Barry had seen in the kitchen window. "Hey, look, Marie, you're rescued," Barry shouted. "Here's fucking Wyatt Twerp."

The old man upstairs had begun to groan at the fall of the drawer, and at last his complaint became words. "Was that a bomb?"

Barry's false geniality turned into contempt as he glanced upward before confronting Marshall. "Put it down, lad, or I'll bash your teeth out with it. Get in the front while you can."

Behind him Darren's mother had straightened up empty-handed to watch. Marshall stepped backward quickly, with a sureness which holding the weapon had lent him. As he came abreast of the front room Darren moved out of his way, then doubled up with pain and clawed at the banister. "Don't just wave it like your dick," he said through his teeth. "It's still loaded."

Barry jerked to a halt outside the kitchen. He looked as though a noose had been thrown over his head, pulling back the corners of his eyes as far as they would stretch. His mouth opened, displaying the wet insides of his lips, and teeth which looked eager to bite. He saw Marshall almost at the front door, and tramped toward him as if trying to crush insects underfoot. "Here I am. Bang fucking bang. I'll be shot, and you'll be locked up, and nobody to guard your arse."

Marshall let go of the revolver with his left hand and groped behind him for the latch. His right hand began to shake with the weight of the gun. The shivering ran up his arm into his body, and he couldn't find the latch. Struggling to keep the gun pointed along the hall, he glanced at the door and closed his free hand around the metal knob. A cramp seized that hand, twisting it off the latch.

He almost let the gun fall. He felt it slump in his fist. He clung to the knob with as many fingers as he could force to work, and strained his elbow up, up. The knob seemed to move only slightly, but he tugged at it with what little strength remained in his hand. The door swung toward him so readily that he staggered along the hall as if the weight of the gun was pulling him toward Barry. That must have looked like a real threat, because it stopped Barry just short of the end of the staircase. Before the man could close the distance between them Marshall stepped backward, sure of himself again now that both his hands were supporting the revolver, and out of the house.

He drew a breath which tasted fresh as sunlight, and kept retreating. Once he was beyond the gate he might feel truly safe, and then, little as he liked to abandon his friend while he did so, he could run for help. The spectacle of his escape appeared to have paralyzed all activity within the house; even the old man had fallen silent. Marshall looked over his shoulder to ascertain that he was several steps away from the gate, then peered down the barrel of the gun. Barry was stalking along the hall, but he no longer seemed nearly so dangerous, however vicious his face was growing. Marshall wasn't prepared to see him grab Darren and pull the boy in front of him, one arm around his throat, the other hand clamping itself between his legs. "Come back here, you, or I'll cripple your boyfriend."

Darren's face crumpled and was all at once much younger. He tore at the arm around his throat with both hands, and Barry grinned more widely. "Do it," Darren snarled at Marshall. "Shoot him. Pull the trigger."

Marshall took one step toward the house, to enlarge the target of the man's face. "Let him go or I will."

"That's it, lad, keep coming." Barry licked his lips, savoring the excitement. "Get a move on or it'll be too late for your lover."

Though his hand at Darren's crotch appeared hardly to stir, Darren's eyes bulged and his mouth stretched wide, the lips quivering around the teeth. His mother ventured tentatively out of the kitchen—Marshall couldn't tell if she was afraid or trying to reach Barry unnoticed—but as the man's head snapped around, she retreated. "Shoot, fucking shoot," Darren screamed.

Marshall stumbled forward one more step, and prodded the muzzle at the sneering target above Darren's agoniaed face, and pulled the trigger. The impact of the hammer on the empty chamber was barely audible, as though it was ashamed to own up to its uselessness. Barry's eyes blazed gleefully, and Darren's face convulsed as his captor thrust the hand up between his legs. "Better not shoot," Barry jeered, "or you might hit—"

Something slammed into the heels of Marshall's hands. The ache of it rushed up his arms to the shoulders, from which it seemed to leap into his ringing ears. For a moment deafness blotted out all his senses, and then he was able to see beyond the muzzle and its wisp of acrid smoke. The agony had drained from Darren's face, which looked almost comically astonished, as if he hadn't believed Marshall capable. Just above Darren's head, Barry's throat was growing bright crimson.

The man wobbled toward the stairs, letting Darren sag in his grip. As the boy's head slipped down the leather jacket, Marshall saw it was leaving a track. It wasn't just the blood which was pulsing out of Barry's throat, he saw. It was pulsing out of Darren too, out of his shattered scalp.

Barry wavered backward and sat down hard on a stair. Darren's limbs began to flail the air weakly and haphazardly. Marshall seemed to be watching a dummy sitting on a ventriloquist's lap—a dummy of which the ventriloquist was losing control. It kicked a little, then its legs flopped, and it tried to reach with one hand for the top of its head to feel what had happened there. The hand rose as far as the forehead before giving up. As the fingertips trailed down again they appeared to pull off the peevish bewildered expression which the face was making an effort to wear, and then it was a little boy's face, slack as though asleep, the lips slightly parted. A moment later Barry's head lolled forward on a neck which was now entirely reddened. His chin poked into the ruined scalp, and a wash of crimson welled down the boy's face, turning it into a red plastic mask.

A clunk of metal recalled Marshall from wherever his mind had retreated. The revolver had fallen from his hands onto the concrete. He watched Darren's mother run along the hall, slapping her hands against the wall and the staircase, and hunch her shoulders nearly as high as her ears when she saw what Marshall had done, and begin to scream. She swung her head almost blindly toward him and came out of the house at a fast jagged walk, screaming words now, too harsh for him to distinguish. Whatever she was calling him, and whatever she meant to do to him, he thought it was less than he deserved. It wouldn't bring his friend back.

He stood waiting, close to welcoming her onslaught. Her nails raked at his eyes, but he felt nothing. At first he didn't understand why, even when he saw her staggering back across the doorstep to sprawl on the floor. It wasn't until his mother stepped in front of him and took his hands that he realized her fist had met the other woman's jaw, knocking her unconscious.

A MAN

As the last bulging suitcase wobbled away along the conveyor belt, Marshall saw a man in the crowd beneath the flight arrival and departure monitors identify him and his mother. She was saying "None" to the woman behind the check-in desk, except that the word changed in his mind as he realized it had only three letters. A gong tolled overhead before a female voice warned yet again that unattended baggage would be removed and might be destroyed. Through the faint hollow echo of the tolling in his ears he heard his mother thank the airline clerk. She turned away from the desk with the boarding cards in her hand, and the man beneath the screens that were shuffling words moved toward her through the crowd.

Marshall swung the baggage trolley in his direction. There was a policeman by the restless automatic doors into the long high booking hall, two more were chatting to a clerk at the Lufthansa desk, and all of them wore guns. He pinched the double bars of the handle together to release the brake, and steered the trolley toward the two policemen and the interior of the airport. His mother was trotting to keep up with him when the man called, "Mrs. Travis?"

The trolley stalled, almost throwing the hand luggage onto the floor, because Marshall's mother had taken hold of his shoulder. One of the policemen glanced incuriously at the incident, which no doubt looked as though a father had just located his wife and son among the mass of passengers. Except that his father was too young, and wore glasses whose narrow lenses were tinted the same dark blue as his suit and cheeks and chin. "Yes, what is it?" Marshall's mother said.

"I wonder if I can ask you a few questions for—" Another gong tolled, and the female voice summoned a member of staff. Marshall stared at the policemen in case they were wanted, but neither moved off. "For what, did you say?" his mother said.

The man repeated the phrase, and Marshall realized that the single syllable was the name of a newspaper. "If you've just a few minutes," the man said.

"I don't know, Marshall. Have we?"

The policemen were taking their leave of the clerk, turning away so that Marshall couldn't see their guns, but he no longer felt the need. "I don't mind."

"If he doesn't mind I suppose I don't either, Mr. . . .?"

"James. Shall we find somewhere to sit? Can I get you both a drink?"

"I could use one. How about you, honey?"

Marshall was trying to decide if James was the reporter's first name or his last; being less than sure of anything about a person made him uneasy now. "Thanks," he said.

"Let me take your bags." Before Marshall could argue, the reporter grabbed both from the trolley and lifted a strap over each shoulder. "You didn't want to keep on pushing, did you, son?"

Whenever anyone called Marshall that, he felt as though they were presuming to be compared with his father. He didn't reply, only looked for armed police as the reporter ushered him and his mother into the next hall, where shops and a bar hemmed in a great many seats fitted back to back. There was a gun, and there another, quite close to the bar where the reporter found three empty stools like puffed-up miniatures of the table they surrounded. "Gin and it it is, and for you, son?"

"Orange in a bottle, please."

"In a bottle," the reporter said as though sharing Marshall's finicality with several Africans in robes and multicolored caps outside the bar, and swung the cabin baggage off his shoulders before strutting to the counter. As Marshall gazed after him, his mother touched his hand. "We really don't have to do this if you don't want to."

"I don't know what it is yet."

"Our farewell to England."

"Sure," Marshall said, and turned the stool and himself to stop the fluttering of destinations on a monitor from plucking at the edge of his vision. His mother eyed him as if she couldn't judge what answer he had given her, and at once he didn't know. He watched while the reporter delivered himself of an ostentatious amount of change into a saucer on the bar and carried over their drinks dwarfed by his own pint of bitter. He set the bottle and glasses on the table, and pulled the creases over his knees, and shot back his cuffs as he produced a notebook from inside his jacket. He hadn't opened the notebook when he said, "So will you be taking any pleasant memories home with you?"

"Of course," Marshall's mother said, and looked the question at Marshall.

"Sure." That sounded as vague as the last time he'd used it, and he backed it up as best he could. "There was the lady who bought my dad's shop."

"Really. She was . . ."

"She paid a lot more for it than we were expecting, didn't she, mom? The last books my dad ever bought were the rarest, but she needn't have said."

"Honest of her," the reporter said approvingly, then set the notebook down so as to take a drink. "And will there be much you'll miss?"

"My videos."

"Really," the reporter said, squinting at him over the tilting glass.

"The police took them because they weren't British. We thought they might give them back for us to send home, but they wouldn't. It's all right, mom," he added as he saw her regretting having signed the videos away when they'd seemed not to matter. "Some of them I don't like much anymore."

Marshall's mother stood her glass on the table with a rap like a gavel. "Excuse me, but what kind of story are you planning to write?"

"As much of the truth as you and the nipper will tell me."

The reporter was presenting an earnest expression to her, but just for an instant Marshall saw another one stir beneath it. Every face shifted like that if he looked too long and hard. "I want to talk about what happened, mom."

"It's up to you, Marshall. If you're sure."

He hoped she would understand when she heard him. He wanted to leave behind an image of himself closer to the truth than the wimp who'd been seen weeping in nearly every newspaper and on maybe every television channel in Britain. Only now that he was being given the chance, he didn't know how to begin. The inside of his skull was growing slippery and brittle when the reporter said, "Whenever you're ready, Marshall."

"I'm thinking, James."

"Actually, it's Mr. James."

"Then maybe you should say Mr. Travis."

"Whoa," the reporter said, or a word that sounded like it, and threw up his palms as though Marshall had pointed a gun at him. The gesture brought Marshall unexpectedly close to remembering, though even as it was taking place the shooting had seemed like a nightmare he'd already had, and the memory found words for itself. "He tricked me."

"You can say that again, son. Drugged you without your knowledge. You weren't responsible in the eyes of the law. Over the worst by now, is he, Mrs. Travis?"

"The doctors say so."

"And what do you say, son?"

"Sure." The question, and the hot noisy kaleidoscope surrounding him, were distracting Marshall from the issues he wanted to clarify, except mightn't they be best kept to himself while his mother could hear? "I was trying to save him," he made himself say instead.

"The other boy, that is. You didn't know then what he'd done to you, obviously. Is it right he was being abused?"

For a moment Marshall thought he was being asked whether Darren had deserved it. "Yes," he said. "I was aiming for the guy who had him."

"To stop it, you mean, of course. Yes." Having answered for Marshall, the reporter raised his pint of beer to him. "I hope you aren't blaming yourself. You always hear them say it in films, don't shoot or you might hit the other person. You'd never handled a gun before, had you? No wonder you missed. I would have."

"I didn't miss."

The reporter lowered his glass slowly as he reached for his notebook. "You didn't?"

"Mr. James—"

Marshall interrupted his mother. "He lifted Darren up just as the gun went off."

"Darren being the boy. Darren Fancy, wasn't it? Some surname. Exactly what nobody would." The reporter had found nothing further to write after all. "Looking back now, how do you—"

"Drink up, Marshall, or bring it with you. They've announced our gate."

"Just another couple of questions while he does that if I may, Mrs. Travis. Is it true you're leaving because of the possibility that someone related to the people who were shot might seek revenge?"

This time the rap of the glass on the table was so sharp that a policeman looked hard at Marshall's mother as she stood up, hefting her bag.

"Tell me, do you make a living asking questions like that? Do you consider yourself to be a professional?"

"I'm sorry, Mrs. Travis, if I—"

"Too late. Get your bag, honey. Leave the drink. I'll buy you another when we're through the gate."

The policeman was still looking, but Marshall couldn't tell whether his hand was flickering toward the gun at his hip. Presumably not, since he turned away as Marshall's mother thrust the strap of the flight bag into Marshall's hand. As Marshall felt his fingers close around it, and his legs begin to walk in the direction his mother was urging, the reporter said, "I'm sorry if I gave you the impression I wasn't on your side. I'll tell you now, son, I think you did us all a favor."

Marshall felt his mother grip his elbow, not so much steering him as driving him past the table, but he hesitated long enough to hear what the reporter added. "Got rid of one bad apple and if you ask me, another that would have ended up just as bad."

Marshall was being urged past the policeman, close enough to reach out and unbutton his holster. His mother didn't slow down until they reached the security check, where a man with a ponytail was advancing and retreating through the alarmed arch, and having to divest himself of keys and coins and his brass-buttoned denim jacket. She visibly didn't relax until both she and Marshall were through the arch, out of the reporter's territory, and not much even then. She bought herself another gin and it, and for Marshall a Coke in a bottle, which felt like being on his way home. He bought a paperback about true crimes from the bookstall, and found his mother rattling the ice cubes in her glass as though she was trying to grind them into water. She seemed to decide not to say what she was thinking, then did. "If anything that stupid insensitive clod said bothered you—"

"It didn't, mom. You don't have to worry about me anymore."

However true that was, it was one more thing he should have left unsaid, because he sensed it was having the opposite effect. At least her concern for him remained silent while he read about executions, which he did on a seat among the duty-free shops, and on another by the boarding gate. Once they were aboard the airplane he concentrated on the faces of those passengers who were already seated, and then the faces which ballooned toward him down the aisle. Few of them looked like criminals, but of course it would be a mistake to think that criminals always did.

The stewardesses offered boiled sweets from baskets as the plane began to taxi through a downpour, and Marshall took a sweet as soon as a basket reached him. It made no sense to suspect everything—you had to learn what to be suspicious of. Once the stewardess was past, his mother nodded at her purse. "Do you want . . ."

"It's all right, mom. I won't need those." The doctor had prescribed him far more tranquilizers than Marshall thought were necessary, but at least his mother hadn't even mentioned them for weeks. He gazed at the rain zigzagging down the window, slicing the view of the runways into jigsaw pieces. He watched the stewardesses enact their safety mime with smiles which must be designed to reassure but which managed to suggest to him that the routine was something of a joke—the opposite of the nervousness with which it had infected him on the reverse of this flight. He wasn't the same person, he thought as the plane gathered speed and the lines of rain on the glass straightened and stretched horizontal before splitting into fragments like a Morse transmission meant specifically for him. Then the land tilted and plummeted away, and the plane pierced the gray sky, which erased a vista of houses that looked poised to slide in disarray down the green fields to the horizon. Grayness arrested the plane, and Marshall's mind too, and he was struggling to work his mind loose of the thick vagueness when it sank past the windows, transforming itself into a sunlit field of white.

The blaze of sunlight felt like a promise of Florida. He basked in it for a few minutes, until his attention was caught by the shadow of the plane on the clouds far below him. It was encircled by a rainbow, and both of them were so small he imagined wearing them for a badge. He turned to point them out to his mother, but she was asleep.

She needed a rest from worrying about him, and besides, he couldn't share everything with her. Soon he'd be able to show her she no longer had reason to be anxious for him. Soon he wouldn't have to keep reminding himself that he was as sure of his life as she was of hers, so that the world ceased to resemble a cartoon of itself which he was trying to inhabit. She was going back to teach in Florida, and he knew what he would be when he grew up. They weren't running away, and it was his duty to ensure they never had to again.

He wished he could have explained to the reporter. If any of Darren's family wanted to follow, let them come. The only one Marshall would have cared about was dead. When he'd heard that Darren's mother was in prison for her involvement with a robbery he'd gone back to the house one day to find out what he could, and had learned from a neighbor that the old man had died in his bed.

Though the news had enraged Marshall, it had also proved him right about the Fancy family. When he'd told the reporter that Darren had tricked him, he hadn't been trying to explain away his own actions. Of course he was responsible, whatever the reporter said. He hadn't missed. Darren had deserved it as much as the man who'd tried to use him as a shield had. However pathetic criminals managed to look, Marshall was no longer going to allow that to matter to him.

His mother gave a small protesting moan, then her eyes ceased to range about behind their lids as whatever dream she was having subsided. He saw the aisle beyond her, and remembered how on the last flight they'd had a trio of seats, his father occupying the far one. Much as he loved his father, there was one mistake for which he might never be able to forgive him. He had to learn from it, so that he at least would keep his mother safe from any threat the world was saving up, not just the dogs.

He shoved his book into the pocket of the seat in front, and gazed at the face of a dead criminal as the plane lanced the sky. Far from running away, he was going back where things were done right, where the law as well as criminals was armed. Once he was old enough he would join the police, and if by any chance they wouldn't let him join—if they failed to understand what he'd had to do at the Fancy house—he would still own a gun. Let George S. and his cronies try to fuck with him then—let anyone. His father had taught him the most important lesson of his life, and so, he was forced to admit, had Darren. "Always make sure your gun is loaded," he whispered, and smiled at his mother as she moaned once again in her sleep.